THE DUSTMAGE

The Dustmage

N.A. Woltzen

Duskenmire Publishing

ISBN-13 (EBook): 979-8-9947462-0-2
ISBN-13 (Paperback): 979-8-9947462-2-6
ISBN-13 (Hardback): 979-8-9947462-1-9

Cover design by: Adam Fyda [adamfyda.com]
Library of Congress Control Number: 2026904196
Printed in the United States of America

To my wife, Sarah,
without whom this story wouldn't have come to life,
and to Edmund and Emmalyn,
who inspire me and awaken my inner child.

Table of Contents

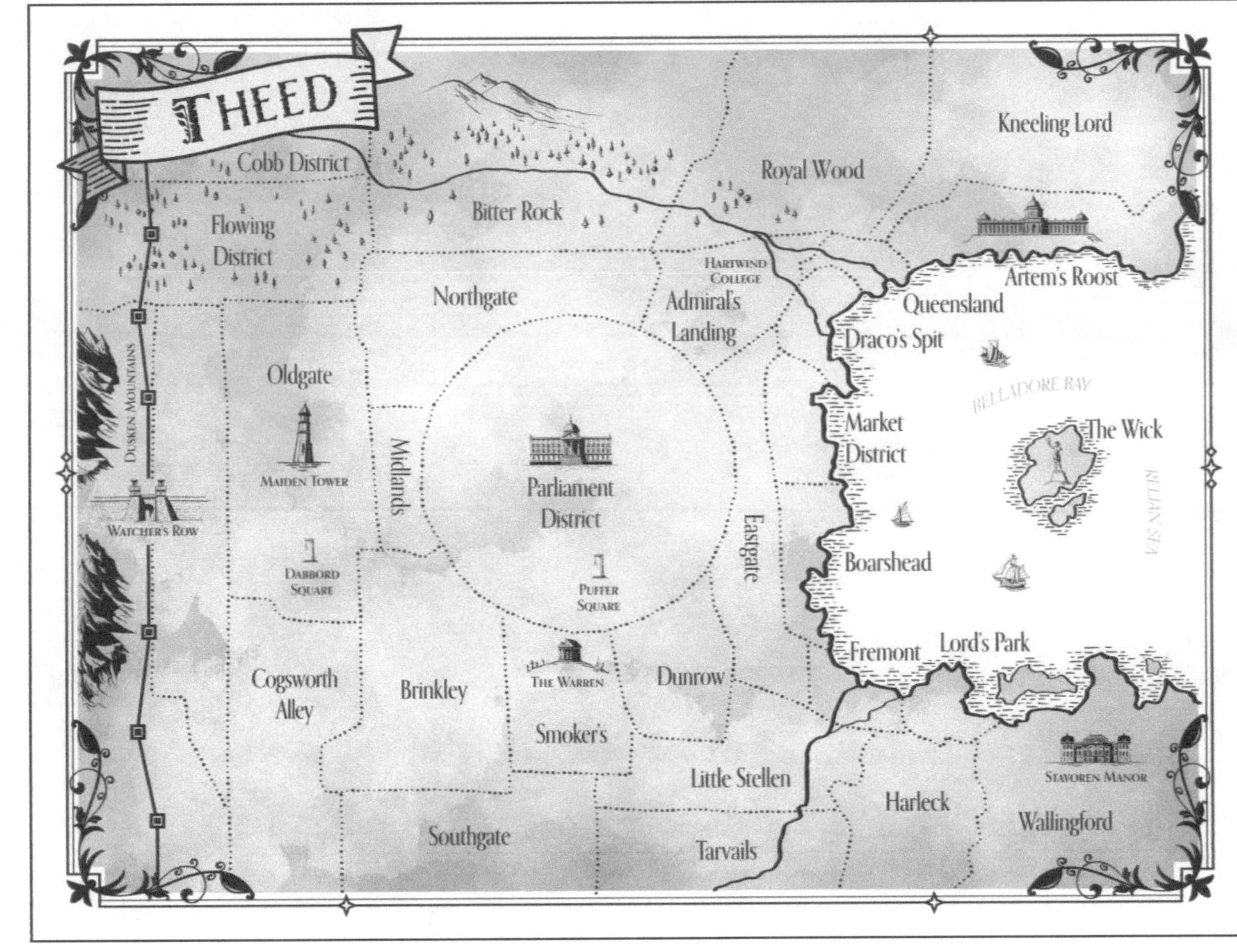

THEED
Cobb District
Dusken Mountains
Watcher's Row
Flowing District
Bitter Rock
Royal Wood
Kneeling Lord
Hartwind College
Artem's Roost
Northgate
Admiral's Landing
Queensland
Draco's Spit
Oldgate
Maiden Tower
Midlands
Parliament District
Market District
Belladore Bay
The Wick
Relian Sea
Dabbord Square
Puffer Square
Easgate
Boarshead
Cogsworth Alley
Brinkley
The Warren
Dunrow
Fremont
Lord's Park
Smoker's
Little Stellen
Stavoren Manor
Southgate
Tarvails
Harleck
Wallingford

Chapter One

Powder hung in the air like mist on a cold autumn morning. If Countess Auriella Stavoren could see better, she might have noticed the disheveled piles of books, stacks of dirtied plates, and half-sipped teacups floating in the air, but she could barely see past her own fingers in her old age. Countess Auriella might even remember the same sorts of objects flying across her living room the other day or the days before that, like an outlandish parade in a fever dream, but her memory was even poorer than her sight.

Auriella's milky blue eyes were glossy and bright from the morning sun cutting through her window as she gazed out over her lush gardens. Her eyes rarely blinked—even when mascara was brushed on her eyelashes, and blush brought life to her sunken cheeks. Occasionally, she would wince when a comb pulled a knot in her long, snow-white hair, but aside from that, she was as close to a corpse as someone exhaling their last rattling breath.

A floating tea kettle made a thud when it bumped into a lamp heading into the kitchen. *That wasn't there yesterday.* Perhaps Madame Auriella moved it this morning. It wouldn't be the first time she got confused and moved things out of place. Katja cursed under her breath as she rushed to fix the egg-shaped dent in the lampshade. Sweat dripped down her neck and beaded on her forehead as the powder room became a musty tinderbox. It didn't help that the countess demanded a fire lit every morning, whether in the middle of winter or the dog days of summer. Katja patted her neck with a cold glass of water and dribbled some down the back of her dress. *The countess won't notice the damp spots anyway.*

"Kitty, is someone here to see me?" Madame Auriella said, a wrinkled smile crawling on her face. "Hugo, is that you?"

Katja. My name is Katja, but the countess made a habit of giving her servants nicknames she thought fit, even if they didn't like it.

"My lady, do you not remember? The count has been dead for over a year now," Katja sighed. She hated how often she had to remind her, knowing the countess would forget moments later.

"Oh no! Not my Hugo! Not my Hugo! Say it isn't so!" Madame Auriella sobbed, thick tears welling in her eyes and running down her cheeks in black streaks.

Katja groaned inwardly. She would have to redo her makeup. It wasn't that she disliked Countess Auriella or didn't feel bad for her in losing her husband of nearly sixty years, but each time the countess forgot and relived the count's death, Katja relived it. In a fatherly way, she loved that old man more than anyone, even her own father, but that was not hard to achieve. Her blood father was only that—*blood*. The only thing her father ever gave her was curly red hair and a fear of dying on the streets, just like he did all those years ago. Count Stavoren died before she could truly know him, but he was the closest thing to a father she ever had. It was all like a tragic poem.

Katja felt mist in her eyes, but after going through this a hundred mornings before, she had grown short of tears. "Yes, I miss him too, milady. More than you know."

Countess Auriella patted her tears with a handkerchief and fixed her eyes on Katja in the vanity mirror. "You were the last one to see him. Did he say anything in his last breath? Anything about me?"

It was strange what the countess remembered and what she didn't. One moment, she forgets her husband is dead, and the next, she recalls the fine details of how his dead body was discovered. It often led to a rather complex conversation.

Katja nodded, but the recollection of the count's body sleeping peacefully at the bottom of his bath filled her with horror. "Sadly, he was already gone when I saw him. I imagine he was thinking of you, milady."

"Is that what you think?" Countess Auriella pinched Katja's cheeks, drawing her face forward.

Katja nodded reluctantly, cheeks warm where the Countess's fingers lingered.

"I will never find love like Hugo again! I will never marry again! Never! They will bury me in the same coffin, and then we will be together again!" Countess Auriella wailed.

"But you are meeting with a suitor tonight! I hear only good things about this new man of yours." Katja pulled away from the countess's grip and grinned.

Countess Auriella smiled for the first time this morning. "Well, I certainly do not want to die alone. Perhaps I will get married again . . . but only if he is as dashing as I am told he is. I used to be the girl who lit up this entire city! When I was young, there was not a single man or woman's gaze I did not own in the whole Commonwealth! Now fix my face!"

Katja pursed her lips and steadied her eyeliner pen to the countess's eyelids. "Only if you sit still so I don't poke your eye out."

Madame Auriella grumbled, but within a few minutes, her smile faded to her usual expressionless malaise. It was strange because Katja could swear that the countess's eyes lit up when she talked about her past life, as if the haze had been lifted from her very irises. But once the storm of her mind conquered, her bright blue eyes dimmed, and her soul seemed to leap out of her chest.

Katja glanced accusingly at the tea kettle, which was wobbling lazily in the air. She watched as the sweeping broom and feather duster wilted with lackluster effort. Then, she pulled a sand-dollar-shaped powder compact from her dress pockets and opened it like a clam.

The powder was the color of lilacs blooming in springtime. Every time Katja saw its light and delicate texture, her mouth watered, and her pulse quickened even though she had done this hundreds of times before. She lifted the soft powder to her face and inhaled it gently. Her nostrils burned, but then a sublime chill ran down her throat into her lungs. A metallic taste soured her mouth like she was sucking on a copper coin. Her heart pounded as *Vigor* filled her limbs and threatened to pour out of her fingertips. Then her heartbeat slowed, her breath deepened, and her vision sharpened.

With a flick of her wrist, the broom handle stiffened, the duster flew across the bookshelves, and a teapot hovered out of the room down to the kitchen stove. She pointed at a pile of disordered journals, and with a swivel of her finger, they flapped in the air like moths and stacked like a dealer shuffling cards. With the wink of an eye, a fresh log plopped into the fireplace, causing the embers to pop and crackle, but not before the wrought-iron screen slid into place to ward off any sparks.

Katja smiled, satisfied. She looked back at her sand-dollar-shaped compact and saw that her reserves were getting low. Finding more magedust soon would have to be her highest priority. She then returned to Countess Auriella's makeup, applying foundation, fresh coats of mascara, and a rosy blush that brought a bit of life into the countess's grave face. The illusion was all that mattered. We all wear masks, and so long as the countess's new suitor was convinced she still had a fervor for life, she wouldn't die alone. However, her inherited fortune was sufficient to alleviate most concerns. The countess was bitter in her advanced age, but deserved some happiness in her last years.

"There you go, Madame," Katja said, finishing the countess's hair with a mother-of-pearl barrette that gleamed in the lamplight. "The lawman will be thrilled to see you as fair as you look now!"

"The lawman? What did Hugo do now?" Madame Auriella asked, crossing her arms.

"The lawman is your suitor . . . Lord Rhys DeGrom. I heard he is a senator," Katja said. "To be so highly esteemed, he must be charming."

Madame Auriella raised an eyebrow and twisted the ruby wedding band on her finger. "If he is half as charming as he is in his letters, then I will be married by the morrow!"

There was a loud knock on the door across the room. Katja cursed under her breath. She wasn't done tidying up yet, but it would have to do for now. She froze momentarily, took a deep breath, closed her eyes, and pulled a few strands of hair from the nape of her neck. Her eyes watered with pain, but as she expected, the broomstick, feather duster, and other floating objects gently landed in their designated spots within cabinets and closets. The front door downstairs opened, rattling all of the windows in the powder room, and there was a shuffle of footsteps.

"Countess Auriella! Your date has arrived!" a high-pitched voice clamored, entering the countess's bedchambers, which were connected to the powder room by a small antechamber. "Are you decent, milady?"

"I just have to fasten her dress. Everything else is ready!" Katja barked, poking her head out of the powder room. "I thought I told you to keep the door shut until I tell you otherwise, Gavin?"

Gavin shrugged. "You have your duties just as much as I have mine. It is not my fault you are so careless in your use of sorcery."

"We had an agreement!" Katja rasped. "You don't mutter a word about my magic, and I don't tell anyone that you write fraudulent checks from the countess's treasury."

Gavin adjusted his tie, which appeared to be suffocating him. "It is only a matter of time before someone finds out. Like I said . . . you have been more and more daring since the count died."

"And what will happen when the countess remarries? Someone will discover your thieving plot!" Katja snapped. "I reckon her new husband will take over signatory duties! Then the honeypot snaps shut on your fingers!"

Gavin huffed. "Lord DeGrom is waiting with his entourage!"

"Is someone here, Kitty?" the countess hollered.

Katja returned to the countess, who was staring at the plum tree outside her vanity window.

"Your suitor has arrived," Katja said, helping her to her feet. "He has brought quite an entourage. You shall never feel lonely!"

Countess Auriella waved at her dismissively like a fly. "When you are as wealthy as I am, you are never lonely!"

Katja nodded in agreement, but deep down, she knew the countess rarely had visitors. Auriella met with a few estate planners, lawyers, and other aging socialites, but even they were slowly dying off. She had hired a matchmaker downtown to secure a suitable companion for her later years, yet months of effort produced only frauds, hucksters, and penny-chasers. The matchmaker only started to take the submissions seriously when the wealthy Lord DeGrom answered. For the first time she had a client who wasn't in it for her purse, a man who already had a fortune from an esteemed peerage. At least that is what the letter from the matchmaker said, which Katja snooped from the countess's mail. Sometimes, she couldn't resist.

Katja inspected Auriella's makeup one last time, fastened the back of her blue dress, shimmering with sapphires, and helped her to her feet and into the bedchamber. When they reached Gavin, he took the countess's hand. He led them down the corridor past numerous other rooms and alcoves adorned with fine oil paintings, tapestries, maps, plate armor, and other curiosities the count had collected over the decades. When they were delicately ushered down the twin staircase into the entry room, a man in waxed boots, flamboyant cream pants, a blue tweed coat, a silky vest, and a long red tie stood in the doorway. His face was long like his horse, and he had a pointy chin. His skin was pale and pocked, resembling a plucked hen, and his nose was long and pointy, like the prow of a ship. A servant in a black tuxedo held a peacock-tail sunshade to protect the man from the hot sun, but sweat still dripped down his red cheeks.

Lord DeGrom stood impatiently, his feet tapping on the cobbles. When he saw the countess, his face looked tortured behind his forced smile. *Thank the Numen Spirit that the countess is half blind, or she might be insulted.* But Katja wasn't surprised by Lord DeGrom's reaction. After all, he looked young enough to be the countess's son.

"My lovely Auriella! You look lovelier than I could have ever imagined!" Lord DeGrom blabbered. "Our carriage is ready!"

He snapped his fingers, and a younger man with black slicked-back hair approached from the carriage with a dozen roses and a bouquet of marigolds. Two other young men who looked similar to him stood anxiously beside the carriage, chatting with the driver.

"Lord DeGrom! The countess and I were just talking about you!" Katja said with false luster.

"And it is the countess that I wish to speak to, not her servant!" Lord DeGrom said through gritted teeth. He reached a hand to the countess, who welcomed it softly. "How are you, my love?"

"Of course," Katja said, curtsying and withdrawing in the background. Gavin gave her a sneering grin.

Katja's smile turned into a frown, but she wasn't unfamiliar with how men in the upper echelons of the capital spoke to their servants. The count was a rarity among his breed, and it wasn't until he discovered her secret that he showed his softer edge to her. She shouldn't have spoken in place of the countess, but she was used to being her mouth and ears.

The countess kissed Lord DeGrom's red cheeks, flush from the heat. She nearly fell but clung to his puffed shoulders, an act that clearly irritated him a little beneath his rosy veneer. "You are young and strong, my dear, but we will find that charm I have been told so much about at dinner."

"Indeed, let's find out!" Lord DeGrom let out an abrupt laugh that seemed to overcompensate for the lack of humor in the countess's voice.

Countess Auriella turned to Katja. "This place had better look spotless when I return! I can smell the mildew and dust you missed! Any other obligation will have to wait! I expect more from the Maiden Tower!"

Katja bowed. "As you wish, milady."

Lord DeGrom and the countess walked away to the carriage, followed by a flock of servants carrying sunshades. When they reached the carriage, the countess nearly fell into her seat, and moments later, the doors slammed shut. Once Lord DeGrom's entourage had boarded the carriage and filled a second smaller carriage riding behind it, the drivers snapped their reins. They mushed away down the street toward downtown, the tall steeples and domed silhouettes jutting in the distance.

"You heard the lady. You have some cleaning to do!" Gavin said, nudging Katja as he turned back into the manor. "I will be in the count's smoking room, enjoying a fine cigar while I look over the countess's mail. Please do not disturb my peace with any of your strange witchcraft!"

When the carriage turned the corner and Gavin disappeared into the smoking room, Katja locked the front door and twirled across the long wooden halls, ordering buckets of sudsy water to fill, mops to slop, brushes to scrub, curtains to straighten, hot irons to unwrinkle, and linens to fold. She set a vinyl disc on the phonograph and let the needle scratch until a satisfying quartet filled the old manor with ambiance.

Katja slipped out of her shoes and slid across the floor, twirling from room to room as the once-cluttered space slowly opened, sending motes of dust into the air. She then tried on a few of the countess's rings and necklaces, which were filled with emeralds, pearls, sapphires, diamonds, and other sparkling gems. Just as the music crescendoed, she tapped up the twin staircases and down the hall to the master chambers. She flicked her fingers in the countess's chambers, and the sheets whipped and tucked into their folds so tight that there wasn't a single wrinkle.

Katja sprayed a lavender perfume on her wrists, took one of the several vintage Stellish wines, and sipped thrice from the bottle so the countess would never notice, even if she could barely remember what year it was. Katja could have a little fun, but she didn't want to get too carried away and caught like an engorged mosquito before it got swatted. She had to be clever or risk losing everything.

Katja looked out the window, imagining the life of a noble, watching the gardeners trim the topiary and orchards. From here, she could make out the dome of the Parliament building, blurred by a cloud of mist. She fumbled through a stack of letters on her bedside, including an opened one from the Board of Stamps and Taxes, another addressed to Count Stavoren, and another from Lord Rhys DeGrom.

Katja couldn't help herself. She took another swig of wine, fished the letter out of the envelope, and read the fine handwritten letters.

My Lovely Auriella,

I will pick you up for our arrangement on the Fifteenth of Springhour. I look forward to our first meeting.

—Rhys

Katja groaned, tossed the letter back onto the bedside, and took another swig of wine before corking it and setting it back in its spot. *What a waste of excitement.*

She then strolled to the edge of the room, where an intricate tapestry hung over the wall. She reached for a small matchbox at the bottom of her purse and retrieved a match, noting she only had a few left and would need to find more in the count's cigar lounge when Gavin wasn't occupying it. She struck the match and lit a lavender candle in a pewter candleholder sitting on a nearby dresser. Once lit, the tapestry swirled with colors and patterns like every thread had been brought to life. She stepped through the swirling fabric and appeared inside a small closet lined with loaded bookshelves and cabinets filled to the brim with manuscripts, odd assortments of trophies from across the world, and wrinkled maps.

Feeling light on her feet from the wine, Katja skipped toward the familiar shrine at the end of the closet. Atop the shrine sat an empty brass holder, but more interesting was the wooden stand at its center, bearing a dusty tome that had transfixed her from the moment she first discovered the room. Surrounding the peculiar tome were clusters of deformed candles that had been melted from use. Her favorite sight, however, was a drawer within the podium where a sheepskin pouch, filled to the brim with lilac-colored powder, was placed beside an ordinary magnifying glass, long pens, and hardened inkwells. *Such a sweet sight indeed.*

She took a few pinches of the powder, refilled her shell-shaped compact, and hid it in her pocket. Her finger scratched the thick skin that made up the bottom of the pouch. Katja's heart sank like a stone in water. Her secret cache was running low. She would have to ration better.

How had she used so much in so little time? The first time she had stumbled into this secret closet was in the dark winter, a week after the count died. She remembered that night well. It was the worst storm of winter, and brilliant flashes flared through the window blinds. The countess, who was much sounder of mind, was occupied in the drawing room. Katja had been busy cleaning the master bedchambers, but being such an unnaturally dark night, she lit a candle beside the old tapestry, which began swirling with radiant threads like gold swirling at the bottom of a miner's pan. Holding the strange candle, she drew closer, inspecting the mesmerizing threads. She reached out to touch it and stumbled into the mysterious chamber brought to life by a candle. That was when she realized there was more to the count, and she had just stumbled upon his dark secret. What great luck that she had a touch of magic herself and now enough magedust to fuel her obsession for half a year.

Katja looked down at the thinning pile of dust. If she was lucky, there was enough for a month.

She shut the drawer, turned to the old tome sitting on the shrine, and grazed her fingers across the leather cover, engrossed with the title "Grimoire" in gold-leaf letters. She fingered through a book nearly as thick as a brick, its spine split like wood, and read the first entry, filled with fine, embellished letters:

The Lockpick's Cantrip: To pick a simple lock, ensure that your Vigor is sufficient, aim your ballast at the lock, insert it into the mechanism, and ask the lock for its creator's name. Depriving oneself of sight can aid this material communication. Once the creator's name is known, utter it in the Elddir tongue, and the lock will be no more.

Katja eyed a locked cabinet in the corner of the room and sat before it, as if she were about to pray. She lacked a ballast, such as a scepter or a wand, but her hands had served her just fine her whole life. Closing her eyes, she pressed her finger to the lock and asked for its master's name like a robber holding up a bank teller.

Silence.

"Who is your maker?" Katja whispered, lowering her gaze to the keyhole, using the candlelight to examine its inner workings. "You are the only cabinet I have not been able to open! Who is your creator?"

Again, *silence.*

Katja tried several more times to ask the lock its master's name in various ways, even in her mother's native Dirkish. Still, she knew she would need to speak the Elddir tongue as the book instructed, which she knew only a few words of, none of which were helpful in picking locks. After giving up, she yanked the cabinet doors, but they wouldn't budge, just like the dozens of times she had tried before. Not even a chisel could split its seams. Surrendering, she flipped through the grimoire's pages, leafing through chapters about common spells, levitation, wards, elixirs, and a few sections about alchemical conversions that she couldn't decipher. The only bits of magic she knew well were so simple a ten-year-old could likely learn them in a proper Glint household—back in the days before magic was outlawed.

Count Stavoren had promised to teach her everything he knew about magic ever since he caught her summoning a brush into her hand while doing Countess Auriella's makeup one morning. At first, she managed to explain it away. But when the count returned home early one day and found brooms, feather dusters, and dishes floating through his halls, there was little she could say in her defense. What she thought would be the end of her employment with the Maiden Tower and a possible report to the constable's office instead turned into an offer of mentoring, which she gladly accepted, even if, at first, she was skeptical of the gaffer's expertise. He never got to tell her about this secret room, but Katja always figured he died before he had a chance. Not even a month after his mentoring began, she found him dead at the bottom of his bathtub, along with her dreams of becoming a properly trained magician.

Katja slammed the grimoire shut, trying to shake his dead, bloated face from her mind. It fell off its stand onto the ground, and something slid out from the folds onto her feet like autumn leaves. When she got a better look at what fell out of the book, she frowned—*three playing cards.* She reached down and picked up the cards, noticing that they were fashioned like ordinary playing cards, but instead of images of kings, queens, dukes, and jesters, they were sketch portraits of regally dressed men and women.

When she picked the cards up, she noted the king of spades, the queen of clubs, and a lowly five of hearts. Atop each card scribbled in red ink were the names *Valery don Scales*, *Boris Hedgewort*, and a red "X" across *Francis Stoker III*.

Former Prime Minister Francis Stoker?

She looked down at the familiar sketch of the prime minister's face and scratched the red ink slathered across it, but it did not peel or chip. Why did the count have these cards? A chilling realization sent a shiver down her spine and prickled every hair on her neck.

Prime Minister Stoker died last summer while he was on a trip to Tarclay for a donor ball and was found dead after a nighttime swim at the Grand Postman's Hotel the morning after. Everyone in the Commonwealth was familiar with the details of this story. It had been a harrowing investigation that made so many headlines in the morning paper that it covered the streets, as people could only be bothered to read the first page before tossing it aside. Everyone in the capital, who was anyone, was almost excited to hear the following report or bits of detail on the prime minister's untimely death. Even if you weren't obsessed, you knew enough to speak broadly about it.

A loud thud rattled the floor beneath her feet. *What was that?*

Katja shoved the cards back into the grimoire and placed it back onto its stand at the shrine before darting through the swirling tapestry. Before she could forget, she blew out the purple candle and put it back on the dresser. She dashed out of the countess's bedchambers and down the long corridor, stopping at the top of the staircase to listen.

Downstairs, a flying fireplace poker dueled its corresponding ash shovel with an iron clang, a broom scraped the floor handle-side down, and sheets of linens danced around the living room like ghouls in a childish nightmare.

This only happened when she was scared.

In the corner of her eye, she spotted a shadow standing in the window, looking in from the gardens. To her horror, a shaded face peered into the living room with an expression of pure awe and something else she couldn't quite place that she did not like. Shivers crawled up her arms. In her fear, she imagined herself resembling a wildebeest with raised hackles. She slid away from view into the entryway antechamber where the crackling phonograph had just finished its final tune, its record spinning with an eerie static.

Katja plucked her hair, making her scalp sting. There was a loud metallic thud as the fireplace poker and shovel clattered to the floor. She reached for the broom's handle before it struck the hardwoods and hid behind a wall. The small of her back pressed against the wainscoting as she held her breath and watched the shadow of the strange peeping man craning his neck between the hedges for another minute before slipping away and vanishing into the garden. When she felt like the coast was clear, she slowly snuck out of her hiding spot and darted to the cigar lounge at the other end of the manor.

Who was that? Did they witness her magic? Of course, they did! Did she really think someone would be peering into an old lady's window to get a better look at her fine books or linen collection? *Boils!* She really messed up this time. And that face . . . they looked like they had seen something completely outlandish. Perhaps she could offer an explanation? But what could she say to make sense of flying broomsticks, dancing sheets, and the other enchantments whizzing around the manor?

Katja rapidly knocked on the door to the cigar lounge, but burst through the door before Gavin could answer her. "Do you know of someone stopping by the manor? A visitor?" Her voice was far shriller than she intended.

Gavin was reclining on a sofa, alternating between smoking one of the count's fancy cigars and sipping golden whiskey in a frosted glass. In his lap was an aging book, among many that lined the walls of the private library, all of their colorful spines resembling a baby's knitted blanket. The smell of cigar smoke reminded her so much of Count Stavoren that it felt like she had stepped back in time.

"Hexes! I told you not to disturb me! Don't you think I would know if we were expecting another guest? Now shoo, girl!" Gavin scolded, his cheeks rosy from drink. "Get back to your witchery!"

Katja slammed the door shut. "I am not leaving! Someone is here . . . in the garden!"

"In the garden? Have you considered it might be the gardener?" Gavin snapped.

"This man . . . person . . . was peeping in through the window!" Katja interjected. "They saw my enchantments!"

Gavin stared at her blankly and then broke into laughter.

"What is so funny? Are you drunk?" Katja scoffed.

"I told you they would find out eventually. I didn't think it would be today!" Gavin giggled. "It was probably one of the queen's Magesleuths sniffing out the witchy stench wafting from Stavoren Manor! Rumors have it that once they catch your scent, they will never forget it. If you are lucky, they won't torture you like some of the others, and the constable will hang you without so much as a trial!"

Even just the mention of a Magesleuth made her throat tighten.

"I thought they only worked at night?" Katja said, her voice croaking.

"I dunno, but I have seen more of them in the last few months stalking the streets with their menacing gowns and sinister sniffing! Do they ever stop sniffing? Why would they when the air is so thick with sorcery!"

Katja turned on her heels, grabbed her purse and sunhat, which she had left beside the front door, and fled Stavoren Manor. The bright sun blinded her as she tilted her sunhat to shield her eyes and marched down the pavement to the main road. Leaving the estate grounds, she peered over her shoulder to see if anyone was watching her from the thick gardens, which were usually a welcoming sight when she visited Stavoren Manor. She needed to act normally, but no matter how much she tried, she felt the awkwardness of a newcomer attending morning prayer at the temple. She fixed her gaze on the ground, occasionally glancing at the traffic and growing crowds, dreading running into the Crown's crimson-clad lawmen.

She boarded the trolley as always, gave the chauffeur a copper, and sat near the back, avoiding the tired gazes of laborers setting off to their next shift. Half an hour passed as the trolley skirted through the bustling capital, crossing two bridges and cutting through Puffer Square, past the domed Parliament building with columns resembling fancy ivory prison bars. When they reached her stop at Dabbord Square, she crossed the street while nearly getting bitten by a draft horse pulling a large carriage. She pushed through a bakery line into a back alley behind an abbey that she had traversed a hundred times, before reaching the Maiden Tower: a tall, ivy-laden turret with a missing clockface and a pointy rooftop that reminded her of a thorn. Although the tower was likely a prominent feature of Theed's vista several hundred years ago, it looked infantile next to the jutting temple spires, immaculate cupolas, and flying buttresses crowding the city.

Katja stormed through the front door, shuffling up the seven flights of steep stairs to her small, shared dormitory. She entered the doorless chamber, dove into her bottom bunk, and hid beneath the covers, listening intently for footsteps and voices. To her relief, the tower was uncharacteristically silent. She rested on the thin mattress, feeling its uneven cushion on her spine. Without anything to distract her, her mind raced behind the black of her eyelids as her heart thumped beneath her ribs. Would that man know that she worked for the Maiden Tower? You would have to be a distant traveler not to know the crimson garb worn by the capital's Maiden Tower. Even the hermits beyond the city walls likely knew it well, only second to the crimson cloaks of the city watch. Did he get a good enough look to describe her to the city watch? Her stomach sank. *What if they blame it all on Countess Auriella?* A thought consumed her like a shadow. *What if the Magesleuths find the count's secret room?* They would arrest Madame Auriella and send her to the gallows with one swift flick of the pen on the death warrant. Better than being strung up by the noose and executed in the city square like the other young witches, right? She felt horrible for thinking it, but the countess was far closer to her expiration, while Katja was barely eighteen. But could she live with herself?

The thought settled like an old castle foundation. Madame Auriella would be blamed and would die for Katja's mistake. The idea haunted her as cold sweat slicked her skin and she rolled on her thin mattress, the wooden bunk creaking beneath her. She had never cared much for the old woman, even at times wishing for the reaper to rap upon her bedchamber door and end the slow misery of age, to reunite her with the count. Still, the countess did not deserve to have her name dragged through the muddy streets and erased from the annals of history.

Katja hid in her bed for hours, head stuffed beneath her pillow as she waited to be found. Once the sun started to dim beneath the curtains, she was startled by the growing sound of clacking heels and boots outside her dorm, wandering from all directions of the tower. At first, she imagined swarms of guards searching every dormitory for her, but she knew it was just the other chambermaids returning from their assignments. She pulled her pillow over her head and tried to ignore the swarms of voices and chatter, and not much later, the supper bells rang. The smell of roast ham, simmering stew, and baked bread delighted the Maiden Tower. The echoes of conversation, laughter, scratching silverware, and clashing dinner plates filled the halls where she knew she would be expected. However, when the prefects called, Katja told them she wasn't feeling well enough to eat. Her stomach growled, but her will to stay hidden was far stronger than her desire for food, no matter how pleasant its scent.

After supper, her other five dormmates burst in, chuckling about something funny that was said at the dinner table. Her bunkmate, Portia Ponvelle, yawned and kicked Katja's leg before climbing into her bunk.

"You alive, Kat? You are still in your day clothes. Boots and all!" Portia said, shuffling into her sheets.

Katja kicked off her boots with a thud and groaned. "I am not feeling well."

Portia's head peeked from above, appearing as a silhouette behind Katja's sheets. "You don't have the pox, do you? Remember what happened to the other girls who got that nasty blight?"

"I don't have the pox! But I do not feel well and wish to be ignored!" Katja groaned.

"The other girls who got the pox acted defensively at first, too . . . and then a few days passed, and they died," Portia whispered. "Best not give it to me."

"I don't have Hexes Pox, Portia!" Katja snapped. "I am more worried about disappointing the countess. At this point, I am more likely to be killed by the prefects for disappointing a patron than the pox! This is already my fifth assignment since signing my contract here, and this one has finally stuck." If she were honest, that was the least of her worries.

"Especially if Prefect Haggerty finds out. She isn't very forgiving," Portia whispered, reaching for something on their bedside table. "That reminds me, Prefect Primrose noticed your absence and gave me some mail to deliver whenever we ran into one another. It looks like it's from the Grand Maiden herself."

"Mail? From the grand maiden?" Katja asked, pulling her sheets from her face to make sure she wasn't mishearing.

"Indeed . . . not something you receive every day. Perhaps it isn't as bad as you think!" Portia stammered. "I also snuck a piece of toast from supper in my gown for you. Don't leave any crumbs, or they will find out someone was eating in their beds."

"Thanks, Portia," Katja uttered. Her eyes were glued to the mysterious letter.

The grand maiden? Katja reached for the letter on her bedside table and felt the crisp paper creasing between her fingers. She slid her fingers to break the envelope seal and pulled out a pale piece of parchment, but could not read it in the dim night. Hands shaking, she crawled out of her bunk and raised it to the sliver of milky moonlight spilling in from a crack in the drapes and read the fine pen strokes:

Ms. Rosdyre,

It has come to our attention that you are assigned to our long-time client, Countess Auriella Stavoren, a Maiden Tower patron of nearly sixty years. Due to recent internal investigations within the Maiden Tower, you, Katja Rosdyre, are hereby instructed under the obligations of your contractual arrangement to search for and report any incriminating objects or evidence within the Stavoren residence and its associated properties.

Failure to report suspicious or illicit findings will result in consequences, including termination of your contract with the Maiden Tower.

Prompt delivery of any such assets will be rewarded.

Grand Maiden Argaut
P.S. This is privileged information.

Katja sighed and shoved the letter in her pocket before returning to bed. Once again, they ask her to spy and steal from one of her clients. She rolled over onto her side, but her mind raced, wondering what caused such suspicions of the countess in the first place. Did they know about the count's secret? Did it relate to her past work as a fundraiser and powerbroker in Parliament? Maybe it was about her suitor, Lord DeGrom, who was courting her in the city. Either way, just as the others before her, Katja would play the spy, take her reward, and move on to the next assignment. It was that or returning to begging in the streets.

Then, an idea struck her imagination like lightning. She already knew what she would take from Stavoren Manor. After all, she had been holding them just a few hours before.

The cards.

This was going to be the easiest bounty she ever earned.
So long as her mysterious witness stayed quiet.

Chapter Two

Katja slid on her dress and apron. She pinned up her thick red hair, powdered her nose, reddened her lips, sprayed the allotted amount of rose-scented perfume on her wrists, and took one last look in the mirror before starting toward the door. She passed a hall of maidens in various stages of undress. Some were tall, others short. Some had skin that resembled alabaster, sable, or cinnamon, with hair long or short, and some fell somewhere in between, depicted in every color one could imagine. Despite their differences, the girls all shared one thing in common: a red dress, white apron, and neat bow on their chest, the signature attire of the esteemed Maiden Tower.

"Katja!" Prefect Haggerty shouted with narrow eyes and a wagging finger. "Your buttons!"

Katja felt the loose flaps of her dress on her back and returned to her assigned vanity, which she shared with her bunkmate, Portia.

"You are up early! Don't worry, I will button you up," Portia said, hairpins sticking out of her teeth like sharp toothpicks. "You must be feeling better . . . or has the countess given you an earful?"

"You could say that. Her condition is worsening, and she is still keen on marrying a new man," Katja said, avoiding Portia's eager caramel eyes. "How is Mrs. Plumett doing? Still fawning over men other than her husband?"

"Unfortunately, but it makes for fun gossip. Jeane and Victoria like to take guesses on when she is going to leave Lord Plumett, but that is a bit sinister, don't you think? She still loves her former lover to whom she was engaged years ago," Portia said, fastening the last button and gasping, sending the pins between her teeth to the floor like coins. "Oh . . . Katja . . . what has happened to your—?"

Katja quickly covered the back of her head and turned to Portia, who looked awestruck, her glossy lips agape.

Katja shifted one of her hairpins to hide a small bald patch. Usually, her hair was so thick that it was easy to disguise the spot, but she must have rushed her hair this morning, distracted by the mysterious stranger at Stavoren Manor and the grand maiden's request from last night.

"Ehm, don't tell anyone," Katja said, taking Portia's cold hands into hers. "Promise?"

"Sure . . . I promise," Portia stammered.

Katja glanced at the dozens of other maidens filling the noisy powder room, too busy gossiping and taking care of their appearances to notice.

"I have a condition. A small section of my hair turned white one day, so I cut it out so no one would notice," Katja lied.

"This doesn't have to do with the Hex Pox, does it?" Portia whispered nervously. "I have heard of very bizarre symptoms—"

"I already told you, Portia! I don't have the pox!" Katja interrupted. She realized she was now gripping Portia's shoulder a bit too intensely. She took a deep breath and turned her clawing fingers into a comforting pat.

"Did you have it checked by a physician?" Portia asked.

"You know I can't afford a doctor," Katja said. "Besides, it is probably something I inherited. I never knew my father, but my mother told me I got my hair from him. Perhaps he got a streak of white hair, too."

"It doesn't look cut . . . it looks like the strands were ripped out of your scalp." Portia pressed her hand against her mouth. "Did someone do that to you?"

Katja glanced at the clock ticking on the wall. "I've got to go, Portia. If you are still curious, feel free to ask me later in private, but I would rather you didn't. It is a sensitive topic, and because of that, I need you to promise not to tell any of the other gals. Promise?"

Portia nodded. "Promise."

"What about the letter from the grand maiden? What was that about?" Portia asked, adjusting her bow.

"Don't talk about that either," Katja snapped. "I will snip your hair in your sleep if you squeal."

"C'mon, Kat! It isn't very often someone gets mail from the boss," Portia said. "I am so tired of boring gossip about who is having an affair and who is running thin on their family fortune. I need something more interesting."

"Maybe another time," Katja said. "I can't risk my contract. Please promise to forget you ever saw that letter."

Portia flinched. "Fine, I promise. Someone woke up cheeky this morning."

Katja sighed and glanced in the mirror before shuffling across the long, buzzing room full of fragrances, powder, and chatter—a three-step recipe for chaos. When she exited the anthill of the Maiden Tower, her face was bathed with gentle rain. Still, in the distance, she could see the sun breaking through the clouds, promising a sunny afternoon.

She darted across town and made it just in time to claim the last seat on her trolley to the Wallingford District, where Stavoren Manor and many other large estates sat upon a raised plot with terraced gardens full of flowering shrubs and bushes in every color. On the streets where she grew up, they called these estates the "Locks," and not because they overlooked a canal or waterway. It is said the term comes as shorthand for "warlock," likely because the only people who could afford to live there came from wealthy families with noble names and magical blood in their veins—a rather fortunate combination.

The door opened before she reached the front entrance. Lord DeGrom strolled past her with a chummy grin.

"Oh, you! You know the countess is not pleased with the mess you left! Even the broomstick was left out on the floor! I would expect more from the Maiden Tower, Miss . . . Miss . . . what is your name, girl?" Lord DeGrom sneered.

"Our beloved Countess Auriella calls me Kitty," Katja said through gritted teeth. "I will be happy to explain everything to *her*."

"Boils! You should thank your guiding fate for not losing your contract. I told Auriella that she should discharge you, but she still appears to have faith in you," Lord DeGrom snorted before strutting toward a stagecoach approaching from the road.

Katja ignored Lord DeGrom but couldn't hide the fact that the comment made her even more nervous about entering Stavoren Manor. Sweat beaded down her neck as she pushed through the front door, where Gavin stood like a candlestick, with a vexing smirk.

"I won't hear it," Katja said before he could speak. She knew what he had to say, and none would ease her nerves.

Gavin chuckled. "I see the Magesleuths have yet to reach you."

Before she entered the living room and marched up the stairs, she turned to Gavin. "Just wait to see what Lord DeGrom does to you when he notices you skimming his inheritance after he marries his future bride. No more cigars for you!"

Katja turned away too fast to see Gavin's expression, but she imagined he was no longer smiling. At least, that is what she hoped.

When she got to the master bedchambers, she expected the countess to be sitting in front of her vanity as usual, looking out the garden window with lifeless eyes, but she was nowhere to be seen. Katja glanced at the tapestry on the wall and felt her throat tighten.

She noticed a cloud of steam trailing from the bathroom. She walked past the vanity and into the bathroom, where a gust of warm air kissed her face. Her heart fluttered as she spotted the familiar lion-paw bathtub in the center of the room, filled nearly to the brim. But where was the countess? She stepped closer, her hands beginning to tremble.

Not again . . . not again. . .

Her stomach lurched when she saw a pale outline resting at the bottom of the basin. She reached into the water, but before she could act, the countess burst from the depths, spilling warm water over the ledge.

"Milady! Are you hurt? I thought you drowned!" Katja shouted hysterically.

Countess Auriella caught her breath and wrung the water from her hair— long, white strands that reminded Katja of cobwebs, so thin they barely veiled her scalp.

"Drown? Kitty, I was only taking a dunk in the bathwater!" the countess said, her eyes bright. "Sometimes I wonder what his final moments were like . . . plus it does wonders for the complexion to scour the skin."

"Please don't do that again, or you will frighten me to death," Katja said, gripping her arm. "I know you don't like to be told what to do, but at your age, it might not be wise—"

"Boils! I have lived a long life and am fortunate it didn't end half as long ago. The bath isn't going to take me out of this world, but that broomstick you left out might!" the countess objected. "Now help me out of this bowl of soup and get me ready for my day downtown! Last night made me miss this city!"

"I presume your courtship with Lord DeGrom went well. . .?" Katja asked.

Countess Auriella smiled, and her face brightened. "Why yes, it is my happiest since my wedding day. We dined, drank, got merry, teased one another, and returned home to dance to fine music!"

"It sounds like a cheery evening," Katja smirked.

"If I am frank, it was very different than my evenings with Hugo," the countess said, playfully splashing a bit of bathwater in Katja's direction. "Old Hugo enjoyed his chair, cigars, liquor, and solitude more than a romantic evening dancing with me."

Katja splashed back gently. "Well, we'd better not disappoint this dashing new gentleman. Let's get you out of the tub and dressed."

Katja helped the countess out of the water and wrapped her with a silken towel. She couldn't help but notice a pep in Auriella's step that had been missing for as long as the count had been dead. There was something about seeing the old lady break from the mold that was holding her back that made Katja smile. It was almost as if the countess was somewhat cured of whatever was tormenting her mind, like a great shadow lifting from her shoulders.

Katja helped Countess Auriella dry off and dress. Today, the countess wanted to feel young again and vibrant in the city, so Katja picked a flowing blue gown from the wardrobe and helped her button it up. She then dried her hair and fashioned it into a bun held together by a sapphire comb that glistened in the morning light. She applied the countess's makeup, drawing neat lines around her eyelids that sparked her blue eyes and dusting warm blush on her cheeks, but noticed she required far less than yesterday.

When she was finished, Katja looked at the tapestry in the mirror's reflection and then at Countess Auriella, who looked nearly a decade younger. Katja was talented at the art of aesthetics, like every maiden who worked in the Maiden Tower, but even that had limitations. Then, a thought struck her. Would she still be able to sneak into the count's secret chamber with the countess so much more vigilant? Would she be able to use enchantments to perform her maiden duties as before? Sweat dripped down her neck.

"You look beautiful, milady! Like a new woman! Who would have thought a man was the cure for all your problems!" Katja joked.

Countess Auriella grinned, but it was short-lived. Her gaze fixed on the tapestry behind her, but she averted it when she noticed Katja was watching.

Did the countess know about the secret room? It wouldn't surprise Katja if it were hard for the count to keep such a secret for sixty years of marriage, let alone in their shared bedchambers.

There were three knocks on the door, and Katja knew it was Gavin.

"The countess's carriage has arrived!" Gavin announced. "Do you want me to tell the driver you will be a bit longer?"

"No! I am ready!" Countess Auriella said, sliding a few flashy rings on her fingers and taking one last glance at her face in the mirror before standing up slowly. It was the first time she had done it unassisted since Katja had met her. She reached for her cane, but Katja wasn't sure if she needed it. The countess slid her purse on her shoulder and followed Gavin out of the room.

Katja's eyes returned to the tapestry, but she knew she must wait.

"Are you following, Kitty?" the countess said, glaring at Katja from the hallway. "You are to be excused early today. I don't have any more for you to do."

"What about the mess from yesterday?" Katja stammered. "I refuse to leave you with clutter. It is my honor as a servant of the Maiden Tower."

"I have already had the mess cleaned. If you had paid attention, you would have noticed that when you walked inside my home this morning," the countess snapped, her blue eyes cold in the pale sunlight. "Besides, I pay for your services by the hour. If there is no mess, you don't need to skim the fat from the family coffers. Now, enjoy your freedom, Kitty Kat!"

Was she being sacked? Since when had money ever been a problem for the Stavorens? Something was off, and it wasn't about the countess's sudden spring of life this time. Something was hiding behind her bright eyes and those pursed, wrinkled lips, now dolled up with red lipstick. She knew something—but what?

Katja followed Gavin and the countess as he ushered her to her carriage. With a whip of the driver's reins, the carriage skirted down the cobblestones to the city. Once the carriage was out of sight, she followed Gavin back to the front door. He lunged at the handle before she could reach it. "You heard the countess. She doesn't want to pay another knot for your terrible services!"

"I forgot something! Let me through!" Katja demanded.

"I can get it for you! Now stay here!" Gavin snapped.

Katja breezed past him and marched toward the stairs. "I will get it myself!"

"We aren't paying you for this!" Gavin said, chasing her heels.

"Suddenly, the Stavoren coin purse runs dry? When did the countess start counting her coins? If so, you would have been caught months ago with your hand in the cookie jar!"

"You can't be here!" he shouted.

Katja jiggled the master bedchamber doorknob, but it wouldn't budge. *When did the countess lock her door?* Did she finally notice the sips of Stellish wine missing from her collection? That couldn't be it. There had to be something more.

Gavin stopped at the door and gently shoved Katja's shoulder. "Leave!"

"Open it! It is locked!" she barked.

He reached for his keyring and clutched the keys so firmly in his hands that his fingers were white. "I would like to see you pry these from my cold, dead—"

Katja felt a prickle up her arm, and with a flick of her fingers, the keys tore from Gavin's grip and levitated toward her. Gavin reached for her, but before he could strike, she ripped all the oil paintings from the hallway walls and knocked over some plated armor on display with a loud clang so loud she imagined the countess could still hear it down the street.

"What have you done?" Gavin screamed.

"The countess won't be happy that her precious decorations are littered on the floor. She would probably normally blame me, but as you know, I am not supposed to be here," Katja snapped, feeling satisfied with her split-second plan. "This will take a while to pick up before she returns."

"Fix it now!" Gavin shouted.

"Let me stay for a few minutes, and we'll have a deal," she smiled.

Gavin sighed, "I hate magic . . ."

He slumped his shoulders in defeat and frantically inspected all the fallen canvases.

"There is dust all over these!" Gavin scoffed.

Katja unlocked the master bedroom and swiftly locked it behind her. She retrieved a match from her purse and ignited the violet candle with a match before slipping into the swirling tapestry.

She smiled when she spotted the grimoire exactly where she had placed it before. She set the candle on the altar and flipped through the pages until she found the cards between a chapter about fire incantations and truth enchantments.

Katja reread the names, uttering them under her breath. "Valery don Scales, Boris Hedgewort, and Prime Minister Stoker." She stuffed them in her purse and jiggled the locked cabinet she had tried to use a lockpicking spell on yesterday, but it didn't budge. She was tempted to try the spell again, but wasn't sure how much time she would have.

What could Gavin really do to her? She had her finger on his pulse just as much as he had on hers, except Katja knew magic. She could ruin the terrible butler with a flick of her wrists. Why shouldn't she try again? After all, she needed to learn more about magic than making objects hover in the air like leaky balloons. Now, with the Magesleuths possibly sniffing for her, it might be her only safe space to do any magic.

Katja remembered the instructions from the grimoire but flicked to the chapter anyway. She placed her finger on the keyhole and closed her eyes, begging for its master's name.

"Who is your creator? Who is your master? Who is your maker?" Katja whispered.

Silence.

Then she realized she knew the answer all along.

"Count Hugo Stavoren," Katja uttered.

Again, the lock did not budge, and then she recalled that the words had to be spoken in the Elddir tongue. She would need to find a translation if she wanted the lockpicking charm to work.

Suddenly, she heard a few heavy footsteps from behind the tapestry. *Gavin.* What would he think about her vanishing into thin air? What if he stumbled into the room by accident? So long as the candle was lit, the portal was open for anyone to slip through.

There was another thud, and she wondered if Gavin had run into trouble putting the suit of armor back into position in the corridor. She picked up the purple candle and carefully stuck her head out of the tapestry.

"Gav—!" Katja shouted, only for her voice to cut short. A hooded man clad in black sat on the end of the bed, reading a stack of letters. When he heard her call, he glanced at her with a look of surprise.

"Fleck! I found the girl!" the man said, a sliver of light revealing bright blue eyes above the mask that concealed his mouth.

Heavy footsteps marched down the hallway, which sounded like too many to be a single person. The chamber door battered open, as if something had detonated behind it. Smoke curled around the edges of the doorway as a man with a red beard and a black wool cap marched into the room, followed by a woman with a blonde bun and cauliflower ears, and lastly, a man wearing a leather duster, with greasy black hair and scars consuming his face.

Katja retreated into the tapestry, her heart pounding out of her chest. They would march right in if she didn't close the portal now. Panicked, she blew out the candle, surrounding herself with darkness. Hot wax dripped down onto her shaky hand as she crawled as far away from the tapestry as possible.

Was she safe in here? Would she be able to get back out? She remembered the matchbox in her purse and that she hadn't refilled it from the count's cigar lounge like she said she would. She dug her fingers into the depths of her purse, fetched the small matchbox, and shook it like a rattle, which proved it wasn't empty. Upon opening it, her fingers felt one match remaining. Her stomach sank as she realized she would only have one chance to light the candle. Even though lighting a match was something she did almost daily, the thought of striking a dud was daunting. If she were a more experienced magician, she might be able to conjure fire with a snap of her fingers, but the count had died before she could learn. She could learn by reading the grimoire, but what use would that be if she couldn't see? The secret chamber was darker than a starless night.

Katja waited in silence for the first hour, listening for footsteps and the loud stomping in the other room, but there was nothing but the sound of her own breath. Occasionally, she felt like she could hear the faint hum of whispers, the creak of floorboards, broken glass, and the strange sound of the wind. Still, when they did not repeat, she figured it might all be in her head. Could you imagine sounds if you sit in silence long enough? She could have sworn she heard the distant whinny of a horse, but she knew that couldn't be true. As time passed, she wondered if the intruders had left, but it seemed odd to have quickly abandoned their plan. The strange man sitting on the countess's bed mentioned "the girl" as if they expected her to be there. Maybe all the silence was part of some nefarious trap to trick her into coming out. She tucked between two cabinets, feeling her shaky arms vibrate against their wooden planks.

After the second hour, Katja left her hiding spot and accidentally kicked something heavy, which shattered on the floor. The metallic scent, which stung her nostrils, confirmed the presence of magedust in the air. *There was more hiding after all.* Her boots stepped on broken ceramic shards scattered about like gravel. She stumbled to the tapestry, placed her face against its rough stitches, and called out to Gavin between coughs after inhaling dust. There was no response, not even an echo. She shouted louder, but still, there was no answer, so she gave up. The quiet started making her more wary than if it were noisy. The uncertainty was enough to drive her mad.

"Gavin! Gavin! Gavin!" she pleaded, pounding her fists against the wall and even attempting to lift the flap of the tapestry, but when she felt behind it, there was only another wall. *Such strange magic.* She had used the mysterious magic like a child with candy, but she didn't even understand how it worked. Already, she could hear the count saying that in his raspy, winded voice. How could she be so foolish? But what was she supposed to do? Let those intruders get hold of her? Who knows what they meant to do with her?

Several hours passed, and her eyelids grew heavier. Her tired mind wandered to her mother. She imagined she was living in some other great city, working as a barber, making enough living to mortgage a small hovel. She imagined the time she wasn't cutting hair was spent waiting for Katja to leave the capital to find her, but she never came. But deep down, Katja knew that her mother was likely still living on the street somewhere or dead. After all, Katja hadn't seen her mother since she was ten years old, after her mother never returned to their shelter one night. Her mother had taught her nearly everything she knew —lying, fighting, stealing, and knowing who to trust in the alleyways during the day and, more importantly, at night. *The answer was nobody, but you would be surprised how many people didn't learn that lesson soon enough.*

Her mother also taught her how to overcome fear, which was commonplace when you didn't have walls or a roof to protect you from the wild. Whenever Katja was scared or anxious, she let her hair down to her shoulders, combed it repeatedly with her fingers, and started to hum. Her mother said nobody who was scared hummed. So, when something prowled or went bump in the night, her mother would hum as if warning them that they weren't the only ones unafraid of the shadows. It was silly, but Katja could count on her fingers how many times it had worked walking alone in this city.

She ran her finger through her hair, imagining she was playing with her mother's long brown locks. It reminded her of the two of them huddling together for warmth during the cold Winterhour. She might have inherited her father's red hair, but received her thick, wavy mane from her mother.

Katja coiled into a ball on the ground beneath a tower of books and parchment. She closed her eyes, her hand forked in her hair, and a hum on her lips.

* * *

Katja woke up in a rustle of paper, wishing more than anything that all this had been a terrible nightmare. To her horror, she hadn't dreamed it. How long had she been sleeping? Did it even matter? She wondered if Countess Auriella had returned from her evening with Lord DeGrom, oblivious that Katja was sleeping a stone's throw away from her bed.

She held the candle in one hand, and in the other, the lone match from her purse, pinched between her clammy fingers. *Please do not fail me now.* She struck the match against the matchbox, but it didn't ignite. She cursed under her breath as sweat dripped down her forehead and fell onto her arms, no longer feeling the chill that once plagued the small chamber. Her eyes strained even though she had nothing to focus on with the lack of light. Strands of long hair fell into her face as she took a deep breath and scraped the match against the box again.

The match sparked so brightly that it hurt Katja's eyes. She smiled excitedly as the flame grew, its fiery prongs growing tall toward the ceiling. The flame quickly slid across the match, nipping her finger. Her heart sank as the match fell to the floor, but instead of snuffing, the flame crawled across the floor with a loud *poof*. Flames clung to her fingers and consumed the fringes of her dress. She jumped to her feet, desperately clasping the purple candle as she watched the small spark spread across the floor, consuming the piles of bone-dry paper until they curled and blackened. Smoke swirled around the ceiling and quickly filled the small closet until she couldn't see further than her fingertips.

Magedust. How could she forget that magedust was more flammable than coal dust?

No, no, no! Her lungs filled with smoke, and her throat burned as she heaved for air. She flailed as the flames crawled up her dress and licked her skin with unbearable pain. She felt the melting purple candle in her hand and thrust it into the growing flame, igniting its wick. Heart racing, lungs burning, she mindlessly darted through the wall of fire toward the swirling tapestry and lunged through it. Once on the other side, she gasped for air and rolled on the hard ground as fire consumed her dress.

"Help!" Katja wailed, rolling on the floor, choking on hot fumes.

A splash of cold water singed the flames and soaked her as she frantically struggled for air. Tears rolled down her cheeks, but no one could tell from the water dripping from her face.

"Countess!" Katja screamed, rolling onto her chest and rubbing the ash and water from her blurred vision. Her mind raced as she tried to come up with an elaborate excuse for her presence and current state.

A shadow appeared from the edges of her vision, and a gloved hand reached to offer help.

"I knew you would come out of your hiding spot eventually, little witch," the shadow said with a grave voice.

Four more shadows surrounded her. Her breath became more labored, flurries filled her vision, and her head felt light. Was she dying? Then she noticed the ground wasn't made of wood, like Countess Auriella's bedchambers. No—the ground was cold stone.

Where was she?

Her vision flickered until it faded.

Chapter Three

"**W**akey, wakey, little witch!"

Katja stirred and opened her eyes. She took a deep breath, but it was shortened by a painful burn deep within her lungs. Dim light flickered off the slimy brick walls, casting long shadows in every direction. A fireplace sat along one wall of the large chamber. Nestled inside the hearth was a bed of hot coals responsible for casting the dim red radiance.

Standing between her and the fireplace was the silhouette of a man with his arms crossed. In the foreground, the silhouette of a lady with long hair paced in and out of the shadows like a moth circling a lamp.

Hexes! Where was she? This was not any part of Stavoren Manor that she could remember. Was it possible that the tapestry brought her somewhere else? She wasn't sure, but she knew deep down that her captors were the same intruders who broke into Countess Auriella's bedchambers.

"Fleck! She is awake!" a woman's voice shouted. "Stav! Give her some bloody space!"

Katja tried to stand, but she was tied to a chair with hemp rope. She scanned the far edges of the room, which she could barely see in detail, but from what she could tell, it resembled what she imagined being swallowed by a massive whale would be like, with curved rib bones serving as arches and tall, crumbling columns resembling teeth. Her eyes fell on the tapestry strung across the far wall; once vibrant, it now lay muted and lifeless.

Two more shadows emerged from the edge of the room. The first stepped close to the fire with arms and legs like tree trunks, a flaming red beard, a barrel for a chest, a bulbous nose the shape of a thumb, a mouth of missing teeth, and a shining bald head with a few wisps red hairs. But it was the second shadow that caught her attention most as it sauntered along the edge of the chamber as if it were stalking its prey. When it emerged from the fringe, it approached Katja, revealing an outline that reminded her of a large bat, its trailing leather duster resembling wings. When the shadow came close enough to see, half of the stranger's face glowed red, revealing a man with cunning eyes, welted and leathered skin, and a toothy grin clamped firmly to a wooden pipe that bellowed puffs of smoke.

"It isn't polite to stare," the man said, his puffed cheeks making a popping sound every time he sucked on his pipe. His face was shiny like glass in parts, while others were peeling like the bark on an aspen tree.

"It isn't polite to hold me hostage either! What do you want from me?" Katja rasped through bared teeth, wrestling with her binds.

"Don't think of yourself as a hostage . . . more as an invitee . . . a guest!" He gestured to the silhouettes behind him. "My name is Fleck, and these people here are my friends. We have been looking forward to finally meeting you."

Katja felt unnerved. Was this a strange ploy to deceive her into gaining their trust? Were they going to rob her? Torture her? Murder her? Something worse? She tried to stop her teeth from rattling, but was too tired and scared to hide it.

"Fleck, the poor girl is terrified. Let's get this dance started already," the man she believed was called Stav said. He stood with his arms crossed, as if he would rather be anywhere else. There was something about him, something in his eyes, that made her stomach turn. She knew it was the same man she had seen sitting on the countess's bed, a mask covering the lower half of his face.

"She is not some ordinary girl. She is a witch!" the stout man with a bald head barked.

"Not a very good one," the lady said, her hair long like dribbled honey and ears knotted and misshapen.

"Obviously no one is as talented a witch as Gwith, of course," Stav said, tongue pressed into his bottom lip.

Gwith smirked and jabbed Stav in the shoulder.

"Very well then," Fleck nodded. He looked to the dying hearth and twirled his fingers, summoning two cores of wood into the embers and causing the fire to roar, crackle, and pop. The chamber grew warmer and, more importantly, brighter, so she could see.

Katja frowned. "You know magic?"

"Oh, that little trick? Sorry, sometimes I forget what impresses people. I could melt iron with fire hot enough to boil every puddle in this potholed street if I wanted, but that would be a terrible waste of dust," Fleck said as the flames flickered blue for a few seconds. "But you wouldn't know about that sort of stuff, would you? No! Like the others, I am sure you will deny your magical abilities until I break every finger on your hand. They all deny it at first, but our eyes do not lie! We have seen what you do when no one is looking, Katja Rosdyre."

"I know enough to do this," Katja said, feeling warmth in her chest. She flicked her finger, and a lump of red-hot coal flew across the room. It hovered inches from Gwith's face.

Gwith stopped pacing midstride. The look of outright horror, but most of all fury, filled her round face. "Get this thing away from my face!"

Katja summoned the coal closer so that it nearly kissed the woman's cheek.

Gwith whacked the hovering coal with a shovel and stamped it into the ground with her boot, spitting on it before swiftly approaching Katja. She shoved past Fleck, slapped Katja across the cheek, and spat at her feet. "Don't ever do that again! Fleck might like you, but I won't stand for your wicked games! If I wanted to, I could paint a new reality on those marble eyes and contort your mind into madness! I could make you see things you would rather die than see! Just with a snap of my fingers!"

Katja clenched her jaw. Her cheek was numb, but she had dealt with blows before. At least it wasn't a closed fist or brass knuckles, or she might have a whole face to fix.

"I am certain I have seen far worse," Katja said through gritted teeth.

Fleck smiled as he puffed a cloud of smoke. "I am glad we can cut straight to the truth. But we already knew you could use basic levitation enchantments. That is what brought you to our attention in the first place. But can you remove the binds from your wrists? Can you free yourself from your prison?"

If he knew about her magic, what else did this man named Fleck know about her? A chill ran down her spine. She didn't like the feeling of being left out of the secret. Living on the streets of Theed made her intensely dislike surprises.

Surprises meant unpredictability, and predictability was your friend on the streets. You wanted your shelter in the same spot as the night before, your food at the same time, and water from the same clear source, if you were lucky to find any. Nothing was worse than returning to your home to find a ransacked shelter destroyed by looters. No one liked missing meals for days at a time, and even worse was finding out that the well you siphoned your precious water from was dry or sealed off when the owner caught on.

Katja wrestled with the hemp rope, but it barely budged. "And why would I tell you?"

"I think you would have done it by now if you could," Fleck said, stepping closer. "But no worry! If you knew fire incantations required to grant your passage out of the tapestry portal, lockpicking isn't far off your docket."

Fleck must think that Katja had summoned fire to light the purple candle. He didn't know she had a match all along. *She could use this to her advantage.*

"That is . . . unless you used a match." Fleck winked. "But I can't imagine anyone would be dense enough to blow out the only portal key without thinking of a way back out!"

Katja felt her stomach drop. Something about Fleck's demeanor made her uneasy. She didn't like how he steered a conversation, and his charm and easy smile struck her as too practiced.

"How did you know I was a... witch. I mean, a Glint?" Katja asked, fearing the answer. Then suddenly, a realization settled over her like hot tar on concrete. "The man that was looking in from the window the other day . . . that was you, wasn't it?"

Fleck smiled. "Not me, but certainly one of us. We have been watching you for a while, Katja Rosdyre."

"Who is 'us'?" Katja shivered. How did they know her name? Only the Maiden Tower and her clients knew her by her full name. She wasn't even sure if her name appeared in the royal records. After all, her mother said she was born beneath one of the canals, far away from anyone who cared to take note of it, like a droplet in a bathtub.

"You already know my name. I am not hiding it," Fleck said. He pulled a wooden wand from his pocket. "We did not find a wand on you. Do you hide it somewhere, or did it burn with the rest of that old mage's closet?"

"I don't need a wand," Katja said, splaying her palms. "My hands have worked just fine. Besides, I can't imagine you can find a wand at any dime store, nor would it be cheap."

Fleck laughed. "You are right on that. I just assumed you were a properly trained witch. Using one's hands is useful, but a wand or other ballast is a sign of someone with a sponsor or academic mentor. Did they not require a wand when you attended one of the great academies in Dirkland?"

"Well, I didn't go to any great college of magic in Dirkland. They wouldn't accept someone like me anyway," Katja hissed, noticing traces of her mother's accent slipping through when she was angry.

Fleck sighed. "You didn't go to an academy? Did you have a mentor? I find it hard to believe a chambermaid could teach themselves the intricacies of levitation on their own."

"I was told magic laws were more lenient to our friends across the Relian Sea," Stav said, combing back his dark hair. "Unlike the Commonwealth, which removed all the high colleges of magic when they signed those dreaded decrees."

"I didn't learn from a college or anything like that," Katja said.

Stav grinned. "Does this seem a bit unusual to you, Fleck? Perhaps my suspicions were correct."

"Possibly. But if not, she must have learned what she knows from someone," Fleck said, glaring at Stav. "I have never heard of a self-taught levitator."

Perhaps they didn't know as much about her as she thought.

Katja smiled, but she quickly noticed and pursed her lips. "I had a mentor. He taught me almost everything I know."

Katja was lying. The first time she knew she was different was when she was eight and could make a stone wobble on the pavement with just her mind when bored. Not even a year later, she won every dice game against the other girls and boys in the alleyway and won all of their bread and sugar. Then she moved on to palming apples off fruit carts and performing a few street tricks for some drunkards in the tavern, which led to speculating rumors about a drifter witch living among the streets. It was then that she decided she needed to leave the streets if she was ever going to learn magic, so she requested a job at the Maiden Tower and was able to use her talents more discreetly. It turned out not as discreetly as she thought.

"Who was this mentor? Was he properly trained?" Fleck asked.

Katja wasn't sure if she should condemn the count, but she had a better answer. "Trust me. He was as masterful at magic as anyone. A shame that he died before he could teach me all of his secrets."

Fleck looked at Stav suspiciously. "See, she had a mentor."

"That doesn't mean I was wrong," Stav said. "We have more tests to confirm."

"Very well then," Fleck said, eyes narrowing. "I think you are ready. I need you to pass three tests. If you pass, we will refrain from reporting your crimes to the constable," he grumbled. "If you fail, we'll just whisper a word in the right ear. The Magesleuths are very good at finding what we want them to find, and they don't ask questions of the shadows. They will interrogate you until your brain is mush, and only then will they sign your death warrant. After that . . . you know the rest."

Gwith slid a finger across her neck, and the unknown man standing behind Fleck acted out as a man being hanged by a rope.

"You would report me for using magic when you have done the same?" Katja scowled. "I know your name."

"Do you, though?" Stav winked, leaning against the hearth. "You have not even the faintest idea of where you are . . . let alone who we are."

Katja looked across the dark room. A beaten iron chimney rose from the hearth, diverting smoke as it bent this way and that until it disappeared behind a wall of cracking bricks smeared with lichen. Surrounding the fire were chairs and a large table covered in maps and scattered parchments. Deep alcoves and shadowed recesses lined the chamber, but one held a messy tent of skins and rope, sturdy enough to serve as a shelter in the alleys of the Smoker District. The ceiling soared nearly ten cubits above her. Where was she?

Katja wrestled her binds. "I am sure the Magesleuths won't have a problem finding where we are, especially with that strong sense of smell. I hear it doesn't take much for them to catch your scent, and once they have it, they will never forget it." She didn't know if that was true, but that is what Gavin told her, and it was compelling enough to make her terrified.

A flash of fear darkened Fleck's eyes, but it was only temporary. "If you pass my three tests, then we don't have to test that theory."

"What are these tests for?" Katja asked.

Fleck swished his wand before walking away. Katja's binds loosened and fell to her side.

"Follow me," he said.

Katja's heartbeat rattled in her chest, and her stomach boiled like a cauldron. She fled to the shady edge of the chamber, striking a key on a piano and stumbling into an alcove lined with shelves of books, candlesticks, flower vases, and other knick-knacks that fell to the floor as she frantically searched for an exit. When she got deeper into the alcove, her hand grazed a stone wall that was slimy to the touch, but then she felt something that made her stomach sink. *Is that bone?* Her fingers jittered as she delicately ran them against the wall again, feeling something rough and brittle with deep crevices, so she pulled back, uncertain of what she was confronting.

That was until a flickering lantern approached over her shoulder, swinging from Fleck's hand, revealing a wall of neatly stacked skulls and bones. Katja nearly stumbled to the floor as she retreated from the pale wall filled with hundreds of deep black eyes and wicked grins staring back at her.

"You won't find a way out. Not like that," Fleck said, raising his lantern to reveal the true horror of the wall, which continued to the ceiling and down a passageway as far as the lantern light was thrown.

"What is this place?" Katja uttered under her breath.

"Welcome to the Warren. It is a haunted place, but that is why we like it. Keeps anyone curious from wandering our way," Fleck said solemnly. "We thank these fallen souls for keeping us safe from those who would stack our bones beside them. Come now, Miss Rosdyre, join me at the hearth. You aren't the first person to be unaware of the thousands . . . millions of bodies this city was built on."

Katja tried to hide her shaking hands as Fleck guided her back to the two moth-eaten chairs before the fireplace. She saw a pinprick of light overhead, catching her attention. Shining in the daylight was a lone vent spilling faint sunlight high above. She watched the bright slits, which looked like a nightmarish tear in the night sky above, and then, to her surprise, something flickered through the light. Then there was another flicker, but before she could determine what caused it, Fleck snapped his fingers in her face and called her name.

"Katja . . . take a seat," he said, puffing on his pipe as the red-bearded man poured amber whiskey into his glass. "It was only a stack of old bones. What you should fear is the living."

"Thank you, Urie," the bald man grumbled, taking a nip straight from the bottle. "Could use some bloody manners in this place."

Fleck rolled his eyes. "Thanks, Urie. I couldn't do any of this without you, old sap."

Urie tipped his head. "Same to you, candleman."

Fleck shook his head disapprovingly, but waved Urie away before pointing to an empty seat. "I promise we're normally more civilized than this," he said.

Katja took a seat in the chair opposite Fleck. Over his shoulder, she could see Gwith leaning against the dusty piano, missing a few keys. She was playfully flicking a silvery wooden wand between her fingers, her burning hate aimed at Katja.

"Civilized? Did you kill all of those . . . people?" Katja asked, gulping down a shiver.

Fleck frowned. His face looked tortured. "They were once just like us. Glints who stood up to the wrong people at the wrong time."

"Why are they here?" she asked.

"The history of this place is a little hazy, but not without its hauntings. It began long ago as a cistern, once filled with water for the city. During the Great Rebellion, the Crown ran out of space to bury all the bodies littering the streets. They stacked them in pits until the maggots had exhumed their pale bones, then moved the remains here, where no one could see the mess they had made. After that, they locked it up, erased any mention of it, and built on top as if it had never existed," Fleck said. "Since we stumbled upon it, we added a few magical touches and made the Warren our home."

"So, we are underground?" Katja nodded, staring at the vents in the ceiling.

"Nice going, Fleck," Stav scoffed, nudging him with his shoulder as he passed.

"As if that detail is enough to make any difference in the matter," Fleck sneered. "There is no escaping the Warren."

Stav waved at Fleck dismissively as he took a bite of a green apple and sat at the table covered in maps and dusty tomes. "Hurry along with the test, old man."

Fleck cleared his throat, drawing her attention to his green eyes with copper flecks near their center. His face was scarred and warped in a way that resembled melting wax. He removed his hat, revealing wisps of black hair.

Her eyes carefully traveled down to his neck, where the scars continued down to the hem of his coat. She hated how her curiosity overcame her. Did it continue across his whole body? She spotted ropey bands of skin on the backs of his hands, confirming her suspicions. *Where did he get those scars?*

Fleck sighed, noticing her gaze. "If you must know, I have had it since birth. Go ahead, touch it . . . it doesn't hurt."

He offered his hand. Katja hesitated to take it, but before she could decide, he reached for hers and smiled.

His skin was thick and lumpy but softer than she expected. She smiled and let go after she felt an acceptable amount of time had passed.

"Thanks." She didn't know what to say.

Fleck smiled, a golden tooth shining back at her. "So, now that you know more about me . . . I have a few questions for you before we start our tests. What brings a talented witch like yourself to be employed by the Maiden Tower? Surely, we know it is very convenient to be able to use enchantments to help with the busy work, so you have time to sip wine from your client's precious cellars, but couldn't you make a decent living as a healer, star reader, mystic, potion brewer in the Outer Realm?"

Katja's jaw tightened like a coil. She was going to ask how they knew she worked for the Maiden Tower, but then she looked down at her crimson dress with its signature bow and swallowed that question. Everyone in Theed knew the signature regalia of the Maiden Tower.

"The Outer Realm? Are you serious? I have only heard terrible stories from out there beyond the city walls. Besides, the Maiden Tower saved me from dying on the streets, and for that, I am forever grateful," Katja said, perplexed by his question. "Magic might be illegal in Theed, but it would be suicide for someone like me to live out there in the wild. I hear there are cannibals out there . . . at least that is what my mother told me."

"They will hang you for many other reasons out there," Gwith scoffed. "You don't even have to be a witch. I don't blame the girl."

"Not many options for a Glint in Theed either," Urie said, pouring a flagon of ale and sipping it so it dripped from his burning red beard. "Unless you have the coin to make the guards look the other way. And I am not talking about a bag of crowns—I am talking a wagon full of Stellish denar!"

"Yes, the Crown has made it clear which heads they lop off," Stav grinned.

"So, why not enlist to become one of the Crown's Magesleuths? I am certain Queen Margot would love some young blood to join their ranks," Fleck said, blowing out a cloud of smoke. Although a little strong, the scent was pleasing. It reminded Katja of an old candlemaker, Mr. Combs, on the edge of Seventh Street in the Boarshead District, whom she would occasionally camp next to. Mr. Combs never reported her for trespassing to the constable and would sometimes give her some bread he had to spare. She always remembered him sitting on his rocker on his porch, eating figs, and smoking his Dusken Ash tobacco pipe until the streetlamps were lit. It was remarkable how a single scent could peel back the sands of time, even for a minute.

"I would never work for the likes of them," Katja spat. "I could never sleep at night knowing I was among the ranks of murderers. I don't even know if it is a human hiding beneath those thick robes."

"That doesn't stop you from spying for the Maiden Tower," Fleck challenged. "I know what that tower does, and I reckon none of it is good."

Katja glanced at the count's tapestry on the wall and then back to Fleck. Did he know about her intention to steal the cards? Were they watching her even when she was tucked away in her dormitory? She shuddered at the thought.

"I don't know what you are talking about," Katja lied.

Fleck smiled knowingly. "Fair. You don't have to answer. But if you want to be released without being handed over to the royal guards, you must pass my next test."

"Next test?" Katja said nervously. She tried to get to her feet, but before she could, Stav brandished his wand in front of her face.

"Your first test was determining if you were a royalist snob or not," Stav smirked, standing at her shoulder. "We don't work with anyone willing to give credence to the anti-magic authorities."

Fleck gestured to Gwith, who was lingering along the edge of the room. She nodded back with approval before vanishing into the shadows.

"There are three trials that I have prepared for you, but you only need to pass one," Fleck said, his jade green eyes flashing in the sparkling flame. "One is a test of stealth. Another is a test of lockpicking, and the last is a test of persuasion. Which direction do your magical capabilities lead you?"

Katja wanted to avoid where this was going. Was this some elaborate trick to get her caught using magic? Did they want to see how weak her magic truly was? A realization settled over her like a cold bath—what if they were working for the Crown? Perhaps they were Magesleuths themselves! They sure seemed to know a lot about them, even suggesting she join them.

"This is a trick! You work for the Crown, don't you?" Katja sneered. "You are doing all this to gather the evidence to prove I am a witch, aren't you?"

Urie chuckled. "I don't think a soul in Theed loathes the Crown more than Fleck. Other than maybe Kristoff."

"He won't be happy you said his name out loud to a prisoner!" Gwith scolded, returning from the shadows. "You know how paranoid he gets."

"He is just paranoid because he knows every dust merchant in this city, and there are no shadier men in the entire Commonwealth. When you hear about a bloated corpse drifting in from the Relian, you know it was a dust merchant or one of their cutthroat soldiers taking care of loose ends," Urie said, tracing a finger across his throat.

"And we wouldn't have a drop of Vigor to share between us without him, so let's keep his name out of your mouth," Gwith said threateningly. "You don't want to see me when I am desperate, Urie."

Urie scratched his head and backed away like a scolded street dog.

Gwith slipped into the dark recesses of the chamber and returned with a small pouch that rested in her palm like a sleeping creature, its weight hinting at something concealed inside.

"What will it be, Katja?" Fleck asked, snapping his fingers to spark a flame that hovered on the tip of his thumb before pressing it into the tobacco packing his pipe. "Perhaps you know nothing at all! Is that the truth? I sure hope not."

Katja scoured her mind, wondering whether she should comply and which test she could pass, but none were in her wheelhouse. Her mastery was levitation, not lockpicking or persuasion. *Hexes!* The last time she tried to lockpick was when she was trying to open the mysterious cabinet in the count's tapestry and was stumped because she didn't know the Elddir tongue. The Maiden Tower trusted her enough to spy and steal for them without getting caught, but the only magic she used was levitation when the situation called for it. She was also not terribly convincing, or else she would have been released by now.

"What will it be, girl?" Gwith said, tapping her cleated boots impatiently.

"Let the girl decide, Gwith!" Stav barked. "It was a lot of work getting her here. We can wait a few minutes!"

Gwith bared her teeth at him in a threatening manner. "I would rather be on a job! But I know you enjoy sitting in your bunk all day!"

"What will it be, Miss Rosdyre?" Fleck asked, ignoring his quarreling teammates.

"How about you let me go, and I don't tell the constable about this strange place and its magical inhabitants when I inevitably get out of here!" Katja spat.

"Well, we know she doesn't know the art of persuasion," Stav smirked, his pale eyes glowing in the flame light.

"You know we are underground, but do you know where?" Fleck asserted, pointing at the ceiling. He waited a moment as Katja fumbled for an answer. "I will take that as a resounding 'no.'"

Stav chuckled. "Not even the Sleuths have been able to find this place. So don't feel too bad."

"Just let me go! I don't want any part of this!" Katja challenged.

"Then I am sorry to say we must bring you to the constable . . . You might not know where we are, but you have seen too much to let you wander the streets," Fleck sighed, hunching his shoulders. He stood up from his chair and clenched his fist. "Lads and ladies! We will have to find another witch or wizard! We lost another one!"

Lost another one? Were there others who had sat in her same seat before?

"Fine! I can pick a damn lock!" Katja spat, her heart racing in her chest. "Just don't send me to the bloody constable!"

Fleck turned to Stav with pursed lips. She could tell he was trying to suppress a smile.

"Urie, you heard the witch! Bring her to the lock!" Fleck roared. He seemed a little too excited. It made him seem oddly friendly but also dangerous.

Urie finished his tankard of ale, retrieved a long key from the pouch, and yanked her from her chair. He was short but very stout, with forearms thicker than tree branches and arm hairs as wild as moss, which complemented his caterpillar eyebrows.

"I can walk myself!" Katja shouted, tearing away from his grip.

Urie glared at her and shoved her forward into the darkest section of the chamber. Fleck followed closely behind, his arms behind his back. Gwith hovered, but she seemed more interested in sharpening the tip of her knife against a whetstone.

Katja stumbled, nearly falling to her knees. She half expected the floor to plummet beneath her and to fall to her death, but instead, she crashed into a set of iron bars.

"Get in!" Urie demanded, his voice gravelly.

"I am making a grave mistake, aren't I?" Katja said, her throat tight and tender from the earlier smoke. "You are slavers, and this is my jail cell, isn't it?"

Urie pushed her deeper into the cell and shut the gate. He then jiggled the lock and turned the skeleton key until it clicked loudly enough to echo across the chamber.

That was it—she would never be free again. She felt sick and hopeless.

Urie moved aside as Fleck approached from behind—the red ember of his pipe lighting half of his molten face.

"Free yourself, and you pass," Fleck said solemnly. "Fail . . . then you meet the hangman's noose like the others. You have until morning."

Katja bashed against her cell. "What then? Will you just let me go? You wouldn't take me and have me go through these tests to release me, would you?"

"Of course not," Fleck uttered.

"Then just send me to the constable if I will be your prisoner! I don't mean to be your vassal!" Katja shouted, spitting at Fleck's face. "I will scream so loud that someone hears up above!"

"Go ahead. You wouldn't be the first to try," Fleck sighed and wiped his face before heading for the hearth.

Katja let out a blood-curdling scream that expelled all the air from her lungs, and she fell to her knees.

"If you pick your lock and free yourself, you will have more options than you ever had at the Maiden Tower," Fleck said, his voice echoing off the tall ceilings as he strolled away with Urie behind him. "You can even get revenge and strangle me in my sleep if you so wish. But I have a feeling you won't. There is a reason you chose the trial of lockpicking and not stealth."

Chapter Four

Sweat dripped down Katja's brow as her wrists craned around the steel bars. Her finger pressed against the keyhole, and she mumbled incoherent words under her breath.

The taste of iron filled her mouth. She realized her tongue was sticking out and licking the prisoner bars. She might have realized it sooner had she been paying attention, but her focus toggled between the lock and the silhouettes pacing around the Warren, with mysterious whispers and periodic glances in her direction.

At one point, a man with long, flaxen hair tied in a bun and a soft voice entered the chambers through a hidden entrance, shrouded in shadow. He wore a deep blue peacoat, a cream vest with silver buttons, a puffed collar and sleeve, a crooked bowtie, pleated white trousers, and buckled boots that gave him the air of nobility if it wasn't for the red stain on his thigh that he clenched with his palm as he limped across the chamber. He sat in the chair across from Fleck, who sighed before tending to his wound.

"You really ought to be more careful," Fleck grumbled. "I used to watch sailors die from tiny wounds. It is the sepsis that gets you."

Katja didn't usually have any issue at the sight of blood. After all, she saw it every day growing up, but there was something about the way the wound shone in the flickering light that made her uneasy. She focused on the lock and tried her best to steady her shaky arms. All she wanted to do was sleep. How long had it been? Looking up at the ceiling, the light spilling from the slits was no longer visible, which meant that it must be night.

Katja whispered to the lock like a madman. "Who is your master? Please, tell me . . . or else I will die."

There was no response, just like the cabinet in the count's tapestry.

"Did you hear me? I am going to die if you don't confess," Katja pleaded. Then, a surge of rage burned in her throat, and she smashed her shoulder against her cell like an angered beast. "Spill it! Is this really how I am to die?"

"People have died for less," the well-dressed stranger said through gritted teeth. "I can name a few."

"Don't talk to her," Urie grunted, tending to a boiling cauldron over the fire. "She might trick you! It wouldn't be the first time a witch has played meek yet deceived with that wicked tongue! Smarter men than you and I have fallen for less."

Gwith smacked Urie on top of his bald head. "You know I am a witch!"

Urie chuckled. "Yes, I do, and I have heard that tongue trill in my ear enough."

"Urie, that is no way to talk to one of our own, even if she is one step above a street urchin. Don't let that red gown fool you," the nobleman quipped. He clenched his armrest and tossed his head back in pain. "Hexes! That hurts! If I were on your ship, you wouldn't have been my first pick to stitch up my wounds! I thought you sailors were all trained better."

"Would you rather have me stick my finger in it?" Fleck scoffed. "Besides, when you are bleeding out on the top of a ship in the heat of battle, the last thing you think about is how pretty the stitches are sewing you back up. Now keep still and bite a wad of that modest peacoat cuff if it hurts so bad!"

"Both of you stop your whining!" Gwith scolded, pilfering a bowl of Urie's stew. "I don't want to hear you two bickering all night!"

"The only voice I hear is yours, Gwith!" Urie scolded. "I hope you burn your wicked tongue on that broth! I haven't even given it the proper seasoning."

"I pity the unfortunate lass that marries you and is stuck with your terrible stews," Gwith chuckled.

"No lady with dignity will be caught at the temple altar with a man who reeks of latrine in a one-knot tavern!" the nobleman teased.

"Tell that to your mother. I borrowed her perfume," Urie challenged, sipping from the cauldron with a large ladle.

"Not to mention all that hair that rivals the floor of a lice-infected barbershop," the nobleman uttered.

Urie grinned. "You would be surprised how many gals like combing their fingers through a real man's chest with hair as thick as an ox! Last I checked, yours was as bare as a plucked hen!"

"Don't worry, Kristoff," Gwith chuckled. "I like a man with less hair than a baby's bottom!"

The chamber grew silent, and Kristoff's shaded eyes narrowed like a sharp dagger's edge.

"What did I tell you all about saying my name in front of prisoners . . .?" the nobleman growled, his jaw visibly clenched.

There was no response, but Katja could tell that this man had held the chamber's collective goodwill hostage many times before. Even Fleck looked distressed as they waited for Gwith to answer.

"Well . . . what do you want me to do about it?" Gwith said, her honey-yellow hair frazzled. "Bash the girl's skull in so she might never remember it? I can do that. It wouldn't be the first time I've beaten someone into a stupor."

The tension in the Warren grew so tight that one could feel it press against their skin. Then Kristoff burst out laughing. "I might have considered a lady like you if you had some manners, a single clean fingernail, and your last name meant more than a heap of dirt. But then we wouldn't have the greatest conjurer this side of the Relian in our ranks."

Gwith stared at Kristoff fiercely, then broke into a smile.

"That is the nicest thing you've said to me!" she exclaimed, hugging Kristoff and forcing a kiss on his cheek. "Who knew you thought so highly of me?"

The group laughed, but Fleck shook his head as he finished stitching Kristoff's grievous wound.

Katja listened to all of this, but she wished to scream at them all to shut up so she could concentrate. It was hard to hear anything over their cackles and banter.

"What is your master's name? Tell me now!" Katja uttered in her mother's native Dirkish, punching the iron with her left fist.

"What is all of that racket? Is that Vostish or Dirkish retching that I hear?" Kristoff shouted. He looked in her direction and then back at Fleck and the others. "Wait . . . is that who I think it is? You didn't . . . did you?"

Fleck frowned. "Do what?"

"Don't play stupid with me, Fleck! The girl, of course," Kristoff snarled. "She was probably expected to arrive at the Maiden Tower hours ago. Don't you think her disappearance will stir up suspicion?"

"Quiet!" Urie shushed. "I spotted a Magesleuth lurking nearby this evening. Mr. Fleck might be confident in how impenetrable this fortress is, but I am not so confident. You can never be certain who listens."

"We haven't been discovered since we found this place many years ago," Kristoff rasped, slamming his fists on his armrests. "But that might change if the Maiden Tower reports the girl missing! If there is someone who could find us, it is the grand maiden and her spies! We should have brought her to a less secure place first before bringing her into the heart of the beast."

"Calm down, Kristoff!" Gwith snapped, kicking him in the boot. "Fleck and Stav have thought all of this through, I am certain."

"Have you given her an ultimatum as we discussed privately?" Kristoff challenged. "We cannot afford to be weak in times like these."

"I told Miss Rosdyre that if she doesn't unlock her cell by morning, we will bring her to the constable. Then the Magesleuths can deal with her," Fleck said, finishing his stitching and severing the loose end of twine with a flick of his wand. "The Maiden Tower has dozens of spies. I wouldn't be surprised if most of the chambermaids they employ were spying on their customers without their knowing. A single chambermaid vanishing won't make a difference. If she gets turned in for crimes of magic, the Maiden Tower won't hesitate to erase her name from their ledgers to avoid being associated with a witch—"

"And if our theory is indeed . . . correct?" Kristoff interrupted.

"We will discuss that if it comes up," Fleck grumbled.

"Good. I didn't know you really had it in you, Fleck," Kristoff grinned. "Turning in your own people to the Crown you despise so much, for them to be murdered by the same laws you detest. I applaud that you have finally grown a spine."

Fleck gritted his teeth. "Sometimes you have to work within the parameters in which you are given before you can change them."

Kristoff raised a finger to protest, but withdrew it seemingly as soon as he realized he didn't have a response. He finished the rest of his whiskey, combed back crazed golden hairs, and grunted before wandering into the depths of the Warren that was shrouded with shadow.

"Let me know if you see my brother! He and I need to talk. I will be in my study!" Kristoff called from somewhere far within the twisting corridors, the screech of hinges following him as he went.

"Good! Sleep off that terrible mood!" Gwith teased, taking Kristoff's seat across from Fleck. She pulled a deck of cards out of her cleavage and spread them across the rickety table between them. "Want to play?"

Fleck smiled and took a card from the table, but Urie snatched it between his fingers before he could pick it up.

"Not so fast, candleman!" Urie grinned, admiring the card and returning to his boiling cauldron. "You aren't leaving me with the scraps this time!"

Fleck furrowed his hairless brow and fetched another card, bending it between the gaps of his teeth like a toothpick.

Katja felt her hand grow numb as she arched it around the lock in an unnatural position. She cursed louder than expected, and her voice echoed along the thick walls.

"What is wrong? Can't figure out how to get out?" Gwith sneered behind a hand of cards. "You aren't going to go far speaking Dirkish."

Katja sighed. She was used to people teasing her about her accent, especially when she was younger, though it was barely noticeable now. "I speak it so I can curse your names without you knowing. I'm not fluent in Elddir, if that's what you're implying."

"No one is fluent in Elddir except maybe a few eggheads at Hartwind College," Gwith chuckled. "We Glints just learn a few words and phrases as needed."

"She is probably plotting and waiting for us to leave so she can pick the lock and sneak off. Shame she will never find her way out." Urie frowned, tossing a set of cards onto the pile with a groan. "At least that is what happened with the last Dustmage . . . or maybe that was the one before the last—I dunno."

"Do you even remember his name?" Gwith teased.

Urie scratched his head. "I suppose I don't. Died before I could get to know him."

"They never last long," Gwith beamed, picking at her fingernail.

Fleck clenched his fist, and the cauldron boiled over onto the fiery embers. The room swiftly darkened as smoke hissed into the air like pale clouds. Gwith and Urie both froze.

"*Simon* . . . his name was Simon!" Fleck growled, teeth clenched in the dim light. "How could you possibly forget? I know it seems like a cruel joke, but I remember every one of my pupils!"

Urie stammered, "Of course, Fleck. I didn't mean to—"

"How could you forget after his terrible . . . passing." Fleck's strong timbre withered as he stared into the flames with a tortured expression on his face. "I still have nightmares about it."

"Cheer up, Fleck! Let's drink one for Simon! The greatest Dustmage in Roth history!" Gwith looked over toward Katja's cell. "Unless she changes that, but considering I haven't heard even so much as a click from that lock, I think our bets are safe!"

Gwith poured a glass of foamy ale, clinked it against the others, and downed it with a loud gasp. Fleck did not partake in the merriment, instead wallowing with his pipe and bottle of firebrandy.

After the three captors ate their hot stew, filled their bellies with spirits, and smoked enough tobacco to leave a thick haze in the chamber, a gust of rancid air wrapped around the room like an uninvited guest. One by one, Gwith and Urie left the fire through the back door, leaving Fleck alone, drunkenly mumbling to himself.

Katja continued attempting to pick the lock, begging for its master's name again after letting her tired arms rest for half an hour. A cool breeze caressed her neck, making her wish she were closer to the warmth of the fire or had a sip of Fleck's firebrandy in her belly.

"Why haven't you saved yourself yet, Miss Rosdyre?" Fleck said, puffing a cloud of smoke. "I expected someone who knew levitation could figure out lockpicking rather swiftly. It isn't a terribly difficult spell. What are you plotting?"

Katja's stomach sank. Of course, it wasn't hard, but she had only a short time to learn from the count, and she had learned only tidbits about levitation from her mother before being forced to fend for herself. Should she confess that she didn't know the lockpicking spell? Would he pity her or get angry? Why did she feel like she owed this monstrosity of a man anything? She was the one who was plucked from Stavoren Manor while she was minding her own business.

"Why would I tell you if I was?" Katja said, trying to regain her confidence, but deep down, she was in a pit of despair.

"I think you are waiting for me to fall asleep to free yourself, and then once you are free, you are going to strangle me as I sleep. Perhaps you will cast a muzzle enchantment on me so no one can hear my screams for help," Fleck said, his tongue heavy from the whiskey. "I wouldn't blame you. I've been a prisoner myself before, and I have had similar thoughts of retribution."

"Perhaps," Katja blurted, not sure how to respond.

Fleck laughed. "Say you did find out how to escape. At least Auriella will be happy to have her hair braided and her book collection dusted. But what does that matter when you can't remember the next minute from the last? Bless her . . . To the countess!"

He raised his drink and swigged it with a harsh swallow.

"You know Auriella?" Katja asked.

"Know her? Of course I know her! We have been casing her ancestral manor for over a month now," Fleck said, clanking his bottle onto the hard ground. "You can thank Stav for finding you. It was all so perfect, wrapped like a present for my name day. Not only were you a witch, but a witch working for the Maiden Tower." He kissed his fingers.

"Too bad you will have me murdered tomorrow," Katja sighed, slumping to the floor.

"You are a good liar, Miss Rosdyre," Fleck laughed. "You are only a few words from freedom, and you know it. You speak your mother tongue and our language here in the Commonwealth. I do not think a few words will be your downfall."

Katja almost wanted to laugh, but she was too mortified about how much trouble she was in. She could lie and brag to the end of her allotted time, but it would all be for nothing if she could not perform a lockpicking spell. Lying is one thing, but performing is another.

Fleck gave her a perplexed look and puffed his pipe somberly. "Where did you really learn levitation enchantments? For many, it takes years of rigorous training to levitate a spoon, let alone a broom, pots and pans, dozens of tomes, and several other things all at once. And that is with the instruction of a master levitator at an esteemed academy of magic."

Katja remained silent.

"I could get any answer I want from your lips with one spell. It would be horrific and agonizing, but I would get my answer," Fleck taunted. "But collecting the ingredients might take me a few days."

"If you get me out of here, then I will tell you," Katja said, leaning back on the cold floor. "And I promise I didn't go to some mysterious academy in the Dirkish Highlands, or anywhere else for that matter. They would never let someone like me in their esteemed doors. I can read well enough, but no one ever taught me to write. Go ahead, find those ingredients. It might even buy me a few more days," she uttered.

"You have to pass my test, Miss Rosdyre," Fleck said dryly. "Nothing changes that."

"It was worth a shot," Katja said solemnly. "Why are you still awake while the others sleep?"

Fleck was silent.

"What happened to the last Dustmage . . . was it Simon?" she asked cautiously. "That seemed to strike a nerve when your friends mentioned him. How did he die?"

Fleck filled his lungs with smoke and slumped in his chair.

"That is none of your concern, Miss Rosdyre. If you don't know a basic lockpicking spell, spare me the time," he scoffed. "Believe it or not, the constable's office is not far."

Was that a slip of his tongue? Katja perked up in her seat, looking at the dark ceiling as if she would suddenly spot a sign in bright red lettering with "Constable's Office" written on it. She turned her attention back to Fleck, but his seat was empty. Where did he go? She scanned the chamber, but there was no sign of life. He was just there mere seconds ago. How did he vanish without her knowing, especially while drunk? He seemed to be getting comfortable.

When it seemed like Fleck would not return, Katja stretched her fingers before attempting the lock again, her arms still tight from raising them all evening. Half the problem was that she couldn't see what she was doing, especially now that it was night. An idea sparked. She drew from the wells of her chest and flicked her finger, summoning five hot coals from the dimming hearth. Stacking them beside her, she felt the warmth seep in, and the faint light gave her a fragile hope.

"What is your master's bloody name!" she hissed angrily, pressing the tip of her raw fingertip against the keyhole. Perhaps she just needed to dig a little deeper. "Tell me now! I beg you! Who is your creator? Please!"

Her voice came back as an echo. She was being too loud. Deep down, she knew she couldn't perform the spell even if she knew the lockmaker's name. No matter how much light she got from the coals, they couldn't teach her Elddir. Even if she knew a hundred words of the Elddir tongue, if she didn't know how to speak the lockmaker's name, then she was damned.

Her blood boiled at her current circumstance. She would not be trapped. Her fingers grew rigid, and her teeth clenched, as she felt something churn in her chest down to her belly. Then, she closed her eyes and raised her hands into the air before waving them like she was conducting a large pit orchestra reaching an unraveling crescendo.

Splintering wood, clanging metal, the roar of the wind, and grinding stone filled her ears as tables, stools, candlesticks, jars, cabinets, plates, and every free-standing item were hurled toward her cage.

Katja fell to the back of the cell and ducked into her arms to shield her face as everything crashed into the iron bars with a sound akin to two carriages colliding, a sight she had witnessed a handful of times before. Shards of pinewood and glass shrapnel launched toward her, and those that missed pelleted the wall, skidding violently across the stone floor. For a minute, all she could hear was carnage, but not long after, there was an eerie silence. When she felt safe enough to lower her warding arms, the chamber was pitch black except for a few pinpricks of remaining coal hissing in a pile of broken furniture propped against her cell like a stack of matches. The prison bars were still intact.

"What was that?" a voice rang out.

A flame ignited, revealing Urie's face as he lit a lantern.

"Looks like the witch tried to break out another way!" Gwith said, cursing as she stepped onto something heavy. "Boils! She ruined our camp!"

Katja felt weak as sweat dripped down her brow. Her pulse felt slow, like her blood had turned to molasses. Then her breathing shallowed, and her vision blurred. She had felt this many times before when her Vigor was low. She needed more magedust.

"Girl! Are you still alive?" Urie shouted, swiftly approaching.

Katja tried to speak, but her lips tingled. She would be alright for a little while, but come morning, she would be dead. The feeling of dread rushed over her. Her heart pounded for one second, only to disappear without notice moments later. Her skin grew clammy and cold to the touch as even a gentle breeze caused her to shiver to the bone. Then, when she least expected it, she felt the warmth of a sweltering summer day broil beneath her skin, making her desire nothing more than to tear off all her clothes.

Katja vomited all over the ashen floor until her stomach felt like it was dry and shriveled. When she felt like there was nothing else to purge, acid and bile trickled up her throat and coated her tongue with a horrific taste, only making her want to vomit more. She could barely catch a breath between heaves as a sharp pain sliced through her ribs.

"She's moving!" Urie blurted. Katja hadn't realized he was standing beside her cell where the heap of rubble was thinnest.

Gwith joined Urie and watched her fall to her side on the ground.

"She doesn't look so good," Gwith said, tilting her head.

"She is a bloody street witch, Gwith! They always look sick!" Urie retorted. He looked at the pile of shattered wood and sighed. "What a mess."

"Did Stav ever come back?" Gwith asked. "Kristoff has been pacing outside his door like a dog waiting for its owner to return."

"I dunno, but I reckon he will be back soon enough. You know, Stav, much like a cat, he disappears for a few days and returns to lick his wounds." Urie frowned. "Kristoff probably just wants to fight him like last time. Those brothers never get along."

"I suppose . . ." Gwith sighed. "Is she going to die?"

"Probably. She just swept the entire room into her cell. Consider herself lucky I took my box of dynamite out of here earlier this morning, or else it might have woken up all of Theed!"

Gwith reached between the bars with her handkerchief and began patting the blood from Katja's shoulder.

"Dust . . . dust . . ." Katja uttered, falling onto her side.

"Dust?" Gwith smirked. "You really think we'd give up precious magedust for you, even if we had it?"

She tossed her handkerchief at Katja's feet.

"I'm going back to bed," Urie said as if breathing was a chore. He then walked away, blew out the lantern, and disappeared into the night.

Gwith struck another match and stared at Katja, her expression shifting from confused to angry to pity. She reached through the bars, combing her fingers through Katja's long red hair, and frowned.

"I am sorry it has to end this way. I really thought you were the one," Gwith whispered. She stumbled back across the room and flicked her match into the corner. "All of that time following you across town for nothing. What a shame."

Katja groaned. Her throat was too hoarse to reply.

"No hard feelings if you can't pick the lock. Not everyone has what it takes to become the Arkan Roth's next Dustmage." Gwith stepped out of the room and slammed the door behind her with a loud thud.

Chapter Five

Katja jolted awake, her hair standing up like sharp quills. She was not alone, and a mysterious scratching sound confirmed this.

"Hello . . .?" she stammered, shivering and feeling sick.

"It has struck me that you never asked for any of our full names . . . not one! I waited for the question, begging fate that you would ask before morning struck, but you never did," the voice uttered. "Why? Why haven't you asked? But then I realized you either possess a kind of clairvoyance I have never seen the likes of before, or the simpler but difficult answer . . . you lack the knowledge of a simple lockpicking spell."

Katja rubbed her eyes, spotting a silhouette darker than the night, like a mismatched patch on a quilt. Sweat dripped down her brow into her eyes, and her body shook uncontrollably. She hugged her knees to keep warm, but she knew this wasn't the kind of cold one could warm up from. She was in the throes of withdrawal, and soon, it would consume her.

Glass shattered on the floor as the silhouette pushed aside the broken furniture resting against her cell door. A red ember glowed bright, revealing a waxy face.

"*You,*" Katja whispered, attempting to slide away from the door. "What are you doing?"

"You are a lost child who has not been taught magic but has had it forced upon her to survive. It all makes sense now. I should have known a simple maiden wouldn't know lockpicking spells. I condemned you to die," Fleck mumbled. "You never had a chance. But that doesn't mean you aren't a Dustmage. The real test will be apparent soon enough. Possibly tonight. But it is a cruel test that crosses the boundary between life and death."

"Are you drunk? You sound crazed," Katja said. "Just let me out, and I won't tell anyone about this place."

Fleck nodded. "Gwith, Urie, Kristoff, the others . . . you must never tell them what happened this night. They will never forgive me. I don't know if I will be able to forgive myself, but even more so if I send you to the constable to die. You are my flesh and blood."

"I won't tell any of them," Katja said cautiously.

Fleck stared at her. "You are weak. I can tell. Your Vigor is failing you. We will soon find out what you are, and if you die . . . I don't know if I can handle it anymore."

Katja nodded. She wanted to vomit, but her stomach was still empty from earlier.

"I will give you more once I get you out of here." He glanced over his shoulder. "You promise to die with this secret? I cannot let another of my kin die. Not another Glint."

"I will not tell a soul," Katja whispered.

"One more thing," Fleck said, his expression tense. "You must stay with us. I will teach you magic . . . lockpicking, fire, alchemy, spellcraft, everything I know."

"And then what?" Katja asked.

"Then you will serve as our Dustmage, Miss Rosdyre," Fleck smiled.

Katja thought for a minute. Her mind raced. With the count dead, she needed a new mentor —someone with training who could teach her the ropes, no matter how basic. She also much preferred this to being hanged.

"I agree." She bowed her head.

"Good," Fleck said, closing his eyes, taking his pipe out of his mouth, and setting the mouthpiece against the metal lock. "First lesson. Identify the lock as I have with my pipe."

"I know this," Katja sighed.

Fleck peeked through one eye. "You do?"

Katja nodded. "I just don't know how to get it to tell me its master's name. Or how to speak, Elddir."

Fleck closed his eyes again.

"You have failed because you have asked the wrong question. You mustn't ask who created the lock, but who was the last soul to seal it," Fleck smirked. "Sometimes, that is the creator, but most often, it is not. That is why I was so distressed by you not asking for any of our names."

Katja's jaw dropped. "That means the name would change . . . constantly?"

"Depends on how many hands the keys pass between. In this case, it is straightforward . . . I don't even have to ask," Fleck whispered, steadying his pipe on the lock. "Urie Mastbilt . . . which translates to *Urie tar Mastbilt!*"

The lock clicked, and with a subtle push, the cell door creaked backward toward her. Katja's heart raced as she crawled to her knees and stood between the newly formed gap so the marred man could not change his mind. *Freedom never felt closer.*

"See . . . once you understand the Elddir tongue, it will be easier," Fleck said, his breath strong with firebrandy. "Naturally, the language is different from what we speak today, but luckily, names of people and things are often preserved through translation because our modern naming conventions only differ slightly from those of thousands of years ago. When the Elddir language was spoken, names were bridged with three simple words depending on the person: *tar* for men, *don* for women, and *var* for all in between. Sometimes, you can still see the remains of this naming tradition in some ancient houses across the Commonwealth, such as the 'Don Bellums,' the 'Varjules,' and the mighty 'tar Scales.' It is also how you get Urie tar Mastbilt."

Katja's fist met his cheek before he could finish his sentence. He stumbled backward, clenching his cheek, nearly falling over the stack of torched wood.

"You . . . hit me," Fleck gasped, reaching for his pipe that fell to the floor as blood oozed out of his nose.

Katja's heart pumped out of her chest as she lunged at Fleck, jumping on him and sending him to the floor. He struggled, but his drunkenness made him clumsy.

Katja pressed her thumbs into his neck as he gasped for air while attempting to wrestle her grip.

Fleck groaned and tossed her into the rubble, which made a loud clatter. Katja felt something jab into her spine, sending webs of pain radiating down her ribcage. She bit her tongue as she held in her cry in an attempt not to wake the others, but she was sure someone would hear their struggle sooner or later. If the others swarmed her, then it would all be over.

"You are a good liar," Fleck croaked, slowly rising to his feet. He plucked the embers from his pipe as if pulling the strings of a puppet, and they leapt to life, hissing and blazing bright. He then shot them toward her, but she escaped all but one of them, which pricked her shoulder like a bee stinger.

"Let me go!" Katja shouted.

"Do you want to learn magic, or do you want to live the rest of your miserable life working in the Maiden Tower?" Fleck blurted through clenched teeth.

"I didn't mind my life before meeting you and your friends," Katja challenged. "Actually, I preferred it."

"That is because you haven't had the chance to know what we truly have to offer," he said. "I don't want to hurt you, Katja."

She hated hearing her name come out of his horrid mouth.

"Too late," Katja snapped, glancing at her bleeding arm. "Let me go, or I'll scream and wake up the others, and I'll tell them that you were foolish enough to let me free."

"I will just tell them you escaped," Fleck said. "And they will hunt you for as long as you live. We do not quickly forget."

"I will leave Theed," she rasped.

"Go ahead then. Leave Theed. As you probably know, the world isn't better outside these city gates," Fleck said. "I could tell you more about that if you stay. Not many people know about what lies outside of the capital."

Katja felt weak and faint. Her last bit of energy was spent fighting Fleck, and if she had anything left in reserves, she would need it to prevent herself from further suffering withdrawals. She needed more magedust, or she would die like all the other mages who spread their Vigor too thin. She could feel the gravity tugging harder on her frame, like there were tiny hooked strings pulling her down to the ground. This was what the count called "Kindling," and whenever he warned her about it, she remembered his eyes darkening and filling with dread as he spoke of its horrors.

"You are running on fumes. I can see it in your face," Fleck said, wincing. "You are dying."

Katja eyed the tapestry across the room. Even if there was an inkling of hope of magedust within the count's tapestry, she couldn't return to it without the purple candle. Where would she find magedust? The unsettling feeling made her nauseous. She was so far from getting relief.

Her arms shook, and her head started to pound. Even though she knew she wasn't on fire, her blood felt like it was boiling beneath her skin. She scratched at her forearms anxiously as cold sweat beaded down her spine.

"I have what you need," Fleck said, reaching out a welcoming hand. "I have enough magedust to get you back on your feet. Join us."

Katja lunged at him, but before she could reach his throat, the floor fell beneath her feet, and a significant weight tugged down on her shoulders like lead. Spots cluttered her vision, and her fingers grew numb.

Then there was nothing.

Chapter Six

"**D**o you think she's dead?" came a whisper.

The voice sounded thick, as if it had been spoken between bites of molasses and honey.

"She's breathing," another voice answered.

Something jabbed her in the rib. Her eyes flickered, and bright blue skies blinded her. She took a deep breath, almost like she was being reanimated back to life. Worst of all, a stabbing pain ached down her right arm.

"She's alive!" a shrill voice called.

"Look at her arm! Those bandages are barely hanging on by a thread!" the other clamored. "Looks like a bullet wound to me."

Katja rubbed her eyes until she could see two pinched, scrutinous faces peering down at her like parents craning their necks over a baby in the crib. She slowly crawled to her knees, but one of them helped her to her feet while filling her ears with concerned questions, but she could barely hear what they were saying.

What happened? She stood on her two feet, feeling her body wobble when left to stand alone. The two strangers propped her up when she nearly fell and eased her toward a stone birdbath. She could feel her fingers sink to the bottom of the shallow basin, the rough-grained granite against them. Her mouth was dry, her lips chapped, and her urge to drink took control of her as she cupped water into her mouth and moistened her lips. The taste was sour, but she didn't care, as her throat felt like a hardened sponge softened by its first soak in water. There were few greater feelings.

With her other hand, she brushed along her arm and felt the slick of cold blood under her fingers. She reached for her face, feeling a massive swell on her right cheek, and looked back at the two men who helped her. Their faces looked confused and filled with the concern a mother has when their child falls from a tree or scuffs their knees.

"Wait . . . I know you," Katja stammered, wincing as her knees wobbled under her weight. "You work for the countess, don't you?"

"We are her gardeners," a rather tall and scrawny man said through a thick blonde mustache. "We always see you inside the manor, but we have never seen you out here, especially in such a curious condition. I hate to ask, but were you robbed?"

"I don't think so . . ." Katja stammered. "Where are we?"

"*Bitter teeth*! She doesn't know where she is!" the other man with a feathered felt hat and a wispy black beard gasped. "We are at Stavoren Manor, of course!"

A chill ran down Katja's spine. The last thing she remembered was falling and everything turning black. She had run out of Vigor, and her body was failing, unlike it had ever done before. *I was dying.* How was she alive? She had seen addicts in the street, pale and lifeless from dust withdrawals, yet here she was, breathing and able to stand another day. She was thankful, but why was she so lucky?

Katja looked around her surroundings and spotted the familiar sloped rooftop of Stavoren Manor overhead. Then, she realized she was standing beside the old plum tree that loomed in the middle of the flowery garden she saw from the vanity window every morning as she powdered the countess's face.

How long had she been here? Did she crawl her way here in a stupor? *Certainly not.* Then something struck her. Did Fleck bring her here?

"Lady! Miss! You should see a proper doctor!" one of the gardeners shouted. "You don't look so good . . . and you are missing some hair!"

"Thanks for your help. I don't know how I will ever repay you," Katja said, before limping away from her curious spectators, cutting through a bed of pink and red petunias and a leafy rhubarb shrub while gliding her hands against the limbs and thick branches to avoid falling onto her face until she reached the familiar entryway.

The Stavorens' front door was as tall as those entering the temple and as wide as a carriage, painted with a bright red sheen that glistened in the morning sun. She kicked the mud off her boots and wiped the dust from her dress, but she knew there was no way to remove the dirt, blood, soot, and grease. Then she roughly braided her hair, her fingers plucking and stringing the frizzed red strands like a harp. It wouldn't look great, but it would have to do for now.

Katja took a deep breath before stumbling through the heavy front doors, avoiding the piercing gaze of Gavin, who was pacing the cigar lounge with a glass of whiskey and one eye watching over the entryway. Her boots clicked on the marble floors, echoing until she strode over the burgundy carpet that always reminded her of a long tongue. Then she darted through the living room and up the stairs just as Gavin's voice hollered after her.

"Katja? Is that you? Where have you been?" Gavin shouted, hurrying out of his seat to chase after her as she crept up the staircase. "I feel like I am seeing a ghost. I could have sworn they were going to find your throat slit and body bloated and washed up at the harbor. The countess was inconsolable in your absence . . . and I don't mean inconsolably sad! She was bitter, and her tongue was like a sharp knife! Are you listening? Do you hear me?"

"I nearly died! Maybe let me process everything a little bit!" Katja spat, her mind rushing as her hand clung to the railing. "How is the countess taking it? You know, the break-in."

"She doesn't know about that, and I don't ever mean for her to," Gavin whispered, pulling her aside and hovering his face uncomfortably near hers. His breath smelled like mulled wine and smoke. "I might be the luckiest butler alive. The bandits didn't steal a thing except for that hideous rug on the wall and . . . you, of course. They fought well, but I warded them away with that saber hanging above the mantle in the cigar lounge."

"I reckon the old gaffer would be proud himself if any of that were true," Katja whispered in his ear. "What really happened? Did they tie you up? Put a gag in your mouth? Slap you until your will to live was broken?"

"You are the one with bruises on your knees . . . and arms . . . and boils! You have them everywhere, Kat!" Gavin said. He looked overly amused by the gray, green, and brown welts on her pale skin. "At least I held my ground."

"Alright, are you done? Have you had your fun?" Katja said. "What do you remember from that night?"

"Well . . . I was going to pick up the mess you created in the hallway, but decided to get a cocktail first, knowing the countess wouldn't return until nightfall. That was a distasteful move of yours, smashing all the countess's precious paintings onto the floor. Luckily, none of them broke their frames, leaving me with only a couple of splinters," Gavin uttered, his eyes tense. "Then I felt a cold breeze and noticed one of the windows was open, and I could hear footsteps shuffling about the manor! I chased down the intruders, but I grew dizzy before I could reach them. Must have been the brandy!"

"Magic wins again," Katja exclaimed.

"Not in the slightest!" he sneered.

"Then what happened?"

"I broke the dizzy spell and fought them off valiantly with that saber until they ran away with the tapestry in hand," Gavin chuckled. "Serves them right."

Katja groaned, shoving his shoulder. "Liar! Tell me, or else I'll tell the countess everything . . . and I mean everything, that you have been doing in that cigar lounge."

Gavin pursed his lips and sighed.

"Fine. I don't remember anything after I got dizzy," he whispered, looking over his shoulder. "I honestly thought I died, but then I woke up an hour before the countess arrived, just in time to clean your mess. You should be kissing my shoes and thanking me!"

"You are delusional," Katja said, shoving Gavin away and skirting past him. "I must talk to her."

"Looking like that?" he sneered. "I have seen scarecrows in the paddy farms with more taste."

"She won't remember anyway," Katja said, strutting down the corridor. "I can't risk losing my contract with the Maiden Tower."

Gavin shouted, "The Maiden Tower had to send someone in your absence because I sure wasn't going to do the countess's maquillage! As a young boy, I couldn't keep a steady hand for glyphs to save my life! I would have poked the countess's eyes out attempting to apply her makeup."

Katja ignored the call and limped up the stairs, praying the wobbly old railing didn't give up on her now when she needed it most. Footfalls scampered behind her, and she picked up her pace.

"Miss Rosdyre! Slow down!" Gavin shouted, his voice ringing off the stone walls. "Are you trying to ruin our arrangement? The Maiden Tower did not seem pleased with your absence! Come here so we can discuss this more!"

Katja reached the landing, entered the corridor, and pressed her ear against the countess's bedchamber door. All she could hear was her own labored breath, beating heart, and the footsteps catching up behind her.

She hesitated before knocking, then turned the door handle slowly, only to find it locked.

"What did they do to you? You really do look frightening!" Gavin said, marching toward her extravagantly, his barrel chest puffing as if someone was pulling a string upward from his heart. It reminded her of an overly proud robin strutting in the morning dewy gardens after plucking a worm from the ground.

"If you don't want me to tell the countess about your little forgery business, then you will help me clean up," Katja whispered harshly. "Got it?"

"Fix you up? You said you weren't worried 'cause the countess wouldn't remember how you looked! What is the truth, Miss Rosdyre?" he chided.

"I can explain a few scratches and bruises, maybe even a dirty dress, but looking like a chimney sweep's wife won't be so easy," she said.

"Please explain the scratches and bruises then." Gavin frowned.

"I fell . . . *hard*," Katja said. "Down the Maiden Tower staircase. They are ricketier than boat deck during a high storm. Is that good enough?"

"You would have gone to the nurse if you had fallen down the stairs. You are a terrible liar," Gavin smirked.

"I will think of something. All I need is a few minutes in the powder room to fix up, then I can remedy this," Katja pleaded. "I know you have the key. Let me in."

"What if you wake her? She will never trust me with a key again. What do you even call a keyless house steward?"

"A *former* steward," Katja corrected. "Also, a handcuffed one for forging signatures. Don't forget that little tidbit."

Gavin gritted his teeth. "Quiet about that."

"I will tell her I stole the key from you."

"And risk me looking incompetent? Again, what more is the resident steward than the master of keys?" Gavin sneered. "Think of something better."

Katja pondered. "I beat you for it!"

"Now I look defenseless! I am supposed to defend this house!" Gavin snarled.

Katja pointed at her swollen eye. "You got me good, but I got you better. Now, you don't look weak."

"And I beat a lady?" Gavin groaned. "That is not a good look."

"Better than a thief and a forger? But if you prefer that alternative, then so be it."

Gavin crossed his arms. "Your threats are as shallow as the grave you'll end up in for dabbling in forbidden arts."

Katja spotted a slight bulge in Gavin's breast pocket where she knew he had hidden the master key. Somehow, despite losing all her Vigor in Fleck's jail cell, she felt a warm, boiling sensation in her chest. Did Fleck give her magedust out of pity? Perhaps he honestly didn't want her to die.

She snapped her finger, and the key zipped out of Gavin's pocket and into her pinched fingers.

Gavin lunged at her, but before he could reach her, she summoned the black tie around his neck to tighten. He clawed at his throat, face red, veins bulging, and she only released control once she had unlocked the countess's door and slipped inside, locking it behind her.

A heap of blankets and pillows moved within the bedsheets across from her. At first, it appeared like one heap, but then it split and became two. The courting between Lord DeGrom must be moving along swimmingly. She hated the way that sounded in her head. To her, Countess Auriella was a precious old lady, not a flirtatious young missy.

Katja bit her tongue and stood utterly still, waiting for a face to appear from the thick blankets, but after a few moments, the heap came to a standstill. She carefully slid across the smooth wood floor, noticing the glaring bare spot on the wall where the tapestry once stood. Then, holding her breath, she snuck into the powder room and shut the door behind her. Just past the powder room was the tiled bathroom fitted with a lion-paw bathtub near the center of the room, where she'd witnessed Auriella's miraculous transformation. She just prayed the waters would transform her to be deemed "presentable." She didn't need to look younger than she was or even beautiful. *Presentable will suffice.*

Katja twisted the brass faucet carefully so the threads wouldn't squeal. Steaming hot water filled the bath, creating a cloud of steam that enveloped the entire bathroom. Once the water had some depth, she stripped off her clothes and gritted her teeth as the hot water lapped at her balmy skin. The water turned a muddy color as layers of soot and dirt washed from her skin.

It felt like she was breaking the law. In a way, she was breaking the law. Nowhere in her Maiden Tower contract did it permit her to use the facilities and luxuries of their clients' homes, and in fact, she might have remembered a tidbit forbidding even using their toilet when you needed a wee. Usually, that wouldn't be a problem, but this was a circumstance in which she was willing to break any law, even if it meant being caught. She would be lucky if the Maiden Tower didn't sack her or put her on probation for missing the assignment of such a highly esteemed client as the Stavorens. Her best course of action would be to appear today before the countess woke up and try to restore the torn relations and forget about everything that happened between her and Fleck's crew.

As she submerged her face in the water, she prayed that she would never see his candlewax face again, but then she remembered the letter and the Maiden Tower's secret objective. The reason she was sneaking into the tapestry the day she was kidnapped in the first place.

The cards.

She held her breath beneath the water, lathering her hair with frothy soap that was far nicer than anything she had ever put in her hair in her life. Then a thought intruded into her mind. *The tapestry was gone from its spot.* She would need to return to Fleck's hiding spot if she wanted to find the tapestry and the cards hiding within. Unless she could find something more damning in Stavoren Manor to report back to the Grand Maiden in time, that is assuming she still had a job.

She could bring back a few bits of mail or stale love letters from Lord DeGrom, but that wouldn't likely intrigue the grand maiden as the cards would. The cards offered her a slim chance of keeping her contract with the Maiden Tower. They might even promote her to prefect if the card opened the case about Prime Minister Stoker's mysterious death. What could the red "X" marked on the dead man's face mean other than him being a likely target of some strange conspiracy?

But it was the count's secret magic room. Could the count really be involved with the death of the prime minister and the others named on the stack of cards? Was the count's death the end of an assassin's plot? Was he a victim himself? Katja's brain throbbed as she scrubbed her armpits and legs, wishing she had time to shave the small red prickles. She was trying to look decent for Countess Auriella, not a date with a handsome man. Suds slid down her freckled skin as she stepped out of the water, pulling the plug at the bottom of the tub, and dabbed her wet skin with a towel so that not a single drop dripped onto the floor. Then she wrung out her hair and tied it in a bun before tossing the towel in the rubbish bin to discard all evidence.

When Katja was mostly dry, she attempted to scrub off the stains from her dress and scented it with a spritz of Auriella's lesser-used perfumes near the back of her collection of mixed glass bottles of varying colors. Then she combed her hair, tied it in a damp braid, slipped into her dress, which still looked a bit scrappy and burnt on the fringes, and put on her boots. Then she wiped a circle in the foggy mirror in the powder room and applied some of the countess's lipstick and makeup, which was a bit off-putting with her pale skin, but beggars couldn't be choosers at the moment.

When she was done, Katja drew open a window to let some cold air into the room and snuck back into the countess's bedchamber, and to her surprise, Auriella was sitting on the edge of her bed looking out toward her window with a mess of white hair. Lord DeGrom's heap sat motionless beside her.

"Kitty, is that you?" Auriella asked, massaging her neck and attempting to turn to see her. "Where has my kitty been?"

"I was not feeling well yesterday. I am sorry, I should have sent you a notice of my absence," Katja uttered.

"You don't have to lie, Kitty," Aurielle said, turning to look at her with a bright expression and only a small sheet covering her naked body. "Where did it go?"

"Where did *what* go?" Katja said, hands shaking.

"Don't play stupid, Kitty Kat," Countess Auriella smiled, scooting off the end of her bed and turning to look at her, as unclothed as the day she was born.

Her skin was wrinkled and old, with age spots covering her hands and feet, but her stride was youthful. Katja had bathed the old countess a hundred times before, so nothing was much of a surprise anymore, but there was something different about her—something youthful and radiant. Even her spine wasn't as bent and her teeth less yellow, but the most noticeable difference was the sparkle in the bright blue rings of her eyes.

"The tapestry . . . my beautiful tapestry," Auriella whispered, eyeing the blank spot on the wall. "It couldn't be a coincidence that it vanished the night that you disappeared. Where is it? It won't be easy hiding it in the Maiden Tower, especially once I report it as stolen."

"Oh . . . that old thing?" Katja said, teeth grinding. Could the countess possibly be aware of the magic room?

"That old thing? That tapestry was a gift from Hugo when he returned from his travels to the far ends of Marath! It was the only thing that kept him warm at night and gave him shade during the day in those vast scablands!" the countess snapped. "It is not just an old thing!"

"I didn't steal anything," Katja challenged.

"I don't believe you, Kitty! And you know I don't like liars!" the countess challenged. She then furrowed her brow. "What happened to your face?"

The heap in the bed started rustling, and a tan arm and leg emerged from its depths.

"Dear, who is that? Why are you so testy this morning?" Lord DeGrom groaned. "Come back to bed and deal with them later."

"It is my chambermaid! I have reason to believe she stole something from me!" Auriella admonished.

"Whatever it is, I can buy you one better," he said, waving his hand. "Just dismiss her already. You only complain about her."

Complain? Other than missing this one assignment, Katja had been nothing but a timely caretaker for the Stavorens. She wanted to scream, but she knew better than that now.

"I need my steward! Gavin!" Auriella blurted. "He will send another letter to the Maiden Tower! I will not enlist thieves within my employment!"

Katja couldn't bear the irony.

Auriella cleared her throat, paced across the room, and draped a silk robe over her body, "Gavin! Do you hear me?"

The doorknob jiggled furiously, and Gavin's voice boomed from behind it.

"Did you lock the door?" the countess asked. She swiveled the lock, and Gavin entered with a flustered red face.

"Gavin, I need you to send another letter! This one will be releasing Miss Rosdyre from my contract and requesting a new and improved chambermaid," Countess Auriella barked.

Gavin flashed a grin at Katja, but it quickly vanished as his eyes met Auriella's.

"What is the crime?" he asked.

Katja stared at him, confused.

"There doesn't have to be a crime! Miss Rosdyre is not to my satisfaction! She will be lucky if I don't press charges for stealing from me," the countess spat. "Ask the Maiden Tower to look for a three-hundred-year-old Marathic tapestry. The one that hung from the wall. It shouldn't take them long."

Gavin nodded. "Of course, milady."

He turned to leave, but before he could, Katja interjected.

"I have something to confess," she said.

Even Lord DeGrom stuck his eyes out from the covers as the words left her mouth.

"What is it?" the countess asked, adjusting the silk robe on her shoulders.

"I know that there is a certain steward in your employment that is hiding something from you . . . something important," Katja said, grinning back at Gavin.

He shuttered. "Katja, please."

Countess Auriella glared at Gavin.

"Continue . . . although I am skeptical of anything coming out of your lying mouth, Miss Rosdyre," the countess scolded.

Katja continued. "Gavin has not been honest with you about—"

"—the stolen tapestry!" he interrupted with a raised finger. "The gardeners stole it! I didn't say anything because it happened under my watch. I plead for your forgiveness, milady."

The gardeners? This was a new low for Gavin, but based on the countess's face, the lie was working at least a little bit.

"Mr. Elysees and Mr. Dassin?" Auriella said, her mouth wide and face tortured. "I can't believe it. They have been trimming our greenery for nearly a decade. Are you certain, Gavin?"

He sighed. "It was hard for me to believe, too. But I had no other theory when I saw muddy footprints leading from the garden up to the very spot where the tapestry hung. I would be lying if their status as fine friends of mine didn't also sway my decision to obscure the crime. We are living in hard times . . . perhaps they were desperate. It seems anyone is willing to do anything for a coin nowadays."

"Tell them to report to my office and wait for me to finish getting ready for the day," the countess said.

Gavin bowed and exited the door without another word.

Katja realized her lies would likely result in the firing of two people and possibly lead to their imprisonment. She had to tell her the truth about the break-in, how she entered the tapestry to hide, and how the bandits took the tapestry and waited for her to get out. She would have to explain the magic candle and how she blew it out so that the bandits couldn't enter the tapestry to capture her, and then she would have to explain how she relit it to escape. But how could she explain without telling the countess that she knew magic and was using it under her roof? No matter how terrible it was, she had to hold her lie. The gardeners would be punished, but they wouldn't be executed, unlike her if she told the truth. Besides, Gavin blamed the gardeners, not her. Either way, it all made her feel ill.

Countess Auriella spared a sympathetic glance at Katja.

"If what Gavin is saying is true, then I will spare the Maiden Tower a letter," she said. "I forgive you for missing yesterday, but never abandon me again! I need to look impeccable for my fiancé and the other clientele I meet with in town."

"Fiancé?" Katja said, mouth agape. "Did I hear that correctly?"

Countess Auriella blushed, her bright eyes batting like a young schoolgirl. She then tugged at her ring finger and, upon realizing it was naked, reached into her drawer and fastened a shiny ruby ring onto it.

"I am aware it is moving along fast, but at my age, time runs at a different pace than for you younglings," the countess said, her smile wide. Her teeth even looked whiter and straighter than before. "He proposed last night, looking at the sunset over the harbor after eating clams and oysters. Imagine me waking up delighted for the future and to show off my giant engagement ring, only to find my chambermaid absent and my bedroom ransacked! I canceled every appointment! I refuse to look like a mummer in public!"

"If I am being honest, countess . . . I haven't seen you look so vibrant since I met you," Katja said, instinctually stepping away from Auriella's outstretched hand. Even the age spots on the back of her palm seemed to be whisking away like crumbs. "Are you sure everything is okay?"

"I have never been better," Countess Auriella grinned. "Now, let's get me dolled up for my meeting in the capital. I have dinner plans this afternoon with Mauve Redd, heiress of House Redd! She and Lord Baylor Redd are expecting a child! Rumor it is a boy!"

"That is great news!" Katja exclaimed, pretending like she didn't wish to be anywhere else on earth, even Fleck's cold cell deep beneath their feet. "I will dress you up so well that you forget all about the trespasses of yesterday."

"I smell like lovemaking and stale fragrances from the night before. Run me a hot bath and let me soak," the countess smiled, marching through the doors into the powder room and further into the bathroom. "Pour me a glass of Stellish vintage while you are at it. These are truly enchanted times in which we live. I must say I am relieved you weren't the one who stole my tapestry. That created a looming shadow over my morning. What relief it is to find out the contrary!"

Katja nodded in agreement, spotting a dark rim of dirt around the bottom of the bathtub bowl. Her heart sank as she ran ahead of the countess to run the hot water and scrub the dirt from the white porcelain before she could notice.

It wasn't perfect, but when Katja helped the countess remove her silk robe and hang it on a rung, the suds on top of the rising hot bathwater had already concealed any stains.

"I still want to know what happened to your poor face," the countess said.

Katja paused, took a deep breath, and then continued.

"I wasn't going to tell you, but I suppose it is impossible to hide," she said. "The reason I was out was because I got the pox."

"The pox? As in Hexes Pox?" the countess gasped, stepping away.

"Don't worry, the nurses say it isn't contagious anymore, but one of the symptoms is a swollen face, like the mumps," Katja said. The lie was so bad she almost couldn't contain her grin. "I am one of the lucky ones. I have a bunkmate who died from Hexes Pox."

"Well, I am gladdened that you aren't contagious," the countess said. "And I am sorry about your friend. It must have been a terrible thing to witness."

"It was harrowing, to say the least," Katja said solemnly. "The tower mourned for weeks."

"And her family . . . they must have been devastated," the countess sighed. "Especially knowing she must have come in close contact with a witch. At least that is my deduction, considering no boys are living in the Maiden Tower, correct?"

Katja bit her tongue and nodded.

"In fact, that might mean you have recently encountered a witch. How horrifying!" Auriella said. "You must be more careful."

"Of course . . . that is terrifying to think about," Katja stammered. "Your bath is ready."

The countess winced as she stepped into the water.

"Is it hot enough for your liking?"

"No! No! It is perfect," Auriella said through gritted teeth before plunging her body into the depths. "You need heat and steam to rinse this old skin properly."

"Your skin looks wonderful. Have you been using something that I am unaware of?" Katja asked.

Countess Auriella chuckled. "You would know if I put any new ointment on my skin. I suppose Lord DeGrom has given me a new lust for life. I have heard love does wonders for your soul."

Could love wipe a decade's worth of aging? The countess's hair was still white, but when Katja applied shampoo and oils, it felt thicker, stronger, and softer than ever. But the most significant difference of all was her mind. Just a few days ago, Katja could set Stavoren Manor aflame, and Auriella likely wouldn't have noticed. To think Katja used to use all sorts of levitation enchantments all in plain sight, now she could barely hide the dirt ring at the bottom of her bathtub. There was something strange about it all, but she already had too much occupying her mind to deal with something inconsequential compared to getting back to the Maiden Tower and figuring out what happened to her back in the Warren. If anything, she should be happy for the old countess, who appeared to have many more years ahead of her, along with a young new fiancé.

Katja poured a glass of Stellish wine and handed it to Auriella. In the past, the countess had been helpless and often put herself in danger trying to clean her arms, legs, and other hard-to-reach places. However, before Katja could start her usual procedure, Auriella tore the sponge from her hand and did it herself, delightfully. Once the room was thoroughly steamed and her wine glass nearly empty, the countess sat back and plunged beneath the water.

"Countess . . . Boils!" Katja blurted, her heart jolting, but then she remembered the countess, her head beneath the water, the other day. *She will be okay.*

Nearly a minute later, before Katja's angst started to spiral, the countess emerged from the bathwater, gasping, and Auriella started to laugh. Katja gave a forced smile, but deep down, something was unsettling about her laugh, which made her miss the old Auriella despite how terrible she felt thinking that. Once the bathwater was lukewarm and before the countess began pruning, she finished her bath and dried off. After a few minutes of rifling through her expansive wardrobe full of dresses, coats, and shoes of varying sizes and colors, Katja dressed her in a regal sapphire gown that danced just above the countess's veiny ankles. Once Auriella agreed on her outfit, they moved to the powder room, and Katja powdered her face and combed her now thick hair. When she was nearly finished, Katja was amazed at how beautiful the countess appeared, with her flowing white braids, blushed cheeks, and glimmering blue eyes, set behind wrinkles that gave her a sense of wisdom.

Once she was satisfied with the countess's hair, Katja touched up Auriella's red lipstick and fastened a brooch to her dress. She bowed and was excused, sending a wave of relief coursing through her body like ripples in a pond. She said farewell and marched out of the powder room and past the master bed, where the heap that was Rhys DeGrom was now missing. She then left the master bedchamber and marched down the corridor and down the stairs, where she spotted the two gardeners, Mr. Elysees and Mr. Dassin, standing awkwardly in the cigar lounge across from Gavin. One of them was on his knees begging not to be sacked from their job, but Gavin didn't show any remorse on his face.

Katja could almost feel Gavin's gaze before exiting through the front door, but she didn't give it any credence as she walked into the bright sun drawing over the entryway. Despite escaping Stavoren Manor mostly unscathed, a sinking feeling settled within her like vine roots, swiftly coiling around her ribcage and strangling her beating heart as she made her way to the Maiden Tower.

Chapter Seven

The moment Katja entered the front doors of the Maiden Tower, she expected to be scolded, beaten, and dragged to the grand maiden's chambers by her scruff, as a mother did to her pup. Instead, she entered silently with her chin tucked into her chest and her eyes at her feet, avoiding eye contact with a flock of colorful maids circling the busy register at the front desk, who were distracted stamping punch cards. The punch cards were just one way the prefects kept track of the maidens' attendance and who was tardy. Otherwise, keeping track of the hundred employees and their assignments while trotting around Theed would be nearly impossible. A hundred was just a guess. There might have been multiple hundreds, but Katja never tried counting and wasn't particularly good at it.

Ecstatic she was not stopped by any of the prefects, Katja hurried up the crooked steps, using the railing to aid her aching body to the seventh floor. The never-ending stairwell was dim and dreary, devoid of any decoration except for a few glowing wall sconces that guided her way, and only half of them were lit. When she reached the fifth floor, her lungs burned, and the spiraling walls looked even more contorted and twisted than usual. She stopped to catch her breath, terrified that she would start seeing spots again if she pressed on too hard. Her bandaged arm throbbed, and she could feel her heartbeat thud between her ribs like a drum. Sometimes, she could have sworn her heartbeat was coming from high in her throat and down her arms and legs, but she knew that wasn't possible. But she also wasn't entirely sure of the limitations of Fleck's magic. All she knew was that he had far fewer reservations about using it than she did—that much was certain.

When she entered her dormitory, the window drapes were pulled, spilling warm light into the musky hovel. Since the dormitories lacked doors, she swiftly undressed. She tossed her red maiden dress and other clothes into a wicker basket and put on her only other outfit—an oversized nightgown the Maiden Tower lent her. She scratched her collar as the itchy fabric pricked her neck and looked out over the view of the city, which was one of the only benefits of living in the Maiden Tower. While several taller buildings obscured the view of the city from her window, she could still make out its winding cobblestone roads, green patina statues, and glimpses of jutting castle spires older than time itself. Katja leaned her head out the window, looking east where a narrow divide split between the clock tower and the abbey. On a clear day, you could catch a glimpse of the Relian Sea's glimmering tides, but tonight, it was shrouded with mist like most days.

Katja snuck down to the laundry room deep into the tower's foundation, which was mostly empty except for two servant girls, whom she had never seen before, folding linens. She soaked her clothes in a bucket of gray water and lye and scrubbed them on a washboard until her knuckles were sore. Then she wrung them out until they were dry enough not to drip and hung them on the nearest line. The burnt hem looked terrible, and she knew she would have to purchase another dress if she were ever to be taken seriously as a maid again.

Once done, she returned to her dormitory, and the sun had set, casting elongated shadows across Theed. Down below, she spotted a new group of maidens sweeping in from the street, returning from their assignments. Feeling paranoid, she dove beneath the windowsill, heart fluttering, but then realized how conspicuously she was acting and peered back down to the sidewalk, which was swelling with crowds. Her heart quickened again when she spotted the blood-red standard of the city watch patrolling the street with their tall bucket hats, shiny badges, and sabers swinging at their hips. Just a few strides behind the guards was a high-ranking constable, identified by a signature white sash and the glint of gunmetal at the holster opposite their saber.

What if they were coming for her? What if Fleck had already reported her to the constable, and they were looking for her? Her throat constricted at the thought of the rope drawing close around her neck.

Katja retreated to her bed and tended to her bandage before anyone noticed she was hurt. She cursed under her breath when she spotted pricks of yellow and red pus inside her sleeve. It was just another part of the entire Fleck affair that she would have to wash clean from herself. She ignored the stains for now and focused on the wound roughly the size of a coin that stung at the touch.

Through clenched teeth, she dressed the wound with a handkerchief from her top drawer and tied it snugly around her shoulder to stop the wound from festering. One of the many things she learned from her mother was how to tend to minor cuts and bruises from slipping on slick pavement, climbing gates, scraps with other drifters, and sleeping on the unforgiving ground.

Loud, strutting footsteps entered the dormitory, and the smell of dandelions filled the room. Katja fastened her nightgown as fast as she could, but she was not quick enough, as Portia's look indicated.

"What happened to you?" Portia gasped. "Where have you been? I have been worried sick that the pox took you . . . or worse!"

Katja raised a finger to her cracked lip.

"Quiet . . . I am trying to lie low," she whispered.

Portia tossed her coat onto the rack in the corner and looked both ways down the breezy corridor before returning to Katja. "First things first . . . are you okay? Do you need to see the nurse?"

"Thank you for your concern, Portia . . . but no . . . like I said, I am lying low and hoping no one notices and everything just resumes as normal," Katja said, carefully buttoning her pajama top and leaning her back against the brick wall that guarded her bed. She could not sit up perfectly straight because of Portia's bunk above her, but it wasn't too uncomfortable if she propped the pillows just right and slouched her shoulders.

"Too late, all of the girls in our dormitory noticed," Portia uttered, resting against the doorway with one eye focused on Katja and the other on the corridor. "I am certain the prefects know already, and if they don't yet, they will soon know when they count attendance on our punch cards. They check attendance every night before they go to bed. That is why the infraction and termination letters always arrive in the morning."

"Well . . . did you tell anyone else?" Katja asked.

"Not that it will matter . . . but only the girls in our dormitory," Portia said, glancing at the two other bunks opposite theirs. "It was hard not to notice, considering we sleep within arm's reach of each other. If it weren't for my worrying about you, then it would have been the best sleep of my life since joining the Maiden Tower. The other girls don't snore nearly as loud as you."

Katja tossed her pillow at Portia and couldn't help but grin.

"And I missed your rumblings and occasional nightmares while locked away!" Katja teased. "I wasn't exactly slacking off in my absence. I was trying to escape from the freaks that kidnapped me."

"You were . . . kidnapped?" Portia gasped. Her mouth dropped toward the floor, and horror burned in her honey-brown eyes.

Katja nodded. "There is a first for everything in this city."

Portia's eyes flashed across the room, her mouth forming silent words she could not say before finally whispering, "By whom?"

"A bunch of thieves . . . bandits . . . whatever you want to call them," Katja replied, her leg wagging anxiously. "They had names, but who knows if they were real. They broke into Stavoren manor and snatched me, among other things." She contemplated for a minute. *Did they take anything else in the manor?* She didn't see them gloating about stealing the piles of jewelry and antiques that littered the countess's estate. *No, they all looked downright miserable, if anything.*

But she couldn't tell Portia that. Who would believe that a bunch of thieves only stole an old tapestry and an unremarkable chambermaid? She remembered Fleck's crew mentioning the need for a new Dustmage, whatever that meant, but she couldn't tell Portia that without admitting she dabbled in magic. Once again, she would need to lie.

"Why haven't we heard anything about this? A break-in at Stavoren Manor would be printed on every newspaper in Theed," Portia said.

Katja sighed. *She's right.*

"I dunno, but I reckon the countess wouldn't notice a few things missing with how impaired her mind has become," Katja whispered, drumming her fingers on her lips.

"And her servants didn't notice?" Portia rebutted.

"If I had to guess, the servants are trying to protect the countess. It has been like walking on glass at Stavoren Manor. No one wants to cause the countess too much distress. Maybe they covered it up," Katja said. "Perhaps they were part of it. You never know."

"You weren't part of it, were you, Katja?" Portia frowned.

"Of course not! I was kidnapped!" Katja hissed, but her voice was barely a whisper. "I just want to move on with my life and pretend like none of this ever happened!"

Footsteps shuffled down the hallway, and Portia smiled at a group of maidens meandering back to their rooms. Once they passed and disappeared from sight, her giant smile vanished, and her attention turned back to Katja.

"The other girls will be back soon. Please . . . I beg of you. Do not tell any of them," Katja whispered. "I am trusting you, Portia."

"But why keep it secret? The whole world should know that dangerous thieves are breaking into our client's homes and kidnapping servants!" Portia argued. "It would be irresponsible not to warn the others in the Maiden Tower, don't you think?"

Another set of footsteps pounded up the stairs and down the hallway, this time entering their dormitory. Claudia led the group, followed by Jeane, Victoria, and Astrid, who slept in the bunks across from Katja and Portia. Most of the girls in the shared dormitory were close and rarely spent a moment apart unless they were working.

Jeane and Victoria were twins, distinguishable only by a red birthmark on Victoria's cheek that reminded Katja of the outline of a fish. They were inseparable, often requesting the same assignments and working as a duo. Astrid, on the other hand, should have been closer to Katja—they shared similar homelands across the Relian and spoke the same mother tongue—but they never agreed on much. That was often the way with Dirks in Theed. Every group could afford only one "across-the-ponder," and two Dirks were one too many, not to mention her people's reputation for stubbornness and inflexibility. At least, that's what her mother had told her.

Claudia was the group's de facto leader, often making decisions for the dormitory, even if Katja and the other girls didn't care much for her ideas. It was for these reasons that Katja kept her cautious distance from her. They tolerated each other, but Katja couldn't be bothered by having two bosses—the Maiden Tower was enough to occupy her completely.

"Hello, Portia," Claudia said. She turned to Katja and frowned. "Oh my! Where have you been? Your client wasn't pleased. I heard she sent a messenger to the Maiden Tower requesting a replacement. They had to send poor Astrid to clean up your mess!"

"I doubt Countess Auriella knew the difference. Dirkish girls all look and sound the same," Victoria teased. "Not to mention the way you sometimes pronounce things."

"You think I look like her?" Astrid winced. "Her hair looks like it is dyed with blood!"

"With blood? Saying stuff like that is why people across the Relian are so strange," Jeane chuckled.

"Yet, you all drool over Stellish wine," Astrid sneered.

"I don't have time for this!" Katja said. "Can you pick some other destitute girl to pick on? At least I don't fill my hair with yellow dyes to look like the girls from the Smoker and Dunrow Districts."

Victoria smirked and sat on her top bunk. "You know I hold you in affection, Astrid. I am only teasing."

Jeane's mousy face twisted with curiosity. "Why are you dressed for bed?"

"Stained my dress," Katja said. "Besides, I haven't been this tired in a long time."

"Not since sleeping on the street and inside brothels, ey?" Victoria grinned.

Katja knew it was a joke, but it was a tired one. The notion that Dirkish women were often ladies of the night was frustrating because, deep inside, there was a sliver of truth.

"I never worked in a brothel. I wouldn't be very good at it anyway, based on some of the comments you girls make about how I look," Katja huffed, fiercely braiding her mess of hair. "I made my money stealing from pretty girls like you with a sharp knife pressed against their throats."

Everyone except Astrid seemed disturbed by the comment. No matter how much she teased Katja, growing up in the war-torn Dirkish countryside had shown Astrid much about humanity's desperation. By the time she was two, she had likely already witnessed hillsides crawling with flies and bloated corpses left in the wake of the Rodnovs' invasion, just as Katja's mother had before fleeing. You could see in Astrid's distant, gray-eyed gaze that she had also seen the darkness.

"You're going to miss pot pies for supper!" Portia interrupted the silence. "Prefect Primrose said it's the last pies until the Hearthward Festival! Do you really want to wait for winter to eat their famous pot pies? I doubt there will be any leftovers once everyone has had their share!"

"Not everyone is this motivated by pot pie, Port," Claudia scoffed. "Katja can have my second slice if she wants it. I refuse to get plump for the winter. Lord Redd doesn't like plump little girls."

"And Lord Redd isn't going to marry a skinny chambermaid either, Claudia," Portia sneered. "I will take my pie."

"Are you still in love with him? You talk about him far too often! He is old enough to be your father!" Jeane laughed. "Maybe granddad, too!"

Claudia rolled her eyes and fell back in her bed. "Some people dream of escaping these brick walls rather than growing into a crotchety old lady and joining the ranks of the prefects. I want to see the world. Theed is just one city of hundreds . . . thousands!"

"And some people dream of escaping with their dignity intact," Victoria teased.

"Like marrying that sweet longshoreman you keep eyeing on our way to the Drummond estate?" Jeane said, nudging her twin sister in the side. "Perhaps he has a twin brother I can marry too."

Victoria blushed bright red and took a swig of water.

Katja was starting to miss the silence of her iron cell. She forgot how much she loathed the gossip and hearsay of the dormitories. Not even a few minutes into talking with her dormmates, her jaw was sore from clenching, and her pulse was quickening faster than a hummingbird's beating wings.

For an hour, she listened to the girls' banter. They discussed every detail of their workday, from subjects as innocent as the Redd family dog delivering a new litter of adorable Larkish hounds, to secret, ongoing affairs between family members and their servants. Once the smell of roasted piecrust filled the halls and wafted to their dormitory, their stomachs rumbled, and the Maiden Tower filled with chatter, laughter, and heavy ruckus as hundreds of girls filed down to the dining room on the second floor.

Not long after, Katja was alone again, except for Portia lingering in the hallway chatting with one of the neighbor girls she had befriended months ago. Unlike Katja, who liked to stick to herself, Portia was a socialite who knew no bounds to her beguiling charm. Katja reckoned her friend knew the names and faces of every maiden and prefect in the tower, along with which room and floor they lived on. She might even know where they were from, something they liked, and their favorite color, all information Katja had no desire to retain. Deep down, Katja knew it was good to make friends wherever possible. It would probably make her a lot happier, but for some reason, she got tongue-tied when meeting new people. It was another reason she was sometimes pleased to have Portia as a bunkmate and often resented it.

Katja enjoyed silence. Her life had always been noisy, and she often wondered what it would be like to live outside the city walls, where she was told that fewer people lived than trees. She had heard of the Commonwealth's great cities, from Krone to Redcastle, but the wilderness was what allured her. So long as the blotters didn't get you. That is, if the stories her mother told her were true.

"Are you sure you aren't coming?" Portia asked. "Are you afraid someone will confront you about your absence?"

Katja nodded. "That's one reason."

"Do you think you're the first girl to miss an assignment? I'm sure you will be fine," Portia said. "Who knows . . . maybe they already forgot?"

"The Maiden Tower doesn't forget," Katja said. Her stomach growled.

"It won't look good if you miss supper again," Portia said. "And while I won't tell anyone what you told me, it will likely do nothing to prevent Claudia and the other girls from speaking of having seen you. Wouldn't it be better for you to address people's questions yourself rather than leave room for rumor?

Katja knew Portia was right. *Damn it, she is always right.*

"Alright, but remember our promise," Katja said, getting up from her bed and following Portia to the noisy dining room.

*　*　*

To Katja's surprise, supper went without a hitch. The three long oak tables were filled to the brim, and their tops were covered with steaming pot pies, cold milk, pudding, and a few stale loaves that were likely from the nights prior.

When she walked into the large, circular dining room, it roared with voices and the sound of silverware scraping on dinner plates. Surprisingly, she only received a few casual glances, but no one paid too much attention to her. In all honesty, it was a relief, and she almost felt more at ease among the bustling crowd rather than in the spotlight of her fellow dormmates, who were now seated at another table at the other end of the room. Portia picked two seats for them next to a few friends she had made on the tenth floor who were far too interested in literature, philosophy, and music to give Katja much notice, with the exception of a girl named Mildred sitting opposite her, who, between talking about the intricacies of breathwork when playing flute, gave Katja a smoldering gaze that made her a bit uncomfortable.

When asked if she played a musical instrument, Katja felt compelled to lie and told them she played the fiddle in Puffer Square with a tin bucket for change when she was down on her luck. Portia gave her a distrustful stare as she spun her lie, which included getting a rather generous sixty-knot tip from a mysterious, well-dressed man that she was convinced was Prime Minister Stoker himself. Unfortunately, that comment reminded her of the red "X" slathered across his face on the card she found in the count's grimoire, which made her retreat into her unfinished pie, still dodging Mildred's gaze.

Once their table was dismissed by the prefects, who barely glanced at Katja from their seats at the heads of the long tables, the girls filed into a line and exited the dining hall. Some tucked bits of pie crust into their blouses, though many were caught along the rickety Maiden Tower steps, which echoed with the bickering and yawns of hundreds of fellow chambermaids.

Before Katja could leave the dining room, a firm hand grabbed her bandaged shoulder, and Prefect Haggerty stared into her soul with a grimace sour enough to turn milk. Katja wanted to squeal in pain, but instead left the line with every eye staring back at her as the spindly prefect dragged her into the corner of the room. She looked like she was angry enough to choke Katja to death in front of every maiden in the tower to show an example of her punitive might.

"I promise I didn't mean to miss my assignments . . . I will make up for it . . ." Katja begged, hands shaking.

"I will leave that to Grand Maiden Argaut," Prefect Haggerty said, her stern black eyes looking down into hers. Despite having the frame of a skeleton, Prefect Haggerty had the presence of a jutting statue, taller than most men Katja had ever known.

"Grand Maiden . . .?" Katja uttered.

Before she could ask any more questions, Prefect Haggerty shoved her into the kitchens, where busy chefs and prep cooks scraped charred trays, pots, and pans in giant soapy basins. A few glanced up as the prefect dragged Katja across the room and stopped at the far wall, where a child-sized door had been set into the wood—a *dumbwaiter*. When Haggerty opened it, the compartment revealed a tiny, abandoned vignette: a half-drunk cup of tea teetered on its saucer with a soggy mint leaf clinging to the rim. An empty wooden box sat on the dumbwaiter floor, its lid slightly ajar. Beside the box lay a notepad with yellowed pages, and a fountain pen, chained to the underside of the box, bore dark, blotchy stains from long-ago leaks.

"Not many people know about this, so keep it close to the chest. If I find any girls sneaking in here to use it, I will know exactly who to seek, and that will be another of many strikes against your record," Prefect Haggerty scolded, wagging a crooked finger. She then took the pen, scribbled something illegible on the pad, and began tugging a rope and pulley for a few minutes until the rope was taut and reached the end of its track.

"Even prefects can't just knock on her door to see her?" Katja asked.

"Grand Maiden Argaut doesn't like unannounced visitors," the prefect said, tapping her fingers together nervously.

Just then, there was a distant rattle, and the rope started slowly sliding downward before crashing loudly back to them, spilling the notepad onto the floor near their feet. There was a small initial in the corner of the page that looked like an eye. Even Prefect Haggerty seemed a bit nervous as she picked up the notepad and read it.

"Follow me," she said, leading Katja back through the kitchens and dining room. She whispered a few quick words to Prefects Nugent and Primrose, who were working with a dozen young maidens selected for cleaning duties that night.

Prefect Haggerty led her up the stairwell. When they reached the seventh floor, Katja saw her dormmates sitting in their bunks, watching her as she skirted by. Her eyes locked with Portia, who gave her a worried look before Katja was tugged up to the eighth floor and beyond, full of boisterous ladies exchanging stories, sharing candies, and bantering so loudly it rattled the windowpanes.

"Uh oh! Someone is getting axed!" a girl, Katja didn't recognize, shouted from one of the dormitories.

"What did you do this time?" a voice shouted from behind her.

"Isn't that the girl who stole from the kitchens?" a shrill cry rang out.

"No! That's the girl everyone thinks is a witch!" a fourth girl insisted. "You can tell by the way she walks. Witches have hooves for feet."

"Talons," someone corrected eagerly. "They have talons for feet and spit that burns like venom."

"And nasty warts. And they cackle in the night," another girl pressed on. "My uncle met a witch once, and she stole his voice. Never heard him speak again."

The smallest of the girls sniffed. "And don't forget the crooked nose, huge and ugly."

Katja took a deep breath and bit her tongue, wishing to scream back at them more than anything, but she knew that was a losing battle. Did they all really suspect she was a witch? Many girls in schoolyards teased each other, claiming their nemeses were witches or hexed to cause a stir, but a paranoid part of her wondered if she was giving off something witchy to the others that she was unaware of.

When they were nearing the top of the Maiden Tower, the prefect took an oil lamp from a rusty rung, struck a match, and lit it. Ahead, the wall and sconces were sparse and unlit, leaving a wall of shadow that, once crossed, felt like entering an unwelcoming yet sacred space. Even the air was thicker, with a musky scent, devoid of the sweet smell of pie crust that had permeated the lower floors.

They marched up the remaining stairs, passing a few strange paintings and wall ornaments depicting gargoyles, owls, moths, and other nocturnal creatures. At the end, they reached a reinforced door with steel hinges. At the center of the door was a carving of a sleeping face, with a piece of its protruding nose broken and one eye open. Below the face was a painting of a thistle, its sharp leaves and bristles faded from time.

Prefect Haggerty pushed Katja toward the door until the carving's broken nose nearly poked out her eye. "Go ahead."

Katja sized up the door, looking for a doorknob, but there was nothing to grab hold of.

She stammered, "There isn't . . ."

"The door can only be opened from within," the prefect said, annoyed. "You must knock first."

Katja hesitantly formed a fist and rapped on the thick door with her knuckles three times.

There was silence, but then there was a creaking sound, and the door pried open at its hinges as if it had been sleeping for an eternity. When there was a crack, Katja reluctantly peered inside, but it was dark except for a faint, distant light coming from around a corner across the chamber.

Katja looked back at Prefect Haggerty for reassurance, but instead, the woman shoved her inside, casting her onto the cold floor. When Katja spun around, she saw a sliver of the prefect's face before the door slammed shut. She slowly climbed to her feet, her shoulder aching, as she patted a layer of dust from her knees and hesitantly limped toward the light. When she shuffled around the corner, the only light source came from a glowing orb emitting moonlight atop a large oak desk. Behind the desk stood a short old lady with black hair, white streaks at her temples, graying skin, and a pointed face. She was clad in a crimson gown and headdress. She was pacing behind the desk.

"Grand Maiden . . . you summoned me?" Katja stammered.

Grand Maiden Argaut stopped pacing and stared at her.

"So, they let you go. Such a shame," she said.

"Excuse me, Grand Maiden . . . who let me go?" Katja said.

"Oh, don't play games, Miss Rosdyre. I am talking about Archie Fleck," the grand maiden said, her small eyes squinting behind circular eyeglasses that sat low on her sloping nose. "And all of the other destitute degenerates he surrounds himself with these days, of course."

Hearing the name "Fleck" felt like a tear within the fabric of her mind. Like the memories of two intertwined worlds that did not mix well, like water and oil. Being imprisoned in the Warren felt like it was somehow recent yet many decades ago, like the memories of her mother before she vanished. Katja used to categorize memories as "before Mother vanished" and "after Mother vanished," but now she thought she might need a new category for "after meeting Fleck." She hated how much of an impression that man had left in her life, though she had known him for less than a day.

"You know? How?" Katja said, her heart pounding.

The grand maiden sighed and pointed at the glowing orb on her desk.

"There isn't much I cannot see once you have signed the dotted lines . . . and even when you don't, I have my methods," Grand Maiden Argaut smirked. "I saw the whole thing. You sneaked into Auriella's bedchambers, and a handful of thieves slipped through a window, cast a paralysis spell on the house steward, and waited for you to return from the portal. I have to say, that was not a bad move, but fairly reckless! If you couldn't relight the candle magekey, you might have been stuck there for eternity! Very risky!"

That is why Gavin didn't recall any of the break-in.

"You could see all of it?" Katja's eyes widened. Was the grand maiden admitting that she knew magic? If so, what sort of magic was this?

"Well . . . not the part where you were inside that pesky tapestry. Portals are tricky bits of magic because they are hard to trace. As far as I know, the other side of that tapestry is on the other end of the world!" Grand Maiden Argaut said. "Or it might be tucked away in a random attic a few blocks down the street, or hidden in someone's cellar just beneath our feet. It is nearly impossible to know without looking deeper into the enchantment."

"You are a . . . a witch?" Katja asked, her face feeling numb.

Grand Maiden Argaut winced. "Witch . . . sure, I guess you could call me that, but that word has lost its meaning to the gnashing mouths of angry *dims*!"

"*Dims?*" Katja whispered. The word seemed familiar, but she couldn't quite place it.

"It is just another word for people who can't conjure magic," Grand Maiden Argaut said. "Have you never heard it used before? I suppose it isn't particularly a kind word for them, but it is hard to feel solace when they treat weeds in their gardens with more kindness."

Katja nodded. She had many questions, but she was having a hard time articulating them.

"So, how did you escape?" the grand maiden asked.

Katja frowned. "I dunno . . . I suppose you would know better with whatever it is you call that glowing thing."

"Seeing stone, scrying stone, crystal ball, ball of voyeurism. Call it whatever you want!" the grand maiden said. "Unfortunately, I could not follow you wherever Archie took you. I could watch the last place you stood before going through the portal, but once they tore the tapestry from the wall and ran away, presumably to their hideout, I lost you. I tried to find you. I scoured until my eyes were dry and bleeding, but I could not find you or those dreaded thieves."

"I don't know how I escaped either. I woke up in Countess Auriella Stavoren's gardens. I almost thought I dreamed it all up, except I still have this to prove it all happened." Katja pointed to her bandaged shoulder. "The last thing I recall was fighting Fleck to escape, and I got this to remember it. Everything turns black after that. I figured I died because I used up all of the magedust in my body."

Katja bit her tongue as the word *magedust* crawled out of her mouth. Even though they were both talking about magic, it was a strange feeling discussing such things with a stranger that would typically lead to her being reported. People were executed for saying far less. There was a side of her that wondered if all of this was just a ruse to get her to confess that she was a witch, but she was already damned as it was. Also, there was something oddly trustworthy about Grand Maiden Argaut. Maybe it was how candidly she talked about magic, or perhaps it was because there was something comforting about how she spoke. She reminded Katja of the count for some reason.

"You can speak freely here. It is one of many reasons I keep this place under lock and key," the grand maiden said. "But back to the story of your escape. The only answer I can come up with is that when you went comatose after running out of Vigor, Fleck spared you and released you somewhere you might not remember his entrapment."

"I sort of had my suspicions," Katja answered. "The night I tried to escape, he was releasing me from my cell contrary to his crew's wishes. He took a risk to let me out."

"Let me guess . . . there was a rather large disclaimer to his kindness," the grand maiden grinned. "Sorcerers like Fleck are clever, but you can smell their desires from a mile away, like when you catch a smell of salt in the air, and before long, you stumble into the sea."

"He wanted to take me under his wing," Katja said, "to join him."

Grand Maiden Argaut frowned. "So you refused?"

"I didn't trust him," Katja said. "And I have been a thief before. I refuse to return to that life. I would much rather work for the Maiden Tower."

"I see . . ." the grand maiden said.

"That is . . . if you will still take me," Katja uttered.

The grand maiden crossed her arms.

"Your absence was not of your own accord, so on that alone, I will not blame you nor punish you," she said, pacing briskly once more.

"Thank you! Thank you! I promise I will be good," Katja exclaimed, falling to her knees.

"Except! The prefects and many of your fellow maidens will expect a punishment, or else it will seem like there was some strange agreement or favoritism that I cannot allow to flourish in this chicken coop!" Grand Maiden Argaut admonished. "I cannot bring more attention to our relationship, and it is my understanding that there is a bit of a rumor already that you might be . . . a witch."

"It is just a silly rumor. Rude girls eventually will call you a witch if you live with them long enough," Katja argued.

The grand maiden nodded. "Indeed, but I cannot take such risks. No one can ever know what was said in this chamber. There are only a handful of prefects who know my secret. It would be the end of the Maiden Tower if rumors were to spread about the grand maiden being a witch herself. No . . . you must be punished no matter how unjust it is . . ."

Katja felt her stomach drop.

"But I will not terminate your contract. You are too valuable to me otherwise," Grand Maiden Argaut said. "But there are some tasks around the tower that might be worse than being tossed onto the street again."

"I will do any of it, and I won't complain. I promise!" Katja begged.

Grand Maiden Argaut caressed her fingers across the seeing stone and tapped it gently, making a dull drumming sound. She sighed and rifled through a bound folder on the end of her desk with her long fingernails. She plucked a sheet of paper and looked over it as if in deep contemplation.

"Am I making a big mistake keeping you, Miss Rosdyre?" she uttered, flashing a long contract at her. At the bottom was Katja's signature from when she first joined the Maiden Tower. "After all, I have not received any new submissions or information about the countess or the Stavorens from you. I was hoping my letter would motivate you."

"I need more time. Besides, I found something I think you will be interested in," Katja lied. Deep down, she knew everything in the tapestry burned to a crisp, and that included the mysterious cards. "I have just the prize you are looking for."

The grand maiden's eyes perked up. "Well . . . tell me."

Katja grinned. "You know how this works."

"Yes, I sometimes forget you are not like the others. That is one of the reasons I have been sending you on these errands since hiring you," Grand Maiden Argaut smiled. "So be it. You are still under contract, and you will get me whatever it is that you are seeking for me."

"Thank you, Grand Maiden." Katja bowed.

"Look out for any more correspondence from me or the prefects," the grand maiden said. "It is rare that anyone gets the pleasure of meeting me face-to-face in my own chambers like this. Usually, a maiden sees me once when they sign their contract and then when they are no longer worthy of service . . . and that is how I intend it."

Katja nodded. "If that is what you wish."

"And now for your punishment," Grand Maiden Argaut sneered. "You will do dishes and laundry duties for the remainder of the quarter. You will not eat with the other girls, and instead, you will take whatever is left from the kitchens and eat it when every dish, pot, and pan is as clean as the day we purchased them. Then, while the rest of the tower is settling for bed, you will be scrubbing dirty dresses, blouses, stockings, and undergarments until your hands are raw."

"What about my assignment?" Katja asked, rubbing her fingertips together, imagining them blistered and bleeding. "It wouldn't make much sense to punish me for missing assignments only to miss more assignments. Countess Stavoren will be sullen!"

"Oh no, you will be tending to your assignments," the grand maiden said. "It is up to you to finish in time. There will be no excuses for absences or having a hair out of place!"

"For an entire quarter?" Katja gasped.

"Would you prefer I tore up this contract, Miss Rosdyre?"

Katja shook her head. "Of course not. I will take on the punishment."

Grand Maiden Argaut pursed her lips, slid the contract back into her folder, and stuffed it inside a cabinet within her desk.

"How do you know Fleck?" Katja asked, changing the subject.

The grand maiden frowned and waved her away dismissively.

"Go on now, Miss Rosdyre. Get your last night of good sleep while you can," the grand maiden said, looking into the seeing stone, which blasted pale light into her face and illuminated her gaze.

Katja didn't budge.

"Did you have another question, Miss Rosdyre?"

"It would benefit us both if I knew more about my captors."

The grand maiden raised an eyebrow, "Oh, really?"

"I have told you everything that has happened," Katja prodded.

"Actually, you haven't revealed much at all. I have seen most of it for myself," Grand Maiden Argaut snapped. "And remember to keep your lips closed. If you tell anyone what happened here today, you will have more to worry about than a torn contract."

Katja refused to budge. She needed to know more before she could sleep tonight. "The item I am seeking is with Fleck in his hideout! I need to know all I can about him if I am to find the bounty I am looking for!"

"People change. I am afraid you likely know more about Archie Fleck than I do," the grand maiden uttered. "We are done here. Be dismissed, Miss Rosdyre."

"Remember that I am always watching," the grand maiden grinned, snapping her fingers. A long rug beneath Katja's feet tugged backward, causing her to fall forward. She caught herself before her face could split on the hard ground, but before she could crawl forward, the rug wrapped around her and slid across the floor, around the corner, and out the grand maiden's door. Katja banged her hands on the door to push it back open, but it slammed shut with a metallic ring.

Chapter Eight

Katja didn't sleep much that night. It didn't help that Prefect Haggerty tore the thin sheets off her and shook her awake before the night could turn to morning. Even the rooster would be too tired to crow if there was one in all of Theed.

Katja dragged herself out of bed, listening to the other girls' snores with jealousy. She slipped on her boots and the manila work clothes the prefect had tossed at her feet, then followed her down into the belly of the Maiden Tower.

The laundry room was humid and warm, which wouldn't be so bad if all she wanted to do was curl up and nap on the nearest pile of linens, but she knew that was not her purpose in being here. Her nose tickled as the pungent smell of mildew, mixed with the scent of detergents, assaulted her senses. She slumped against a steaming tub of dirty water, which would have made a fine bath for a troll, which used to be a central feature in many of her mother's nighttime stories. Sometimes, a fairy story was the only thing that could distract her from the horrific noises.

Prefect Haggerty steered her toward a middle-aged lady with a bulging belly and introduced her.

"This here is Miss Frisbie. She runs the laundry facilities here at the Maiden Tower, if you didn't know that already." Prefect Haggerty beckoned. "While I am sure you have cleaned your gowns in the past, there are a few lessons you must learn when cleaning hundreds of gowns."

"Thousands, if you include every article of clothing from dirty stockings, aprons, robes, ribbons, scarves, and undergarments alike," Miss Frisbie corrected, rubbing her belly. She was clearly uncomfortably pregnant. "Sometimes you even run into some rubbish accidentally discarded through the laundry chute that makes a mess you have to clean. Those are not good days."

Katja didn't want to say it, but based on many of the girls she knew in the Maiden Tower, those "accidents" were no more an accident than a well-planned coup.

"Indeed," Prefect Haggerty said. She looked annoyed. "I will let you take it from here. Remember, you still must complete your assignments, Miss Rosdyre. No excuses for being tardy either."

"Yes, Prefect Haggerty," Katja said, waiting for the prefect to vanish through the door before fetching her burnt-red dress, still hanging where she had left it.

"Is that yours? I nearly threw it away," Miss Frisbie said, hanging a pair of damp stockings onto a drying line. "Burns are not easy to fix."

Katja was disappointed to find her dress still damp, so she hung it back on the line before stirring a pot of gray water filled with towels, sheets, and pillowcases.

"It will have to do for now. A replacement would be expensive," Katja sighed, pointing to a heap of tangled red dresses and linens. "Is this all our dirties?"

"All? Don't make me laugh!" Miss Frisbie smirked. She pointed to several additional heaps of mostly red clothing piled along the other end of the room. "We haven't even made a dent."

"We are supposed to get through all of that today?" Katja gasped.

Miss Frisbie nodded. "Unless you want to do it later, but I reckon those piles will be even larger by the time the girls return from their assignments."

Katja nearly choked on her spit. "I have supper duties tonight. There is no other time."

"Then I guess you have your answer. Hurry up now! The sooner you get your hands dirty, the sooner you can hurry off to wherever else you have to be . . . and the sooner I can go home and rest on my rocking chair. I swear this child will be the death of me! Their weight tugs at your joints in all the wrong places!" Miss Frisbie exclaimed, grunting as she pulled a tangled mess of socks and brassieres from the bottom of the clean pile.

Katja glanced at the clock on the wall. "I have three hours. Do you normally do all this alone?"

"No, normally, some of the other prefects help if they don't have some other poor girl in here because they broke house rules," Miss Frisbie said. "Put a core in the fire and start filling the pots with dirties. The detergent is over there in the bins under the counter. Only need two spoonfuls, some stirring, and some time, and then we will be on to drying!"

Katja groaned inwardly, deposited a few logs into the flame, and nearly fumbled a box of detergent all over the floor, but managed only to powder her feet. Miss Frisbie started singing a song that sounded familiar, something perhaps from the temple or maybe even the royal anthem that was occasionally blasted from horns around town. Either way, Katja knew she hated it.

*　*　*

A few hours passed, and Katja's work clothes were soaked with sweat and dirty laundry water. Miss Frisbie's lips grew tired, so she started humming, which was a small mercy. Katja soon began to take refuge in the tune because when the humming stopped, the room fell into an eerie quiet, and she could hear the distant creaks from a tower that had long since passed its expiration. Even though she loathed the constant snores in her dormitory at night, there were times that she could hear haunted whispers, shifting floorboards, taps on the windows, and strange groans seeping in through the vents, which she found far fouler. Everyone who lived in the Maiden Tower knew it was haunted, and even the skeptics turned believers after spending one night in its halls. However, most avoided discussing it, as if it were some insider secret, because they all knew the truth behind the tower's bloody past, and it was far more terrifying.

The Maiden Tower was the only remnant of the old Theed wall, dating back hundreds of years. It was also common knowledge that the reason it was the only part of that wall that still stood was that it was used to imprison, torture, and murder enemy captives who dared to stand up against the Crown.

When all the dirty laundry was washed and dried, Prefect Haggerty arrived with another hamper full of clothes that had been missed the night before. Katja was going to protest, but instead, she bit her tongue, curtsied, and added the dirty clothes to the pot.

Once the last dress was hung to dry, she cracked her sore neck and quickly fetched her maiden dress from the line, which was disappointingly still damp. It would have to work for today, and she would have to do her best to keep it clean to avoid washing it in the coming days unless she wanted to wear a damp dress again. Then, out of the corner of her eye, she spotted a perfect crimson dress with a neat, silky white bow hanging on the wire that looked just her size and was perfectly dry.

No, Katja told herself. She couldn't stoop so low to take another girl's dress and ruin her morning just because hers was starting terribly. She was already at risk of being turned in for magic and had the grand maiden breathing down her neck. Adding more trouble to her life was the last thing she needed.

But the allure was too much to resist. After all, was it stealing if she returned it before anyone noticed? Most girls were already stuffed in their outfits for the day and heading out to their assignments, so perhaps some lucky maiden was fortunate to have two dresses. Claudia and the other girls in her dorm had multiple dresses for different occasions because they could afford them. Meanwhile, Katja had used magic as a child to steal coins from tip jars and apples from fruit stalls, and long ago she accepted it as a means of survival.

Katja watched for Miss Frisbie, who was distracted, scrubbing a stubborn grass stain from a pale stocking. She swiftly snagged the dress from the line, stuffed it under her arm, and hung her burnt dress to dry in its place.

"I will be back tomorrow morning!" Katja said, overly enthusiastic. She was acting suspicious, but Miss Frisbie had little reason to think anything of it and dismissively waved her away without even a glance.

Katja stormed up the stairs to the dressing and powder rooms, which were already nearly empty. From those left, she received devious stares, but their gazes quickly retreated to their laps when she locked eyes with them.

Katja splashed water on her face, slipped out of her work clothes, put on her new dress, powdered her nose, tied her ratty hair into a formless bun, and dashed back to her room on the seventh floor. She stashed away her sweaty work clothes in her lopsided bedside table, put on some clean stockings and boots, and then nearly jumped down seven floors of stairs to the entry room before making her way to the trolley.

When she finally got to Stavoren Manor, the countess was thrilled to see her and talked about how charming Lord DeGrom was in their last meeting. Katja was thankful she did not find him still sleeping in the bed, as the day before, which had only made things awkward. She was also grateful that the countess was not disturbed by her being almost late and still smelling of detergent, but sometimes one got lucky.

While she attended to Countess Auriella, she entertained the woman's town gossip and vapid political claims with silent nods and vocal "oh's," "aha's," and "mmhm's" to sound remotely interested and engaged, though that couldn't be further from the truth.

Gavin was mostly silent throughout the day, spending most of his time reviewing paperwork and interviewing new gardeners to replace Mr. Elysees and Mr. Dassin. She still felt terrible about being the sole reason for their termination, but selfishly, she knew the alternative was to admit she had learned magic, and to admit that was no different than surrendering your own life.

Once the countess left for her evening meeting with an estate lawyer, presumably to discuss marriage considerations, Katja cleaned the house the old-fashioned way, which reminded her of how terrible the other maids had it in the Maiden Tower. The temptation to whisk away a pile of books, summon a broomstick, or transport a heavy bucket of soapy water across the floor was intense. Still, she would need to conserve her Vigor now, without her usual magedust reserves to draw on. Burning flames swelled in her mind as she remembered all that precious magedust burning in an inferno in mere seconds and cringed. She should consider herself lucky not to be trapped in the tapestry closet or burned to a lifeless crisp. She went back to wallowing, remembering her favorite sand-dollar compact, another victim to the flame, where she stored her rationed reserves in times of need. *And just like that, a perfect system was ruined.*

Katja sighed. Everything was going so well until Fleck entered her life.

When she was done, the red dress she borrowed was far dustier than she wished, and her body far sorer than she had ever felt after an assignment. She locked the door as she left and barely made her trolley to the Maiden Tower, which looked like a crooked toothpick on the horizon once they were close enough. On the trolley, a young girl and boy stared at her beneath their mother's arms, and Katja flashed them a smile. It was then that she noticed they were staring at a dark, wet stain on her shoulder where her wound was struggling to scab over. She covered the stain and awaited her stop at Puffer Square before running off the crowded trolley.

Once back at the Maiden Tower, she hurried to her empty dormitory and found a bleached pair of work clothes and an apron waiting on her bunk. She changed quickly, shoved the stolen dress down a laundry chute several floors below, and marched to the kitchens. There, a dozen chefs in white gowns rushed to bake bread and simmer tomato bisque for the evening. In the scullery further back, the washers scrubbed plates until their knuckles bled.

Prefect Haggerty was waiting in the scullery with an unpleasant grin. She pointed to a pile of cutlery, bowls, and cutting boards sitting in a deep sink bowl. "This is just the start. Once supper is over, you will have dirty dishes up to your elbows!"

Katja tiredly nodded and started splashing steaming water over the stack of crusted pots and pans, and began scrubbing them until her fingers grew accustomed to the scorching heat. Once Prefect Haggerty stopped breathing down her neck and made for the other room, Katja slackened her aching shoulders, rolled her head, and closed her eyes as the trickle of warm water nearly lulled her to sleep. Thankfully, a loud shout and the shattering of plates woke her before anyone noticed.

Once supper was served, the dining hall was filled with laughter, muffled by the swinging doors leading into the back kitchen and scullery. Bored to death, Katja listened for any remotely interesting conversation, but the words were too jostled to make sense of them. Her stomach grumbled as she watched the buttered bread leave the kitchen and slide onto the table in the other room. All she needed was a tiny crumb to satiate her for the next hour, but by the time an hour came, stack after stack of dirty plates, silverware, and cups of varying sizes filled the trolley beside her just as the prefect forewarned. And these dishes were far fouler than what the chefs handed her. These plates were full of half-eaten mutton, yoked-up eggs, sneeze-filled napkins, and tangled hairs marinated in the juices.

It wasn't for another two hours that she finally got a bite to eat—two bites of leftover pasta and what was left of a burnt loaf of bread. She dipped the hardened bread in warm milk and scarfed down the burnt ends like a child dipping cookies in milk. If she were honest, it didn't taste all too bad, but she might have also just been *that* hungry.

Once she was done wolfing down her supper, she entered her dark dormitory while the others were fast asleep in a whirlwind of snores. She let out a breath of despair before slumping onto her bed.

* * *

The next few days were mostly the same, but each day, she grew progressively more tired and sore and even more desperate to find the place Fleck dubbed "the Warren," where she could finally find those cards and deliver them to the grand maiden. Perhaps then the woman would lighten Katja's punishment and restore some of her life.

What if the cards burned to dust? Katja's stomach sank at the thought, but she let it pass like a cold breeze in the night and kept her head down while she stirred a boiling stew of dirty socks.

It wasn't until the second week that her body began to adapt to the fatigue. Her shoulder wound had scabbed over into the shape of a red coin, and her arms and calves had become hardened from the long hours of lifting everything from slopping wet gowns to broom handles to massive wrought-iron pots filled to the brim with slick oil and water.

Around the third week, Countess Auriella started to get antsy about her newly found engagement to Lord Rhys DeGrom, who had taken up second residence in Stavoren Manor since the proposal. During the long days, many guests arrived at the manor with expertise in décor, patterns, flowers, fabrics, dresses, party promotion, and estate planning. The countess inevitably got so busy that Katja rarely got to see her as much as she used to, as their conversations were cut short the moment she finished dressing and powdering the old woman's cheeks. By the time her earrings were poked through the holes in her ears, the countess was already marching out of her bedchamber to catch her driver or meet an important guest.

It was all so strange. Katja recalled Auriella being one of the loneliest people she knew, isolated by her expiring mind and body, but nowadays, no one would suspect she was crawling on death's doorstep just weeks prior. How could someone go from being unable to remember if they drank their morning tea to suddenly orchestrating an entire battalion of visitors? Katja was happy for the countess, but couldn't lie about being slightly disturbed by it all.

It all reeks of magic. Despite this, Katja knew the countess was as anti-magic as they came. After all, the wealthy families in Theed were loyal to the Crown and vilified magic whenever possible.

During the fourth week, Katja never arrived late to her assignment with the countess. She also didn't arrive too early, which was good because she wasn't there to see Lord DeGrom roll out of bed with the countess in nothing but the skin on their backs. One morning, Prefect Primrose dropped off a dozen pillowcases soiled with honey after some girls on the other floors played pranks on the girls from the fifth floor, with whom they were scrapping. Prefect Primrose got the brunt of that joke, her face bright red and distraught that morning as she had to figure out how to remove globs of honey from a chambermaid's hair, which left Katja dangerously close to being late for her assignment.

Another morning, while Katja was combing the countess's hair, the countess sniffed and wrinkled her nose as if she had smelled something foul. Katja sniffed herself but had to admit she was growing blind to her stench, which had turned unpleasant over the last month. When did she have time to bathe in her crowded schedule? No matter how much powder or oils the prefects lathered on her in the morning, nothing could replace the scent of dirty swamp water, old sweat, and soiled dishwashing rags. It was like she was a skunk immune to the smell of its spray.

Eventually, the countess recoiled at her scent and made a condescending complaint. Katja waited for the countess to leave for a meeting before snagging one of the lesser-used bottles of perfume on the counter and sliding it into her apron before leaving for the day.

One night after another long shift of washing dishes, she scarfed down a plate of leftover pasta and headed to her dormitory. Katja knew she needed to fill her stomach or else she wouldn't have the strength for tomorrow, because her dress was starting to feel loose against her ribs.

Once at her dormitory, she tiptoed into the dark room, slipped out of another borrowed dress, apron, stockings, and shoes, untied her bun, and hid the stolen bottle of perfume in her bedside table. She then quietly rolled into her thin sheets and buried her face into her pillow, feeling the tug of sleep on her heavy eyelids.

Her eyes fluttered open when she heard a stirring from the bunk overhead, followed by a muffled sniffle in the darkness.

"Portia, are you crying?" Katja whispered, doing her best not to wake up the others.

"Kat?" Portia's nose was plugged as she spoke.

"What is wrong?" Katja asked. Portia poked her head over the ledge, her hair dangling like ivy. A sliver of moonlight illuminated the wet streaks on her cheeks.

"I am leaving at the end of the term," Portia sobbed.

"What? When did this happen?" Katja asked, her heartbeat quickening.

Portia took a deep breath and sighed.

"What is it, Port?" Katja asked. "Did you get in trouble?"

"No, it is my grandfather. He died three nights ago . . . he was old, nearly eight span, so it wasn't unexpected," Portia whimpered.

Katja sighed. "I'm sorry to hear that. Was he ill?"

"He had been sick for a while," Portia said. "The problem is that my parents came upon a sizable inheritance when he died."

"Isn't that a good thing?" Katja asked, wishing her tone sounded less callous.

"Yes, but it means I must leave the Maiden Tower. My parents are moving into my grandfather's old home and expect me to attend a nice school now that they have the funds. Before, we barely had a crown to our name, but they hope to act like everything is back to normal now that we have grandfather's fortune. He nearly wrote my father out of the will after he lost all his money, but never got to it before he got sick."

Katja stiffly patted her on the back. "I am sorry to hear that . . . but at least you get to leave this place. I would kill to go to school and learn something. It sounds much more interesting than staying here the rest of your life."

"But I will miss my friends here! I don't fit in back home!" Portia exclaimed, but turned her voice to a whisper when she realized she was being too loud. "Money has only caused trouble for my family. They will have all of these expectations for me, like marrying a boring, wealthy man and living like all the other socialites in this terrible town."

"To be honest, you would be really good at being a socialite," Katja smiled. "You know just about everyone there is to know in this tower. If you marry an old man and he dies, you can marry again, just as Countess Auriella did. She is happier than ever," Katja said. "It could be worse."

"Of course. I have no right to complain. After all, money is hard to come by these days. I shouldn't have been so insensitive," Portia sighed. "But I will miss the Maiden Tower. Despite all the rules and terrible prefects telling us what to do. I have never felt freer."

"Living on the streets sometimes felt like freedom too . . . but sometimes too much freedom only cripples you. It put me in many difficult situations. I needed the structure of the Maiden Tower, or else I would be locked away somewhere," Katja chuckled. "But I know you're different. You will do well with this opportunity, Portia. I've got a feeling."

Portia slid down to Katja's bunk and embraced her. Warm tears pressed against her neck.

"Promise me when you become wealthy beyond imagination, I can be assigned to you so I can powder your nose," Katja smiled.

"I am here for the rest of the term of my contract, but after that, I will be home for the start of the Winterhour," Portia sniffled. "I tried to tell Claudia and the other girls, but they were too busy. You're the first one I have told."

"Thanks, I'm honored," Katja said, lying back on her pillow, her eyelids heavy. "We should sleep. Perhaps we can talk again tomorrow."

"I don't know if I can stay up this late again to catch you, but I can try," Portia said. "Can I sleep in your bunk tonight?"

Katja reluctantly said yes and squeezed to the end of the small bed as Portia tucked herself into her like a small child.

Portia sniffed. "Katja . . . on the other hand . . . I might sleep in my bunk. I don't mean to be rude, but you smell like dirty dishwater."

Katja chuckled, relieved her stench had some benefits. "That is because I am covered in dirty dishwater. Don't worry, I don't take offense."

Portia climbed to her bunk as quietly as she could. "Also, I noticed your dress is burnt. I pulled some money from my trust earlier. I want to give you some to fix it at the tailor's or get a brand new one."

"Portia, I can't take your grandfather's money," Katja uttered, eyes now peeled open. A fixed dress would do her wonders if she were honest, but she couldn't admit it.

"One of the girls from the ninth floor complained about missing a red dress she sent down the laundry chute. Later, she told us at supper that she found it, but it was dirtier than when she put it in the laundry, to begin with," Portia whispered. "You couldn't have been involved, could you? After all, I know you spend your mornings in the laundry room."

Katja gasped. "I am not a thief, Portia."

"No . . . but many in your situation might do the same and justify borrowing a dress to keep their contract," Portia said, her head peeking over the railing as a silhouette. "I am just saying, if that was you, you don't have to do it anymore and risk getting another strike against your record. I can't imagine the leash is very long between you and the prefects these days."

Katja nodded. "Thanks, Portia. I will repay you one day."

"I also noticed you are without a purse," Portia whispered.

"Yes, the kidnappers took it," Katja sighed. "I have been carrying everything with me every day, or just not bringing anything at all."

"You can have my old one," Portia said, reaching down to their shared cabinet and pulling an embroidered purse from her drawer. It was hard to tell in the dark, but Katja remembered that it was pleasing to the eye and had a long drawstring cord to strap around the shoulders, unlike her last purse.

"I can't take that. What will you do?" Katja asked.

"The first thing I bought with my allowance was a new purse from Briston Row; you know, where all the fancy shops line the streets," Portia whispered. "My old one is nice in its own right and should serve you well."

"Thank you, Port," Katja said, her heart fluttering. Honestly, this would help her almost as much as the new dress. "I won't forget your kindness."

"Don't tell anyone, but the money is under my mattress. In the morning, when no one is looking, take thirty crowns and take your dress to the tailor. That should cover it with a little extra. It is the least I can do for an old friend," Portia chuckled.

Katja was going to open her mouth and tell her friend that the mattress and pillowcase were the first places a thief would look for hidden money, but instead, she turned over and dreamed about her beautiful new red dress before falling asleep.

Chapter Nine

The walk to the tailor was brisk. Katja woke up an hour earlier than usual to finish her laundry duties and tucked a clean red dress from the drying line beneath her armpit. She promised herself she would never steal another dress again once hers was repaired. For some reason, repeating the promise under her breath made her feel better about the whole thing, but deep down, she knew she was trying to convince herself she was a good person. *Your mother taught you to steal before you could walk. None of this was your fault.*

She wasn't convincing anyone. Not even herself.

One of the perks of waking early in Theed was that the crowds were thinner at the crack of dawn. The reason: a mixture of fear of being mugged and a sense of self-respect in allowing themselves to sleep like a well-adjusted person. Although sparser, the streets and trolley lines would be crowded if her errand wasn't done quickly. She allowed herself just enough time to stop at Puffer Station, reach the tailor, and then hop back on the trolley to Stavoren Manor in time for her assignment.

When Katja arrived at Puffer Station, the world was still cloaked in darkness, though wisps of the earliest sunlight brushed the eastern skies with gold. She felt the six knots—thirty crowns in total—tinkle against the countess's glass perfume bottle at the bottom of her new purse, like tiny discs dancing in celebration. Relief washed over her. At last, she had something to carry her things, which was far better than the tiny apron pockets that barely left room for two fingers side by side.

The purse bounced proudly on her hip, a beautiful thing with a pewter clasp and floral embroidery, making her feel like someone for once. Now she only had to carry both red dresses to the tailor. This route took her south past the old theater and through a stone gate into the merchant quarter of the Parliament District, an area far more refined than the famed markets and bazaars of Little Stellen, Boardshead, and the Market District. She crossed several crossroads, and walked along a line of fruit stands buzzing with bartering foreign traders dressed in an assortment of outlandish uniforms and gowns. She gazed down at her stained work outfit that wavered loosely on her arms and legs and dreamed about one day wearing the bright tangerine, goldenrod, azul, jade, and other wondrous colors worn by the Stellish men and women babbling among each other as she passed, their lips moving so quickly that they appeared like the beat of butterfly wings. Their lips were dyed with vibrant pastes, which always helped her differentiate Stellish and Priz-Stellish merchants, who were less numerous and wore exclusively black lip paste.

When Katja reached the end of the fruit stands, the pink morning light peered through the distant clouds, catching her a rare glimpse of the royal palace shining high upon the jutting bluff known as Artem's Roost. The palace looked over Theed, usually wrapped in a cape of mist and fog from Balledore Bay to the east.

Katja and a few other bystanders froze in the street, some standing in front of traffic as the mists swirled with a gentle breeze, revealing several jutting turrets topped with massive glimmering domes that resembled three shimmering gemstones: emerald, ruby, and sapphire. The palace was too far away to see its finer details or see through its windows. Still, one could spot the crimson and gold banners clinging tightly to their poles in the wind, swooping buttresses, rainbow stained-glass windows, and tiered balconies overlooking the bay and further to the Relian Sea. She could only imagine Queen Margot and the royal family sitting atop those balconies when the warm trade winds blew in from the sea to watch a magnificent sunrise or sunset on clearer days.

When the breeze gave up, and a cloud of fog covered the palace once more, everyone who had stopped broke from their trance, shook their heads, and continued walking as they were, many still looking somewhat dazed as they walked to their original destination.

As she entered the tailor's at the Kroner and Redd Street crossroads, the bell above the door rang, and she saw people heading back down the street to Puffer Square, the silhouette of the Parliament building standing far off on the horizon like a hulking stone fortress. She approached a slender old man with tufts of white hair poking out from a shiny bowler cap that reminded her of cotton. His face looked malleable, as if it were made of taffy. He spoke to his young apprentice, who was cutting fabric with a long pair of scissors, and his wispy eyebrows, which furrowed as he looked Katja up and down from toe to forehead, reminded her of the wings of gulls.

"Good morning, dear!" the tailor exclaimed. "You came at the right time. I had a line forming outside the door until they heard there would be another hanging at the square. It would appear death is a better business than clothing."

"That is probably true for most things, sadly," Katja said.

"And you have no interest in watching another neck split by rope?" the tailor smirked.

"Not in the slightest. I have seen enough of that in this city," Katja said, jostling the coins at the bottom of her purse. She then set her burnt dress on the counter. "I need this dress repaired."

The tailor grimaced repugnantly as he examined the dress like an antique map. "This is going to be a lot of work . . . burns are not an easy fix."

"I have twenty crowns. What can you do with that?" Katja lied.

"For twenty, I can certainly throw it away for you," the tailor teased, tossing it back onto the counter. "You work for the Maiden Tower, I wager. I could recognize that red gown and white apron from a mile away. Not to mention, I have supplied the Maiden Tower with plenty of dresses over the years here at Needle & Spool."

"So, can you make me a deal?" Katja smiled.

"A deal? Certainly not. I run on tight margins! But I know how little you chambermaids make. Twenty crowns are likely over a month's work for you," the tailor said, scratching the space beneath his long nose.

"You aren't wrong." Katja nodded. "And most of that goes toward meals, taxes, and an occasional outing. I had to save for a while."

"I won't cut you a deal, but I can only offer you this because I am friends with the Grand Maiden," the tailor said. "You give me twenty crowns today, and in return, I will make you a whole new dress. It won't be flashy, but it will undoubtedly be nicer than that pile of rags."

"Twenty crowns will cover that?" Katja gasped. She reached out to shake his hand, but the tailor shied away. "Deal!"

"Not quite!" the tailor said, pulling out a ledger and dipping a pen in ink. "You give me twenty crowns now, which covers the materials, and then you give me fifteen more crowns for a total of thirty-five when you pick it up in a few days."

"You know I don't have that sort of money!" Katja lied. "You even said you know how much we chambermaids make."

"We can write you a loan if you don't have the money," the tailor smirked.

"I can't afford a loan," Katja huffed. She would still owe five crowns if she used every knot Portia had given her, and after losing her last purse she wasn't sure she had enough for her expenses. She still hadn't been paid for a month's work. Not to mention she had been dreaming of a hot meal and a glass of ale from one of the taverns in town, and she couldn't bear to let that dream die. The thought made her mouth water. "How about I promise to bring you the rest later?"

The tailor chuckled. "What is your name, girl?"

Katja debated telling him, but conceded. "Katja . . . Katja Rosdyre."

"Katja Rosdyre . . . memorable enough not to forget." The tailor frowned. "If you don't come back with the money, I will march to the Maiden Tower myself, and my apprentice and I will shake you upside down. I know where you live, and I know your boss well."

"You have got a deal," Katja grinned, setting four knots worth twenty crowns onto the counter, each displaying the shiny mint of Queen Margot's regal profile.

The tailor eyed her suspiciously but shook his head and then scribbled something onto his ledger.

"Come back in three days, and you shall have your dress," the tailor said. "I don't normally accept handshake deals, but for some reason, I trust you, Miss Rosdyre. Just don't come back penniless, or we will be forced to write a loan, which won't be cheap."

"I will be back in three days," Katja said, feeling the two coins remaining in her pocket. She would give them to the tailor in time, but for now, she figured they could prove useful elsewhere. "But first, can I use your changing room? I need to touch up my lipstick."

The tailor pursed his lips and nodded. "As you wish."

Katja trotted to the back of the tailor's room, where walls of mirrors and stacks of different fabrics, in every color, were organized on neat shelves. She entered the changing room and locked it behind her, then pulled the red maiden dress she had borrowed earlier and quickly slipped it on, checking the mirror to ensure she looked reasonably presentable. She then snuck out the front door before the tailor could utter a "goodbye," but she reckoned he was confused as she walked by wearing another red dress despite all of that desperate haggling.

Once on the street, she noticed the street heading to Puffer Square was even more crowded than before, and provocative chants started to echo off the tall brick walls. She backtracked her footsteps back toward the station, but got stuck behind a wall of people. After wading through the ranks for what felt like an hour she entered the square, where she caught glimpse of the main attraction at the gallows, two men and one lady standing at the noose, each having a thick rope fastened around their necks by executioners whose faces were hidden beneath shrouds.

Katja looked away in disgust, but something morbid from deep within her gut compelled her to peek just as the lever was pulled, and the three bodies flailed like perch on the end of a hook. Her stomach sank as she lowered her gaze to the feet of the crowd and passed through Puffer Square to the trolley station.

At the platform, she waited for her trolley to arrive, which appeared to be running a few stops behind based solely on the number of angry faces and impatient toe-tapping among the crowd. A man standing beside her glared at her and inched away like he had seen a rotting fish in the harbor that was more pleasant to look at. In response, Katja reached into her apron pocket and sprayed three spritzes of the countess's perfume on her neck just as the trolley arrived. Once she boarded, all of the seats were filled, so she resorted to leaning on a slim slice of wall between two other bobbing passengers to keep herself from falling over with exhaustion.

After a few minutes, the trolley clanged its piercing bell at pedestrians crossing the tracks. Her eyes flicked open. How long had she been sleeping? Did she miss her stop? Then something caught her eye.

A small boy was staring at her, dressed in a flat-billed hat, fingerless gloves, worn knickers, an off-white shirt, overalls, and holey leather shoes. There was something innocent yet unnerving about the child. His youthful red cheeks, a dusting of freckles, ear-length brown hair, and buck teeth were endearing, but his beady eyes were distressing, for lack of a better word. His eyes were nearly black, dilated to the rim, yet the whites were a yellowish hue and bloodshot. His gaze was heavy with an unwavering hold that made her wish to hide.

Katja grinned awkwardly and gave the boy a timid wave, but he did not return the gesture, and his gaze was unfocused. Perhaps he had a condition or was sick? Maybe he was another dust addict. She wasn't so sure about that, though. She had seen desperate eyes before, but nothing like this. His eyes looked wicked, like the eyes of a ghoul.

"Can I help you?" Katja asked.

The boy remained unfazed by her question as they approached the first stop. Several people shuffled as passengers departed, and more boarded, cramming the small space even more. But the boy did not budge.

"Is there something wrong with my face?" Katja asked, wiping her cheek.

"Is this man disturbing you, miss?" a man with a dark walrus mustache asked.

"No . . . we're fine," Katja said.

The boy then stared daggers at the walrus-mustached man and swiftly dashed across the trolley despite the conductor's protest. He jumped out the window onto the street below and darted back toward the crowded square.

Katja's heart skipped a beat as she half expected to be attacked or, at least, robbed, but not many thieves were so brazen as to do so in front of so many witnesses. Not many would let someone get away with thieving on a crowded trolley, even in a town as sick as Theed. *But then again, one may never be certain.*

After a few moments, everything settled back to normal. A young girl with long red braids sat in the boy's empty seat. The girl reminded Katja of herself at that age, and, thankfully, her eyes were not haunted, which put her at ease. She had almost forgotten the strange encounter by the time she reached her stop in the Wallingford District. She arrived at Stavoren Manor ten minutes early, noted by Gavin, who flashed his pocket watch the instant she walked in like a jockey timekeeper.

Katja ignored Gavin's gossip and bickering as she paced across the manor, picking up a few messes along the way, which she would have usually done with the flick of her wrist. She knew it was silly, but it pained her to spend time doing things that once were done with magic. When she reached the centrally located drawing room, Countess Stavoren greeted her impatiently as she basked on the sofa, smoking a long cigarette.

"Countess! Good morning to you! Why . . . why aren't you upstairs in your chambers?" Katja asked. "Is Lord DeGrom here this morning?"

Gavin cleared his throat. "I have been trying to tell you. The countess and Lord DeGrom have been sparring. I am afraid."

"Why are you speaking like she isn't in the room to hear you?" Katja asked, glaring at the well-dressed steward.

"You can determine that for yourself," Gavin whispered through clenched teeth.

"Kitty, is that you?" a voice croaked from the sofa. It was a voice she barely recognized anymore.

"Countess? Are you alright?" Katja said, stepping closer. "Are you sick?"

Countess Auriella groaned, and that was when Katja noticed her blue eyes were milky and distant, and her wrinkles seemed deeper and more widespread—even worse than before she met Lord DeGrom.

Katja turned her attention back to Gavin, angling her body away from the countess, and lowered her voice to a whisper. "What were the countess and Lord DeGrom sparring about? They seemed so happy, and the wedding seemed to be coming along smoothly," she insisted.

"I didn't have it in me to ask," Gavin said. "But it appears our countess is heartsick."

"Heartsick? She looks like she is knocking on death's door," Katja whispered so the countess could not overhear. "This has to be some strange magic. None of this makes sense. She has aged a decade in a day, like she was before meeting Lord Degrom."

"You are the witch. You tell me what to think of it," Gavin spat. "Wickedness! This whole city is rotten to its core!"

"Come with me," Katja said, helping the countess to her feet and ushering her up the stairs to her bedchambers. Chills ran up and down Katja's spine. This had to be some strange enchantment or curse. She should have trusted her gut when she saw Auriella pounce out of her bathtub, spry and full of youth, that one day. She doubted a practitioner could explain such a reversal of one's condition. The countess could barely remember where she was, plagued with a sickness of the mind, and now that enchantment had been broken, she was somehow far worse. Was this Lord DeGrom's doing? Perhaps some sort of evil love curse? She could not say.

Katja delicately ran the countess's bath and massaged her fingers through her scalp. To her horror, clumps of long white hair coated her hands like wispy cobwebs.

"Countess Auriella, are you feeling alright?" Katja asked. "You don't seem well."

The countess smiled. "I saw Hugo today. He was walking through the gardens with his large straw hat. I spotted him through the window . . ." She drifted off, but Katja snapped her fingers in her face. ". . . I went downstairs and saw him peering in through the window. He was so young and handsome with that long dark hair, but he lost it when the boys were born. The boys were born with a full head of lush locks. I reckon they took them from him for themselves. You know how children are."

She cackled manically, drool running down her pointy chin.

Katja sighed. "Hugo is . . . never mind . . . what happened to you and Lord DeGrom?"

"Lord DeGrom?" Countess Auriella whispered as she nearly fell back into the tub.

In a panic, Katja lifted her by the shoulders and stared into her milky eyes. "Your fiancé! You are both to be married! Certainly, you couldn't forget?"

"Forget? Of course, I didn't forget. Rhys has called off the engagement. I don't reckon I will ever see him again. He was so handsome, too," Countess Auriella said. "Can you tell Gavin to reach out to that matchmaker again? What was his name? I think it started with a 'K' . . ."

Matchmaker? How could she so quickly move on from the new love of her life? None of this made any sense.

"What happened between you two?" Katja asked.

Countess Auriella smiled. "Sometimes men love with short wicks and long ones." She paused, her gaze drifting. "Sometimes, that fire snuffs out faster than you ever imagined."

"Faster than you could get married? What about all the reservations? The dress? The ring? The wedding?" Katja exclaimed.

Countess Auriella nodded, and her eyes wandered across the room as they had in the old days. Katja could tell that she was likely done talking for a while.

Katja sat momentarily to think of what to say or do, but then decided to finish her assignment. There were too many things to worry about, and this engagement was neither her problem nor her business to address. She pulled the countess from the bath, dried her, picked an outfit, pinned up her hair, powdered her face, and cleaned up the mess at a backbreaking pace. She was so tempted to draw Vigor and cast a spell—after all, how bad could one spell be? But she stopped herself before she could feel the boiling bubble in her chest and took a deep breath. Without more magedust, she risked death even with something so simple.

She punched the tile countertop and recoiled.

It serves me right to even think I could use magic at this time. The pain of kindling was far, far worse than a stinging knuckle.

When Katja was finished, she handed the countess off to Gavin, who brought her back downstairs while Katja cleaned the bedchamber. She noticed the prominent pale spot where the tapestry should have rested and longed for the days when she could light the candle and enter the count's wonderland to refill her reserves, but she knew those days were over. All of that magedust burned up the instant she struck that match anyway.

Katja took a small break, sat on the countess's soft bed, and massaged her aching knuckles. She uncorked a bottle of Stellish wine and took a large swig, dripping a speck of red on her dress. Thankfully, her dress was already red. Then she rifled through the countess's mail on her bedside table, where a few manila envelopes, some open, were stacked untidily as autumn leaves beneath a balding tree. It only took a glance to realize none of the letters looked remotely interesting. She sighed, corked the wine bottle, and returned to work, swapping the countess's bedsheets with a new cotton spread smelling of fresh lavender. When she whipped the sheet to fit the bed's length, to her surprise, a small piece of parchment slid to the floor.

Katja's heartbeat pounded as she glanced at the parchment, which, to her disappointment, contained a list of ingredients and shops where she could purchase them. She cursed under her breath, set the note on the bedside table, and tidied the bed before continuing the rest of the afternoon, fixing up the rest of Stavoren Manor.

When she was done, Katja bid the countess farewell. She made for the Wallingford trolley to Dabbord Square without any incident except for the usual beggar hassling trolley-goers for spare change, which she could not afford to give. Even when she was living on the street, she was lucky not to have to rely solely on begging for her meals, but perhaps if she hadn't been fortunate enough to learn what she knew about magic from her mother, it would have been her only option. The thought made her feel forlorn, but also relieved to be where she was—a rare feeling these days.

Once she arrived at her stop, she wandered across the crowded square but diverted to a shortcut she had often used down the alleyway between the abbey and a crumbling inn known as a hive of gamblers, smugglers, and ladies of the night—a wholesome union.

Overhead, the crooked Maiden Tower peaked through a sliver of sky caught between the abbey and the inn. The light was fading into a deep violet, casting deceptive shadows that would have made her hackles rise if she were a cat.

Her breath caught at the sound of a boot scratching pavement that echoed in the alley behind her. She dashed for the Maiden Tower, too panicked to look behind as she anticipated a pair of hands reaching for her arms and tripping up her tired legs as they hammered the concrete.

Thankfully, those hands never reached her, and when she breathlessly reached the Maiden Tower doors, two prefects were hovering around the entrance in a heated debate, and a maiden with bouncing braids was sweeping the porch. None of them paid much attention as Katja pressed her sweaty back against the cold brick wall where she felt safe and gasped for breath.

When she looked back at the alleyway, no one was chasing her. Nothing at all but a collection of rubbish bins and last week's copy of the *Daily Kroner* littered across the damp pavement like grease-soaked napkins. The street was empty.

"Miss Rosdyre, you are getting dirt all over yourself!" Prefect Nugent said with an appalled expression. "Why were you running anyway? A proper maiden doesn't run!"

Katja swallowed her breath and pointed back at the alley. "Someone was chasing me!"

"From over there? You know best not to sneak around those dark places. You should know better than anyone that there are spots in this city filled with wickedness," Prefect Primrose hissed, her face still flushed from arguing with Prefect Nugent.

"Are you seriously blaming me for being chased?" Katja retorted. "I always come through that way and have had no problem. Maybe a panhandler here and there, but they are mostly harmless if you aren't jiggling your coin purse in the open, and even then, they are mostly too dazed from their dust withdrawals to do anything."

"Watch your tongue, Miss Rosdyre! Remember, you are balancing on a razor-thin line with the grand maiden! You are on probation!" Prefect Primrose shouted, adjusting her bonnet around her head.

Katja bowed. "Yes, Prefect Primrose. I am sorry."

"Just hold that tongue of yours, dearie!" Prefect Primrose said. "You've got to watch your back out there! People have been getting more and more desperate. Ever since Prime Minister Stoker died, the streets have gotten seedy!"

Prefect Nugent nodded in agreement. "I will warn the other girls to avoid that alleyway if that makes you feel better."

"I . . . I just know someone was chasing me. They were running. I could hear them," Katja said. "Did you see someone following after me?"

"I saw them!" a voice interrupted from overhead.

Katja craned her head toward a window on the fourth floor, where a young maiden with black braids and skin the color of cinnamon was dangling her feet out of the window. She was knitting a blanket that nearly reached down to the window below.

"What did you see?" Katja asked. She recognized the girl but couldn't place her name.

"All I know is that it was a little boy with a round hat," the girl said, deftly plucking the ball of yarn with a long copper needle. "I only saw him briefly, but I noticed something was off about his eyes before he drifted back into the shadows."

Chapter Ten

For the next two nights, Katja dreamed about Count Hugo and her mother. Those dreams were mostly pleasant, except every time they ended, her stalker was hunting her—the boy with yellowing eyes and a round hat. When she woke up, her mattress was soaked with sweat. Her dormitory window was still dark, which meant it was not yet dawn.

Katja was feeling particularly sullen this morning. She reached for her new purse with the remaining ten crowns and the countess's perfume clanking at its bottom. She slipped on her stinky beige work outfit and joined Miss Frisbie in the laundry room until she finished her duties. She reached for the red dress she had now gotten used to borrowing and smiled, realizing she would no longer need to steal another girl's dress after today. While she waved farewell to Miss Frisbie and left the Maiden Tower, she took a moment while basking in the pink morning sun to collect her thoughts.

Not caring that she looked like a sweaty ratcatcher in her work gown, she returned to the tailor on the other end of Puffer Square, avoiding the abbey alleyway on her way to the trolley. Thankfully, the square seemed less busy than usual, and she got to the tailor's half-timber shop before the line was too long. She figured the streets were emptier because it was the first frost of the year, as evidenced by the glittery cobblestones, smoky chimneys, and biting wind, but the most eerie was the lack of songbirds tweeting, which made the city of Theed as quiet as a corpse. The people were also more rushed than ever in the

Winterhour as they clutched their frock coats and clenched their jittering teeth as cold breath bellowed from their mouths like a smokestack.

"Hello again," Katja said as the bell rang jovially when she entered the tailor's store. "It has been three days. I hope you have my dress as you promised."

The tailor scrutinized her as if he couldn't place her face, but gasped with recognition.

"Ah! The poor maiden girl with the dismal dress!" he beamed. "Do you have the full payment, or will you require a loan?"

Katja jingled the two knots in her purse. "I will pay in full."

"You got that fifteen crowns swiftly," the tailor grinned, "but I won't question how you got it. I run a business, not a bank."

"Oh, I thought we agreed on five crowns. I have the five today, but I will get you the rest by the end of the month," Katja lied, doing her best to put on an innocent face.

The tailor crossed his arms. "We agreed on fifteen crowns. I'll need to write you up for a loan for the additional ten."

"I won't have those ten for a few months. Everything is expensive these days," Katja pleaded. "Can we make a deal without a loan? I promise I won't use another tailor while I live in Theed."

"Running this business is expensive too," the tailor said. "I'm sorry, I can't make a deal. Either pay up or take the loan. Besides, I hear more than one coin in that pocket, and they sound like knots to me."

Katja sighed. "I have ten crowns . . . but I was hoping to have something to spare for other costs." Her dreams of a hot meal evaporated like mist.

"Fantastic. I'll write you up for a five-crown loan and you can take your dress with you today. It will only take a moment to rifle through my orders, and then I will bring it out here for you to try on," the tailor said. "I think you'll be delighted with how it turned out."

Katja let out a breath of anguish. It felt like receiving a present and a slap at once. It was clear she had lost her bartering charm after being away from the street all this time.

"Feel free to take a seat or admire my other works hanging on the wall," the tailor said. "I know you work hard for your money, but it doesn't cost anything to look."

Katja waited for the tailor to vanish into a back room before perusing through the vibrant ball dresses, wedding gowns, capes, dirndls, and cocktail dresses. On the other side was a row of tuxedos, coats, and fine cotton doublets. In a drawer, she found stack after stack of colorful socks, gloves, neckties, scarves, shawls, and silk ties so numerous you could wear one each day of the year and never repeat a style.

Before long, she got carried away and was a couple of aisles into the store before she spotted a boy in a bowler hat looking into the shop from across the street, among a meandering crowd.

Her heart skipped a beat, and she dove out of sight behind an oversized saddlebag hanging on its own. She slowly snuck behind a white wedding gown and peeked back out at the street, but to her surprise, the boy who haunted her dreams was looking around aimlessly.

He looks lost. Was he looking for her?

Katja caught her reflection in the glass and remembered that she wasn't wearing her vibrant crimson maiden gown, but instead her beige work clothes. Perhaps he didn't recognize her without her outfit. But did that mean that he knew she would be at the tailor's? Was he waiting for her to arrive in her red dress? Was this all just a coincidence? Her heart told her it wasn't.

Then, it struck her. Was the boy working for the Magesleuths? There were all sorts of legends or rumors about who the Magesleuths were and if they were even human. Some said they were formless, while others claimed they were a part reptile and part human travesty. However, one thing common to these stories was that they were paid in magedust due to their rabid addiction and exceptional hunting skills, which haunted the imaginations of both magic folk and non-magic folk alike. The worst part was the *sniffing* as they hunted the scent of magic out of the air like flies to a rotting corpse. But even if the Magesleuths were human, the boy seemed far too young to be one of the Crown's mysterious inquisitors, but it wouldn't surprise her.

Perhaps they kept tabs on her to see if she would slip up and use magic. She had to be vigilant. And she could not be caught wearing her new and improved maiden gown, as that left less risk of being followed—or worse. No, she would need to wait—or perhaps she needed to take advantage of her impromptu disguise. She held her breath as footsteps erupted from the back room, but before the tailor could return to the front desk, Katja slid out the door and joined the crowd. She snuck down to the end of the street, where she spotted a tall streetlamp, which she leaned against, pretending to be preoccupied with something in her purse while keeping an eye on the boy.

He was right there, blind to her advance, like the child he was. *Would Magesleuths stoop so low to hire young children to do their bidding?* She was sure there was a long line of young boys and girls willing to do almost any work for a copper or, if they were addicts, a few grains of dust.

Katja shuddered at the thought as she continued to watch the boy, noticing his beady, wandering eyes. He glanced at her briefly but then continued scanning the busy street. She needed to find out who he was and why he was stalking her, but she was also afraid of the answer. Was she foolish to want to confront him? What if she wasn't as lucky the next time he followed her down an alleyway? She couldn't live her life looking over her shoulder more than she already did. Time was running out. She could tell the boy was getting antsy, if not from boredom. It was undoubtedly from dust withdrawals. He could bolt at any moment and become another hidden face in the crowd for eternity.

Her heart fluttered like a mackerel pulled by fishing line out of Balledore Bay.

An epiphany came to her as her fingers pinched the two coins at the bottom of her purse. Her dress would have to wait. Timidly, she dropped the coins onto the road, took a deep breath, felt the warm boil in her chest, and raised an instructional finger. At the command of her finger, the coins hovered mere inches from the cobblestone as passersby crossed the street with barely a notice.

I've missed this. But she knew she couldn't hold it long or risk kindling again.

Her eyes fluttered back into her skull as tears brimmed at the corners.

"Girl, are you okay?" a bearded passerby said, waving his dirty hands in front of her face with a concerned look.

Katja broke her trance, and the crowns fell to the ground, but by luck, the man did not notice. Of all the times someone would check in on her well-being, it had to be now. Of course. She never received more than a "Hello" or "How are you?" when she lived on the street, but they noticed now that she was occupied with something as important as this.

"No . . . I am fine," Katja said.

"You don't seem fine," the man asked, scratching his mustache.

She sighed. "Thank you . . . but I am only praying. May the Shining God deliver you great blessings."

The man smiled, pulling a copper chain from around his neck with a circular piece of glass hanging from its end. It looked a lot like a monocle, but Katja knew it was worn by those who followed the Shining doctrine. It was similar to the one her mother had worn before she was forced to pawn it away for low-quality magedust, often referred to as *dust* by those unfortunate enough to know the difference.

"Shine bright, sister," the man said before walking away.

Katja refocused. She needed to be calm. It had been a long time, and it felt wonderful, and she couldn't break her concentration this time. Slow and easy, she lifted her finger and levitated the coins across the street, dodging carriages and swishing horse tails, until they hovered directly in front of the boy's anxious face.

Startled, he stumbled backward, nearly falling onto the pavement. When he noticed what was hovering before his face, his eyes widened, and he reached for the coins, but Katja flicked her finger, tugging them like strings luring a playful tabby cat into the busy street.

When the road was mostly clear, she hovered the coins further across the street as the boy continued snatching at them furiously. When he could not reach the coins, he stopped and spun around, hoping to find his bewitcher.

Katja reached into her purse for anything she could use as a weapon, but only found the countess's glass bottle of perfume. The realization struck that she was not well-equipped for a skirmish. But she figured she was safe on a crowded street for the most part, so she swiftly hovered the coins toward her direction just past the streetlamp. The boy cautiously followed, occasionally lunging at the coins until they were just an arm's length from her shoulder. Then, she summoned the coins to her palm.

"Why are you following me?" Katja said, hand gripping the perfume bottle. She could smash it against the side of his face if she needed to. That would deal plenty of damage to allow her escape.

The boy's eyes widened. "You! What are you . . .? How are you . . .?"

He looked like he might take off down the street, but Katja clenched the fabric of his muddied frock coat before he could.

"Don't run just yet," she spat. "Tell me why you are following me!"

"Unhand me!" the boy shouted, tugging away from her grip.

"Two knots can buy a days worth of dust," Katja teased. "Are you sure you don't just want to tell me why you're stalking me?"

The boy sighed and stopped fighting, but Katja did not let go of his coat.

"Give me the coins first," he growled, his pupils slit like those of a cat and as black as tar.

Katja gave him one knot. "The other is for when you have completed telling me who you are working for."

The boy cursed under his breath.

She avoided his gaze because the usually white spots were an unsettling bright yellow.

Why did the boy have those eyes? She looked at the rest of him, expecting to find a swishing tail on his backside or other catlike features, but there were none. *What is wrong with this boy?*

"They don't have a name," the boy said. "All I know is they are hunting a young witch with long red hair who works for the Maiden Tower. That's all they told me."

Katja's stomach sank.

"And they told you I would be here? Picking up something?" she asked, chills running down her neck.

"I've been following you for a few days." The boy flashed a toothless grin. "No one goes to the tailor just once. Repairs take a few days."

"Why do they want me?"

"I dunno, they never said," the boy answered, body shaking with tremors. "All I know is they want me to ensure you haven't left the city."

"You know more," Katja said threateningly.

The boy groaned. "Sorry, ma'am, I will faint if I don't get my dust."

Katja reached for her purse, but before she could say another word, the boy broke her grip with a swipe of his arm and dashed down the street, pushing past the crowd toward the square.

Katja tore after him, spotting a glimpse of her beautiful red dress with its neat bow on the tailor's counter. And now she was a coin short. *How could I be so stupid?*

The boy plowed through the street, nearly knocking over passersby, who reacted with disgruntled curses. Katja followed the mayhem, focusing intently on the back of the boy's hat as he zigzagged through the crowd to slip away towards the masses of Puffer Square. She nearly crashed into a line of preachers, then stomped into a puddle of water used as a bath by a flock of pigeons, and skirted past a busy tea stand. She stumbled into a massive wall of a man, glancing off his iron pauldron onto the ground. The man frowned as he reached for a long switch tied to his leather girdle fixed around his wide waist. He spat at her feet and cursed in a foreign language.

"Sorry!" Katja shouted, painfully pouncing to her feet. "That boy stole my money!"

The man stroked his long, bright blue beard, which complemented his red eyebrows. He looked across the crowd, towering, and pointed. "I do not like rambunctious children, but nothing is worse than a thief! Your burglar is over there! I'd better not run into you again, child!"

Katja nodded thankfully and followed the man's sausage-thick finger through the crowd, squeezing between the gaps of grumpy and statuesque passersby who often refused to budge or allow an inch of inconvenience upon their busy days.

"Stop that boy!" Katja shouted, but no one paid much attention to her. "Thief! Someone help me!"

A few in the crowd offered token sympathy, only to shrug before returning to what they were doing. The majority looked annoyed as if her short cries for help hindered their entire day. To them, she probably looked like a simple street urchin in this worn-out gown smelling of detergent and stale water. *Just another stupid girl begging in the streets.* She could almost smell their hatred as they looked her up and down like she was a lame horse at one of those fancy derbies.

Katja ducked past a caravan with no business moving through such a crowd, cut through a large marble fountain where children often played in the water on hot days, and nearly slipped on a smooth sheet of pavement, but caught herself before her face could meet it.

Panicked that she had lost the boy, she scanned ahead, searching for a disruption in the crowd, but most importantly, that black bowler hat fixed on the back of his big head. But hats like those were a dime a dozen in the city. What were her chances of finding him again? In the distance, a flutter of pigeons took off, and there was a commotion. Just by chance, she spotted the boy's reddened cheeks and horrific gaze through a brief window in the crowd. As though every limb, head, hat, cloak, wagon, and everything else that wandered the square parted perfectly to create a hole large enough for her to see her target.

But the hole revealed one thing: *He was getting away.*

With a wave of her hands, Katja felt the warmth boil in her chest, took a deep breath, and focused all her thoughts on that bobbing bowler hat. With a flick of her wrist, the hat forcefully slid over his brow, sending him stumbling into a tall bystander, who shoved him with a look of displeasure. She forced herself through the crowd of wayfarers until she came within a few strides of the scurrying boy.

"Get back here, thief!" Katja shouted.

When she was an arm's length away from the boy, she instinctively reached out a hand, feeling the bubbling in her stomach. She couldn't continue her brazenness. She was already risking too much.

Instead, she settled the warmth in her stomach and lunged at the boy, tugging his shoulder and knocking his hat onto the hard cobblestone.

He turned to her for an instant, his yellow eyes now full of fear.

"Let go of me, witch!" he shouted, flailing from her grip. "Witch! Witch! She is a witch, I tell you!"

Katja's stomach dropped as passersby stopped to listen, giving her repulsed glances like she was worse than the grime beneath their boots. Moments later, others were shouting "witch!" and hailing the guards scattered across the square. It wouldn't be long before they answered those calls, and it would be even worse if it brought the attention of the Magesleuths. She made a terrible mistake using magic, even on something so small as a hat. If the Magesleuths caught her scent even once, there would not be a single stone in Theed she could hide behind to save her.

The boy shot her a sly grin before starting towards the end of the square.

Katja bit her tongue. She reached for the countess's crystalline perfume and threw it at the boy, causing it to break into a flowery mist that coated everything in a small perimeter. But the boy continued running, hunching low to sneak between the gap behind the seat of a parked stagecoach, whose driver looked unamused by his escapades.

She cursed under her breath and continued chasing the boy, now emitting a strong lavender scent. Some stranger grabbed Katja's shoulder and scolded her, but the stranger didn't have long as Katja tore from their grip and darted past the parked carriage and back into the stirring crowd. The crowd seemed angrier, tired of their antics, as they hollered after her and the boy. It was only a matter of time before the city watch took notice, and her fears were further confirmed as the horns and whistles broke through the air, and the crowd became wild with fear. Mothers clenched their sons and daughters, grandmoms and grandpops were ushered out of the street, and babes cried and latched to their mother's breasts as the square turned to complete disorder.

Using magic, even subtly, was a mistake. *Bitter teeth!* She would hang for this if she were caught! Why was she so rash sometimes? It was like something took over her—some deeply rooted fear or lack of control.

Hexes! And now every guard in the Parliament District was descending on Puffer Square.

Before she knew it, she was near the end of the square, which was swallowed by a wall of tall buildings and towers. She was trapped. The clock chimed the noonday summons to worship and the midday fare, its clamor only increasing the disorder. Then, she spotted the gallows out of the corner of her eye, the long ropes swinging in the wind, and her stomach clenched.

The crowd thinned as the whistles approached, blaring off the walls like shrill banshee screams. Her heart pounded, and for a moment, she froze, unsure of where to run. Then she spotted the boy running along the edge of the gallows and climbing behind them with a loud clack of his leather boots on the pavement.

Katja followed, climbing up the gallows and leaping behind them just the same. Her feet struck the ground like a hammer on an anvil. It was a more significant drop than anticipated, but she stumbled off the gallows ledges, which were far higher than expected. She had jumped from high porches, windows, off dry docks, and into shallow wells, all to prevent capture, and only rarely was she ever caught. But she had only been seen by the city guard once, for stealing seeds when she was young. The other times, she was caught by people like her or by store owners who preferred to leave the guards out of the conversation. It had been years since the guards last seized her, and they would show no mercy now that she was older.

Her skin ached at the thought of the floggings she had received years ago. As an eight-year-old, she received ten, but for magic, she'd be hanged in front of an enraptured crowd. Her heart pounded against her ribs as she chased the boy with legs that felt like they might fall beneath her at any minute from exhaustion.

"Stop!" Katja screamed, her voice hoarse. But the boy did not respond.

They pressed on toward an underground tunnel barred by fencing and a line of round bollards, each stamped with bold warning signs proclaiming

HAZARDOUS and **DO NOT ENTER**. Katja paused, her breath hitching as she studied the unlit passage—a dark, gaping mouth descending into the city's belly. The hesitation lasted only a heartbeat. If she let it pass, she might never get another chance to catch her stalker.

She vaulted the obstructions, her boots skidding on loose pebbles before she regained her balance, then plunged down the uneven stone steps, swallowed quickly by the darkness below. Her heart raced, and her lungs burned in her chest. Everything inside her, including her mother's sweet voice, told her not to go down those stairs, but her determination said otherwise. She had already risked everything for this, and nothing could stop her now. She leaped down the stairs after him, heels striking the steps deep into the cool shadows.

"Stop running! I won't hurt you!" Katja shouted. But all she heard was more thuds and her voice echoing back.

What is this place?

Suddenly, a shrill sound echoed off the walls, but after listening for a second, it was clear it was a whistle. Not a guard's whistle but an *eerie* whistle. The sound tapered off and rang through the stony subterranean hall in an almost shrill melody that was beautiful and haunting but leaned more toward the latter, given the situation. As she moved deeper and deeper into the darkness, the whistle grew, accompanied by quick footsteps clacking on the steps as they sank into the nightmarish abyss.

But it wasn't long before she realized the only footsteps she now heard were her own. Was the boy standing in the middle of the stairs waiting for her to pass? Chills ran down her neck at the thought, and she stopped running and listened to the droplets dripping from the ceiling. She was consumed by darkness, fearing that at any moment, her stalker with his yellow cat eyes would lunge at her. Her breathing was loud, and she could feel the beat of her heart pound against her ribcage like a drum.

How could she be so foolish as to come down here?

Katja heard a boom deep beneath her feet, sending goosebumps up her arm. She dashed back up the stairs like a child running for their mother in the night after a foul dream. The darkness widened her imagination, and she pictured phantoms and ghouls grabbing at her heels as she used every ounce of strength to push her body back up the stairs to the light.

Then she slipped, and a cold breeze passed over her. Her quick hands caught the ground before any real damage could befall her, but she knew her hands would need mending. Absolute horror struck her as she sat trying to control her breathing with her sticky, warm palms pressed to her lips as she tried to listen. Hot tears welled in her eyes.

Then a scent filled her lungs, but it wasn't foul like the stench of death as she was expecting. No, the smell was familiar, like freshly blooming lavender mixed with vanilla.

The countess's perfume! Katja sniffed the vigorous scent, so strong it felt like running through a densely packed garden of flowers. The further she ascended the steep stairs, the stronger the smell got, only to nearly disappear as she strayed too far. She quickly retraced her steps to where the scent was strongest.

Katja stopped there for a minute, her mind racing, before slowly patting and sliding her fingertips against the smooth stone wall, half expecting the boy to stand before her in the dark. But instead, her hands continued to graze until catching something raised along the wall's perimeter, causing her to pause. Her fingers fumbled upon it, and she slowly painted a picture in her mind of a tiny, embossed spider with a fat body and eight spindly legs. She didn't mind spiders and even thought of them as small pets when she lived in the nooks and alleys of Theed, and she became used to them thatching their nests in the corners of walls. Occasionally, one would wander into her camp in the middle of the night, and she would use a twig to guide it back to its nest. In a way, they were a lot like her. They were always looking for a safe place to make their home and find food, and because of that, she never killed them like the others in the alleyway. There was even one notoriously large spider that all the drifters and vagabonds knew about that lived at the mouth of a spout on Smallshire Street. Katja only found it once, but she could have sworn it was nearly the size of her hand.

Anxiously, Katja raised her nose to the embossed carving and sniffed. It couldn't be a coincidence that the boy vanished like a phantom, and now this stony spider smelled like the countess's lavender perfume. Perhaps it marked an entry or served as a secret portal, like Count Hugo's magic tapestry. But what if she didn't want to enter wherever her stalker disappeared? What if he was working with the Magesleuths and this was some strange passage to their headquarters?

Katja took a deep breath and pressed the embossed spider, but nothing happened.

What if it were part of an unlocking spell, like the one she used to escape from the jail cell in Warren? If true, she wouldn't have much luck because she would have little chance of guessing the boy's name.

A loud crash of steel echoed from the top of the stairs, followed by the distant holler of voices. Katja held her breath. *The guards.* Why did she have to resort to magic? All that risk to end up lost in some abandoned passage, nowhere closer to discovering the identity of her pursuers.

The footsteps were numerous and coming fast, and Katja was caught like a gnat in a spider's web. Her heart raced, and her fingers shook with adrenaline as she desperately twisted, pressed, pulled, and rubbed the strange spider. A loud, piercing whistle echoed off the walls, which she recognized as the same one she had heard earlier.

The whistle. Why was the boy whistling when he was doing his best to hide from her? What other reason would he have other than to alert whomever he worked for? Katja pressed her forehead against the cold wall, feeling it vibrate from the oncoming party.

Katja remembered the strange, ghoulish notes the boy had created, but couldn't be confident of their accuracy. Recalling the tune as well as she could, she let out three long, breathy whistles and then a series of high, shrill bursts. Silence answered her. Faint flickering lanternlight danced across the ceiling. Between labored breaths, she could hear the guards shouting at each other.

Hurry! Hurry! Hurry!

Katja whistled again, this time three long notes with two wavering shorter ones between them, like a heartbeat. Her lips trembled so violently she could barely shape the sound, and for a moment she thought the whistle would die on her lips—but she forced out a few thin, ragged notes, each one sounding like it might be her last.

A faint red hourglass-shaped light broke the shadows like a single star on a moonless night. Katja continued to whistle desperately as she spotted a bright lantern swiftly approaching from the stairs above. Without thinking, she pressed the spider inward with her thumb, and a sharp, needle-like prick sent pain down her thumb into her palm and down her arm.

Her teeth gritted like a goat with lockjaw as she swiveled behind the wall and was flung into the depths.

Chapter Eleven

Katja winced and looked at her bleeding finger for only a second before she spotted the long-legged spider creeping into a dark recess near the perimeter of the swiveling door, presumably to its place on the other side, where it would stand to watch for its next victim.

She had fallen into a pile of coarse hay, with a few stray apple cores and chicken bones submerged at its bottom, pressing uncomfortably against her. Slowly, she pulled herself to her feet, noticing a black bowler hat among the pile of yellow hay, and looked around her new surroundings.

A quiet fluttering sound flapped near her ear, and the scruff of a white goat whisked against her cheek. She jumped away from the creature, which bleated once between sideways bites of hay. When she stood up, a dozen brown birds with black specks along their elongated necks gazed at her with cautious expressions.

Are those quails?

The quails fluttered into the corner of the room, using their short beaks to peck small grains from the dirty floor. The white goat charged a younger spotted goat across the room with a crash of horns. Then, a baby goat jumped onto Katja's knees with its hooves and sniffed her closed fists, searching for food.

"What are you doing down here?" Katja whispered, stepping through the hay, nearly stepping on a pile of small eggs speckled like moldy bread.

The wall behind her started to rattle, sending dust motes to the floor. She backed away from the wall, hearing shouts behind the spider trapdoor from which she had fallen into a pile of hay moments ago.

"Bitter teeth! What was that?" a panicked voice shouted.

Katja spun on her heels and waded across the room, stepping in a pile of neat pebbles she knew was goat dung. Across the room was an entrance with a half door, presumably to keep the quails and goats from escaping between this chamber and a dingy hallway where the voices seemed to be coming from.

"Did you bring every guard in the bloody district along with you? Bullocks, boy!" the voice shouted again, echoing off the stone walls.

That wasn't the voice of a young boy.

She entered the hallway and snuck toward another door, but it was locked when she wiggled the doorknob. There were several other doors of varying shapes and colors scattered on the walls, but she decided not to test them in case she ran into someone. Where was she? An old strip mine? The Magesleuth headquarters? Something even more nefarious than that?

It wasn't until she spotted a large, rusty steel door standing ajar near the far end of the hall that she found cover. She slipped inside and pressed herself against the wall beside the doorway, leaving a narrow slit of sight into the corridor. She barely had time to steady her breathing before footsteps approached.

"Take your cursed payment! I'm getting out of here! I'll go check the barriers!" the man shouted.

His boots hammered closer, echoing off the concrete, until his shadow stretched across the doorway. He strode past, close enough that she could see his shape briefly framed in the dim hall light—a black silhouette moving away from her down the corridor. She remained frozen as he continued toward the tunnel entrance.

There was a rustle of materials, followed by a sharp pause. Seconds later, the same footsteps returned at a run, racing back the way he had come—then stopped just short of her door. They resumed again moments later, fading quickly as he turned and disappeared down the hall.

Katja could feel her pulse beating in her ears as the echoes of his footsteps skimmed along the featureless walls. She waited a moment to see if the man would reappear, perhaps forgetting something, but everything became eerily silent, and she knew it was her chance to move.

How can anyone see in this place? Katja reached around the room's edges, looking for a candlestick or match, but there was no such thing. She carefully snuck out of the room and found another chamber adjacent to hers, lit by some strange green phantom light. She stuck her head into the room and didn't see anyone occupying the room, but she did spot something shockingly familiar hanging on the wall: *the count's tapestry.*

She was . . . in the Warren? How did it take her this long to figure that out? Of course Fleck and his crew would send someone out to hunt her down after somehow escaping! How could she be so lucky?

Chills and excitement crawled down her spine as she pinched the tapestry between her fingers. Its colors looked slightly different in the strange jade light. She looked around for the purple candle, but it was nowhere to be seen. It couldn't be far.

Katja crept into the familiar central chamber, the same vast room where her iron cell still hunched in the corner, embedded in the stone like the ribcage of some fallen subterranean beast. She moved carefully across the space, rifling through stacks of books, parchment, pens, and wood shavings scattered throughout the cluttered room.

The sight of it all dragged her backward in time. For a moment, it felt as though she were reliving the nightmare of her imprisonment months ago. She slipped behind a crate used as a makeshift end table, memories pressing in: the sharp scent of the burning fireplace, Fleck's chair pocked with old scorch marks, the lofty ceiling spilling thin slivers of sunlight down the walls.

She stilled and listened. To her surprise, the only sounds were a low mechanical hum and a guttural snore.

Sitting opposite Fleck's chair was the boy, now hatless. His face was smeared with pink stains, and to her horror, his beady, yellowing eyes were fixed in her direction. Katja raised her hands slowly, signaling for his attention. He did not react. The stare never wavered. Relief washed through her as she realized his body was motionless, save for his stomach, which rose and fell in an uneven rhythm.

Dust. She sprang from her hiding place and approached the boy, noticing the bubbling pinkish drool dripping down his chin. It was how most of the addicts looked once they finally got their fix. Magedust came in four varieties as far as she was concerned, but pink and green were the most common. She never quite understood the differences, but that was probably because it was a forbidden topic, and the people likely selling it to you didn't even know. They were looking for their own fix anyway.

It was then that she spotted it. The purple candle was sitting on the ledge of a desk, drooping like a neglected houseplant. A swish of air, followed by a distant creaking sound, groaned from the unknown depths shrouded in shadow. She looked out as far as she could see, her gaze following the gill-shaped light beams striping the high walls to her left, but just to the right of that, there was a wall of featureless darkness. It was impossible to tell how deep the hideout went. It could have gone as far as a stone toss or as far as her mind could wander. The idea made her shudder. She plucked the purple candle up, levitated a lump of hot coal from the embers, lit the candle wick, and darted back to the tapestry.

She nearly walked straight into the tapestry, now swirling with color, but remembered her near-fatal mistake last time. She willed the red-hot coal upward, and it hovered above her shoulder, obedient and burning. She wondered whether the coal could pass through the portal with her, or whether it might spark the drapery aflame. Despite this uncertainty, she rolled the dice and leaped into the count's closet, except that when she entered it this time, the only similarity it had to her memories was its three walls.

Soot and ash piled high along the sides. The nails and fasteners were all that remained of the bookshelves and altar that once graced the space, giving it such a unique, arcane ambiance. *How could anything survive this?* She reflected on how lucky she was not to be among the ashes. All the result of a little flame and a whole lot of magedust. It was almost reckless now that she reflected on it. How could the count have allowed himself to hide his most precious magical findings in what was essentially a powder keg?

Carefully, she bent to her knees and started shoveling the ash from the ground, her fingers combing through the gray, white, and black remains as she choked on the foul air that stirred up. She carefully sifted her fingers across the floor, trying to feel anything solid the flames could have spared. After what felt like hours, she felt something hard and heavy near the furthest wall, near where the altar once stood.

She clawed the ash from what now appeared to be an iron cabinet blackened by flame. When she brushed the face of the cabinet clean, she could make out a small keyhole that sparked intense memories—the lock.

It was the same cabinet she had never managed to unlock, no matter how many times she had tried. She couldn't help but grin at the find. Even the fires of the underworld couldn't open that cabinet, and here it was taunting her, or rather, daring her to try and open it once more. If she couldn't find the cards, maybe there would be something equally valuable for the grand maiden inside. Whatever the count put within must have been even more critical than the grimoire and cards, or at least that is what she convinced herself of as she stuck her finger to the keyhole and cited Fleck's teachings.

You mustn't ask who created the lock, but who was the last soul to seal it. All this time, she had been speaking the name of someone she thought had created the lock, but it was the user all along, and it had to be spoken in the Elddir tongue. *It all seems so simple now.* Did the rule include dead people? Katja was prepared to find out. She channeled her concentration, felt the slowly depleting Vigor bubble in her chest, and closed her eyes. She called Fleck's instructions, trying to remember if men went by "var" or "tar" or if it was neither.

"*Hugo var Stavoren,*" she mumbled. Nothing happened, so she changed it up. "*Hugo tar Stavoren.*"

Nothing. She couldn't give up now.

"*Hugo don Stavoren?*" she tried, wincing because she knew that sounded wrong.

Still nothing. She rattled the cabinet to see if maybe all it needed was a little shove to open, but when nothing happened, she turned back to the swirling tapestry, disappointed and defeated. Was Hugo not the only person to use the tapestry, or did she misremember Fleck's quick training? How would she ever expect to be a talented Glint if she couldn't remember three simple words?

As she stepped out of the tapestry, she quickly retreated. A new light came from a closed wrought-iron door across the passageway.

Katja's throat tightened as she raised the ember like a weapon before sneaking back out and extinguishing the candle. She cursed when she realized the ember was now blackened coal. She diligently plucked a short hair from the back of her head, causing the extinguished coal to fall to the ground.

She crept back to the quails and goats to see if she could find a way back up through the trap door, but it was far too high, and the wall was utterly void of cracks or ledges to attempt to climb. She snuck past the lit room back into the larger chamber where the boy was still snoring in his chair, but this time noticeably more slouched.

There had to be a way out of here. Katja scanned the edges of the Warren, looking for the identifiable rectangle of a doorway or some indication of a direction to flee, but there was nothing. She looked overhead into the rafters, but even if there was a way out, it was far too high for her to climb or reach.

Panic began to rise as the walls seemed to close in on her. She approached the sleeping boy and shook him violently, but he barely budged.

"Tell me how to get out of here! I will get you more dust! Just tell me!" Katja ordered in a hushed voice, patting his face, but it was useless. The boy might as well be dead.

"There is no escaping. Trust me. I have looked," a grave voice whispered from behind her.

It came from the jail cell.

Katja slowly turned. She approached the cell with her candle in hand. "Is someone there?"

A pale set of hands gripped the bars, and a face appeared between them with a mess of tattered gray hair. His face looked beaten and emaciated, with dirt caked into his deep wrinkles.

The old man slouched against the bars as she approached.

"They put a bag over my head when they took me, but I have had plenty of time to see them come in and out of this place. They are wicked . . . all of them . . ." the man cursed.

"Why did they put you in here?" Katja asked.

"An unsettled debt . . . jealousy . . . revenge . . . you pick . . ." he said. "You'd better hide while you can. The man with the freakish face will return soon."

Fleck.

"One of them already came back after scaring off a bit ago. It was the first time I thought I might get out of here . . . the guards were so close," the prisoner spat.

"Did they give you a test? Were you instructed to unlock your cell?" Katja asked.

The old man was silent, tilting his head. He looked confused, as if he had never heard those words uttered to him before.

"If you know the name of the person who locked you in here, I might be able to help you," Katja whispered. He would be an extra distraction, giving her more time to find a way out.

"It was the man who was just in here moments ago. I didn't catch his name. He put me in this dreaded place!" the old man spat, rattling the bars. "But if you can get me out of here, I can try to see if there is a way out that I missed. I will do anything to get out of here."

"I can't help without his first and last name," Katja said.

"You sound just as batty as they do! Why do you need their name? Do you think the bloody monsters that live here would tell me who they are?" the man growled. "Besides, what would that information even offer you? Good luck reporting the name to the guards without a way out of here."

Katja scoffed, "Your loss. I'm not the one in a cage."

"Alright . . . please . . . let's start over. I will give you anything I own, even my ring. It is worth a pretty fortune in the hands of the right dealer. There are only two that were made, and the other one belongs to my father, who would pay tenfold the asking price," the man stammered, anxiously tapping his large ring against the bar emblazoned with the letter "D" on a large red ruby.

That answers one question: *they didn't mean to rob him.*

The man paused. "You . . . you look familiar . . . but from where?"

Katja stepped forward, but not too close for him to swipe her. Her eyes widened as trace light illuminated the features of his face. Chills ran down her spine.

No, it couldn't be! His face was far too old and his pockmarks resembled the deep dimples in dough kneaded with too much yeast. She eyed the "D" on his ring again and envisioned the man twenty years younger.

"Lord . . . DeGrom?" Katja gasped.

Rhys DeGrom's eyes widened. "You are Auriella's terrible chambermaid, aren't you? What are you doing here?"

Suddenly, there was a brush of foul air and a swish of water like the pipes of an old house.

"He is back! Hurry! Run!" Lord DeGrom stammered.

A few moments later, a pinprick of red light appeared behind Katja's shoulder, and the smell of tobacco filled the air.

Chapter Twelve

"**Y**ou shouldn't have come back," Fleck said, exhaling a cloud of pale smoke.

"He . . . he was following me. I didn't know he would lead me back here," Katja said, pointing at the boy spilling out of his chair beside the fire.

Fleck placed the back of his hand against the boy's sweaty forehead. "I was keeping an eye on you. I guess my hired watcher wasn't sneaky enough, though."

"Why is he here?" Katja pointed at Lord DeGrom, who was surprisingly quiet. "You know who he is, right?"

"He is one of Stav's prisoners," Fleck said, waving his hand dismissively.

"He is Lord Rhys DeGrom. Senator DeGrom. Do you realize the trouble you are in? His family is nearly as powerful as—"

Fleck cut her off before she could finish what she was saying.

"I know who the DeGroms are. They are a terrible bunch, and this miserable piece of crock is among the rottenest. Just hearing him talk makes one want to leap from the tallest window in Theed," Fleck cursed, returning to his seat by the fire and reclining. He pulled a bottle of brandy from the depths of the cushion and poured it into a used glass. "But I shouldn't underestimate Rhys's lordly father. That man is scum. Our people will release a relieved gasp when he dies!"

Katja frowned. She didn't like the man either, but there was clearly more to the DeGroms than being a snobbish merchant family.

"There is a lot you don't know, Miss Rosdyre," Fleck said as if he heard her thoughts.

"What are you doing?" Katja asked. "Aren't you going to toss me into the cell?"

"Is that what you wish?" Fleck said, his eyes glowing a caramel hue in the firelight.

Katja shook her head. "Of course not."

"Good, then, I was hoping to enjoy the silence before the others returned," Fleck said through a forced smile. "Did you return for the book?"

Katja's heart fluttered. "The book?"

"The one in the portal," Fleck said. "Turns out Stav knew about the secrets of the tapestry and found the grimoire in the ashes. Its pages are enchanted with some flame-retardant ward . . . very complex stuff indeed . . . but you wouldn't be interested in learning more about pesky wards and spells. You would prefer to be a chambermaid until you die in that tower and the prefects toss you to the rats in the alleyway!"

"The grimoire survived?" Katja gasped, stepping closer. "Let me see it, and I promise I will never come back again! I won't cause you any more trouble!"

"I heard that before, and here you are, standing in my home once again," Fleck growled. "Besides, you lied to me. I saved you from your prison, and you took my trust and tore it to pieces when you attacked me! It took betraying every impulse in my body not to let you kindle to death on the floor!"

"Do you want a Dustmage?" Katja blurted, barely hearing what he was saying. "If you give me the grimoire for one minute, I will join your ranks and serve you to my dying breath."

Fleck spat, "We will find another Dustmage. Once Urie arrives, I will have him send you straight to the city watch, perhaps the constable himself! They aren't far!" He pointed casually toward the ceiling. "Sometimes, when it is quiet, you can hear the necks break when the executioner drops the rope. But most times, that sound is swallowed by roaring cheers and screams of elation over yet another dead Glint."

Katja remembered chasing the boy past the gallows in Puffer Square and the dark tunnel that led her here. *It was beneath my feet this whole time.* Her trolley stopped in Puffer Square daily on its way into the Wallingford District.

Never could she have guessed the Warren was mere miles from her bed in the Maiden Tower. Chills crawled down her neck.

"I promise I won't break my word again. I know every nook and cranny in Theed. I can find anyone for you if you give me their name! There were not many pickpockets in the entire city that were as clever as I! Imagine . . . I can fetch you whatever you want!" Katja pleaded. She was embellishing her abilities a little, but it wasn't a whole lie. Her ability to levitate made her uniquely skilled at survival, no matter the cost.

Fleck sighed. "I know a liar when I meet one. I can trust the bad liars because I can read their eyes, but you are a rather talented one. I don't spare good liars if I can help it. Isn't that right, senator?"

Rhys slammed against the iron bars. "I will destroy you! Every Magesleuth enlisted in the queen's ranks will be searching for me, and once they find out who did this to me, they will do all sorts of terrible things to you! The legends of their torture methods are far too kind, if you ask me!"

"I could end you right here and now if I wanted," Fleck barked.

"You do know whose orders they follow, don't you?" Rhys sneered.

Fleck's jaw tightened like damp leather.

"Of course you know. Anyone with a bit of intelligence knows they bow down to one or two names," the senator said. "Queen Margot . . . and the DeGroms. My father."

"It doesn't matter," Fleck scoffed. "Your name and title mean nothing down here."

"You will be begging for death!" Rhys screamed.

Fleck drew his wand, flicked it, and Rhys's sweaty face cracked into the bars, sending him to the hard ground. "I can't stand his screaming."

Katja stared at Rhys's limp body on the ground. She knew he was alive, but it was unsettling. "You are really going to kill me. After all of the risk you took to let me escape?"

Fleck groaned. "I can't trust you. I am sorry. And now you know where the Warren is located. There is a reason this place has never been found despite being beneath the constable's feet."

"And what you do down here is so pious and charitable? Aren't you all a bunch of thieves, cutpurses, and kidnappers? Sure, I lied, but I never kidnapped anyone!" Katja spat, anger welling in her arms and legs like tight coils of rope.

Fleck chugged his brandy and smashed it on the floor. "We aren't thieves! We are vigilantes!"

"If you steal things that are not yours, you are a thief," Katja smirked. "And if you murder someone, that makes you a murderer."

Fleck rose to his feet with a tense face and stared at her as if deciding if he would murder her then and there, but instead took a breath of his pipe and sat back down in his seat.

"We do not murder," Fleck sighed. "Not anymore."

Katja was going to pry, but based on Fleck's withdrawn demeanor, she decided she would wait for another time if she ever got it.

"Let me try unlocking the cell again. Test me, and I will be your Dustmage!" Katja said.

Fleck smiled. "You already know I saved you from failing that test. Showing you how to unlock that padlock is the first and last time I tutor you on anything related to magic."

Katja didn't know how to respond, but she knew she had to say something, or else she was doomed to meet the city watch. Part of her wondered if the man had skin thick enough to send a young girl to the gallows. There was something soft within him that she could barely see from the edges of his eyes, a glimmer of a soul, but she dared not risk it. Not tonight.

"What are you going to do to this man? You know he is a lawman. He is the heir of the DeGrom family with enough gold to purchase a castle in Stellen or Legria if he wanted," Katja said. "He was my client's fiancé. Do you plan to kill her, too?"

"No, but I am going to make damn sure he never sets another foot in Theed again," a raspy voice hailed from the hallway. A tall man with dark hair, a red bandana, stubble, and a hawkish nose appeared before them.

"Stav! I should have known you were here! Can you escort the girl to the constable? Urie has not yet arrived, and I am tired of waiting," Fleck snapped.

Stav swatted Fleck on the back of his head. "Too risky! This place has drawn too much attention for one morning. Besides, she's your problem. I say to hell with finding a new Dustmage! They are too hard to keep alive anyway."

"Not if they are properly trained!" Fleck said. "And you are the one who gave me the lead on this one."

"This was all Kristoff's idea, not mine," Stav jabbed. "You know he is always brewing some stupid new plot shrouded in mystery. I don't know why you trust him. He might as well be working for himself."

"You know why I keep him," Fleck scoffed. "If it were up to me, he would have gone with the others ages ago."

The Warren grew silent as Stav leaned against the brick mantlepiece and petted a cat that Katja had not noticed due to its jet-black fur. The cat stretched onto its back, exposing white patches as it purred.

"Why is she back?" Stav said, resting his hand on the hilt of his scabbard

"She found our spy. And now she wants me to be her tutor," Fleck uttered painfully.

"The girl passed the test, after all. I guess she must have changed her mind about wanting to be something more than just a chambermaid." Stav frowned. "I am impressed that she found this place . . . not even the bloody Magesleuths could do that. Now you either slit her throat or tuck her under your wing. One option is much more bloodless, and I know you value that more than anything, Fleck."

Katja watched Fleck wince. Only the two of them knew the truth of her escape, and telling his crewmate that he unlocked her cell to save her life would not bode well. *Look who's the liar now.*

"I . . . let her go because she was incompatible," Fleck said. "She lacks symmetry. She would be a terrible cloaker."

Stav slowly paced toward Katja, drawing an invisible line down her face, with his tongue sticking out and one eye closed. It made her feel like an ugly sculpture in some fancy museum.

"Fleck, are you blind? The girl has fine symmetry, perhaps a freckle or two out of place, but that is it," Stav scoffed. He looked down at her body and gasped. "Or is there something I am missing?"

Fleck sighed, "Indeed."

Katja gasped at the implication. "As if he would ever know! And stop looking at me like a piece of meat!"

Stav smirked. "I like you! Fleck needs to hear more rejection in his life. He gets a bit high and mighty from time to time when he goes too long without someone putting him in his place."

"What does symmetry have to do with any of this?" Katja asked. A wave of dizziness started to creep into the back of her eye sockets. Her stomach also started to twist and turn beneath her navel.

"It means everything when it comes to cloaking," Stav laughed, then bit his tongue. "Sorry, I forgot you didn't get proper training."

"Yes, I am just a pathetic little street urchin who broke into your 'secret lair.' Bear me your pity," Katja spat.

"Of course, my liege!" Stav bowed as if addressing royalty. "No matter, you learned from someone. No one could learn levitation without a tutor. Who taught you what you know?"

"My mother taught me levitation," Katja said. "And I learned from another magician in hiding how to use magedust and a few other basic concepts . . . but he died before he could teach me everything he knew."

Stav's eyes perked up. "Peculiar . . . but for such a little street urchin, you are quite advanced in levitation. Shame we must send you to get hanged."

Katja reached into the wells of her chest, feeling what little Vigor remained in her body. Stav noticed and reached for her arm, but before he could, she parried his advance, levitated the crooked oak wand from his pocket, and palmed it. Then she backed toward the dark corner, brandishing the wand threateningly at them.

"You will have to kill me yourself!" Katja shouted, her blood boiling beneath her skin. She didn't know how a wand worked, and she thought that it was a knife or something more practical at first glance, but she figured it was better than nothing. "Let me go, and I won't bother you again!"

Stav stared at her with awe. "You took my wand."

"Yes, she bloody disarmed you! How could you be so careless? Have I taught you nothing about warding your wand?" Fleck snarled, reaching for his own. "The first rule of magic is to keep your wand guarded!"

"I had it warded," Stav said, his pale eyes wide. "How . . . could a novice . . . less than a novice, witch, do such a thing? Unless she knew my wand's—" He glanced at Fleck with a look of horror. "How could she know?"

"Did you tell her something about yourself that you shouldn't have?" Fleck chided.

"No! Did you? You are the only one who has spoken to her alone!" Stav shouted.

"Was the ward properly sealed?" Fleck said, head tilted, eyes full of rage.

"As secure as the Warren itself!" Stav spat. "The only way she could have controlled my wand is if she . . ." He shook his head and paced in front of the fire as if Katja wasn't aiming a wand directly at him.

Despite stealing his precious wand, he still did not fear her.

"Stop pacing!" she barked, focusing the wand at the strange, lanky man with ear-length locks drifting across his face as he paced.

"I have decided!" Stav blurted, raising a finger. He seemed a bit unhinged. "I am going to train the girl!"

"Just a moment ago, you were going to escort her to the constable?" Fleck scoffed. "I do not trust her. She is a liar!"

"I don't care. I am a liar, too," Stav grimaced. "My name isn't Stav, and neither is yours Fleck. See, we are both liars!"

"Those are just names!" Fleck spat. "Her lies are the worst kind of lies! The kind you can't come back from."

"Okay, then what were those lies?" Stav asked, tapping his chin ponderously.

The color left Fleck's face, which now resembled a churned bowl of goat butter. Katja grinned—she could see he was trapped, squirming under his own pitiful lies.

"Well, that settles it!" Stav said, glaring at Fleck suspiciously. "Rather than have another young Glint murdered, we will take her in under our wing, and I will take her in as my pupil!"

Fleck glared at Katja. "It is too risky! She knows where the Warren is!"

"I hope so, because she is going to spend a lot of time here," Stav grinned. "It will take a while to get used to this place and understand its inner magical workings, but once you get the hang of it, you will feel at home. Perhaps even more so than the Maiden Tower!"

Fleck sighed. "This will not be without tribulation, Stav."

Stav gave her a somber look. "Of course. We have our bylaws. We will get to that later."

Fleck took a sip of brandy. "Just let me know when she has mastered cloaking, and then we can continue with our plans for Operation Pagemaster."

"I have never had a pupil before. Do you think I'm ready?" Stav said.

"Not if you lose your wand to an over-glorified street magician!" Fleck groaned, sitting back into his chair. "But I do believe you are plenty ready. You have had more formal training than I ever had at your age.

"Perhaps that is what the Dustmage position has been missing all this time . . . a breath of fresh ideas," Stav blurted, rubbing Fleck's shoulders. "This place could use a bit of youth and positivity for once. I think Miss Rosdyre is just what we need!"

"Fine! But you will train the girl and take responsibility for her," Fleck said, breathing in heavy smoke through his pipe. "If you don't fail, we will give her work when you have completed her training."

"You won't regret this," Katja said, her tongue suddenly heavy. *Now I need to find the grimoire.*

Stav stared at her in horror. "Are you bleeding?"

Katja tasted iron in her mouth and wiped blood from her chin. She felt suddenly very sick and clammy.

"*Kindling* . . . I need dust . . ." she pleaded, dropping Stav's wand to the floor with a muted clanking sound.

"That isn't kindling as I have seen it," Fleck said, puffing his pipe. "If you were to bleed while kindling, that would be considered a good thing."

Katja stared blankly at their blurring faces as their voices swirled and slithered in her ears.

"You got here through the spider gate, didn't you?" Stav said, reaching her as she started to wobble.

"Spider?" Katja muttered, but the world was slowly shifting in her vision. "Oh yes . . . I pet a spider to get in here. He liked my whistling."

"I am going to guess the boy didn't give you the antivenom before he decided to take a dust nap," Fleck said casually. "Stav, fetch the bloody serum before she dies."

Katja could tell in his eyes that he would have preferred it if she did.

Stav helped her across the room into one of the chambers, where he sat her in a rocking chair. He then fumbled through a drawer in a side table next to a torn mattress in the corner of the room, retrieving a red serum in a glass vial.

"Drink this, and you should feel better. Not perfect, but better," Stav said, his blue eyes full of worry. "Would be our luck to lose a new Dustmage on the first day."

"Reassuring . . ." Katja said before swallowing the serum, which had a foul metallic taste—*or was that the blood?*

"Normally, we take the antivenom shortly after the bite. It might take a while to feel better," Stav said.

There was something familiar about his eyes, but she couldn't tell where she recognized them from.

Stav paced around the small bedchamber, taking the purple candle from her and setting it on his bedside. He then placed his hand on her forehead, grabbed her hand, and inspected her palms. Then, he sat at eye level and bounced his gaze back and forth between each of Katja's eyes. He snapped his fingers, igniting a small flame that extended from the tip of his thumb like an elongated fingernail. When he was satisfied, he pulled her up to her feet.

"Is everything alright?" Katja asked nervously.

Stav grinned. "Your pallor looks good, and I see no sign of toxicity, but then again, I have as much healing knowledge as the district executioner."

"I would like you to do a little light reading while I think of what a horrible decision I made taking you under my wing," he said. "You can read, right?"

Katja frowned, still dazed. "Of course, I can read."

"I do not mean to insult you, but you never know with someone of . . . your background," Stav said, looking like he regretted waking up this morning.

Katja snapped, "What sort of glamorous background do you come from to think a lady from the Maiden Tower does not know how to read? But then again, I shouldn't be too surprised, you are a thief whose wand got stolen."

"You got a bite, I'll give you that," Stav smirked. "I'm going to regret this, aren't I?"

"If you don't, then it will have all been a failure on my part," Katja rebutted. "Though I should warn you, the last person who tried to teach me magic died a tragic death."

Stav seemed to perk up at this comment.

"The countess! My assignment! I'm going to be late!" Katja blurted, remembering how her whole morning started. "My dress! Stav . . . if I miss another assignment, the grand maiden will skewer me and send me to the streets! You have to let me go . . . I promise to return!"

Stav shushed her, which she did not like in the least.

"New plan—no reading until tonight. We are going to visit Stavoren Manor," he said. "We can't afford to have you lose your seat at the Maiden Tower."

"How did you know I work at Stavoren Manor?" Katja asked.

Stav laughed. "Don't you remember where this all started? It was there that we found you in the tapestry. He glanced at a silver pocket watch in his coat pocket, engraved with the letter "S", and clicked it shut. "You have to be there in twenty minutes."

"Twenty minutes? That isn't enough time to get to the Wallingford District! The countess is going to murder me!" Katja said. She didn't even bother asking about the creepiness of his memorizing her schedule, but nothing made much sense down here.

"Don't worry—I know a shortcut," Stav smirked, grabbing her hand and leading her down the hall, past the fireplace where Fleck was sorting through notes. "I am taking the tunnel."

"Did you repair the corner after last time?" Fleck said, tapping the tip of his pipe on his teeth loudly. "Also, it could use a dusting."

Stav waved Fleck away dismissively. "Neither is required for it to function, and we are running late for the ball."

"The ball?" Fleck asked gravely.

Stav sighed. "It is a figure of speech. Do I have to explain everything to you, Fleck? I am going to Stavoren Manor. I will be back."

"Please! Let me go!" Lord DeGrom screamed from his cell. "I will give you anything if you take me with you!"

Stav chuckled. "Look who decided to join us! You are going nowhere, DeGrom!"

"What are you going to do? Keep me here forever? Someone will come looking for me!" Lord DeGrom shouted, bashing at the bars. "I know many of the district constables by name! They won't be lenient in your sentencing when they hunt you down!"

Stav's heels pounded on the ground as he marched to Lord DeGrom's cell. He reached in, grabbing the old man by the back of his hair, and stared into his eyes.

"You tried to defraud a dying widow, but in the end, you were a fool just like the others! You will never step foot in Theed again! You don't even realize that it will be doing you a favor to never return to this place! The old matriarch never gives up a grudge and always plans to get even! It is because of morons like you that death will come back to our streets like never before, and you don't even know it!" Stav shouted.

"You have won now, but there will be victory bells ringing throughout Theed when I get out of here," Rhys said as if a sworn promise.

Stav released Lord DeGrom, spat at his feet, and walked past Katja without a glance.

"Follow me," Stav said, leading her into the darkness along the edge of the room. He then picked up his wand from the floor where Katja had dropped it. He examined it briefly and then eyed her with that same look of disbelief before tapping it three times on his head, which made it illuminate at its tip in a way that reminded her of a firefly.

"Can you show me how to do that?" she asked.

Stav didn't respond. Instead, he revealed a glistening mirror hidden behind a sheet at the far end of the wall, its silver surface marred by blackened spots. They reminded her of the dark patches on the moon when you stared at it on a starless night. She joined him at the mirror, but when she looked into it, there was nothing to see.

Katja went to graze her finger against it, but before she could touch it, Stav pulled her away.

"You will find out there are a lot of magical and enchanted things in this place," he said, reaching into his pocket and uncorking a bottle. "Traveling through glass is taxing."

Stav took a swig of the drink, winced, and handed it to her. "It tastes like cat piss, but it works better than magedust if you ask me."

"That stuff is unnatural!" Fleck yelled from a distance.

"Ignore him. He is allergic to novel ideas!" Stav said, loudly enough for Fleck to hear.

Katja took a sip, and instantly, her stomach started to boil with Vigor.

"I am allergic to falsehoods!" Fleck retorted. "I am fine with novelty. But I've learned sometimes things are too good to be true."

Stav held his breath and stepped into the mirror, pulling Katja along with him, and after a strange shattering sound that rang in her ears for a few seconds, they waded into a large, dark cavern sparsely lit by his wand's firefly light. He approached a raised rectangular platform carpeted with a familiar but outlandish pattern. It was a white, seafoam-like color with bands of silver and pale blue, edged with bright, honey-colored frays. At the center of the carpet was a strange rune that appeared to be made of strands of molten sunlight. A small tear attempted to steal her attention in the corner until Stav jumped onto the center of the raised platform and pulled her along with him.

"What is this?" Katja asked.

Stav smiled and uttered a few words under his breath. Katja stumbled and hitched forward as the carpet forced upward from the platform and wavered beneath her like a fluttering flag. She took Stav's helping hand to get back on her feet, with little success.

"It can take a while to gain your sea legs . . . or rather flying legs," Stav said, barely wavering from his stance, which looked more like a crouch. He extended his long arms forward and pointed down the large cavern, sending the hovering carpet onward so fast that the wind whipped her hair, like strings of red thread on a kite. The wind tore at her eyes, sending tears down her cheeks, and the mixed smells of waste, piss, and dust filled her lungs.

"Stav! What if we fall?" Katja screamed, barely able to keep her eyes open to see the tip of his wand stream a trail of golden light behind them like a banner atop a spear before battle.

"What? Hold on tight!" Stav shouted, his blue eyes reassuring. "Stopping is the hardest part!"

Katja curled her fingers and dug them into the wandering fabric, which danced like it had a mind of its own. The swift motion made her stomach feel all sorts of vile outbursts, barely improving when she closed her eyes. She gripped so hard she thought her fingers might break like stiff, dry twigs, but before she lost her will to hold on, the carpet came to a stop, lunging her into Stav's legs, who nearly stumbled off the ledge but was able to regain his balance.

"Hexes! I told you to hold on!" Stav shouted. He then noticed her scared expression and sighed. "Right . . . you are new to all of this. I *am* going to regret picking up a pupil," he sighed, until something ahead caught his eye. "Follow me."

The carpet slowly rose toward a rugged iron grate in the high ceiling. Katja told herself she wouldn't look over the edge, but there was nothing to see but darkness when she did.

When they got close enough, Stav twisted a wheel lever on the grate and opened it with a loud squeal. Bright sunlight beamed onto their face as the grate slid out of the way. Stav climbed through it and pulled Katja through with a grunt.

When Katja's eyes adjusted to the light, she realized she was standing at the end of an alleyway. She let go of Stav's sweaty hand and took a few steps down the narrow path, noticing a cat hiss and scurry away through a vent with its hair on end. Stav slid the grate over the hole they had crawled through, which she realized was a sewer cover like the ones she had walked over with little notice all her life.

Stav marched down the alley, where a young man sat in tattered clothes with green stains around his nose and bloodshot eyes. He stopped at the man, knelt to his level, and quickly peeled back his flickering eyelids before continuing down the alleyway.

"He won't remember a bloody thing, thankfully," Stav said. "Otherwise, we might have had to remedy those pesky memories. Beats killing him. Believe it or not, there was a time when the Roth might have killed a man for seeing less."

Katja had many questions, but felt her mouth did not align with her thoughts. She felt as though she was dreaming and that some strange saint was guiding her. She always envisioned some strange wizard or crone plucking her out of her terrible life to teach her everything about magic and the way of her people. But why did it feel like she was making a huge mistake? In those dreams, her savior was old, with white hair, wearing long robes and a large, pointy hat, and sauntering around on a knobby cane, but Stav looked nothing like that. *I just need to survive another day.* She could escape when she found the grimoire with the cards and completed her mission for the grand maiden.

They turned down a few corners, right, left, and even diagonally, until they reached the familiar street leading to Stavoren Manor with its extensive frilly gardens full of chirping wrens, juncos, and other songbirds.

Stav checked his pocket watch. "Perfect, we are two minutes early."

Katja looked at her work clothes, and a realization struck her.

"I don't have my dress!" she blurted. "I left it at the tailor's! You don't know any magic to turn this dress red, do you?"

"Certainly not," Stav said. "But I will explain everything . . . don't worry about it."

They walked through the boisterous, overgrown garden, which had been neglected since the gardeners had been fired. Katja still felt terrible about them being blamed for stealing the tapestry, but she knew the alternative too well. She would pay them back one day.

Once they got close to the front door, Stav held out his hand, demanding she stop.

"You go ahead and knock. I will be right in," he said, slipping off around the side of the house and leaving her alone.

"Stav!" she shouted, but he was gone before the words left her mouth.

Katja felt nervous as she knocked on the front door. Thankfully, not even ten seconds later, Gavin appeared like a phantom, grimacing as he assessed her outfit.

"What is that you are wearing?" he said, standing as straight as a plank and reeking of cigars.

"Just let me in. I'm going to change," Katja lied, pushing past Gavin and wandering up to the countess's bedchambers. Still, before she reached it, she spotted Stav sneaking suspiciously down the hallway toward her from an open door that led from the larder and kitchen.

"Hugo, is that you?" the countess's voice echoed from the other room.

Good—it was the version of the countess who wouldn't remember a thing.

"No, it is just your Kitty! Sorry, I am underdressed, but I will make up for it with how well I dress you for today's occasion!" Katja said, bursting into the chamber with a wild smile. The room was empty.

She entered the bathroom and spotted the countess combing her hair with a brush. Her eyes were bright and clear.

"You . . . look well this morning," Katja said, approaching the vanity and tussling Auriella's long white hair.

The countess smiled. "You look terrible. What happened to your dress?"

Katja quickly tried to conjure a lie, but her skull felt full of cobwebs. It must have been the side effects of insufficient sleep and the spider venom, which was still draining every ounce of energy from her emaciated body.

She almost wanted to tell the countess all about what happened to her and Rhys DeGrom, but she couldn't be sure she would be safe to say anything. It was as if she were a lone split piece of wood wedged into a woodpile, unaware if being pulled would cause other sections of the pile to collapse and fall apart. It was too dangerous to divulge now. Besides, who knew what Stav was up to? He might even be listening as she spoke. She might have managed to take his wand, but she knew he was likely a master wizard beneath that aloof façade. If he decided to take her to the city watch—or worse, Magesleuths —she doubted she could stop him.

"I will give you a pass today. I have been very impressed with your work lately, Miss Rosdyre," Countess Auriella said, tapping her front teeth with her long fingernails. "I have a meeting with my matchmaker this afternoon, and after that, I have a reservation at Clyde's Theater this evening."

Katja nodded, running the bath and scattering perfumy salts and sudsy soap into the hot water until it was foamy. "I take it your engagement with Lord DeGrom is irreparable, then?"

Countess Auriella's eyebrows perked. "Oh, Rhys? It was a rather clean split. It's nothing like dealing with a dead husband, that's for sure. Wills and inheritances are always messy."

Cold. She was months away from marrying the man, but now she acted like he never existed.

"Have you heard from him since?" Katja pried.

"Of course not! I imagine old Rhys has sailed somewhere across the Relian or south to Tordaluga by now to try and trick another seasoned lady of my status out of their money!" the countess roared. "The man was unmarriageable! I should have known from the start that it would never work. That youthful spirit he shared with me when we first met burned out, and it didn't take long for a lady as old as me to feel like I was marrying a man with one foot in the grave. He was like a leech, willing to take everything Hugo and I had built together. I wish I had never met him!"

Katja had no idea they were having so many problems. Whenever she saw Rhys and the countess together, they seemed happy and intimate. Sometimes more intimate than she wished to have seen. Katja pursed her lips and used every bit of restraint not to tell her the truth.

"I am sorry to hear that, milady."

"Just don't marry if you ever want to remain young," the countess smiled. "I am getting older just talking about that dastardly man!"

She submerged into the tub and bathed, using oils and soaps to exfoliate her now far less wrinkled skin. There was no doubt this was the work of magic, but how could someone turn back the hands of time so quickly? The other day, she was feeble-minded, frail, and ancient compared to just one day later. Even when she was engaged to Lord DeGrom, it had taken a while for her to smooth her pruned, leathered skin and polish the fog from her eyes.

There was a frantic knock on the door, and not even a minute later, Gavin entered with sweat dripping from his brow and his long nose. He patted the sweat with a handkerchief and caught his breath before speaking. When he saw the countess naked, he looked away toward the wall.

"I am sorry to intrude, countess, but I believe you would want to hear my most recent sighting!" Gavin gasped.

Auriella seemed unbothered by the intrusion.

"Get out of here!" Katja demanded, shoving him out the door. "Don't you see the countess is bathing!"

"Milady! It is your son! He has been spotted!" Gavin shouted, wrestling past Katja and avoiding casting his gaze upon the countess's naked body. "I saw him for myself!"

Auriella looked surprised by the news but didn't respond at first. Instead, she splashed water on her face and rose from the bathwater. Katja wrapped a bathrobe around the countess and tied it firmly around her waist.

"Well . . . where is he?" Countess Auriella said. She looked sullen, like a sad, wet statue erected in the middle of a fountain reservoir.

"I spotted him in the garden! Should I tell security to escort him off the estate?" Gavin shouted. "I only mean to protect you . . . considering both of your histories."

"Is it weird that I had a feeling he was nearby? A mother knows when their babies are home," the countess smiled. "Fetch him and bring him here to me."

Gavin looked perplexed. "Are you . . . sure?"

"If you can catch him," she grinned. "Knowing Hugo, he has already run off to somewhere else. He is more like a ghost than the boy I once raised."

Gavin bowed and exited, hustling out the door with loud grunts.

Stav. How did she not figure that out, Katja wondered? *Stavoren . . . of course!* She felt a chill run down her neck when she caught the countess's bright blue eyes flashing at hers before she stepped out of the bath and sat before the vanity in the powder room. It all made sense! No wonder he hated Rhys DeGrom. Locking him up in a jail cell was a bit cruel, but if the lord was genuinely trying to steal Stav's inheritance, she could understand a little. Count Hugo had mentioned that he had sons, but he never went into much detail about them, and as far as she recalled, they never once visited. Even in her delirious state, the countess never whispered anything about her children. She would call out for Hugo, but Katja had never considered that it was also her son's name. But something didn't sit right with her. She had to know more.

"Your son . . . he was named Hugo, too?" Katja said, wiggling a knot free with a comb and letting the countess's damp white hair fall to her shoulders.

Auriella frowned. "Why men name their firstborns after themselves will always be a mystery to me. Perhaps it is ego, or it makes them feel like they are reincarnated. But I know he wasn't named Hugo because he was my husband's favorite. That would be the younger brother. Hugo was much more like me when I was a child. Always getting into all sorts of trouble that dragged the Stavoren name through the mud, to my husband's dismay. It's never pleasant to read your son's name in the morning paper with unflattering exposition . . . even worse when you hear others whispering about it when they think they are out of earshot."

"I am sorry to hear that. Does he work in the same family business that the count did?" Katja asked.

"Yes . . . and no," the countess said. "He took everything we built and made it worse! He is unwilling to make the hard, cutthroat decisions needed to succeed. Being passive in this business only leads to your death."

Katja tied up Auriella's hair with pins and started powdering her face. "So, he is still involved in the family business?"

The countess glared at Katja through the mirror. "You sure are curious this morning, dear! Just get this makeup done . . . and done right so I can move along with my morning."

"Perhaps he is here to apologize," Katja whispered.

"Apologize? Good one! My son never apologizes! If anything, he is here to steal something he thinks is rightfully his . . . if only he knew I struck him from the will years ago! He won't get a single bent knot out of me!"

Katja opened her mouth to say something, but the countess glared at her before the words could exit her mouth. When Auriella's makeup and hair were all perfected and her dress fitted, there was no sign of Gavin. For a moment, Katja was surprisingly worried about the terrible man. She didn't like him, but didn't want him to run into trouble with bandits like Fleck's crew. Although it might be satisfying for a few minutes, she didn't want to find Gavin on the other side of the prison cell, standing next to Rhys DeGrom, begging Fleck for a puff of his tobacco and a sip of firebrandy.

When Gavin finally returned, he came back defeated, coat tattered in pine needles, and unbearably sweaty. Countess Auriella wasn't surprised by Gavin's empty promise; instead, she acted like nothing had happened, headed down to her carriage, and rode down into town without saying another word about her troubled son.

Stav . . . Hugo . . . Who are you? Katja pondered as she pulled the drain in the bathtub.

Once the countess was gone, and Katja was sure it was only she and Gavin wandering the manor, she felt the good bubble in her stomach, remembering the vial of liquid magedust Stav had given her hours ago. She had never felt more filled with Vigor in her entire life and figured she might not find a better time to practice a few minor levitation spells. She swished her hands, and the broom and duster flew across the house. Then she sorted the countess's closet, summoning dresses, pantyhose, shoes, gloves, and scarves to their allotted hangers, cabinets, and dresser drawers in what would have taken her an hour prior. When she was finally done, she plucked a hair from the bald patch hidden in the back of her hair and said farewell to Gavin before slipping out the front door. It felt exhilarating to finish her job with the aid of magic after breaking a sweat chiseling a single hardened morsel off a dinner plate over the last few months.

Outside Stavoren Manor, the sun was setting, painting the sky an orange hue. She curiously searched the gardens for the elusive Stav, checking over her shoulder to ensure Gavin wasn't watching. She stepped through a spiderweb and nearly onto a path of daffodils that would have been devastated by her stomping boots. Frantically, she swiped the webs from her arm and face and watched the fearful garden spider flee across the remains of its masterpiece into a line of boxwood hedges bordering the edge of the lawn. She then cautiously waded down a path circling a small pond dotted with red and white fish surrounded by shrubs, colorful flowers, and well-manicured orchard trees that added a sense of safety to the vast leafy plot. She searched the cluttered gardens but couldn't find anyone human—only gnats, flies, mosquitoes, and buzzing bumble bees dancing from pistil to pistil.

"Kat . . ." a voice whispered. "Up here."

Sitting atop the tiled rooftop of Stavoren Manor was none other than Stav, who was basking in the setting sun with his pant legs and sleeves rolled up. His skin was tanned but a bit red from running away from Gavin, or sitting a bit too long in the sun. In his hand was a bottle of Stellish wine, which dribbled down his chin, and in the other, a bag.

"What are you doing up there? Someone could see you!" Katja hissed. "She was right about you."

He waved at her to join him.

"I can't get up there unless I crawl outside a window, and I would rather not." She scowled.

Stav simpered. "Guess you won't get your little red dress back then."

"My what?" Katja asked.

Stav teased her by pulling a red sleeve from his bag, "I know you want it."

Katja cursed under her breath, but deep down, she had never felt more relieved. She spotted a gutter running up the corner of the manor and heaved herself up, but could barely get halfway up before slipping back down to the ground. She tried three more times, but it only resulted in her embarrassment and a tear in her work gown that she was thankful wasn't revealing.

"Think about it. You know levitation, Kitty, why don't you use it to give yourself a lift?" Stav asked, peering his head over the ledge. His smile was infuriating.

"I can only levitate objects," she whispered, looking over her shoulder. "Levitating flesh and blood is something completely different."

"And what do you call the shoes on your feet? You might not be able to fly like a bird, but it might give you the extra push you need to climb . . . a small gutter."

"You shouldn't speak so loudly," Katja said nervously. "Anyone can hear us."

Stav grinned and scanned the garden wall. "You are right . . . the frogs might be working with the dreaded Magesleuths!" he said, annoyingly louder than before.

"Stav . . . stop!"

He suddenly lunged over and reached an arm down toward her. "If you are so paranoid."

Katja hesitantly grabbed his arm and pulled herself to the roof from the rickety gutter, nearly stumbling off to a broken neck before finding a seat next to Stav.

He passed her a half-empty bottle of wine.

"Have you been sitting here all this time getting drunk?" she said, noticing a red stain on his teeth. "You know, the countess's steward said he found someone sneaking in the gardens and chased after them. I figured it had to be you. Do you want to get caught?"

Katja wasn't sure whether to mention that she knew his parentage, so she kept the description vague. She just needed to be trusted long enough to see the grimoire and take the cards. There was no reason to take unknown risks. There was a reason he avoided his mother, and she wouldn't lend him "a single bent knot."

"They couldn't hire someone fast enough to keep up with me," Stav said, reaching for the wine, but Katja kept it from him and stole his sip.

"Figures you didn't really care about some stolen wine," he chuckled. "You stole a fair share when you thought no one was looking.

Katja returned the bottle, pulled her crimson-red dress from the small bag, and held it out proudly. It was perfect and far more beautiful than any of the other dresses in the Maiden Tower. It was just in time for her to never wear it again if she lost her job at the Maiden Tower or made another mistake. Sitting here on the roof was probably one of those mistakes, but she smiled as she felt the silky fabric and neat bow between her fingers. All that laundry and dish soap had rubbed her hands dry, but the silk made them feel like she had never lifted a finger in her life.

"How did you know where to find this? I hadn't even paid for it in full. Still owe the tailor fifteen crowns." She suddenly remembered where one of those shiny knots went. "That's what caused all this trouble in the first place."

"I wager it goes back much further than that," Stav said, voice gravelly.

"Did you pay the loan?" Katja asked.

He sucked his teeth. "Let's just say I really don't want you to lose your Maiden Tower gig. It will be advantageous to us once we start Operation Pagemaster. And before you ask . . . don't. Fleck and I are still fleshing out the scope of everything. But mostly because I don't trust you one bit."

"Well . . . thanks," Katja said, taking another sip of wine. He must have trusted her a little, or she was as intimidating to him as a dandelion seed, but she decided to let him underestimate her.

There was a pleasant silence as they watched the sun set behind the western hilltops and jagged peaks, where rays of light pierced the clouds, which looked like dirty cotton on the horizon. Balledore Bay sparkled like burning oil to the east, where faint light revealed the pale masts and faint outlines of schooners, freighters, and fishing ships returning to the harbor. In the middle of the bay, an island rose like a dark jewel, crowned by the Duskwarden, a colossal statue of a man holding a lantern toward the sea. Missing one arm, it still towered above the island like a guardian of stone. From this vantage, they could see the outlines of Theed, including the domed Parliament building, temple steeples, clock towers, and the distant cliffs concealed in the mist, where the royal palace sat perched on its magnificent roost.

"I should be heading back to the Maiden Tower. I have scullery duties to attend, and if I don't show up on time, the grand maiden will wring my neck," Katja sighed, the wine warming her cheeks. "If you don't want me to lose my seat at the tower, you will agree."

Stav nodded, and they both climbed down from the roof, snuck out of the garden, and followed the path back to the alley to the sewer entrance. He then unlatched the manhole door and jumped into the darkness, only to land back on the flying carpet. He helped Katja down to join him, and once she was holding on tight, she felt the warmth of Vigor boil in her belly before they flew into the underground labyrinth.

They flew what felt the same way back to Fleck's hideout, but they swiftly turned down a narrower section of the sewer until they reached another coin-shaped grate door, which Stav shimmied open with a few thrusts, thumps, and twists. When the grate opened, Katja stepped through to find herself on the side lawn of the Maiden Tower, behind a holly bush.

She hauled herself through the hole and scanned the surroundings, heart hammering, but no one was watching. Only a handful of curtain-covered windows loomed above. When she turned back to the manhole to ask about the reading, she found nothing but darkness. Stav and the flying carpet were gone.

Disoriented, Katja slid the sewer door back into place and made her way to the Maiden Tower before anyone noticed she was missing. The seventh-floor dormitory was empty when she returned, a relief. She tucked her new dress into a drawer and headed down to the kitchens, where she spent the next two hours scraping custard and chicken bones from plates. The work barely registered. Vigor still glowed warmly in her chest, carrying with it the lingering fear and exhilaration of learning magic from a stranger.

From the son of the man who had promised to teach her everything he knew before he died.

Chapter Thirteen

"**K**atja! Get up!"

Katja jolted awake and rubbed her eyes, only to see Portia standing by her bedside with a look of worry on her face. Portia was dressed in her crimson and white maiden gown and looked ready to leave for her assignment.

"Hexes! I am going to be late!" Katja shrieked, leaping out of her bed like a wild animal.

"I have been trying to wake you for a while. Are you sure you are okay?" Portia said, face full of concern.

Katja nodded, but if she was being honest, she felt like the room was a bit lopsided. She shook her head and rubbed her eyes, and the world started looking slightly more level. Perhaps her body had finally had enough of the lack of sleep and decided to take matters into its own hands, or maybe it was the remnants of the spider venom? Either way, she knew she didn't have time to mull over it for long.

"I haven't been getting much rest, but I'm fine," Katja said, rubbing the sleep from her eyes as she marched into the stairwell, where she nearly collided with a flock of red-clad maidens who shot her judgmental glares. It was then she realized she was still wearing her dirty clothes, streaked and stained from doubling as her laundry and dish outfit. She rarely had the time to change between shifts and was often too tired to even bother, so she fell into bed smelling of sweat and dirty water after a long night of scrubbing plates.

Portia followed Katja closely, like a shadow. "Are you sure? It took me forever to wake you! I kicked you with the heel of my boot! You gave me a real scare!"

Katja nearly stumbled down the spiral stairs to the entryway, where she spotted Claudia, Astrid, and the twins, Jeane and Victoria, clustered near the entrance. She did not have the time to get caught up in whatever they were talking about, so she slipped further down into the belly of the Maiden Tower, into the laundry room where Miss Frisbie was hard at work churning pots of dirty brown water. Her face was flush, and her brow was slick as fresh pavement on a rainy day.

"Where have you bloody been?" Miss Frisbie barked, blowing strands of frizzed hair out of her sweaty face. "Hope you told your client you aren't making it today because we got nearly double our usual load this morning! Not to mention the news going around!"

"What news?" Katja quickly grabbed a pile of dirty clothes, shoveling them into a pot of water, and then dumped lye and detergent into it, much like making soup.

"A girl has been arrested," Portia said, standing in the doorway, panting. "I tried to tell you, but you wouldn't slow down. It is the talk of the tower."

"Arrested? Who? And for what?" Katja asked.

Miss Frisbie sighed. "All I know is the crimes were of a wicked nature."

"It was Gabrielle on the tenth floor. Thinking back, it was probably she who spread the Hexes Pox around. To think we had a witch sleeping among us, beneath our noses," Portia said, wiping her hands on her hips as if talking about a witch would dirty her hands.

Katja didn't know anyone named Gabrielle. However, if anyone did know, it was Portia, who seemed able to befriend anyone who breathed.

"Well, what is going to happen? Have the prefects said anything?" Katja asked. Deep down, they all knew the answer. She didn't know what else to say on the matter.

Portia started wiping the mist from her eyes. Despite how disgusting Katja must have smelled, Portia hugged her, then took off through the door without another word. *That was strange.*

For the rest of the morning, Miss Frisbie was primarily silent except for a few curses muttered under her breath between chores. Halfway through Katja's duties, another pile of red dresses crashed through the laundry chute to the ground in a pile. How was she ever going to get all of this done, reach the countess in time, complete her duties, and meet up with Stav again? Now that she thought about it, she wasn't even sure how Stav expected her to enter the Warren. Clearly, the spider door was a path of desperation unless it was customary to constantly poison and resuscitate yourself every time you returned to the burglars' nest.

Prefect Haggerty entered the room with a rather large smirk.

"There is one more load coming down in a few minutes," she said. "The girls want all their outfits washed after hearing about who lived among them. Wouldn't want to take any chances getting hexed, cursed, damned, jinxed, . . . or worse, especially when evil incarnate sleeps among the litter!"

Katja ignored the prefect, but something about her speech made it sound as if she were threatening her directly. *Does she know something?* After all, the grand maiden was proclaimed "evil incarnate," but the grand maiden told Katja that not all the prefects knew about her abilities. Was Prefect Haggerty one of those she could not trust enough to tell her inner secrets? If true, Katja didn't blame her.

"Miss Frisbie, I would like you to take the rest of the morning off," Prefect Haggerty bellowed.

Miss Frisbie looked perplexed and signaled to the piles of laundry around her. "Are you serious? You just stated more work is coming."

Prefect Haggerty frowned. "It turns out Miss Rosdyre has earned more punitive labor on her docket! Now go! Return tomorrow and enjoy your day off."

What was she in trouble for now?

Miss Frisbie bowed uncertainly, grabbed her coat and purse, and left the room without another word. When the door shut and her footsteps faded, the prefect turned her attention to Katja.

Katja groaned inwardly. She would be lying if she weren't a little nervous, especially after the news of the arrest.

"The grand maiden is growing rather impatient. Has there been any update on your promised acquisition?" Prefect Haggerty said, tapping her toe.

Katja sighed with relief.

"What do you know about that?" Katja asked, hanging a few socks to dry.

The prefect did not seem pleased by her answer. "I know enough."

"I'm getting closer. It has taken me a while to gain some trust, but I must be careful," Katja whispered. "Tell her I will have what she desires soon."

"Soon?"

Katja nodded with pursed lips.

"The grand maiden has told me she wants it by the end of this week. That gives you two days," the prefect said.

Katja dropped a sock on the floor. "She told me I had until the end of the quarter! I still have several weeks before then!"

"I am only the messenger, Miss Rosdyre! And I want to remind you that you are speaking to a prefect, not some peasant on the street!" Haggerty scoffed. "You have two days and even less time, considering you don't have Miss Frisbie's help this morning."

She seemed to enjoy torturing her.

Before Katja could protest, the prefect spun around on her heel and slammed the door shut behind her.

Katja's heart raced as she daydreamed of slapping the grin off Prefect Haggerty's face, but instead she started punching wads of bloated dresses bobbing in the hot water, splashing grimy water in her own face. Her anger felt like trying to scratch an itchy scab that she could only dab with a cloth to avoid reopening the wound. Once there was a puddle of dirty water on the floor and her dress damp with the smell of mildew, she began imagining the dresses hanging from the drying line; each resembled every prefect that had treated her poorly, including a particularly fancy blue dress that she imagined was the grand maiden, who had sentenced her to a task that anyone would fail, left to their own devices.

Although she felt righteous, when she woke up from her fantasies, she was only halfway through the large heap of stinky clothes towering in the corner of the room. She would have to send a letter to the countess to tell her she would miss today, but would the countess believe her when she inevitably came up with a terrible excuse?

A quiet tapping sound broke over the bubbling water and popping suds, catching her attention. When the sound didn't come back, she continued stirring the laundry pot. A few seconds later, a loud thud from the laundry chute rattled its rusty siding.

Great. Another large load.

A few dresses slid from the chute to the pile, but that didn't warrant such a loud sound. Then the pile started to move, sending chills down Katja's spine. She backed away from the shifting pile in horror, knocking a bucket of detergent flakes onto the slick ground and nearly stumbling onto her tail end. The pile began to grow, and within moments, a person stood before her, a corset strung around their face and shoulder.

"It smells terrible in here!" a voice whisper-shouted.

"Stav . . .?" Katja uttered.

The corset caught flame, and black smoke rose to the ceiling.

"Oh, fire was a terrible choice," Stav said, his voice muffled.

"Are you trying to burn this place down?" she said, wrestling the burning corset off Stav's head and frantically tossing it into a pot of water with a loud hiss. The smell was indeed terrible, made even worse by being set ablaze.

Stav stumbled off the pile of laundry and kicked a few dresses from his ankles before approaching her. "This place is horrible. I have no idea why you chose to work and live here."

"When the other option is sleeping in the piss-soaked alleys, then 'horrible' doesn't sound so bad," Katja challenged. "How did you get in here? Did you know I was going to be here?"

"I snuck in, of course! After you told me you had chores to work at the Maiden Tower, it only took a few guesses to figure out where you were. I checked the kitchen, and you weren't in the larder or boiler room," he grinned, but after no response, continued. "Lo and behold, I found you . . . that is all that matters."

"You should leave before someone sees you!" Katja said. "Besides, it is awfully odd to sneak through a laundry chute."

"Is it?" Stav said, scratching his neck. "Anyways, I need you this morning . . . and I promise you won't be late for your assignment or whatever it is you call it."

Katja glanced at the door. "No one saw you enter the Maiden Tower? Boys aren't allowed in here, and if they—"

"Thankfully, I am not a boy . . . I am a man," Stav smirked.

"A man who just came barreling through a laundry chute, tangled in a corset. But that doesn't matter! You don't work here!" Katja said through gritted teeth, trying not to make too much noise. "Someone could find you."

He dashed toward the door, put his ear to it, stuck his finger toward the lock, turned it like a key, and pretended to swallow it playfully.

"I used a cloaking spell, of course. It is the first bit of magic I plan on teaching you, so long as you don't get a blemish on that sweet little face," Stav said, twirling a lock of peppery beard hair. "It isn't the simplest of spells, nor is it for beginners, but from my examination, you are a passable levitator, and you were able to escape Fleck's lock. Not many even know how to pick a lock properly. Isn't that embarrassing?"

Katja's jaw clenched. "Yes, very embarrassing . . . but I can't go anywhere unless I get through all this laundry."

"Oh, this old mess?" he said, retrieving his wand. "Why don't we start with a little exercise?"

Stav swirled his wand in the air, and dozens of damp clothes flew and were clipped to the drying lines. After tapping three pots, the gray water started to spin on its own. He glanced at the pile of clothes, flung them up like a flock of seagulls, and sent them plopping into the pots in rapid succession.

Katja gasped in horror. "No! Stop! Someone will find us!"

"Don't be silly! The door is enchanted! No one can enter unless they are a very talented sorcerer!" Stav grimaced. "Hurry up and join me, and it will be even faster! We will be out of here in no time!"

"Stav! A girl was arrested earlier . . . I don't want to take any chances!" Katja said, swatting his wand to the ground. "Besides, you said your wand was protected with wards yesterday, but I got hold of that just fine."

Stav stared at her and then at his wand. He looked like he might murder her for a minute, but then he took a deep breath. "If you want to work for me, then you must be willing to use magic, especially when it is risky. Of course, we want to be calculated based on our risks, but you must be willing."

"You lack empathy," she scolded. "A girl is going to hang because of magic."

"And unless we succeed, then more girls and boys will be murdered! That is why the stakes are so high! Once you fall under my wing, you must be willing to give your life to something greater!" Stav rebutted. "Now, hurry up and join me so we can get out of this dreaded place."

Katja sighed. She wanted more than anything to run away, but her curiosity about Stav, Fleck, Gwith, Urie, and all the other sorcerers living in the Warren was too great. Not to mention, she might as well learn a little magic while she was doing the grand maiden's bidding. She felt the boiling bubble in her belly, closed her eyes, levitated several dresses across the room, and joined Stav until every article of dirty clothing had been accounted for and was hung up to dry.

He might have won this time, but she wouldn't back down so easily. Should she confront him about his true identity? Should she ask him the real reason why he has his mother's ex-fiancé locked up in a cell? The temptation was strong as her curiosity grew.

When they were finished, Katja turned her attention to her next task. "I need to get ready."

"I'm going to follow you. That is part of why I need you this morning," Stav said, reaching for the doorknob.

"I am *not* going to undress in your presence!" Katja sneered.

"I am *not* going to watch!" Stav sneered back. "I have other plans."

"Such as?" she probed. "I am your apprentice, after all."

"You are my apprentice . . . but I do not fully trust you yet," Stav challenged. He pressed his finger to the lock, muttering a name under his breath that he thought he was hiding. The door clicked open. "I will be cloaking myself so no one spots me. It will look like an ordinary morning for you, walking up to your dormitory."

Stav took a deep breath, pressed his wand between his clenched palms so that it divided his face, took several heavy breaths of varying intensity, and uttered, "*Tudor vasa.*" Suddenly, his body vanished with a strange popping sound. When Katja reached for the spot Stav had stood just moments ago, she felt nothing and gasped.

"I can't even feel you . . ." she whispered.

There was no response, but Katja opened the door and trotted up the staircase to the seventh floor. There was no door on any of the dormitories, and she wasn't sure where Stav was hiding, nor how he was being so quiet. So, she dressed beneath her sheets and headed to the powder room, which was thankfully barren, to comb her hair and powder her nose quickly. *I must be running late.*

"Stav? I need to be going," Katja whispered, feeling like she must appear crazy talking to herself.

Upon getting no response, she strutted out the front door onto the crowded plaza. Just as she entered the alleyway, a popping sound rang out, and Stav appeared, sweaty and delirious.

"Have you walked to the grand maiden's chambers before?" Stav asked, out of breath and leaning on the rotting brick walls. "Have you gone past the twelfth floor?"

"Not often," Katja said. "Is that where you snuck off to? You could get us both in trouble."

"I told you already. I was scoping . . ." Stav uttered, ". . . another lesson in cloaking—you cannot speak when invisible. When you cloak, your physical body folds upon itself along the heartstring like two perfect halves. You will read about it more in the grimoire, but symmetry is so important in cloaking magic, and I cannot talk or be felt under its spell. You cannot touch anything when you are folded in two."

"What word did you use again? I could barely hear it," she inquired.

"*Tudor vasa*," Stav whispered. "It is from the old Elddir word for 'fold thee,' which is quite fitting if you ask me."

Katja nodded, wishing she had a pen to write it all down.

"So, how will we get to Stavoren Manor on time? Is there a secret manhole or sewer entrance we can enter nearby?" Katja asked anxiously.

"I need to get back to pondering my findings with Fleck and the others," Stav said, pacing back and forth. "There must be some enchantment blocking people like me from passing the twelfth floor . . . very curious."

"Stav! I am going to be late!" Katja shouted.

"Go ahead to Stavoren Manor. When you are done, return to Puffer Square and wait for me," he whispered, deep in thought.

Stav then reached into his pocket, where he palmed a glowing green glass orb. He kissed it once and tossed it into the wall, emitting a bright green flash that became a bright crack in the brick until he passed through it and vanished. Katja stood there in awe, staring at the spot where Stav had stood just moments ago, which quickly disappeared without a trace.

Magic is insane . . . and maddening.

Katja cursed under her breath as she ran down the alleyway and across busy streets to the trolley. If she were lucky, she would be only an hour late, and Gavin would greet her with the most infuriating grin imaginable. But despite being abandoned, she couldn't help but obsess over the idea of cloaking and meeting Stav after she finished his mother's makeup.

Chapter Fourteen

The crowd was dense at Puffer Square for another prolific hanging, but for some reason, Katja's heart fluttered like she was going to meet someone she would fall in love with for the first time. Her eyes scanned the faces as they passed by in the street, doing her best to appear like an inconspicuous bystander. Theed was an enormous city, so her crimes, including being chased by the city watch, were already long forgotten, but she could never be too careful. Occasionally, she spotted a red-and-gold-clad patrol strolling one way or the other, but most of the time, they seemed too occupied by navigating the crowd and bashing boisterous pedestrians with batons to take notice of a basic chambermaid, and for that, she was thankful.

Katja watched for nearly an hour as the crowd grew denser, noticing a gangly executioner standing at the gallows, inspecting the trap door mechanism. She always felt uneasy when she caught a glimpse of the Crown's executioner. He wore a black pointed mask with slits for eyes and acted so nonchalant about his murderous profession. She didn't watch the gallows long and mostly avoided looking in their direction. She refused to be part of the gnarly spectacle known as public execution. If she was honest with herself, though, it was hard not to notice that three prisoners were standing solemnly by their ropes. *Three? The Magesleuths have been busy.* Her stomach sank as she glanced at the overly decorated constable who took the podium. He hollered to the crowd as he read from a long scroll, but she could thankfully only hear every other word.

Look away. Look away.

She turned her head away, forcing herself to look at anything else, but her eyes kept drifting back. When they landed on the prisoners again, the details snapped into focus: a middle-aged man, an old woman, and a young girl, each with a noose around their necks.

Someone tapped the top of Katja's head, and when she spun around, Gwith stood there, arms crossed, with a cold expression.

"I drew the shortest stick," Gwith grunted. "Follow me . . . and don't get bloody lost in the crowd. I am not turning back to find you."

Gwith shoved past her and slipped into the crowd swiftly. Katja followed closely behind, occasionally glancing at the gallows as the constable finished reading his statement. A priest rose to the podium with a censer swinging back and forth, puking white smoke into the air. *It won't be long now.* She felt disgusted as she snuck past chanting spectators licking their lips at the sight of adding three dead souls to the gallows' grim tally.

The closer they moved toward the gallows, the denser the crowd grew and the faster Katja's heart pounded. She called for Gwith, pleading with her to slow down, but the woman never once turned around to ensure she was still following. The priest's incense drifted through the air, faint at first, then growing stronger with every step as they drew nearer to the gallows. She could now make out the deep wrinkles on the other prisoners' faces, but the young girl's face was smooth and unlined, only bruises and welts remaining, and her expression was lifeless.

Gabriella. Was this Gabriella from the Maiden Tower? The girl who was arrested? Katja's heart chilled, but before she could react, the platforms dropped, and all three souls fell through the gallows with the loud mechanical swooshing sound of the lever. Thankfully, she was not close enough to hear the cracks of their severed necks, but nothing could hide the roaring cheers that followed.

"The witches are dead! The witches are dead! The wicked witches are dead!" the crowd cheered.

It was then that she looked back toward Gwith, but the illusionist was no longer in front of her. Instead, Gwith stood beside her angrily, staring at the swaying bodies.

"You came back for me," Katja asked, tears misting her eyes.

"Are you alright?" Gwith said, breaking her trance and continuing behind the gallows where the crowd was starting to thin. "Follow me."

Katja followed her down a narrow path through a gate of tall yew trees, then cut along the edge of an old abbey with tall glass windows, its façade patinated by vines and moss. At the back of the abbey, to her surprise, lay a muddy yard filled with lopsided pitchforks made of iron, copper, wood, stones, and wicker sticking out of the ground like horns. She stopped in her tracks, bewildered by the sight. If she had to guess, there would have been hundreds of pitchforks littered like spilled toothpicks. Among the heap were candles, flowers, dolls, runestones, lanterns, and broomsticks.

"Hurry up!" Gwith snapped. "The objective is not to be seen if you can avoid it!"

Katja broke her trance and carefully stepped through the yard, the mud sucking at her heels with every step as she weaved between the rows of rusty pitchforks to avoid getting impaled. Beneath her feet, a few small gravestones were embedded in the ground, some broken, split, or nearly consumed by the dirt. In the distance, pale stone mausoleums dotted the horizon of varying size, age, and state of decay, one of which they swiftly approached.

The mausoleum Gwith was leading her toward was one of the nicer ones, if that said anything. It was three armlengths wide and six in length, with a ceiling nearly twice her height. The door was embossed with what looked like tree thistles, but even that was unfortunately marred by scratches that appeared to be the work of vandals. Once they got closer, she noticed a few words etched on the front door: "*Knock the wicked dead.*" Other words showered the door, including "*burn forever,*" "*murderer,*" "*leech,*" "*dead warlock,*" *and* "*the only good Glint is dead,*" among some insults in other tongues she could not read. The door was barred with chains, metal brackets, and a long plank.

Katja ran her finger against the engravings. "What is this place? How have I never seen it?"

"I am not surprised. Not many people come here because most are wise enough to avoid it," Gwith said. "The less attention they give people like us . . . the better."

"Is this the entrance to the Warren?" Katja asked.

Gwith slapped her across the cheek. "Never say that out loud. You never know who is listening!"

Katja rubbed her stinging cheek. "If you slap me again—"

"—You will what? Strike me back? I would like to see you try," Gwith spat. "Are you coming or not?"

Katja sighed. She would have to bite her tongue if she wanted to get close enough to snatch those cards. Instead of combating, she changed her approach.

Katja followed quietly, flicking a spiderweb out of her hair and pulling it into a bun.

Gwith pulled the door open after unshackling the bolt and entered the mausoleum. Katja observed the intertwining chains and planks, which had nails that were too short to penetrate the wall. *It was a trick door. Clever.* She entered the recess of the mausoleum, which contained a small chamber with two coffins filled with dust and cobwebs. Between the two coffins was a gargoyle with buggy eyes, short horns, thick brows, sharp claws, tiny wings, and a wide-open mouth with jutting teeth.

Gwith reached for a small marble in the gargoyle's mouth and smiled.

"Kristoff is home. This should be interesting," she muttered, setting the token along the ledge of an altar behind the gargoyle. She then took a thimble from the altar beside a six-faced die and placed it in the gargoyle's mouth. Then she cleared her throat and spat onto the right coffin and knocked three times on its lid.

"*Kristoff tar Stavoren,*" Gwith whispered.

Suddenly, the coffin to the left opened with a loud creak, and a gust of foul air stung their nostrils.

Kristoff Stavoren? Did she hear that right? Was the other son here, too? Once the coffin opened, she noticed a rickety staircase plummeting into the mausoleum's shadows. Gwith dangled a leg into the coffin and waved for her to follow as if it were the most normal thing ever to happen. At first, Katja hesitated, but when Gwith knocked three times on the coffin again, it began lowering back into place. Before the lid came to a halting thud, Katja slipped through the narrow gap and scurried down the creaking stairs as day became night.

They traversed deeper into the mausoleum's underbelly.

"Gwith! I can't see a thing! How are we supposed to make sense of where we are?" Katja said, carefully wading forward.

"You will get used to it," Gwith said, her footsteps moving onward.

Katja reluctantly followed down, relieved when her hand came upon a handrail that gave her splinters, until the walls lit up with a warm, flickering light. *Fire.* When they got to the bottom of the stairs, a surreal feeling dizzied her when she spotted the same burning hearth, two chairs, and jail cell that had plagued her nightmares. She glanced at the cell in the dark corner, which now appeared empty. *Where is Rhys DeGrom?*

"Stav! I have fetched your bumbling protégé!" Gwith shouted.

Stav peeked out from one of the back rooms and waved her over. She could hear whispers as she walked past Fleck's chair, noticing a pipe resting on its armrest, and cautiously entered the chamber where Stav was residing. She had almost reached the door when a man with jaw-length golden hair and a sullen face stomped past, taking a swig of pale green Vigor from his coat pocket. Before she could speak, Stav gently tugged her into the room and slammed the door shut.

"It would be most wise of you to never talk to that man," Stav said. "He only brings trouble and misery!" He yelled it as if hoping the golden-haired man heard him. "He may be my bloody brother, but he has more ambition than cunning if you ask me, and is someone to be avoided if you want to keep your wits about you!" Stav said, flipping his wand between his fingers as he paced in what appeared to be a study filled with tomes, glass beakers, empty glass vials, parchment, inkwells, and other knick-knacks, including a large bone that was certainly too large to be a chicken or pig. She prayed it wasn't human.

"You didn't tell me the Roth was a family affair," Katja said.

"You and I only just met. When was I supposed to get to the specifics of my extended family with your schedule?" Stav shouted, but before he could holler more, he glanced at her, and his eyes softened. He took a deep breath and placed his hands on his hips. "Sorry, sometimes my family consumes me with rage. It isn't any reflection on how I think about you as my pupil. That is still to be determined."

Katja nodded. "You already lied to me. You said you would find me at Puffer Square, but instead, you sent her?"

Stav raised a finger. "I was going to meet you, but I got caught up meeting with my brother . . . or rather, screaming at him . . . so I asked Gwith to go in my stead. I hope that did not cause you too much distress, Kat."

"You said you had a book for me to read?" she inquired, inspecting the small hovel where the man also slept.

Stav reached for a leatherbound book and set it in her lap. She recognized the gold-foil lettering instantly. It was the count's grimoire. Somehow, it had survived the fire despite everything being devoured in magedust-induced flames, except for a single bewitched cabinet that failed to open. Her eyes lit up, and her pulse quickened. *Perhaps the cards survived, too.* After all, the cards were hidden within the grimoire's pages.

She flipped through the pages feverishly but caught herself and paused. Although Katja felt like she could trust Stav, she barely knew him, so she would have to fetch the cards when he wasn't looking. She then flipped to a marked page titled, "The Art of Cloaking."

"I want you to absorb every word on cloaking, and then we can start the hands-on portion of my first lesson," Stav said, his blue eyes murderous. He was still not over his argument with his brother.

Katja nodded. "I will bring the book back to you tomorrow."

He laughed. "I will not let you leave this room with that book! I could never risk losing it! It is worth more to me than my right arm!"

Boils! Katja sighed.

"Fine. But you trust me enough not to report the location of the Warren to the city watch. That is more trust than you would afford a stranger on the street," she teased.

Stav smirked. "Trust or leverage? Because, despite what you might think, you have more to lose than I do. You have a contract with the Maiden Tower to lose. What can you take from a man that has nothing?"

"Besides a boy's bedtime story?" Katja said, pointing to the grimoire.

"The book belonged to someone I loved. But this is all beside the point. Consider yourself lucky . . . I trust you for now, but the moment I don't, I will have Fleck do what he has wanted to do to you ever since your last meeting. What was it? Did you spit at him? Tell him his mug looked like a cow's udder? Perhaps an old tree knot?"

"No," Katja said. "Why would someone tease him like that?"

Stav tilted his head. "Tease? Fleck? Oh, do you think he needs defending? You have a lot to learn about that man. He used to be a pretty man and flaunted it like he was the first smiling face under the sun! Then he got cocky and bit off more than he could chew!"

Katja wished he would disappear and leave her to the grimoire, but he kept hovering around like a fruit fly.

"I still don't like bullies," she chided.

"You think I am some schoolyard bully? I don't think that is a way to talk to your mentor!" Stav said, tsking like a stern headmistress.

"I have yet to be taught," Katja sneered. She could feel the air thicken with tension.

Stav opened his mouth to speak, but instead marched outside the door and locked it behind him.

Perfect.

She waited a few seconds for his heavy footsteps to fade away. She could hear him cursing up a storm in the other room, but thankfully, the words were too muffled to hear. Her heart fluttered, and her hands started to shake as she flipped through the grimoire. Her stomach sank as she frantically rifled through each page for the cards, but after numerous checks, they were nowhere to be found.

They have to be in here. Where else would they be? She had put them back in the grimoire before Fleck and his band of pirates took her. Did someone find them? Stav must have seen them and put them somewhere . . . but where? Katja set the grimoire on a desk and rummaged through the cabinets, beneath a bedside table, but the cards were nowhere to be found. Defeated, she kicked a tall stack of tomes onto the floor, not caring who heard, and paced, glaring at the grimoire as if it were depriving her of the cards' locations.

"Where are you?" she muttered to herself. Then something struck her.

Kristoff. What if Kristoff took the cards? The grimoire was just as much his father's as Stav's.

Katja tried to open the door, but it didn't budge as expected. She then took a deep breath, placed her shaking finger on the lock, and felt the Vigor boil in her chest so much that it nearly came up her throat like bile.

"Hugo tar Stavoren Junior," she uttered.

The lock clicked, and a smile crawled across Katja's face. She did it! She finally unlocked something and no longer needed to learn a new language. Her body filled with excitement and pride, but she had to reel it in as she snuck out the door, looking down the cold passageway. Stav was pacing in front of a large dining table with mismatched chairs clustered around it. On top of the table was a large map of some sort, along with piles of coins, pens, paperweights, and what looked like a crystal ball. Gwith was sitting next to the fire across from

Fleck, who must have entered the hideout recently. Just the sight of Fleck's back gave Katja shivers.

When everyone looked away, she crept down the passageway and snuck past the room where she had found the tapestry the other day. She peered inside the room but quickly saw a silhouette emerge from the candlelight. She retreated just in time for Urie to burst out of the door and start hollering toward the others like a foreman screaming at his dockers moving cargo at the port.

"The plot is on! We got a letter from the college! Sealed in wax by the professor herself!" he exclaimed, waving an envelope as he approached the others in the other room.

"Good, I look forward to meeting the old crone again!" Stav shouted, giving Urie a celebratory pat on the shoulder.

"Are you, Stav? I thought you didn't like royalist zealots? If I recall, Professor Gill wrote a whole book on the role of a subservient Glint class destined to live beneath the Crown's lofty boot," Kristoff hissed. "I never cared for her, but I will gladly take something valuable off her hands."

Katja wanted to continue listening, but knew she couldn't waste time. She slipped into one of the back rooms and carefully shut the door. She found a candlestick and matches beside the entrance and lit the candle before carefully exploring the strange room she had just entered. Compared to Stav's chambers, this room was neat, with tall oak bookshelves perfectly stocked and organized by volume. In the corner of the room was a bed tucked at the seams so tight that she wasn't sure a penny could fit beneath the sheets. On the far end of the room, beside a small hearth, was a polished black wood piano with ivory keys. She set the candle on the piano ledge, observing the booklets of written music by names she had never heard of, except Pierre var Hummel, one of the most famous Astlani composers in the world, that even a waif in the street would have heard about. The name *Kristoff Stavoren* was written neatly on the edge of each booklet.

She was tempted to push one of the keys, but knew it would make too much noise to risk it. She had never played the piano before. The inns and hotel lobbies were filled with pianos and music-making late at night, which she would often listen to in the alley outside if the bricks were thin enough for hearing. But if she dared enter, the valets and hoteliers were quick to shoo any vagabonds drifting through their doors.

Katja abandoned the piano and her daydreams as she brought her candle to the large black safe in the corner of the room. She fidgeted with the safe's metallic dial, which gave a satisfying click, and wondered if something like this could be unlocked with a simple lockpicking spell.

Again, she closed her eyes, raised her finger to the safe, and muttered, "*Kristoff tar Stavoren*," but nothing happened. It was worth a try, but it made sense to find a better lock, considering his brother could easily unlock it and access his belongings. She wondered what could be in the safe after years of banditry on the streets of Theed. She couldn't shake the thought of the cards being in there, separated from her grasp by a few lengths of steel. *I have to open it.* Would she ever get another opportunity like this?

She cursed under her breath, glancing back over the room like a desperate, scurrying hare, and spotted a long black coat hanging on the back of the door before blowing out the candle. Her heart raced as she reached into its pockets, returning with a few spare crowns, a pack of cigarettes, and—to her delight—the three cards from the tapestry. Kristoff must have taken them from the grimoire. And if he had, they must be more valuable than she had previously thought.

Katja nearly fell as she dodged the door smashing open, and Kristoff entered the chamber. She pressed her hand to her mouth to refrain from screaming as he muttered something under his breath and shifted the wheels of the safe a few times before opening it. He shoved an envelope inside, pulled another envelope out, and slid it into his vest pocket. Katja didn't get much of a glimpse, but she could have sworn there were piles of opened envelopes and colorful vials that she reckoned were filled to the brim with magedust serum.

Kristoff then locked the safe and tugged his coat from the back of the door as he briskly exited the room, the wind of his stride smelling like smoke and lemon zest. She was thankful he never questioned the smoking candle on his bedside table, but he seemed too distracted to notice something inconsequential, including a stranger standing at his door jamb.

When she felt confident her heart wouldn't burst from her chest, and no one else was approaching, she snuck back to Stav's room, but she felt a call to return to the tapestry that suddenly consumed her. Katja went into the dark room, lit the purple candle, and then entered the tapestry. The chamber was still dusty, but to her surprise, there was a broom in the corner of the small room and a neat path in the dust that someone had carved. *Did Stav do this?* she wondered as she set the purple candle down and knelt before the remaining cabinet.

"*Hugo tar Stavoren,*" Katja muttered, but there was nothing.

Then she wondered. If it wasn't the count, maybe it was . . . A shred of horror crawled down her neck. It would begin to explain a family of Glints.

"*Auriella don Stavoren,*" Katja said, and there was a click.

Inside the cabinet was a slightly bent wand carved with embossed vines and flowers along its hilt and a large rune on its body. Katja tucked the wand near her chest, shut the cabinet, left the tapestry, blew out the candle magekey, and snuck into Stav's bedchambers before her luck could run out.

By the time Stav checked on her again, she had hidden the wand along the crease of the grimoire and pretended to be deep into studying.

"You are going on your first job," he ordered. She noticed him suspiciously glance at the padlock.

"I have dishes to clean," Katja stated.

"Then you aren't sleeping," Stav retorted.

"But you heard Fleck, I am not ready," she said. "I haven't even begun to learn cloaking."

"This job won't require cloaking. Besides, you are my apprentice, not his. He made that very clear," he said. "Finish studying, and we will finish your training tomorrow."

Finish? When had Stav even started to train her? In the last few hours, she had learned more on her own than he had taught her. She bit her tongue, but her frustration was swelling.

"Where should I go?" she asked.

"Meet me at the college in Admiral's Landing across town. Do not bring anything with you, not even your purse," Stav said, his face grave. "It will be a night of festivities."

Chapter Fifteen

S tav was mainly silent during the flight, focused on something far ahead or deep within his mind. He didn't even say farewell to Katja when she pulled herself into the alleyway. So, she slid the lid back over the sewer hole without a "goodbye" or "meet you later." He should be pleased. She had finished reading the entire chapter about cloaking, but Stav seemed unimpressed or too distracted when she told him. To get his attention, she was tempted to confront him about his lies, such as why he failed to mention that Countess Auriella was his mother or why Rhys DeGrom had been locked in a cell. She wasn't even sure if she wanted the answer to that last question. Nonetheless, the timing didn't seem right, and she needed to gain his trust.

Deep down, Katja had to focus on her main goal: the three strange cards stuffed in her bosom. She would deliver the cards first and then worry about the mission later tonight. Her head spun with questions about the countess. Did she know Katja used magic to clean during her assignments? Was her swiftness too suspicious? Did she know who her sons worked for? Katja's mind sorted through questions about the countess and Rhys, but she wasn't sure the answers would ever come to light. She should have taken more seriously into consideration that the countess's sudden revival was of an arcane origin. How was she supposed to know that it was possible to stop time or turn the hands of time backward? If so, could one become immortal? What else was she missing about the capabilities of magic? She felt anger at how much she had been deprived due to a bitter queen and a few loyal lords who had struck the decree, agreeing to forbid magic a long time ago.

The Maiden Tower was bustling with life when she arrived. She tied up her mess of red hair, put on a hairnet, and joined a few other sullen-looking girls whose fingers were already pink and raw from scrubbing porcelain and glass. Katja spent over an hour cleaning, and once the other girls had finished their portion, she discreetly levitated pots, pans, lids, ladles, forks, knives, and skillets across the tables, mere inches from the surface in case someone barged in and she needed to hide her misdeeds by dropping them into the sudsy basin.

Once done, she scarfed down a plate of cold pasta marinated in oil and basil, scraping a chunk of rye bread into a red sauce until the pot was almost clean enough to shelve. She chased the meal with a glass of lukewarm milk and then walked up to her dormitory, which was as black as night. When she entered the dormitory, she could hear the familiar sound of snoring from Astrid's bunk, but also heard whispers and the shuffling of bedsheets, which suspiciously stopped when she stepped into the room.

Katja slipped the embossed wand beneath her mattress. She would have placed them here before clocking in for dishwashing duties, but she knew that sometimes the prefects did their sweeps of the dormitories, looking inside pillowcases and the seams of mattresses for anything out of place. It was a risk hiding a magic wand in her bed even at night, but she expected to return before sunrise, before the first prefect woke for morning roll call.

Katja waited a few minutes in bed until she sensed everyone in the dormitory was sleeping. She even pretended to sleep herself, adding a few guttural grunts to sell it. When enough time passed, her legs slid quietly off her mattress, and she headed out of the dorm and into the empty hallway. For once, she was thankful the dormitories did not have doors as she stepped up the spiral staircase, passing the eerie paintings of owls, moths, and gargoyles up to the grand maiden's quarters. When she reached the large steel door, she retrieved the three sweaty cards and hesitated before slipping them into the small mail slot beneath the sleeping face with its broken nose.

That is it—the nightmare is over.

A floorboard groaned somewhere from behind the grand maiden's door, sending shivers down her neck. She fled down the spiral stairs. The tower's dark halls felt like something might clutch her heel at any moment. After all of these years living in the Maiden Tower, she had memorized the steps, the creaky ones, the crooked ones, and the ones that made you nearly tumble to your death. Without fail, she reached the bottom of the Maiden Tower without making too much sound, which was a testament to a building that had likely seen kingdoms fall and rise over the centuries.

She hovered outside the tower entryway, spotting the glow of the front desk, where the Maiden Tower clerk, Elisa Humphry, stood guard, reading a newspaper while smoking a thin cigarette. Thankfully, Ms. Humphry wasn't paying much attention to the stairs, so Katja slipped down a passageway to the rear door exit. The door was locked, but it only took one guess to figure out who had last locked it, and that was the same Ms. Humphry smoking at the front desk. Everyone in the tower knew the secretary's naughty habit of sneaking out the back door for a smoke during the day and smoking freely at night while the prefects slept.

"Elisa don Humphry," Katja mumbled, looking over her shoulder as the lock clicked before storming out onto the back street as the wind tugged at her hair.

"Katja . . ." a soft voice whispered from behind.

A girl in a nightgown with a familiar pale face propped open the door. Her face spoke where words couldn't.

Katja could see it in her eyes, in the tight line of her mouth, in the way she held herself. She was worried.

"Portia?" Katja panted, taking a few steps closer and darting her attention to the dormitory windows overhead. Thankfully, they were all dark except for one at the top, where the grand maiden lived.

"What are you doing out here?" Portia whispered. Her face looked tortured. "It is late."

Katja fumbled for words, but none of them came.

"It is dangerous out here at night. You aren't leaving, are you?" Portia said, foot wedged in the door. "If you need money to get by . . . I can help."

"Port . . . I have somewhere I need to be," Katja said defensively. "And if you are worried about me, remember where I came from. There isn't much that can scare me."

"Where could you possibly need to be at this hour?" Portia asked, crossing her arms. "I am worried about you. You look sick, and you rarely sleep."

"Go back inside, Port," Katja said, shivering as a cold breeze scraped across the city.

"What about that boy stalking the alleyway across the street? What about Gabrielle? It has gotten bad out here. You shouldn't walk alone."

Katja whispered, "I left in secret because I didn't want you all to worry about me. I will be back by sunrise."

Portia looked offended but swallowed her pride.

"I will follow you as far as you will allow me. How about that?" she challenged. "Besides, I leave soon. My family needs me sooner than expected. I will be gone next week. I would rather spend my nights walking around town with a friend than sleep a couple more hours."

Katja shook her head. "No. I must go alone. Go back inside where it is warm so you don't catch the pox!"

Portia looked like she was debating challenging her again, but took a deep breath instead.

"I will see you tomorrow morning," Katja said reassuringly.

"I am going to watch you until I can't see you anymore, and then when I get back upstairs, I will continue watching you from the window," Portia said. "And if I see anything that makes me suspicious, you better bet I am going to march out this door to find you."

Katja felt terrible about how she was acting toward her one and only good friend. But she knew what she was about to do had far larger implications. She was determined, above all, to find out more about Stav and the Arkan Roth—*about magic.*

"I would only expect that from you, Port," Katja said. "But I will be fine. I can stand my own."

She then stormed across the street, down a side street, and headed to the famous Hartwind College, which stood like a spiked crown overlooking Admiral's Landing.

* * *

Even though Katja had acted bravely around Portia, there were things that truly scared her about walking through Theed at night. After all, fear kept you alive—it was foolishness that led to one's demise. Only a fool was fearless in walking the unlit sections of the district. The lampless alleys were ripe with cutthroats, robber barons, dust lords, and every bit of filth that, unlike flowers, only seemed to grow in the shadows. She did her best to avoid those shadows. She also feared the ruminating thoughts that were never to be underestimated. Her mind could conjure every terrible scenario, turn every dumpster or enclave into a night stalker, and without someone to dispel the nightmares by calling her a "nit," they would grow and deepen. Those lonely thoughts were enough for her to take longer strides while looking over her shoulder like a field mouse after hearing the screech of an overhead buzzard.

But her biggest fear was reserved for the Magesleuths.

Katja approached Admiral's Landing, the sleepy burrow living in Hartwind College's shadow and its labyrinth of towers. This burrow would be filled with academics, professors, and squires in the daytime, but it was as silent as the grave at night. She scanned the lines of buildings and shops with blackened windows, but there was no sign of Stav. She caught something in the corner of her eye, stalking along the fringe of a distant lawn. The wind left her breathless, but she did not scream as a figure in a blood-red robe prowled the square's edges. For a heartbeat, she caught sight of a pale mask with deep-set eyes and a long, narrow nose before it slipped back into shadow. She thought she heard it sniffing, though she couldn't tell if the sound was real or imagined.

"Stav . . .?" Katja whispered.

There was no answer, but she spotted a pinprick of fire across the courtyard, and the smell of tobacco leaves filled her nose. She swiftly approached, but before she could get close enough, the pinprick vanished along with the smell of smoke.

"Fleck?" Katja stammered.

The smell of smoke returned, and she spotted the flame up the crawling stone stairs that led like switchbacks up Deacon Hill toward the college. When she reached a platform atop the first flight of stairs, the flame vanished again and reappeared further up the stairs, where distant music began tickling her ears. Further onward, she could make out the buzz of conversation and the cackle of laughter echoing off the tall towers, turrets, and walls of Hartwind College, a congregation of ancient castles welded together like intertwining vines. Looking out of her vantage spot, she scanned the streets to see if the Magesleuth had returned, but it was thankfully nowhere to be seen.

She looked at the college's glowing balconies, wavering banners, and magnificent flying buttresses with the same awe she felt when she first caught a glimpse of the wondrous college and dreamed of walking its halls as a student.

Deep down, her mother probably knew Katja would never have the coin or smarts to attend the most prestigious college in the Theed and the entire Commonwealth. Still, it didn't stop her from invigorating her daughter's delusional childish dreams whenever they passed it on their way to the market to steal something. While fear kept you physically alive, dreams kept your soul aglow when you lived in squalor.

Katja approached the pinpricked flame again, but it did not vanish this time.

"Hello, Fleck," she whispered.

"Good," Fleck uttered gravely as a tall shadow appeared, coming down the stairs. "I thought he was leaving me out to dry."

Stav huddled in next to them. He wore a tan waistcoat with a black double-breasted suit, and a white cravat fastened tightly against his neck. Beneath, he wore white pleated trousers that made his legs look long and gangly. When Fleck stepped into the lamplight, he was also dressed in a fine suit, this one in a deep blue with a red bow tie. Suddenly, she felt underdressed in her work gown, which was stained with sweat and had lost its color from detergent.

"Was I supposed to wear a dress?" Katja asked.

"You? A dress? Absolutely not," Fleck snapped.

"I am afraid you will not want to wear anything particularly pretty or exciting tonight," Stav smiled. "Your job will be to look as boring and uninteresting as possible."

"Get to it, Stav. We don't have all night," Fleck blurted. "I spotted a Magesleuth snooping around the square a little while ago. There is no saying it won't come back. Let's get the amulet and go!"

"Amulet?" Katja asked.

A lady dressed in a green ball gown, with clacking heels, a lacy umbrella, and a matching bonnet, tapped down the stairs and joined them. It was Gwith.

"What are you all waiting for?" Gwith said. "I am already working my magic on the professor . . . well, one of her colleagues. I can't decide whether to mention that I came with a date. One option sounds far more exciting."

"How many people are there?" Fleck asked.

"A few hundred, if I were to guess," Gwith said, locking her arms with Stav. "Does the girl know where to go?"

Stav put a warm hand on Katja's shoulder and looked at her with the countess's pale blue eyes.

"Your job is to sneak into the professor's study while we distract her at the ball. Professor Gill isn't particularly a rabble-rouser and tires early in her old age, so we need to do our best to make sure that she doesn't turn out of the Hearthward Ball early so that you have ample time to fetch her amulet," Stav whispered, looking over his shoulder as a few drunken guests stumbled past them.

"What is so special about this amulet?" Katja asked.

"You don't need to know that yet," Stav said, tapping his brow. "But believe me, it's far from an ordinary piece of jewelry."

"Why doesn't one of you just get the amulet? I have only just started to learn," Katja uttered.

Fleck nudged Stav. "Just like what I said. She isn't a Dustmage yet."

"You cannot become a Dustmage without practice," Stav grumbled. "Besides, her greatest strength is levitation. That is all we need from her tonight."

"The girl is a better levitator than all of us except Fleck, if I were to wager," Gwith interrupted. "I don't have the patience for it."

"And that is why you are the *siren* and not the Dustmage," Fleck said, puffing his pipe. "Where is Urie?"

"He is inside, ready for when we need him," Gwith said. "But unless the professor has the amulet locked away in some complicated lock safe, then I don't think we will need him much tonight."

"Good," Fleck said.

Stav pulled a crumpled map from his pocket and handed it to Katja. The map was a detailed outline of the college's eastern wing, or at least that was what it appeared to be at first glance. She could even spot a sketch of the stairs where they stood, leading up to the main foyer, labeled in fine ink.

Stav pointed to a room on the other end of the map marked with a faint red "X."

"That is where you ought to go. Professor Gill's study," he muttered. "There will likely be a few professors, students, and monitors walking along these long corridors, which is precisely why we didn't want you dressed up for the ball, lest someone notice you walking away from the ball with likely a very terrified and perplexed expression on your face. The more you look like a college custodian, servant, or perhaps unenthused student, the better."

"And when I get to this professor's room, then what? Will the amulet be in an obvious place?" Katja whispered as the sound of upbeat drums danced off the walls.

"That is when things get more complicated, and we hope your experience from the Maiden Tower comes in. Who would know places powerful and influential people hide important things more than the servants who clean, fix, and care for said powerful and influential people," Stav said. "We do not know where the amulet is located . . . precisely, but we know it is in that study. That is for certain. Which is why I've arranged for a few of us to be there. We'll keep her company, keep her drinking, and make sure she doesn't slip away."

"What does this trinket look like? It seems easier if one of you did it," Katja rebutted, wishing she were sleeping back in her dorm.

"Trust me, Kat . . . I made that argument myself. I wouldn't send a rookie recruit either." Fleck's tone suggested they had argued for a long time, which made her want to do it to spite him.

Stav glanced at a lit window high on the balcony, then back at Katja.

"The professor and I know each other. Our history is complex, but I used to be one of her students," Stav grimaced. "It was through her invitation that I am attending this ball tonight, and through my pestering, she will not only accompany me to the ball but also relish in it long enough for you to swipe her amulet. I can speak all night about that woman, but we don't have the luxury of time."

"Why do we need this amulet in the first place?" Katja asked.

"You are a greenhorn, girl. You don't get to ask questions," Gwith said, slightly too loud. "Do you want to get away from that dreaded tower?"

At the moment, being back at the Maiden Tower was all she wanted, but she knew that was the easy road. She could watch the sands of fate without any prophetic magic at all. Like Prefect Haggerty, she would end up stowed away in the same tower her whole life, neglecting the dwindling flame of her dreams of mastering magic. That was if she didn't get caught using magic all those years. She had to bite into this opportunity with her teeth, or it would slip away.

"Are you ready to prove your loyalty?" Stav said, reaching out his hand.

Katja clenched his hand firmly until it hurt, ripped the map away, and began memorizing it.

"Follow us," he said, waving the others up the stairs. "Once we reach the entryway, there will be a list-checker to let us in, but your name will not be on the list. You will instead open a locked side door past the hedges. The college steward, Sir Geoffrey Poissont, mostly uses the door to smuggle dust for his private collection. Gather from that what you want."

Katja nodded, sucking her cold teeth. She looked down toward the square, making sure there was no more sign of the Magesleuth before following Stav, Fleck, and Gwith up the marble stone steps that zigzagged the hillside until they reached a fortified entrance with iron doors large enough to accommodate trolls and their entire troll families. Crimson banners were drawn from the stone façade, and a heraldic shield displayed the castle's coat of arms over the entrance: a fiery salamander proudly perched on a round stone. Splitting the entryway was a covered tollbooth with a lantern swinging loudly on its rung in the wind, which had gained ferocity the higher they climbed.

"Now?" Katja whispered as they approached a set of gatekeepers in savvy tunics.

Stav did not answer, but Gwith turned to her and mouthed, "HURRY!" with a fierce expression.

Katja tucked her head down to her chest and darted quickly toward a row of hedges on the edge of the castle entrance. Wind blew in her face as she felt someone might call for her at any moment. She pushed through the thick hedges, her cheeks grazing through dense brush and cobwebs until she reached the other side, but to her horror, someone was standing just outside the door.

Her heels dug into the pavement, and her body stiffened.

"Hurry . . . hurry," the middle-aged man whispered, his long nose sticking out of a drawn hood. "Hold on . . . you are a new face. Do you work with Stav?"

Katja didn't know what to say and couldn't tell who was hidden beneath the hood. Was it Kristoff or Urie? Wouldn't they recognize or expect her?

"You don't work for him, do you? Oh . . . this is not ideal," the hooded man uttered, his beady eyes darting like an oversized rat, fearfully watching every directions. He pulled a wand from his pocket and aimed it at her heart. "I am sorry . . . you know too much. Come with me."

Katja waved her hands frantically. *I'm going to kill Stav.* "No! No! I work for Stav! I am his pupil!"

"Pupil, ey? I didn't know Stav had it in him to take on a student," the hooded man chuckled. "Stav told me to meet out here for my delivery at eight this morning, but when he didn't show up, I figured he must have meant eight in the evening and made a mistake. I have been waiting all day for this, so it better be good!"

"Mr. Poissont?" Katja asked. "That is your name, correct?"

"Sir Geoffrey Poissont . . . but that doesn't matter now," he stammered. "Do you have my order?"

Katja looked over her shoulder. "Let's go inside. I saw a Magesleuth snooping around earlier."

Sir Geoffrey's eyes widened. "A bloody Sleuth . . . in these parts? The gall these bastards have after all the college has done for them in terms of recruitment. Come inside, but don't bring any attention to yourself. The castle is busy tonight. It is the Hearthward Ball after all."

Katja followed Sir Geoffrey into the room and was instantly swarmed by the smells of incense, rotting wood, dusty books, and an ashy fireplace. Hartwind was everything she ever imagined as a child. The halls were adorned with tall crystal chandeliers, candelabra, and dripping wall sconces, revealing a richly decorated castle full of leather furniture, elaborate tapestries, expansive maps, vases filled with bright flowers, hanging globe ornaments, and alabaster statues of strange men and women in various states of undress. The numerous doors, alcoves, staircases, and passageways led to all sorts of intriguing unknowns snaking through the labyrinth-like structure, beckoning them to explore. Light dimmed as they whisked past a set of twin doors. Alternating wall sconces were lit, leading down a long hallway beset by doors of varying colors and sizes. They then swept up a staircase through a door, up another flight of stairs, until Katja wasn't sure she could ever figure out where she was on the map stuffed in her pocket.

"We are almost to my office. It will be safe to speak in there," Sir Geoffrey whispered once they got out of earshot of a few robed passersby. "Can't let just anyone see what we are doing."

She knew she didn't have any magedust to give the strange man. She needed to find the perfect escape, and luckily, other than the side streets of Theed, there had never been a place easier to get lost.

"I am in no rush," Katja lied.

He led her through a set of doors, glancing back at her to see if she was still following. Katja played along through a few more doors and down a set of halls until she spotted her escape—a set of dimly lit stairs in a lone alcove. She darted to her left, up the stairs, and down a narrow corridor past a few young girls reading from thick textbooks. She then slid through the gap of a door into a chamber occupied by a boy with long black hair who was standing at what looked like a butcher's bench, chopping ginger root into a boiling pot that billowed noxious red fumes. He was holding a sharp knife with nubby fingers. Her heart pulsated when she realized they were cut above the knuckle. Just looking at the boy made her want to run for her life.

"Er . . . sorry," Katja gasped before slamming the door shut and dashing down the corridor past a sleeping tabby cat napping on a desk and up another flight of stairs until she was sure the steward couldn't track her.

She caught her breath as a group of formal ball guests passed, smelling of delicate perfumes, sandalwood, and bergamot. When no one was near, she pulled the map from her pocket, raised it to a nearby wall sconce, and tried to figure out where she was. For a moment, her heart dropped when she remembered that this map didn't include the entire castle, and the possibility of being in uncharted territory terrified her. Still, she spotted the "X" marking the professor's door on the third floor just below the library, which, based on the neat sign on the wall, was directly in front of her.

Relieved, she continued down the corridor alongside the enormous library until she found a narrow staircase, which she descended. Squeezing past a few students stuffing their faces with desserts and bowls of pudding, she entered a dark hallway, the foyer lit by a few scattered candles. She glanced at her map again, tracing her fingers to the foyer on the opposite side of the hall of the professor's study.

When she spotted the door with chipped green paint, her heart fluttered, and she couldn't remember the last time she had breathed. Should she knock, just in case? She checked the hall for passersby, but it was eerily silent, which almost seemed too perfect. Perhaps Stav was more of a professional than she thought.

To be safe, she gently knocked, but to her relief, there was no answer. She twisted the doorknob, but as expected, it was locked. *Easy.* Stav never told her the professor's full name, probably because he was too afraid of listening ears or something of that matter. Still, thankfully, there was a nameplate on the door, and a few faded derogatory carvings that were probably whittled by estranged students and pupils over the years. The worst of the carvings were "blood traitor" and "hang the foul," which were unfortunate to read.

Katja read the nameplate and repeated it to herself as she turned the doorknob. *"Beatrice don Gill."*

The door creaked open, and Katja slipped into the study like hot oil sizzling in a pan, barely making a click as she shut the door behind her. The study was poorly lit, with only a sliver of moonlight from the western-viewing windows to outline the room's edges. Stretched across the window was a large oak desk covered with neat stacks of pamphlets, paperweights, quills, inkwells, and a few intriguing items, such as a brass scale and a centuries-old globe fading with age. Opposite the study was a leather sofa with dimples cratering the cushions from wear, and a large fish tank that looked haunted by looming phantoms in its inky black waters.

Katja spotted a fireplace on one of the walls, pulled back the heavy screen, and thankfully spotted a tiny ember. Quickly, so that it did not burn out, she levitated the ember from its ash bed and blew on it, invigorating its glowing core. Scattered across the room, she spotted dozens of half-melted candles, which she lit with the coal before it crumbled into ash across the floor. She would need to clean that. When there was enough light, she summoned the ash back to the hearth, set the screen back, and pulled the thick curtains over the window so she could get to work in private.

With a bit more light, she wandered across the carpeted floor, noticing the features she had not seen before, such as the enormous shelves lining the walls filled to the brim with books of assorted sizes and jacket colors. The phantoms in the fish tank became bright and bloated goldfish, some with strange appendages on their heads that reminded her of balloons. The pamphlets on the desk were now legible, revealing the leery title *Royal Plots: The Assassination of a Prime Minister* embossed in gold lettering. Inside were sketches of Prime Minister Stoker, along with gruesome depictions of his death, blood scattered around his toilet bowl.

Did the professor know about the assassins who scribbled a red "X" on Francis Stoker's card? She wanted to continue reading, but knew she had to find the amulet. She wondered how Stav, Gwith, Fleck, and Urie were doing at the ball and if the professor was buying their distractions. But she knew Stav was a convincing man if not persistent.

She spun around the room slowly, investigating the high bookshelves, dreading the possibility of secret hiding places among them. The professor might have hollow books with carved-out pages, making a perfect hiding spot for a small amulet, but would an aging professor go to such lengths? The professor would probably put it somewhere clever but within arm's length. She scanned the desk, opened the cabinet and drawer one by one, and sifted through the clutter, but she did not find it.

Something grazed her leg beneath the desk, causing her to jump, but when a black and white cat leaped onto the fish tank and started licking its paws, it put her at ease. She sighed in relief and carefully petted the cat, who purred as she slid her fingers from its ears to the tip of its tail.

"Is this your home, Mr. Cat?" Katja whispered. "You sure are friendly to burglars."

The cat ignored her, stretching its long hind legs, and stared down a small vent at the fish hovering in the water below. Its green eyes focused intensely, and then, in one swift strike, the cat clawed the goldfish out and chewed it viciously until it died.

"I don't know if the professor will like what you did there," Katja said, watching the other goldfish scurry around the musty water. "Do you know where the professor hides her jewelry?"

The cat ignored her and continued scarfing down the fish.

Katja checked the rest of the room, looking through the first two rows of books on the shelf, beneath and under sofa cushions, underneath the flaps of the carpet, on the mantle, resting on the windowsill, the next row of books, and even inside the cavity of the fireplace and within the ashes. Although it seemed like a stretch, professors were usually eccentric, and she had seen the strange places where people on the streets hid their prized possessions. Sometimes, they buried, ate, hung, or even tossed them to sink to the bottom of Balledore Bay to varying success.

Sink them. Maybe . . .

Katja glared at the fish tank and pressed her face to the glass. The goldfish scattered in every direction at the disturbance as she looked for any sign of a amulet somewhere at the bottom. When there was nothing, she stuck her hand down the vent, and the cat seemed amused by this, as if she would come back up with a goldfish and split it with him for giving her the idea.

Her hand dug into the pebbles, sifting through slime and what she could only imagine was fish scat until she felt something metallic buried near the bottom. Excited, she lunged, spilling water onto the carpet, and retrieved a mother-of-pearl amulet from the watery depths, holding it by its long silver chain. She wiped her wet hand and thanked the cat with a long pat. Then she soaked up the water on the carpet with the fringe of her work gown, tidied the loose cushions, picked up the coal dust from the rug, and shelved the scattered books with a quick flick of her wrist before plucking a hair from the back of her head. Her eyes teared up as she began blowing out the candle, but before she could finish, there was a whistle followed by footsteps outside the door.

Katja stuffed the amulet in her work gown pocket and dove behind the desk, causing the cat to dart across the floor.

The door jostled and opened. The whistling came to an abrupt halt.

"Bitter teeth! What has gotten into you, Freckles?" a soft voice said. "Did you get into the fish again? Your paws are wet!"

The lady waded across the room, the floor groaning beneath each step.

"That wasn't lit before . . ." she stammered. "Did someone break in again?"

"Sorry . . . sorry!" Katja stood. "I was cleaning! Sir Geoffrey let me in to finish up my duties," she said through clenched teeth, which were desperately trying not to clatter.

"You are cleaning?" the lady asked, her expression fierce.

"Did you not want your quarters cleaned, professor?"

The lady frowned. "And how did you manage to get through my locked door?"

Katja quietly reached for a heavy paperweight off the table. Her heart drummed in her chest.

"Don't throw it!" the lady shouted. Her face resembled a red tomato, her hair was so gray it was nearly blue, and half-moon spectacles hung from the tip of her pointy nose. You wouldn't turn that second-age Rohnish stone into a murder weapon, would you?"

"I won't throw it if you let me leave," Katja rebutted, breathing heavily. She eyed the window behind her and tried to size the surface below, but it was far from a survivable leap.

"Who are you?" the lady asked, stepping forward.

"I am a servant." Katja bowed.

"A servant, but you resort to hiding and violence when a tenant returns to their chambers? What did you take from me? Are you one of my students?"

"No."

"Did someone send you? You do not look like an experienced thief or . . . anything, for that matter," the professor said, her deep wrinkles furrowing in her brow. "Poor thing, you are so skinny. Is it food you need? You only had to ask."

Katja eyed the window again and then the door.

"You won't survive jumping unless you suddenly spurt wings," the professor said, straightening her green ball dress. "If you go for the door, I will scream so loud the guards will hear me from the other end of the college."

"Then you leave me no choice . . ." Katja's hand tightened around the weight.

"What? Murder? Do you think you have it in you?" the professor said, petting Freckles, who leaped onto her desk. "You are so young . . . shame . . . did the Arkan Roth put you up to this?"

"Arkan Roth?" Katja asked.

"Don't pretend. Stav, Mr. Fleck, and those other goblins have got you tangled up in this, don't they?" the professor sneered. "They have been stealing from me for ages. Just admit that they sent you! You aren't the first foolish thief to come stumbling into my study, rifling through my things!"

How does she know about all of this? Katja's heart pounded out of her ribcage.

Katja shook her head. "I have no idea what you are talking about."

The professor chuckled. "Will you put that to a test?"

"What do you mean?" Katja said.

The professor sniffed the air and smiled. "You are a Glint."

A chill ran down Katja's spine.

"I hope you aren't just another doomed replacement to serve as their Dustmage. Poor thing . . . you will be dead by the end of the Winterhour. You have no idea what you are signing up for," the professor continued.

What else does she know? Katja wanted to ask, but knew that would mean revealing her alliance to Stav. No matter what, she would ask Stav more about this when she saw him again—*if* she saw him again.

She gritted her teeth and shook her head. "I dunno what you are talking about."

"I will report you to the Sleuths if you don't tell me now," the professor said. "There is so much trace magic littered in the air that it might as well be a bloody crime scene, and once the Magesleuths catch your scent, they don't forget it."

Coming here was a mistake. She should have listened to Portia and stayed at the Maiden Tower. She would hang like Gabrielle and the other witches before the temple bells tolled.

Katja threw the paperweight at the fish tank, cracking it and causing it to leak onto the floor. She dashed for the door, but before she reached the handle, a concussive blast drove her into the sofa, busting her ribs. She rolled onto her back, but the professor was aiming a wand directly at her breast before she could get to her feet. The old woman had a strange smile, like someone who would finally get their revenge after years of injustice.

"Good try, little witch," she hissed. "Now tell me who sent you before I use a truth enchantment on those pretty lips of yours!"

Katja felt the words form on the tip of her tongue, but she swallowed them instead. She would be dead anyway. Why bring the death of more along with her? How could she even consider sending Stav, Fleck, Gwith, and Urie to their deaths? Fleck was rude sometimes, but didn't deserve to hang for this. She took a deep breath and resigned herself.

"I came alone," Katja said.

The professor flicked her wand, muttering something in Elddir under her breath. An invisible hand tugged her hair and yanked it three times before pulling her into the air. Katja swiped and screamed as her scalp burned and tugged, her hair acting like thousands of small hooks digging into her head. One by one, threads of hair snapped, sending agonizing pain down her forehead into her jaw. She screamed and screamed, tears welling in her eyes until she fell back onto the sofa.

"Tell me, or next time, not a single hair will remain!" the professor spat.

Katja's lip quivered. "I told you!"

The professor flicked her wand, sending her into the air again, but Katja wouldn't go down without a fight. Her skin started tingling, and her arms shivered as she reached for the bookshelf to find somewhere to hold onto, but instead, she only sent books tumbling to the ground with loud thuds.

She tumbled to the floor again, this time landing on the spine of an old tome.

"Ready to confess, witch?" the professor scowled, her frown devious.

"I came alone," Katja uttered.

"I think she has had enough," a voice whispered. It was coming from Freckles, who was perched on the desk. "I think she passed."

The professor took a deep breath but lowered her wand. Then, with a pinch of the professor's arm, the study began to vibrate and then swirl around them, transforming into a desolate and seldom-used larder or storeroom with shelves full of bottles, barrels, crates, and a few dusty books with breaking spines and pages instead of the elaborate book collection Katja saw a moment earlier. Instead of a fish tank filled with fish, it transformed into an iron barrel filled with brackish liquid. The fireplace and desk were mostly the same, except that instead of a cat sitting on top of it, a stout man with a long beard sat in its spot. Standing in place of the old professor was Gwith, still dressed in a fanciful green ball gown, although more fitting to her stature.

"I think you went too far this time, Gwith," Urie said, arms crossed, twirling his messy beard hair. "Last time I messed with a girl's hair, they nearly killed me."

Gwith grimaced. "She will be fine. Better off than if she betrayed us, don't you think?"

Urie licked the top of his hands but caught himself before continuing. "I think you are getting too good at this . . ."

Gwith smirked.

Katja's mouth felt like it would never close again. *It was all my imagination.*

"You . . . you tortured me . . ." she stammered, slowly massaging her scalp, pulling a few red strands like freshly cut hay. "I got the professor's amulet! Was this all just a test?"

"It is just a part of our initiation," Urie said, raising a finger to his lips. "We have already made a loud commotion. Let's level our heads and get out of here."

"Initiation?" Katja said.

"It was a test!" Gwith said, her expression stern. "Just be happy you didn't fail!"

"Was there ever a mission?" Katja asked, pointing an accusatory finger at Gwith. She was going to murder Stav for this.

Gwith chuckled. "Oh, there was a mission. It was just on the other end of this bloody castle. Did you think we would send a rookie Dustmage on such a massive heist? You don't know all the spells you need to know to be a true Dustmage."

"Did Stav invent the whole story about him and his old professor?" Katja asked, her blood boiling.

"Professor Gill is very real. Stav didn't lie about that," Gwith smirked. "If we are lucky, he has already stolen the map from her study on the other end of the castle. Urie, have you heard the signal yet?"

"Just a few moments ago. I will see you back at the Warren," he said, uncrossing his forearms and poofing into a cloud of smoke with a snap of his fingers.

"Quick, come with me," Gwith said, opening the door and spilling into the dark corridor.

They ran out of the corridor, down some stairs, and through a door, before Gwith pulled her out of view and huddled them against the wall.

"Did you see that? Castle guards . . ." she whispered, her face so close to Katja's ear that it tickled. "They look like they are searching for someone. If Stav got caught, I would give him so much razz."

Katja remembered Sir Geoffrey Poissont and wondered if he had reported her after abandoning her, and if he was even real. Would he risk them asking what the castle steward was doing, allowing a stranger in through a secret side door he used for smuggling dust? Perhaps he had enough sway over the guards to keep their lips sealed. No matter. There was a chance the guards were searching for her.

"Someone saw me earlier. I barely got away," Katja whispered. "They might be looking for me."

"You could have told me sooner," Gwith blurted, opening the door just a crack to peer through. She then slammed the door shut with wide eyes and hair standing up on her forearms.

"What is it?" Katja whispered.

"A Magesleuth . . . there is a Magesleuth in the castle," Gwith uttered. "Boils! I could use siren magic to slip past the guards, but a Magesleuth changes everything. We need to get out of here . . . with Stav and Fleck or not. Wicked hearts! I was not prepared for this! Damn it, Stav!"

Katja's legs started to shake, and her body still ached from earlier. She was not one to go into fear in times like these, but going from thinking she was going to die to it all being an illusion and back to fear was enough to paralyze her. Was this a test, too? Was it the same Magesleuth she spotted earlier in the square below? They needed to escape this place, and they had to do it without magic.

Gwith tugged on her arm, and they started running back down the corridor. Looking outside the window, Katja could see they were still high in the castle, as the pinpricks of city lights clustered beneath them and the dark horizon consumed the castle like a cape. They wandered into a crowd of laughing students and straightened their posture as they approached a lone guard berating a group of young girls.

When they were out of earshot of the guard, they hurried down a set of stairs. They continued until they reached a solid platform overlooking a crowd of ballgoers stumbling drunkenly to their bedchambers or wherever students and attendees went after they were done merrymaking. They slowed down to avoid drawing suspicion, walking in the opposite direction of the crowd, until they heard the hum of stringed instruments and distant laughter. The air grew warm, and the smell of mixed perfumes, fireworks, tobacco smoke, and sweat surrounded them as they headed nearer to the ball.

"Are you sure it is wise to go this way?" Katja asked, tugging Gwith's dress.

Gwith glared at her. "First off, if you tear my dress, I will murder you. Second, we can blend in better with a crowd. Third, we know an exit exists because that is how we entered."

"You don't think my lack of dress won't bring attention my way? The steward probably tipped the guards off to look for someone dressed like a servant."

"We won't stop and mingle. We are going straight for the exit," Gwith demanded.

Katja had a sinking feeling in her gut. They headed closer to what she hoped was the exit, swimming past crowds of elaborately dressed ballgoers, all with enough pomade and sprays in their hair to replace the mortar on every brick in this castle. The corridor led to a large ballroom with tall ceilings, adorned with chandeliers, strings of pearls, marble statues, balloons, streamers, flowers, wreaths, and various flags and banners. They nudged through the crowd, passing butlers with platters of cheese, tartlets, biscuits, grapes, mead, wine, and other fine refreshments. Katja plucked an olive and a glass of wine and pretended to blend into the crowd despite wearing her servant rags, which made Gwith respond with daggers for eyes.

"I should have torn out every strand of hair from your head," Gwith mumbled.

As they inched toward the front of the ballroom, it became even more crowded as people shuffled away and headed for home. Katja had no idea what time it was, but it felt very late. A breeze of old air wafted their faces, filling them with hope of an exit, but just as their hopes rose, they were dashed as they spotted a crowd of guards swelling at the front door.

"Keep close," Gwith uttered.

They slipped through the front, avoiding eye contact with the guards until Katja spotted the Magesleuth standing like a statue on the steps down into the square. Would it be possible to smell her because she used magic earlier? She wanted to vomit as she tried to avoid its shrouded face, but her curiosity overcame her. Her eyes darted to the Magesleuth's hood, catching a glimpse of a face that looked like some mix of a shrew and an owl, with black orbits for eyes.

The sniffing grew louder and louder.

"Gwith . . ." Katja stammered.

"Keep your head down," Gwith whispered.

Katja held her breath as she instinctively looped her arm in Gwith's. She diverted her eyes to the approaching stairs, but she could see the black shadow in the corner of her eye as she passed. The sniffing grew so loud that it was all she could hear, pulsing against her eardrums and rattling inside her skull. Just before passing the Sleuth, she could have sworn its long, blood-red robe swayed just enough to see monstrous black talons for feet. Still, she couldn't be sure because once they were down the first flight of stairs, Gwith dragged her arm, and they took off into the night, desperate to get as much space between them and that terrible *thing*.

Chapter Sixteen

The walk to the Warren was quiet. A halo glinted on the eastern horizon when they entered the abbey mound and waded among the hundreds of graveyard effigies. When Gwith swapped the small tin soldier toy with her pewter thimble and uttered the name "*Hugo Stavoren*" under her breath, it was the first time they had said anything for over an hour.

It wasn't nearly as silent when they stepped down the coffin stairs and into the hideout.

"Your foresight is lacking! You refuse to see the evidence dangling in front of your eyes and make a decision! I should never have given you so much authority! You weren't ready!" Fleck shouted, pacing in front of the crackling fire.

"You should be thanking me! I got the map! This will set up our plans for the remainder of the year! Once we get the grand maiden's log, we can make even more plans using the two resources together! No one will see it coming!" Stav shouted, leaning over a yellowing map draped over the long dinner table.

"But at what cost?" Fleck said, puffing his pipe and blowing smoke out of his clenched teeth. "You saw the Magesleuths! We all used magic at some point, so we are all at risk of being caught! Our scent is wafting through the halls of that castle like a bakery full of treats! If the Magesleuths don't start knocking on our doors in the next few days, we will be lucky!"

"What will they do without a name or face for the crime? Catching the scent of magic is one thing. Connecting it to a person is another," Stav said. "It isn't like people aren't secretly casting spells and cantrips behind closed doors at that college anyway. Our scent is a strong westward wind, you know, the ones that smell like cow manure coming from the pastures of the Cobb District. It takes just a change of the wind coming from another direction, and our trail will be gone before it leads them to us!"

"I do not like your analogies," Fleck spat, "and I do not like how risky it is here even now! I am leaving!"

"Leaving?" Gwith said as they approached.

"Not for good, although if I want to keep my neck intact, I should consider it," Fleck said. "I will be back in a few days . . . maybe weeks. I do not like this 'smell' in the air and want to ensure no one is hunting my scent."

"And what about us?" Gwith said.

Fleck glared at Katja as her face appeared from the shadows.

"Someone must have tipped the Sleuths off about our doings at the Hearthward Ball. It isn't like them to show up uninvited to crowded events like that," Fleck said. "I suggest you all lay low, too. If you need me, you will have to wait."

Fleck jabbed a finger at Katja's shoulder. "Consider yourself lucky you didn't squeal our names. It might have been our prized *siren* asking you those hard-hitting questions. Next time, however, it might be a district guard, mobster kingpin, or even a bloody Sleuth, and they will do much more than torture you. They know magic far fouler than the pits of our soul are capable of understanding."

Katja didn't know what to say. Nor could she tell if she was being applauded or berated.

Before Katja could respond, Fleck flapped his coat and disappeared into the shadows. The three of them were silent until the iron door slammed shut, and the sound of trapped air hissed off into the distance.

"Boils! Of course, he took the bloody carpet!" Stav said, punching the table. "Guess we will be wandering on foot until he returns."

"Where is he going?" Katja asked.

Stav turned to Katja and frowned. "We never really know, but I think he likes it that way. Probably somewhere far away from Theed."

"He always smells like piss when he returns, so I imagine it is somewhere out by Fox Den," Gwith sighed. "If you have ever been, it is an apt description of what most small villages outside the city walls smell like."

"I was born across the Relian, but Theed is the only home I remember. I don't have any memories of going beyond its tall walls," Katja said. "My mother told me it is a wild place filled with wicked cults, murderous clans, and changelings—part men and part beast."

"That is what they tell everyone, but I imagine it isn't so bad," Stav said. "But if Fleck feels more comfortable out there, maybe it is as terrifying as your mother told you."

"I was born in Krone," Gwith scoffed. "It isn't so bad if you have a keen eye and don't wander on your own on the Royal Highway. Using the old forest roads might take longer, but you will live longer and sleep better. There are numerous stars out there, too, like in a painting. Not like what we see here in the capital."

"And it is lawless," Urie said, entering from one of the side rooms. "You can be truly free out there. Our people can use magic as long as they like it and as long as they have the resources they need."

"And most people don't," Gwith challenged. "Magic might be legal outside of Theed, but good luck finding a speck of magedust. There is a reason people tell stories of wandering blotters rampaging through travelers. They take almost everything they can burn, cook, trade, or bleed. A horrific way to go."

"And you said it isn't so bad out there," Stav smirked.

"That is why you've got to have your wits about you," Gwith said. "Blotters are some of the worst people you can meet, but they are about as slow as any other dust addict in the street. They cut themselves so deeply that they grow weak and tired. Some have gotten so desperate that they are missing fingers, ears, and even full arms and legs, and their wounds fill with gangrene! You can ask Fleck all about it when he comes back. He knows all about blotters."

Katja's stomach turned.

"Alright, Gwith . . . enough," Urie said, sitting across Fleck's chair. "We don't know anything about that. You might have grown up in Krone, but that does not represent the entire Commonwealth. There are wild lands out there beyond the great cities."

"He told me some things when drunk," Gwith said.

"I don't want to hear it!" Urie said, taking a swig of firebrandy.

"Don't you wonder about those scars? 'Cause we all know his story about being born with them is a crock," Gwith teased. She sat in Fleck's chair, removing her boots and rancid socks before placing her calloused feet next to the fire.

"You speak foully of the man and take his seat? Do you have any respect left in your stony heart, Gwith?" Urie grumbled, brandy dripping from his lips into his beard.

"You would have any left if you knew what I know," Gwith leered.

"Shut it!" Stav shouted, pounding his fist on the map. "I am trying to concentrate. We might have succeeded in our plans, but we have more to accomplish than gossiping! Fleck is gone, so I will need all of you to work with me!"

The chamber grew silent except for the occasional crack of embers. When no one responded, Stav turned to Katja. "I want you to continue reading about cloaking. It will be useful in our next plot."

"I have already read the entire chapter."

"Read it again! Then we will continue our lesson," Stav insisted.

Katja interrupted. "I have laundry duties in the morning. I think rest—"

"Laundry duties will have to wait then!" Stav shouted.

"I will get in trouble! I am already on a short leash at the tower!"

Stav appeared to be debating his next few words before speaking. "It is a risk I am willing to take."

Katja's jaw dropped, but when his face only emboldened, and he returned to the map, she realized he was serious. She could, of course, leave, sleep in her bunk at the Maiden Tower, and do as she pleased. She had already earned his trust. But there was an itching part of her that couldn't find herself interested in the affairs of the Maiden Tower tonight. The world seemed to expand around her, and watching Gwith turn a plain storeroom into an elegant professor's study made her hunger to know more.

She gazed at Urie. *Gwith had turned him into a cat.*

Chills ran down her spine as she marched to the grimoire. She was done serving. Now, she wanted to learn.

The Maiden Tower could wait.

* * *

Katja's eyes blinked heavily as the letters started to blur and contort on the page. Her forehead fell into the book fold, but she bobbed it upward before drooling over the pages. When Stav entered the room, she didn't notice until he gently patted her on the cheek with the back of his hand.

"I am sorry I was so harsh earlier," he said. "That man, Fleck, knows how to get under my skin. It is always a bit of relief when he leaves."

Katja shook her head and stood up.

"I am not a child. Do you think I haven't heard worse in the soup and bread lines? I was born with people shouting in my ear," she growled, rubbing the sand out of her eyes. "I wasn't the one born with a ruby soother in my mouth!"

Stav tilted his head. "I came in here to apologize, not argue anymore. You are my pupil. I would like you to act like it."

"Weren't you once Fleck's pupil? I hear how you speak to him." Katja knew what she said was uncalled for, but she was tired.

"Fine, do you want to fight? Or do you want to learn how to cloak? The choice is yours," Stav said, returning to the door. "But, if you want to make assumptions about my upbringing, I won't accept it. It isn't what you think."

"Then don't make assumptions about mine either."

Stav's blue eyes softened. He reached for the doorknob but then decided against it.

"A few days ago, I locked you in this room to read, and when I returned, it was unlocked. At first, I thought, 'Does she know?' but then I considered that maybe I forgot to lock it," he said, eyes fixed on the doorknob. "But I didn't forget . . . did I?"

Katja was silent.

"I should have suspected you would figure it out," Stav smiled.

"Not many people are named Stav in Theed. In fact, I have met many people and learned their names, and I have yet to meet one Stav," Katja said. "I knew your father, Hugo, for a little while. He was my first master, but he died before I could learn much more than how to use magedust properly."

"And even your knowledge of magedust is severely lacking." Stav nodded. "I considered that when Fleck asked me to take you on. If my father saw potential in you, then who was I to say otherwise?"

"I was there . . . when he died," Katja whispered, "not exactly when, but I was the first to find him."

"In the bathtub . . . I am sorry you had to witness his murder," Stav said, sitting beside her.

"His murder?" Katja said, although she had always considered it in the back of her mind. "That is a heavy accusation. How do you know who did it?" But deep down, she knew it to be true.

"Yes, but that is a story for another day. Like the story, you will tell me, describing what you did when you went rogue and unlocked this door using my name," Stav grinned. "I've changed my mind about letting you return to the Maiden Tower tonight. Now is the time for your first lesson in *cloaking*."

Stav pulled a wand out of his pocket along with a vial of Vigor.

"We are going to need a lot of this with what we are about to do," he said.

Chapter Seventeen

Stav carefully traced a midline down Katja's face with a pen, marking her forehead, the bridge of her nose, splitting her lips, and down her chin. When finished, he inspected each side of her face so close that his stale breath brushed against her cheek. He wiggled her ears a few times and checked the inside of her mouth with his pen, examining her teeth and tongue before taking a few steps back, pacing with his wand in hand.

"The first thing you need to be wary about with cloaking is *symmetry*," Stav said proudly. "The more symmetry one has, the easier it is to split along the midline and cloak. Oddly enough, becoming a good cloaker is about maintaining appearances, so avoiding fights, brawls, cuts, or bruises unless you want to make it more difficult. It is one of the few materialist forms of magic, but there is no skirting past the requirements. A single pimple is enough to throw off even a talented cloaking enchantment. It is why not many have what it takes to become one, as there are other worthy forms of magic to study that aren't so fleeting."

"Yes, I read this in the grimoire," Katja said. It was complicated to understand, however. She had learned to read from street signs and a few tattered books whenever she stumbled upon them; books were rare finds, especially ones in decent condition.

"One of the reasons we selected you was your symmetry—and because you worked for my mother and the Maiden Tower," Stav said.

"Are you saying I'm pretty, Stav?" Katja batted her eyelashes.

Stav frowned. "One does not have to be pretty to be symmetrical. Even ugly people can be symmetrical."

Katja blushed. "It was just a joke."

He tied his ear-length brown hair into a bun. "Maybe even more important than symmetry is keeping proper tally of your Vigor. Not knowing how much your body spends to stay invisible is dangerous and has led to more-than-terrible ends for those who failed. If you thought kindling from running out of Vigor regularly was excruciating, imagine doing so while your body is folded upon itself! There aren't many worse deaths, and if you do survive, the deformities are often debilitating."

"Be wary of my Vigor, got it," Katja said, reaching for the vial before it was swatted away.

"First, I want you to acknowledge what reserves you already have," Stav said. "Even you know it is wise not to waste previous Vigor."

Katja sighed, closing her eyes and folding her hands on her stomach.

Stav tapped her shoulder after a few seconds of waiting. "You don't know how to measure your Vigor, do you?"

Katja shook her head. "I make a poor witch, don't I?"

"You learned what you could. Many Glints are wandering the streets without an idea of what powers dwell within them, but despite this, you learned levitation," Stav reassured. "My father never taught you about tallying your Vigor reserves?"

"My mother taught me how magedust works, but nothing beyond not taking too much and only using magic when necessary. She was always afraid I would get caught or end up addicted like the others," Katja said, tapping the side of her nose. "As for your father, he never knew I found his secret cache in the tapestry. He never asked me how I got what little amounts I got from the streets. I imagine he would rather know the truth now."

"Where did you find it? You didn't get intertwined with dust merchants, did you?" Stav frowned. "A terrible bunch, all of them."

Katja nodded. "I always knew to avoid them. But if the truth be told, I was always fortunate to stumble onto some unfortunate soul's hidden stash and steal it. The stuff has a strong scent, so I always knew when it was nearby."

"A true Dustmage," Stav said. "Do you know the ability to smell magedust is not normal? Are there other things you smell that no one else seems to be able to detect? Perhaps the smell of hot iron or rusted metal?"

Katja nodded. "That is what it smells like! Are you saying you can't smell magedust?"

"It is a scentless powder, Kitty," Stav said, opening a pouch of green magedust and pinching it between his fingers. "And most people cannot take it raw as you have; that is why we have these fancy serums that turn it into a liquid. It contains enzymes that allow us to tolerate it better. Without that, we turn into the people foaming out of their mouths on the street corner."

"So that is something only a Dustmage can do?" Katja asked.

Stav nodded. "Fleck says that only one in five hundred Glint are born with the ability to smell and digest raw magedust like you. I am one of the four hundred and ninety-nine who cannot."

"And that is why you need me?" Katja asked.

"Those are the reasons we first noticed you, but it doesn't hurt that you work for the Maiden Tower, one of our next targets," Stav said. "But let's not get ahead of ourselves. First, let me cover the basics, and you can tell me what you don't understand."

Katja nodded, but admittedly, she wanted to ask more about why the Maiden Tower of all places would be a target for thieves. There wasn't any gold, gemstones, or anything of high value that she had seen within the whole tower. If anyone knew of the tower's treasure, it would be Katja.

"Let's start with the basics, then. If you want to measure your Vigor, it is quite simple, especially compared to levitation. Some sorcerers have tried to invent gadgets and various devices to measure it, but none have been more accurate than the breath test."

"*Breath test?*" Katja repeated.

"Yes, cup your hand to your mouth and take a sniff," Stav said, doing exactly that. If it smells sweet like honey, then you have plenty. If it smells like iron or blood, you don't have long before the kindling begins. Fleck always told me the sweet spot is somewhere in between. I liken it to the smell of wilting roses—sweet but decaying."

Katja sniffed her breath. "What if it smells like cabbage?"

"Then you probably need to rinse your mouth, but you likely won't die. You will know when it gets bad. You might even remember the taste from the last time you kindled. It tastes like you are sucking on a ball of pig iron," Stav said, puckering his lips. He uncorked the vial of Vigor and handed it to her. "Take a nip."

Katja sipped the vial and handed it back, choking on the sour taste.

"Next, I want you to stay seated. The act of cloaking can be a bit disorienting at first," Stav said, raising a finger to his lips as if to shush her. "Then I want you to place your finger here and close your eyes, focusing on your breath. It doesn't matter what you use to touch your line of symmetry. It could be a twig, a knife, a wand, or even the bones of your enemies—it matters little. We mostly do this to help guide your mind rather than serve any practical need."

Katja followed his instruction and placed her finger across her pursed lips. She followed suit when he closed his eyes, but occasionally, she peeked while he started to take heavily drawn-out breaths. After a few seconds, he breathed so deeply, his face so relaxed that he appeared asleep. She almost snapped him out of his slumber, but before she could, he uttered a word under his breath and vanished, folding from his shoulders like a book.

"Stav?" she gasped.

There was silence, but before she could panic, Stav reappeared, folding outward from his center. Instead of standing in front of her, he was across the room with a mischievous grin.

"Although becoming invisible in this method has many advantages, it does not come without a cost," Stav said. "You cannot speak, touch, smell, or even hear, much like you would imagine a ghost. Fortunately, you can see, but not as well as you do now. It's more like someone looking through a spyglass. It takes getting used to."

"That sounds terrible," Katja said. The thought of it made her feel squished, like she was being buried alive. She thought turning invisible would be remarkable, but if it meant she could only see, then she wasn't sure how intriguing it sounded.

"You are free to find other spells that make you invisible, but most take years of learning or are only available through enchantments," Stav said. "If you want to learn those, you might need to leave Theed."

Katja sighed. "How do you pronounce the Elddir word again? They didn't say in the grimoire. Was it, thudor var?"

"Trill your tongue more. It is more like your mother tongue than mine," Stav said, tapping his tongue on the roof of his mouth. "It is pronounced '*Tudor vasa.*'"

She closed her eyes, took deep breaths for a few minutes, felt the Vigor boil in her belly, and muttered, "*Tudor vasa.*"

As she expected, nothing happened. It never happened the first time with magic, be it levitation or lockpicking, so she was used to it by now. It probably wouldn't work the second or third time either, but she was determined to learn it before returning to the Maiden Tower, no matter how ambitious and unrealistic Stav believed it to be.

"You have to imagine being split . . . folding your material body along the symmetry like one folds a piece of parchment so that it has equal halves," Stav said, dragging his finger down the tip of his nose and chin toward his heart. "Sometimes doing this motion helps."

Katja ran through the steps repeatedly, dragging her finger across her face like a knife and focusing on her breathing so much that she nearly fell asleep. She jolted awake and spoke the magic words, but again nothing happened.

"Nothing," Katja said disappointedly.

Stav nodded. "I still see you clear as day."

"What else can I improve?"

"Just keep trying. Sometimes the key is repetition and diving deeper into meditation," Stav said. "Once you do it, you will know how deep you must plunge into your consciousness. After a dozen times, it will come quickly, and you can do it without much concentration, but getting to that point is difficult. Not everyone can figure out cloaking, including Gwith and Urie."

"Is that because of symmetry, though?"

Stav chuckled. "Perhaps, but even people without perfect symmetry can cloak with enough practice. Sometimes, certain Glints have natural affinities to certain types of magic. There is a whole study on the subject if you want to learn about it one day. It is theorized to have something concerning the stars, but others think the immortal gods chose it."

"And how do you then become *uninvisible* . . . I mean, visible, again?" Katja asked, sweat dripping down her brow as she focused.

"What have you been doing to dispel your levitation enchantments?" Stav asked. "I recommend you do the same."

Katja tugged a lock of frizzy red hair as if rehearsing it. The thought of becoming invisible sounded almost too good to be true. A deep thrill was vibrating in arms and legs as she imagined being able to vanish whenever she pleased and sneak about the Maiden Tower without any of her bunkmates knowing. She would be lying, though, if she said it didn't equally terrify her. What if plucking a hair didn't work and she was stuck invisible forever? More realistically, what if she were stuck being invisible until she ran out of Vigor and died? How knowledgeable was someone like Stav or even Fleck? Her only choice was to trust their intuition, but trust was something she usually didn't offer easily.

In the next hour and a half, Katja attempted to split herself in half to the point that a red line formed on her face. To her displeasure and Stav's impatience, each attempt didn't bring her closer to becoming invisible. In fact, by the end of the lesson, she felt like she took up more space and was more visible than ever. Like a lone ballerina on a stage failing to perform in front of an audience, even though Katja knew it was only an audience of one.

When Kristoff arrived, the first lesson was marked as over, which made Stav let out a weary sigh and cross his arms. She could tell that Kristoff's appearance had changed Stav's mood entirely, making him stark, impatient, and deep in thought. This was made worse when Kristoff loudly knocked on the door and called Stav to join him in his study.

Stav nearly left without saying a word, but then remembered Katja and looked at her with a regretful smile. "We will try again tomorrow."

Katja left the small, dingy room and waved farewell to Urie—who was laboring over a pot of porridge—before making for the stairs to the mausoleum. She took two steps up the steps before a voice grumbled behind her.

"You can't go that way!" Urie hollered, looking up from his boiling pot. "What do you think people would think seeing people come in and out of this place like a damn bathhouse? They would have found the Warren ages ago!"

Katja looked at Urie tiredly. "Then how do I leave?"

Urie pointed his dripping stirring spoon to the door Fleck had gone through earlier, which she knew led to the flying carpet.

Katja frowned. "But there is no—"

"Carpet? Yeah, tough luck! You must do what everyone else without a flying carpet does and climb through the manholes! You don't have to make it more complicated than that," Urie scoffed. *He's tired, too.* There wasn't much sleep being passed among the Warren, so nerves were bound to be raw.

"With your abilities, you don't even have to worry about doors and strange exits, do you? You know . . . being able to poof away as you can," Katja said, wandering slowly to the door along the recesses of the dim chamber.

Urie glared at her.

Katja took the hint and reached for the door, but it was then that she realized that she didn't know Fleck's full name. She turned to Urie, who looked like he would vomit into his bubbling porridge. She wondered if teleporting took a toll on him. Was that why he looked so deathly pale?

Urie groaned, marched to the door, and glanced over at her before whispering something faint under his breath and letting her through the door without another word. She was tempted to ask him why it was so secret, but it didn't seem wise to upset him further. She entered a tunnel on the other side of the Warren wall, which, like before, was dim with undefined edges and bricks coated in a layer of grime.

The door slammed behind her and locked.

With the word *tudor vasa* repeating in her head, she spotted a pinprick of faint morning light beaming through a sewer cap overhead. A series of metal rungs embedded into the brick led to the manhole, and when she climbed it, her hands and boots nearly slipped on their slick surfaces.

When she reached the top rung, she took one disorienting look down and used all her might to slide the manhole cover, droplets of rain pattering on her face. She peered out of the hole and looked in every direction, but she was surrounded by wooden beams that acted like a roof over her head. She watched as boots stomped across the streets just beyond the wooden fortress, like hundreds of matches striking the strip on a matchbox—the dust cloud in their wake resembling a flash of smoke.

She stepped out of the manhole, slouching beneath the wooden beams and roof, slid the cover back over the hole, and scurried to a less busy portion of the road lined with hedges, which provided the spot with considerable privacy. When she could finally stand, she peered at the wooden contraption she had stumbled into and realized she had come through the bottom of the gallows.

If only the guards knew what's brewing just beneath their feet.

Katja snuck through a gap in the hedges and joined the dense crowd, making way for the trolley to bring her back to the Maiden Tower.

Chapter Eighteen

When Katja arrived at Maiden Tower, the morning dew was still beading on the ends of every blade of grass like shiny gemstones that washed away on your shins before you could collect them. In the distance, fog was retreating from its dominion over the long lawns and alleyways like narrow ghoulish fingers crawling back into the caves of the underworld as light conquered the night. Mornings in Theed were lovely, if you didn't have anywhere to be, but like most times, Katja was running late.

Her shoulders were slouched, her eyelids felt heavy and swollen, and her legs felt like they had been beaten with a cobbler's mallet. She received a few judgmental glances as she dragged her tired body up the stairs to her dormitory, but for once, fear didn't have that similar taste in her mouth as it usually did. Katja felt defiant, as if she had just found the love of her life—or something far more important than anything this crooked tower could possess. The girls stared at her as she entered the doorless chamber, but it wouldn't be long before her training would be complete and she could vanish before their eyes—then, their stares would be meaningless.

"Where have you been?" Claudia said as Katja entered their dormitory.

"Probably getting in scraps with the other beggar girls in the alleyways," Astrid said with a heavy tongue.

Jeane and Victoria giggled but seemed too mortified at Katja's ragged appearance to say anything. If Katja was honest, she didn't look fit to live in civilized society with her sweat-stained work clothes, rough palms, sunken face, and dastardly tangled locks that looked more like red moss than hair.

Katja didn't mind them, but she started panicking when she noticed the sheets, pillows, and linens at the ends of every bunk, only to find bare mattresses.

"They did sweeps today?" Katja said, her fingers quivering.

"Yes, is something wrong?" Claudia said. "You don't have anything to hide, do you?"

"No, of course not," Katja lied, eyeing her pillowcase on the floor. *The wand is gone.*

Her heart pounded as she checked around the bed and in her drawer, but there was no sign of that wooden rod anywhere.

"Sure seems like you were hiding something," Astrid grimaced.

Katja was too tired for this. "When did the prefects come through?"

Jeane glanced at the clock on the wall. "Half an hour ago."

Katja didn't care what the others thought. She tore through her pile of bedsheets and even delved into Portia's, which were stacked next to hers. She checked under the mattress, under the frame, in her cabinets, and in every possible place the wand could have rolled off to, but it was nowhere to be found. She was as good as dead. They had found a magical item hidden among her things and would report it to the city watch. They would drag her out of the Maiden Tower just like Gabrielle and hang her in front of the roaring crowd above the Warren for all of the Arkan Roth to see.

She cursed under her breath. Before she left, she knew the possibility of a dormitory sweep, but she got too distracted. Too distracted, gaining the trust of thieves and learning sorcery. When she repeated it in her head, it all sounded like the work of nightmares. The kind of life that mothers and fathers warned their children about while they sat around the dinner table. *Don't get caught up with magic folk. Don't do something that will get you hanged.*

"You aren't ever going to get it back," Claudia said, pointing to her identical cabinet. "I hid a few knots in mine and never saw them again. They even took the ivory brooch my grandaunt gave me in her will."

"You are right, Claudia," Victoria said, tapping the fish-shaped red birthmark on her cheek. Without it, they would never be able to tell if it was

Jeane speaking. "They took a pair of socks from me that were not part of the Maiden Tower uniform. I think they secretly loathe us all. I bet they took that lovely red dress from that girl on the ninth floor who finally found hers after it went missing for weeks. They tried to blame one of us, but we know it was a lovely dress, and Prefect Haggerty would love to fit into one of them again to revisit her glory days.

"Shhh . . . not so loud, Vic!" Claudia shushed. "I hear someone coming."

Portia turned around the corner, her face surprised when she saw Katja.

"We should leave before we are late," Astrid said anxiously. "Good luck finding what you are looking for, Kat."

As Portia entered, Claudia, Astrid, and the two twins squeezed through the doorway like a flock of sheep, the smell of mixed lavender, rose water, and honeydew wafting by as they left. When their footsteps disappeared down to the powder room, Portia pulled Katja by the sleeve, leading her across the hall into the seventh-floor bathroom, filled with steam, running water, and the distant singing of a showering girl echoing off the tiled walls. The singing was off-key, but Katja had heard far worse over the years.

Portia pulled her into an unattended shower in the bathroom and drew the curtains so no one could see. She pulled Katja's wand out of her back pocket. "Missing something?"

Katja gasped. "Where did you . . . why do you have that thing?"

"Thing? I think you know damn well what this thing is," Portia snapped. "If it weren't for me finding it beneath your mattress, the prefects would have dragged you to the gallows themselves!"

"Someone must have hidden it there," Katja muttered out of habit. She could tell by Portia's frowning face that she was not convincing.

"You want me to believe it was one of the other girls? Claudia? The twins? Astrid?" Portia whispered, her tongue slicing the air like a knife. "I thought you were smarter than that . . . than to hide something so dangerous in such an obvious place. The Maiden Tower is no place for storing a secret diary, let alone this."

Portia wiggled the wand in the air, then pressed it into Katja's chest.

"What are you going to do?" Katja whispered, arms shaking nervously. "Are you going to tell?"

"I should . . . but of course, I am not going to report you, Kat," Portia said, her gaze softening. I can't stand hearing of another girl being harmed in this tower, let alone my friend."

Katja didn't know what to say.

"Where did you go last night?" Portia asked. "You didn't have anything to do with the news at Hartwind, did you?"

"News?" Katja asked.

Portia sighed. "Yes, about the professor. It was all over the morning paper."

Katja remembered the map that Stav and the others had stolen, which they had draped over their war table. Portia had always been loyal to Katja and the closest thing she ever had to a friend in the Maiden Tower. Katja's life was in her hands. She wasn't used to trusting people, but had no other choice, like walking out on a narrow tree branch.

"It was just a robbery. The professor has been working against my people for decades. She isn't a good woman," Katja said.

"*Just a robbery?*" Portia gasped. "The professor is dead."

"Dead?" Katja said a little too loudly, and the echo reverberated through the bathroom.

Portia nodded, her eyes haunted. "You didn't . . .?"

Katja grabbed Portia's shoulders and hoped she could read the truth in her eyes. "Of course not! I would never!"

Portia handed her the wand, and Katja stuffed it in her pocket. "I promise you I did not . . . *murder* . . . anyone."

The thought of Stav, Fleck, Urie, Gwith, or any of them murdering Professor Gill ran a chill down her spine. Suddenly, she felt very ill, like she was going to vomit. Was she such a fool? Of course, a group of bandits living beneath a cemetery could kill someone. Who were those buried in the yard above? She had lived in the streets among men and women far less organized than the Arkan Roth, who had murdered. Why would she believe more sophisticated people wouldn't? Just because they were Glints? She lunged onto her knees and gagged, but nothing came up except for a guttural belch. Her arms shook as she wiped drool from her chin.

Had she been too distracted by the smoke and bright lights of magic to see the ghouls behind it all? She wanted to march to Stav and confront him now, but with the news in the morning paper, he likely already knew that she knew.

Could she ever return to the Warren? Was it safe? Her head spun as Portia rubbed her back and tried to hold her messy hair back from her face.

"Your secret is safe with me," Portia said. "But once I am gone, it might be hard to protect you. If Claudia found out, you already know the guards would be raiding the Maiden Tower."

Katja straightened. "Thanks, Portia."

Portia nodded. "I am leaving soon. If you need a safe place away from those not in the Maiden Tower, you're welcome to come to my family's estate in the Lord's Park. We live across from the old lighthouse. It is a bit famous over there if you haven't seen it for yourself. It is crooked, like a poorly tapped nail. Sort of like the Maiden Tower."

"Thank you, Portia," Katja said. "But I should be fine."

Portia rubbed Katja's shoulder. "You are going to leave them, aren't you?"

Katja pursed her lips. "I dunno. I need answers."

"Just be careful out there," Portia whispered, peeking through the shower curtain. "I should leave before someone notices us. Next time, don't hide that . . . *wand* . . . in the Maiden Tower. Do you want Prefect Haggerty to be the one to hand you over to the guards? She would be too pleased."

"Thanks again, Port," Katja whispered. "I will be fine."

Portia stepped out of the shower but, before leaving, twisted the shower knob. "First things first. Take a shower. You smell like a barn."

Katja would have customarily been annoyed, but instead, she basked in the lukewarm water as thoughts swarmed her mind like a rising tide. She closed her eyelids as visions of Stav driving a sharp blade into her belly flashed before her eyes. Images of warm blood gushing down her legs and swirling into the drain filled her mind. But instead of blood, brown, dirty water circled the drain as she stripped off her grimy work clothes that clung to her skin like strands of cooked noodles. The distant toll of the clock tower chimed just as she turned off the water, which meant it was too late to join Miss Frisbie downstairs for laundry duties. Her heart sank once more as she braced for the inevitable punishment that would likely come her way. She took a deep breath, determined not to fail two daily obligations. She stepped out of the shower, the steam thick and swirling around her as she wrapped a fresh towel around her body and dried off before making it back to her dorm to get dressed.

When Katja was dressed in her red maiden gown, she made for the powder room, where she joined the rest of the maidens to get dolled up before their assignments. She took a seat, and Prefect Haggerty tugged the comb through her knotted red hair firmly, as if there was some pent-up anger behind each forceful yank.

Katja barely noticed as she gazed past her reflection in the mirror, the horrors of the night before repeating in her mind like a nightmare. It wasn't until Prefect Primrose set an envelope on her vanity with a grunt that she broke her trance and remembered where she was.

"From the grand maiden," Prefect Primrose said before turning to comment on another girl's hair. Prefect Haggerty did not seem pleased by the arrival of the letter.

Katja took the letter and broke the grand maiden's wax seal with trepidation. When she started reading the letters, her jaw nearly dropped.

Ms. Rosdyre,

Your delivery has reached my hand, and your findings are most curious. In recognition of this service, I grant you ten knots and declare your penal debts settled. You are hereby released from your duties.

Should you stumble upon further curiosities, bring them to me as our pact demands.

Grand Maiden Argaut

Katja could feel Prefect Haggerty breathing down her neck as she tried to read the letter.

"She is letting you off easy. It would have been a year of labor if it were up to me," the prefect sneered, finishing powdering Katja's cheeks.

"Thankfully, it isn't up to you," Katja smiled before getting up from the vanity. The wand stuffed in her stockings pressed firmly against her thigh, obscured by her dress. She left the Maiden Tower and made for Stavoren Manor, retracing many of the steps this morning.

She boarded the trolley, looking over her shoulder as a sinister feeling overtook her. She felt paranoid, like the kings and queens of old, marked for death in their final days. But instead of finding usurpers with drawn knives, she found bystanders and people going about their lives. Occasionally, she would hear the faint sound of sniffing breaking through the mundane chatter of the crowd, but it would disappear before she could pinpoint where it was coming from.

For the first time, it was a relief when she spotted Stavoren Manor's tall roof jutting over the horizon as she entered the countess's garden, which always felt like entering another world. She approached the front door, noticing the overhang where she and Stav had sat days earlier, half expecting him to be basking in the sun among the shingles, but the ledge was empty.

The countess was not there this morning—a relief, as thoughts ruminated in Katja's head. She dusted the blinds, wiped the countertops, watered the flowers, scrubbed the floor, and cleaned the countess's heap of delicate dresses and skirts, all with the help of a swish of her finger. At first, she tried using the wand like she imagined the wizards in the old stories, but it didn't respond, so she put it away and continued her day. Perhaps there was something she still had to learn to use correctly.

She debated whether she would return to the Warren. Thieving was one thing, but murder? Kristoff chased Lord DeGrom into the wilderness. What chance did a simple chambermaid have against their crew if she decided to separate from them? There was no way they would trust her to keep her lips shut all her life. Even if she were silent for five years, who is to say she could stay quiet for decades? An entire lifetime? Her heart sank at the prospect.

If they could murder the professor, they could murder her—but she had to return. The opportunity might never arise again to learn magic beyond basic levitation. Then she would work for the Maiden Tower until she was gray in the temples like Prefect Haggerty. She would know how to cloak, leave, and never seek the Arkan Roth again. After all, she might as well learn from them while she had gained their trust.

When she was done with her assignment, Katja plucked a hair, wiped her brow in the bathroom sink, took a few sips of the countess's Stellish wine, and left for the Warren without having to say a word to Gavin. She could smell the scent of cigars burning in the count's old study before leaving and waved to a set of new gardeners trimming a hedge, basking in the golden sun. She still felt guilty for the last gardeners, but she bowed her head and marched toward Puffer Square, which was surprisingly bare due to the lack of hangings.

She snuck past the abbey alleyway toward the graveyard, where she noticed a few new additions to the shrine, distinguished by their lack of rust and fresh wooden handles gathered near the front. *Pitchforks. Why pitchforks?* She pondered as she noticed a pile of splayed roses, tulips, and thistles sitting at the prongs stabbed into the ground. She saw a pale stone with disturbed dirt further into the shrine, where someone had recently been buried. The headstone was blank like all of the others.

When she reached the mausoleum, she felt relief from the glaring sun and tied her hair into a bun. It was sticking to her neck, slick with sweat. She found a small tin soldier sitting in the gargoyle's mouth and returned it to the altar. What would she use to replace it? She returned to the shrine and plucked a thistle from the pile, hoping the departed wouldn't mind giving up one flower.

"Mind if I borrow this?" Katja said, patting the pitchfork before returning to the gargoyle and setting the violet thistle flower in its mouth before spitting into the right coffin and knocking three times upon its rickety lid. "*Hugo tar Stavoren*," she uttered.

The coffin slid open, revealing the familiar staircase leading into the shadows. Katja took a deep breath of rancid air, wondering if she was making a terrible mistake before stepping into the Warren, where she knew Stav would likely be stirring.

Katja lowered into the Warren, but it was eerily dark and silent. She squinted, using the wall as her guide and the faint light beaming in from the ceiling. Wading through the shadows, she came upon Fleck's chair and took a seat. Her senses alerted as something scurried along the chamber's edges.

"Stav?" Katja whispered.

"Is someone there?" a strained voice called from the back of the chamber.

Katja straightened. "Stav, is that you?"

She fumbled her hand along the floor next to Fleck's seat and the mantlepiece, coming upon a box of matches, books, balled-up newspapers, and a few empty bottles of firebrandy, which clanked loudly against each other. She struck the match, walking closer to the voice down the corridor, and stumbled upon the pen full of quails and goats whose glowing eyes approached her excitedly. In the corner of the room, she found the haystack she had fallen onto days prior. When she brought the fire nearer, she saw a pair of yellowing eyes and a boyish face staring at her.

"You . . ." Katja said, taking a step back with surprise. "What are you doing here?"

"Hello . . . do you have any dust? I can barely move," the boy said, crawling on the floor in agony. His pale skin looked wet, and his ear-length brown hair was slick. "I just need a little bit and will be out of your way."

"You are poisoned. You need the antivenom, not more magedust," Katja said, lighting a new match as the flame drew near her fingers. "Do you know where they hide it?"

"Dust . . . dust . . . dust!" the boy shouted. "Give me dust, witch! I don't need anything else!"

Katja debated letting him die. Would the goats eat his corpse? She pet one of the eager goats, found a metal bin full of fresh hay, and fed it to them, making them excitedly flock to the gate. She then tossed a few handfuls of hay into the crowd and some pellets to the quails.

"You would feed them before you save me?" the boy shrieked, crawling across the floor, his hand smearing a pile of goat scat.

Katja shrugged before beginning her search for the antivenom, recalling Stav fumbling through a drawer in his bedchambers. When she entered Stav's room, she was relieved to find it empty. She discovered several glass vials full of red serum and took one and returned to the yellow-eyed boy in the quail pen, who had once filled her nightmares.

"This isn't what I asked for!" the boy shouted.

"But it is what you need," Katja said, watching him clench the vial in his hands. "If you break it, I won't get you another. You will die a horrible death if it isn't too late already."

The boy clenched his teeth, reluctantly chugged the vial, and shattered it against the wall. "Now, kindly get me the dust that I was promised."

"Promised you?" Katja said. "For what?"

"It's a secret," the boy smiled. "You are that red-haired hag I was paid to follow, aren't you? I remember that gown. I sure tricked you! You thought you could fool me with two knots! You are a fool, girl!"

"You are a child," Katja snapped, blowing out the matches as they threatened to sear her fingers and struck a couple more. "I got what I needed, and you led me straight to the Warren."

The boy frowned. "I would have thought you would be dead by now. Now go fetch my dust, hag!"

Katja clenched her fists, but a cool breeze caressed the back of her neck before she could respond.

"Here is your payment," Stav said, tossing a small pouch at the boy's feet. "If you ever call Katja a hag again, I will ensure you never spot another morsel of dust. You hear me, Jasper?"

Jasper nodded. "Yes, of course, Mr. Stavoren."

"Stav . . . call me Stav!" Stav said. "Don't make me regret hiring you."

"Yes, milord! Of course!" Jasper bowed, fingers fidgeting as they pulled the drawstring.

"Good," Stav scoffed. "When you are done, I want you to collect all of this quail and goat dung and get all the good eggs. Remember, I will rip out your tongue if I see you stealing anything!"

Jasper spilled green powder onto the ground, but he didn't seem bothered as he buried his nose into the heap, staining his skin a sickly hue. Stav blew out Katja's match and wandered down the corridor to Fleck's chair and jabbed his wand toward the hearth like a dagger, sending fiery tongues to lick the brick mantlepiece.

"You really shouldn't feed his addiction. Besides, that is a lot of magedust that could be used better, don't you think?" Katja said. She couldn't help but see him in a different light. Those same eyes likely watched the light leave Professor Gill's eyes. Her sinister feeling returned.

"The boy will be lucky to make it to adulthood," Stav said, sitting next to the fire, searching for an unemptied bottle of firebrandy. He found one with a bit of brown liquid left and took a heavy swig. "He is better used doing something useful for his fix rather than cutting purse strings on the street."

"What did you hire him to do this time?" Katja asked, not sure she wanted to know the answer.

Stav swept his thick hair out of his face. "He has been keeping tabs on someone I worry about dearly."

"Your brother?" Katja asked.

Stav chuckled. "No, not Kristoff. My mother."

"The countess? Why?" Katja asked. Then she remembered that Countess Auriella had been absent today with no explanation. "Did something happen?"

"It is a long story," Stav said.

"I've got time," Katja smiled. "The grand maiden was nice enough to give me a pardon from my extra duties."

"Is that right? Do you know why she would do such a thing?" Stav asked, his thick brow furrowed.

Katja couldn't tell him about the cards she had stolen. "I guess she pitied me."

"I have heard the grand maiden isn't compromising, so that comes as a surprise," Stav said, looking at her suspiciously. "She might be the most secretive woman in Theed aside from Queen Margot herself. I have tried to send spies to the Maiden Tower before, but she has some unbreakable enchantments preventing us from reaching the highest stories of the building. I predict it is a very ancient magic, but how the grand maiden learned it . . . I would love to know."

"Why do you want to spy on the grand maiden?" Katja asked, perplexed.

Stav chuckled. "I already told you why we selected you. Not only were we spying on my mother, but we also happened to stumble upon a far greater treasure than we had ever expected—a Glint employed with the Maiden Tower. You will play a significant role in our next major move. But now we must wait for the guards and Magesleuths to lose our scent and for Fleck to return from his hiding spot."

"You want me to break into the Maiden Tower?" Katja asked, a shred of horror crawling down her neck.

"Not 'break in.' You simply enter your own house! So long as you are contracted with the Maiden Tower, you are free to walk within it, correct?" Stav grinned, taking another swig of brandy before passing it to Katja, who took a seat.

"As far as I know, but I still don't know how to cloak," Katja said, sniffing the brandy before taking a small sip. It burned down her throat all the way down to her belly. "And Hartwind College was just a test."

She hoped he would go into the mission at Hartwind College and dismiss her fears about his involvement in the professor's murder, but instead, he moved along.

"Well, that is why we will review your second lesson today," Stav said. "So long as we don't get too drunk."

A foul wind swirled into the chamber, and a black silhouette entered. Kristoff crossed the room swiftly, disrobed his coat on a rung, and paced before the map—the professor's stolen map.

"It's good to see you, brother," Stav said, his eyes like daggers. "Where have you been?"

"Only quelling the flames you created, brother," Kristoff scolded, turning to look at them. He revealed a bloodied bandage covering his right ear. He had the same eyes, nose, and chin as Stav, except his skin was paler, his hair a dull wheat color, and his mouth bore a permanent scowl.

Stav leered. "What happened to you? Mother finally smack you hard enough to draw blood? We all know Father wouldn't lay a hand on you, but Mother didn't mind."

"Mother wouldn't lay a hand on me," Kristoff spat, revealing a bandaged fist. "I ran into some trouble on the road. Where is Fleck?"

"Hiding again," Stav said. "Jasper said Mother found another man. She has been having a lot of success trying to replace the empty hole our father left her at her age. She has more success with the opposite sex than either of us ever had. Strange, wouldn't you think, given her age?"

"She is the dowager countess with prestige and wealth," Kristoff said. "She has aged well for someone eighty years of age. Some people have all the luck."

"She has aged a little too well. I'm not sure if I would attribute it entirely to luck. Perhaps divine intervention," Stav chuckled. "But you are right, brother. Mother could be a rotting corpse, and someone would still try to marry her."

Katja wanted to blurt out that she knew their mother was a Glint like their father and that Auriella had operated the tapestry all along. She reached for the wand, intending to show them she knew the countess's darkest secret, but she still wasn't sure what she was permitted to know and what knowledge endangered her life. What if Portia was right? What if she was making a big mistake and should never have returned?

"You don't have to talk about Mother with such a harsh tongue," Kristoff said. "It hasn't been the same since she got shackled to that manor, and then Father died. Before then, she was brilliant. I am sure that brilliance is still in there deep down inside if you are willing to find it."

Stav nodded. "Brilliant if you mean at destroying everything our family stood for . . . sure, I will give you that."

Katja felt uncomfortable as an awkward silence filled the air.

"Kat, let's practice cloaking. We can do it right here, and if Kristoff has any advice, he can give it as he pleases," Stav said, raising his wand. "However, he won't be much use with that bandage on his face. No amount of natural symmetry can fix that."

Kristoff waved at his brother dismissively and sat at the table, scribbling notes onto the parchment so fast it seemed his fingers might tear. Did he notice the cards missing from his coat pocket? If so, would he ever suspect her?

"Pay attention!" Stav said, flicking Katja's forehead.

"Don't do that!" she barked, diverting her attention to Stav's warm face.

How could that face murder? He sometimes seemed hardened, but was he capable of taking a life? Her worries melted away slightly as she watched him close his eyes, press the length of his wand against his nose down to his lips, and mutter the Elddir words:

"Tudor vasa."

Chapter Nineteen

Hours passed, and the light shifted across the chamber, turning a radiant red hue as the sun crossed the evening sky, but Katja was no closer to turning invisible. Nor was she any closer to finding out what truly happened the night the professor was murdered.

Sweat dripped down Katja's brow, and her eyes grew weary as she focused on the boiling fire in her chest. Her finger, now shaky, pressed against her dry lips. Her shoulders felt heavy, and her neck kinked as even Fleck's leather seat grew uncomfortable. No seat could prove comfortable after three hours, and she was far less drunk than Fleck usually was when he sat here late into the night.

"*Tudor vasa*," Katja said, her lips quivering.

Stav sighed. "Still nothing. Is there a scar or mole I do not see, hidden somewhere on that face? Perhaps behind an ear? Maybe beneath all of that makeup?"

Katja snapped, "How do you expect me to be able to focus with you sighing all the time? Could you make it any clearer how you feel about my progress?"

"I'm just breathing. It is hot in here," Stav said, pulling back his hair, slick with grease.

Katja closed her eyes, pressed her finger to her lip, and focused every fiber of her being on turning invisible and folding along where she felt her body was perfectly centered. Exasperated, she gasped for air, not realizing she was holding her breath the entire time. Once again, the results of her efforts were dismal.

"You rushed that time," Stav sighed heavily.

"See!" Katja pointed. "You are always sighing. Just admit you regret picking me as the next Dustmage!"

"You do sigh often, brother," Kristoff interjected as he looked over the maps.

"Just keep trying, but don't rush this time!" Stav grumbled.

"Maybe you aren't as good a trainer as you think!" Katja scowled.

"You read the book. I am only manifesting the text physically so you can see it work. I have not doctored anything!" Stav groaned. "Try again . . ."

Katja clenched her fists, but heard a loud bang followed by a puff of smoke before she could counter. Urie walked from the center of the cloud, his thick brows furrowed and his expression grim.

"I spotted a Sleuth snooping around the perimeter," he whispered breathlessly, "sneaky bastards."

Stav straightened. "Hexes! Where about?"

"It's just north of the abbey. Too close for comfort if you ask me," Urie said, looking up at the ceiling.

"And you are sure none of them caught your scent? It only takes a little bit," Kristoff said, elbows digging into the table as he massaged his temples.

"I am certain," Urie said, although his face looked frightened, "and if anyone were to get caught, it would be Fleck, but he is far away from the Warren now."

"Where is Gwith?" Kristoff said. "Is she accounted for?"

"I don't follow everyone around, Kristoff," Urie scoffed. "I am not her handler, but I am going to keep watch." His face was tense. "I could use some help."

"I will go with you," Stav said, standing up. "Katja, keep practicing in my absence. I will be back."

Urie and Stav disappeared into the shadows, leaving Katja with Kristoff in a den of eerie silence. She glanced over her shoulder and into the vents where the crowd's footsteps sifted overhead. She imagined the Sleuths' blood-red robes, horrific masks, and haunting snorts as they stalked the yards above their heads. She closed her eyes and tried to focus on cloaking, but the thought of a Magesleuth tracking them like a hunter and its prey was terrifying.

"You are missing something," Kristoff said.

"Missing what?" Katja said, tying her hair back.

"The trick is to hum," he said, lighting a skinny cigarette between his teeth. "It stimulates the cleaving process required for cloaking."

"Humming? I didn't read anything about that in the grimoire," she said, resting her head in her palms.

"A lot of things are not in that grimoire," Kristoff said, dipping a nib into ink and jotting across a scroll. "My father was a talented sorcerer, but his mind wasn't open to experimentation. Some things are best learned outside of rules and books. One of those is humming."

Katja sighed and reluctantly tried his advice. She began humming so deeply that her teeth rattled. She pressed her finger against her lip, closed her eyes, and uttered the enchanted words. To her surprise, a jolt of static prickled down the grooves of her spine to her toes. When she opened her eyes again, one of her hands was missing. Her heart fluttered as she noticed not only was her hand missing, but half of her body was fading and iridescent.

"With enough practice, you will be able to cloak the rest of your body," Kristoff said, glued to his writing. "My brother is a serviceable wizard but lacks patience in his studies. How can anyone expect him to extend what was already thin to a new pupil?"

"You would take me in for yourself?" Katja asked.

"I could, but I am more interested in what doors you open."

"You are interested in my lockpicking skills, then?"

Kristoff turned to face her, his deep-set blue eyes nearly black. "No, I simply like your access to the grand maiden."

"I don't have as much access as you might believe."

"More than I." He licked the tip of his quill and started scribbling wildly, "My brother, Urie, Gwith . . . Fleck . . . they are too cautious. We must strike when the iron is hot, and when the grand maiden least expects it."

"I was told I need to be able to master cloaking before our next mission," Katja said. "And what of Fleck?"

"We do not need Fleck. He is too paranoid anyway," Kristoff said.

"So, what would you have me do?" Katja asked. "Raid the Maiden Tower, half invisible?"

"You will sneak into the grand maiden's chambers, and once you do so, you will find the Maiden Tower's dossier and bring it back to me," Kristoff said, folding his arms. "The dossier is reported to be notated on an enchanted scroll that appears blank and only reveals itself when the correct words are spoken."

"I am not going to risk being caught to appease someone I barely know," Katja declared. "I would rather discuss this further with the rest."

Kristoff nodded. "Wise, but that won't work. As I said, the others work far too slowly. We will be caught, arrested, quartered, and hanged before Stav and Fleck feel confident enough in you to finish this assignment. This might be the most crucial operation we as a team work on because the rest of our work hinges on the success of this one."

"And your answer is to rush in unprepared?" Katja admonished.

"Your thoughts are so . . . limited," Kristoff scoffed. "This is why Stav and Fleck are both mediocre sorcerers at best and why it has taken years to even get to this operation. Sometimes, I question if they truly want to change the world and make life better for our people, or if they are so bloody used to death and darkness that they have accepted it. Every day those monsters murder another Glint is another strike against us, and they become more emboldened."

"What are you talking about? I thought you were just a group of sophisticated thieves using magic, hoping to strike it rich," Katja said, unable to stop herself from pacing in front of the roaring fire.

"Of course; Stav never told you?" Kristoff uttered. "Have you ever taken a second to wonder why a bunch of magical thieves are still living in squalor? We barely have a stack of crowns to our name, and we dress nearly worse than beggars! We steal maps, books, and other things your typical crew of vagabonds is tossing away in search of gold and silver! No! We are onto something more extraordinary than fleeting wealth. My family has fought that battle for many lifetimes, but it has done little to make us stronger. Once Stav and I die, the Stavoren line will be dried up and buried in the annals of time, but if we carry out *this* . . . we might be immortal in the eyes of Glints who come to arise long after we have died."

Katja stumbled upon her words. She was both invigorated by Kristoff's passion and horrified at the same time. Why were Stav and the others keeping her in the dark about something like this? She had just figured they weren't very successful bandits all this time, but it was strange that a crew with such magical talent wouldn't have walls of solid gold or even a semblance of money. If saving Glints was their plan, was there a motive to kill the professor? Her mind wandered, but it didn't come closer to a reasonable answer.

"Tomorrow night, I want you to sneak into the grand maiden's room," Kristoff whispered, eyes like daggers, "and then I want you to take the dossier and bring it to me. We will be one step closer to saving our people. Isn't that what you want? You saw the many shrines and offerings in the abbey graveyard, so numerous that it is hard to see the ground beneath your feet. I dare say there are enough pitchforks stabbed into that hillside to arm a small riot or uprising. More are added every day! In a strange, spiteful offering by the gods, we have been given a burrow beneath the very gallows that chokes the life out of us like some punishment for being complacent! We can hear the screams of our people in death and the cheers of those boars as they watch. We must do something, or else we will be next!"

Katja could see the fire in Kristoff's eyes that had been hidden all this time. It was a passion his brother had, but far more intense, as if it had been unraveling and repressed for ages. She didn't like how his face looked like a wild beast prowling on its prey.

"I never knew you spoke this much," Katja said. "We should consult with the others first."

Kristoff sighed. "Then I have failed, and another day . . . month . . . year will go by with more nameless graves. Surely, they will run out of space before long."

"I have to complete my training," she said. "If I get caught or fail . . . then you will be even further from succeeding in whatever you are all planning."

"I will tell them your secret," he threatened.

Katja stammered. "What . . . secret?" Her heart raced.

Kristoff was silent for a minute, but then spoke.

"I know you took the cards," he uttered, his voice hushed yet stern. "You didn't think I would notice them missing from my coat pocket? You took my mother's wand, too . . . she won't be pleased when she finds out."

"How?" Katja gasped.

"I am always watching my bedchambers. I have a scrying ball just for these purposes," Kristoff said. "I also know you snuck into the tapestry because the cabinet where my mother locked away her wand all of these years had been reset. Remember to cover your tracks next time you use a lockpicking spell. The next person might guess your name correctly."

Katja's eyes widened. She was caught, and there was nothing she could do about it.

"Stealing from the Arkan Roth is an unforgivable act . . . especially another's wand," he spat. "Such treachery . . . betrayal . . . is on a whole other level."

"I will get them back . . . I swear," Katja said, feeling a wave of nausea.

Kristoff frowned, closing the gap between them with his outstretched wand aimed at her. "I am sure you delivered them to the Maiden Tower the other day, no? That is when they vanished from my coat pocket, and I doubt you would wait to get your reward. I know chambermaids aren't paid well, and . . . we all have needs."

"I can make this up to you," Katja said. "I promise . . . I will get them back."

"You did exactly what you were contracted to do, like a good little witch, and now it is too late. The grand maiden has seen the cards, and there is no forgetting that," Kristoff said. "The damage has been done. But there is something you can do for me that would make me more likely to forget this atrocity."

Katja knew precisely what he was going to say next. Her stomach sank before the words even left his lips.

"Get me the dossier, and all will be forgiven," Kristoff smiled. "Tick tock, Miss Rosdyre."

Katja's fingers clutched the countess's wand stashed in her stocking.

Kristoff's sharp eyes noticed, and his smile grew. "Perhaps if you succeed in fetching the dossier tomorrow night, I will let you keep the wand."

"Tomorrow night?" she said, horrified.

He nodded. "Haven't you been listening? Action is needed. I would not want to be the little girl who fails to complete this plot. If Stav discovers what you did . . . you will have five sorcerers hunting for your head. Not even the Maiden Tower can protect you if that happens, but something tells me the grand maiden doesn't put too much stock in loyalty. You heard about the other witch who got caught using magic among you. I have never seen a execution so swift. Terrible . . . terrible . . ."

"How do I know where the dossier is or even what it looks like? I am sure the grand maiden has hundreds of documents stored in that room."

"Look for a large scroll, perhaps with a marking of an eye," Kristoff said, tapping his cheekbone. "I imagine she keeps it close to her hip. It won't be far from where she sits. It might be the most precious thing she owns."

Katja's hand tightened on the wand as she tried to formulate her thoughts.

"You don't have long," Kristoff said, waving her off with his hand. "Stav and Urie will return soon, and I don't know if I can keep a secret."

Katja fled to the shadows, unlocked the door, and climbed up the slimy rung to the street above, cursing the tears welling in her eyes.

Chapter Twenty

That night, Katja devised a plan.

After she left the Warren and failed to fight back her tears, she remembered something that instantly dried her eyes—*the dumbwaiter.*

The kitchens had a dumbwaiter that traversed through the walls from the undercroft to the grand maiden's quarters at the top. Memories flooded of the night she was first hailed to meet the grand maiden, but it wasn't the terrible meeting that fated the next few months of punitive labor that excited her. She recalled Prefect Haggerty receiving a note through the lofty dumbwaiter—the message: a small inky eye drawn on the corner of the page.

She also remembered the prefects delivering the grand maiden steaming mugs of herbal tea every night. Fortunately, the glowing crystal ball the grand maiden used to spy on her had a limitation. It simply could not see through the tapestry portal, leaving the maiden blind the moment she stepped inside.

That could be a problem. It was unlikely Argaut watched the scrying ball nonstop, but Katja couldn't count on that. Without confidence in her cloaking, she'd have to be very careful to sneak into the grand maiden's chambers unseen.

When supper arrived, Katja was late but sat a few seats from Portia, who cast her curious glances as the sounds of scraping dinner plates and slurping gullets filled the room.

The entire time, Katja kept an eye on the door to the back kitchen, watching the familiar faces she worked with all those months walk in and out like ants. She also took note of the prefects, especially Haggerty, as they scanned the tables and occasionally stared at her as if they knew she was up to something.

One of the prep cooks meandered out from the kitchens and delivered a small yellow note to Prefect Haggerty. Without hesitation, she followed the young cook into the back. Katja recognized the yellow parchment, but she could not read what was on it.

A few moments later, Katja excused herself quietly. She marched to the kitchen door, escaping suspicion thanks to her prior arduous dishwashing duties. Some of the chefs and cooks likely didn't even know the news of her duties being rescinded. But for her plan to work, she had to verify when the grand maiden called for her nightly tea.

In the corner of the kitchen, she spotted Prefect Haggerty swirling a concoction together and adding a mint leaf from a private pantry on top before setting it inside the dumbwaiter. The grand maiden hailed for her tea near the end of supper, just as suspected. Katja turned her back toward the action, facing a sink full of dirty dishes. When the prefect hoisted the dumbwaiter upward and returned through the swinging doors to the dining room, Katja casually opened the pantry with the mint, emptied the drawer, and placed the sprigs of mint into her pocket. Then, she scrubbed a few more plates nervously before returning to the supper table, praying no one would notice that she smelled like peppermint humbugs. Now she just hoped there wasn't another cache of mint somewhere else in the kitchen, but there was no time to confirm.

Katja joined the rest of the girls as they meandered to bed, and listened to Portia and the other girls gossip about their high-society assignments. When Prefect Haggerty came in to snuff out the lights, Katja turned to her side, stuffed the countess's wand up her shirt, and struggled to fall asleep, pondering the next few hours.

The exhaustion of the last few days finally consumed her to the bone, and she had a dreamless night.

* * *

The morning dragged on, and her fingers fidgeted as she drove a pin through her loosened hair to hide the bald patch. She no longer let the prefects touch it, for fear of accusations.

She got ready as usual, darted across town to Stavoren Manor, and, like the previous day, tended to an empty house. According to Gavin, the countess had disappeared again under undisclosed circumstances. He winked as he told her before locking himself into the count's smoking room, likely forging the countess's signatures on checks as was tradition. For a moment, she wondered how much money he had siphoned from the Stavoren war chest. Still, the newly pressed suit, ruby cufflinks, and heirloom ring gave her a hint as she conserved her Vigor and avoided using magic to clean the mostly spotless home, which looked as though it had not been lived in for some time.

The thought of the yellow-eyed boy used to fill her with dread, but discovering what Jasper truly was had stripped away her fear. While she still puzzled over the Arkan Roth's intense interest in Auriella, she tried to convince herself she was overthinking it. Perhaps the Countess was simply on an extended holiday, or had found a new lover. Yet, it seemed impossibly odd that she hadn't notified the Maiden Tower or, at the very least, left a letter.

When she finished her work, she made her way to the Warren, but, as she had the first time, she went through the cold underground staircase that led into the subterranean abyss beneath Puffer Square. She wondered if it was an abandoned path to the dungeons or an armory because it was near the constable's station beside the hangman's block, but she was unsure.

She started whistling, and when she got close enough to the Warren's secret entrance, the creeping spider crawled out from the edge of the wall. Instead of pressing her finger into its fangs, she pulled a glass ampule from her pocket and gently pressed it against the spider's fangs, which looked to be made of brittle glass.

When a few drops of yellow venom filled the bottom of the ampule, she capped it and made her way to the Maiden Tower. Part of her was curious and wanted to enter the Warren to see if there had been any news or what had come of the Magesleuths sneaking around the abbey, but she thought otherwise. She didn't have time. Kristoff gave her this one night, and she could not fail or lose her only hope of learning magic and leaving her life behind.

Supper was mostly the same, but Portia insisted on sitting next to her this time, which was distracting. However, Katja was so nervous that a distraction wasn't so bad. They ate cold porridge and buttered bread for supper. She tried to scarf down a few bites to draw away suspicion, but anything more than that made her sick.

She was too bloody nervous. She took a deep breath and closed her eyes before swigging watered-down milk.

"Is everything alright, Katja? You seem tense," Portia said, her comment drawing the attention of Claudia sitting ahead of her.

"Do I?" Katja said, her voice squeaking. "It was just a long day."

Portia whispered almost inaudibly, "Did you hide it?"

Katja coughed. "Sort of."

"No wonder you are nervous," Portia said.

"Why are you nervous, Kat?" Claudia interrupted. "You have been acting off lately."

"When is she acting normal?" Astrid said.

Claudia nodded in agreement.

"Did you hear about that raid at Puffer Square? Probably one of the biggest by the city watch in ages," Astrid said, her eyes wide. "They haven't announced, but I reckon it has something to do with the murder at the college."

Puffer Square. The Warren. It sat on the very edge of the square, and if one squinted, perhaps the graveyard could be said to spill into the Smoker District. Maybe it wasn't them. *Maybe.* But her stomach twisted anyway. The thought of the city watch marching past the rows of pitchfork murals up the hill to the mausoleum made her chest tighten, a cold spike of fear that refused to fade.

Portia glanced at Katja.

"Serves them right," Claudia snarled. "I must admit that I will be walking the streets more comfortably now, knowing those ghouls aren't sharing it with me anymore."

Prefect Haggerty darted her attention to Claudia and then Katja, her eyes like daggers.

"Let's talk about something less wicked, girls," she scolded. "Just talking about witchcraft spoils my appetite."

"What would you prefer we talk about then?" Claudia scoffed.

The prefects at the ends of the table glared at Claudia in unison, which killed the conversation.

Katja eyed the back door to the kitchen, where a server entered with a pitcher of water. She excused herself, slipping away so fast that Portia's "Where are you going? You have barely eaten" was a whisper in a storm of heartbeats.

She shoved through the kitchen doors, her head down, and started picking up crusted pots and pans, putting them in the sink next to the dumbwaiter. For a few minutes, she waited and waited for the dumbwaiter to slide down, and just when she was about to lose hope, she heard the pulley squeal, followed by the ring of a bell.

At the sound of the bell, a prefect reached for a teacup, filled it from a steaming kettle, and reached for the pantry for mint, but frowned when she realized it was empty.

"Where did our mint go?" the prefect asked the entire room, but everyone was too busy to stop and listen. "Does anyone know where our mint went?"

Katja slid closer to the dumbwaiter, shakily pulled a shiny mint leaf from her pocket, and placed it in the steaming mug of tea before the prefect could object. "Don't worry, I always have a leaf or two on me. I pluck it from the countess's gardens on my way home to freshen my breath."

"To freshen your breath, ey?" the prefect said sternly. "That is very odd, my dear. Very odd indeed."

"You never know when or where you are when you meet the love of your life," Katja grinned nervously. She hoped no one noticed the slick and wilted appearance of the mint leaf, but there was nothing she could do about it now.

"Do you want me to take it out?" Katja asked. "Although I am not sure the grand maiden would appreciate plain boiling tea. What do you think?"

The prefect scanned the room, stress pouring out of her eyes. "No, it is fine."

For a moment, Katja wondered if resorting to poison was going a step too far. Was she no better than the cutthroat in the street or Stav for murdering the professor? If he did murder her, that was. The grand maiden was a powerful sorcerer. If anyone could create an antidote, it was her. But Katja had nothing to fear. She had no other choice.

Before she could ponder more about her decision, the prefect pulled the dumbwaiter up to the top of the Maiden Tower and then waited. Katja nervously stood around for several minutes, waiting for the tea to be served to the top of the tower. When the dumbwaiter returned empty, relief and terror filled her.

There was no going back now.

She continued cleaning the dishes and wiping down the countertops for a few minutes until supper was finished and the prep cooks had left, leaving only the unfortunate few to do the dishwashing duties.

When the kitchen was empty, and she was certain no one would return, she tidied the corner, pressing a finger to her lips, closing her eyes, and murmuring the words, "*Tudor vasa.*" She tried twice more, but the spell still refused to take hold. That was alright. Cloaking would have been convenient, but the mission did not depend on it. Even if she found the dossier, she would not be able to carry it while invisible. She would have to prepare again, casting another cloaking spell to accommodate whatever she chose to take with her.

Katja levitated a heavy pot out of the packed sink and dropped it into the sudsy bath, making a loud clatter and leaving a soapy mess on the floor. When everyone was focused on her convenient distraction, she slipped into the dumbwaiter, folded her knees, and pulled herself up through the shaft, which was far smaller than she had previously estimated.

It took a while, and there were moments when she thought she might get stuck, but eventually she reached the top of the shaft, where only her shallow breaths filled the silence. Everything was shrouded in darkness except for the bluish light of the grand maiden's scrying ball and the faint candlelight nearby.

Katja waited a moment to see if anyone had heard the scraping of metal from the dumbwaiter. When there was no response, she carefully stepped out and held the brake so it wouldn't crash to the bottom of the shaft.

She crept around the chamber's perimeter. The scrying ball and oak desk shone faintly, while a flickering light deeper in the chamber hinted at another space she had not seen before.

Was the grand maiden unconscious? Asleep? Dead? Her stomach sank. She wandered toward the desk near the center of the room, flanked by tall bookshelves with endless volumes. Off to the side, tucked into a shadowed corner, the curious orb glimmered, casting a phantom light on everything it touched.

Her eyes lingered on the back room, flickering with firelight, before she turned her attention to the desk, where a pile of mail sat beside a collection of pens and inkwells in varying colors, a bronze bust of an unknown figure, a letter opener, a ticking clock, and a birdcage that held no bird.

When she reached the chair set at the desk, she slid it back quietly and rummaged through the cabinets, which varied in size and shape. Some of the cabinets were locked, but before attempting to unlock each, she spotted a roll of parchment on a podium beside the crystal ball.

Katja abandoned the desk and crept toward the crystal ball, its depths swirling with pale blue mist. She reached for the roll of parchment and carefully unfastened it from the podium. As she did, it spiraled into a thick scroll, securing itself onto a golden rod adorned with ornate mother-of-pearl end plates, each engraved with the symbol of an eye.

Katja's heart skipped, and her fingers fidgeted, as she knew then that this was the dossier Kristoff had told her about. There was no way that this wasn't it. She unraveled the scroll and brought it close to the orb's glow, revealing a fine list of names and other columns that she could not read in the dim light.

It looked like a ledger. Why would Kristoff need a ledger? Questions swirled in her mind, but she knew her mission wasn't finished. She trotted toward the dumbwaiter, set the scroll on the platform, and started to crawl in herself when she heard a faint cry from another room.

Katja froze in terror, sending the hair on her neck up like the quills of a feather. She listened as mumbling and gasping echoed off the hallowed walls.

The grand maiden . . . she was dying. Could Katja leave her like this to a terrible death? Did she have any options? She didn't have the antivenom and cursed herself for not fetching some in case she needed it earlier, but she hadn't had time. In the corner of her eye, she spotted the glistening of metal resting on the end of the desk. A dagger.

Katja sighed and hid the dagger behind her back as she crept to the far end of the grand maiden's grand chamber and down a narrow hall toward the darkened back room—somewhere she'd never known existed. She pressed herself against the wall and listened.

"Hello? Is someone there?" the grand maiden choked, her voice shaky. "Please . . . help."

Katja debated leaving and living with the guilt of murdering someone on her conscience forever, but the pain in the old grand maiden's voice was too hard to ignore, no matter how cruel she had been sometimes.

If Katja turned invisible, perhaps she could get away with everything she had done tonight, but she wasn't confident. Instead, she found a coat hanger draped with a black wool coat and slipped it on, draping the hood over her face.

After hearing more wails, her guilt won, and she entered the firelit chamber. To her horror, sitting nearly lifeless on the bed was the grand maiden. Her legs were beneath the thick blankets, and her top was wrapped in a silken nightgown. Her face was pale and shiny from sweat. The grand maiden's eyes were sunken and dark, and her mouth was agape and bloody. Every breath came infrequently and of varying depth.

"What have you done . . ." the grand maiden gurgled.

Katja deepened her voice. "I don't have the antivenom. I heard your cries. I didn't mean for you to die."

The grand maiden eyed her tea and then looked back at Katja. "What did you use?"

"I suspect it is a type of spider venom," Katja said, but she wasn't sure what an arcane spider conjured by magic would genuinely be working with.

The grand maiden's eyes fluttered as she went in and out of consciousness.

"If you have the antivenom, I will find it and give it to you," Katja said, scanning the room and ensuring the hood still concealed her face. "So long as you give me ten minutes to escape."

"Five," the grand maiden muttered, foam forming in her mouth. "But you must hurry."

"Deal."

The grand maiden's eyes flickered before pointing to a cabinet in the corner of the room, filled to the brim with glass containers, beakers, vials, tubes, and jars of botanical ingredients, meticulously labeled. An assortment of grinding mortars of varying sizes was displayed in ascending order from smallest to largest. It was an impressive display.

"Dandelion root, garlic, crow's feet, ether, owl pellets, and . . . asp venom," the grand maiden strained, clutching her throat.

Katja was thankful for the grand maiden's meticulous labeling because she was able to find all the ingredients except for the asp venom until the grand maiden pointed to another cabinet across the room that opened up with a few vials of Vigor, which Katja pocketed, and a long vial of pale asp venom.

"Crush everything together in the order I told you," the grand maiden said. "Then give it to me."

Katja did as instructed, finely grinding the dandelion root and garlic, which, if she were honest, felt like cooking until she got to grinding the crow's feet and owl pellets, which had a foul sound and smell. She was careful not to show her face as she handed the results to the grand maiden, along with a beaker of clear ether and the venom.

"You will pay for this," the grand maiden groaned as she slowly mixed the ground ingredients into the beaker of ether, hands shaking with tremors. "You will pay dearly for this, I am afraid. You should have left me to die."

A chill ran down Katja's spine, and her fingers clenched the dagger's hilt until her knuckles whitened.

"I can rip it all away right now if you want me to," she threatened.

"But you won't." The grand maiden scowled, adding the asp venom to the beaker, which began to steam and turn a bright violet color. "You are not a murderer . . . not yet."

Katja pictured swatting the steaming beaker from her hand, but the grand maiden was already chugging it, and it was too late. Despite this, a wave of relief succumbed to her.

Katja walked to the exit.

"Do not follow me. If you do, I will finish what I started," she spat, entering the main chamber.

Katja dashed across the dark room and forced herself into the dumbwaiter, but it was a tighter fit this time, with the long scroll taking up an awkward amount of space.

She froze, hearing a faint whisper. "Goodnight . . .Ms. Rosdyre . . ."

The firelight flickered in the grand maiden's room, and then suddenly, it blew out, and the room was completely black. Even the glowing crystal ball was snuffed out.

A cold breeze grazed her face from across the room. It smelled foul, like rotting flowers. Katja yanked on the rope, but it didn't budge.

Her eyes stared out into the darkness as she sensed something swiftly approaching. Her heart rattled against her ribcage, and the hairs on her arms and neck pricked like dried shoots of ryegrass.

Katja leaped into the darkness, leaving the scroll inside, and, with the dagger, cut the rope, sending it rattling down the shaft so loudly that it probably alerted the entire tower.

"Ms. Rosdyre . . . I thought we were becoming friends. Those cards were exactly what I have been looking for on Auriella Stavoren," the grand maiden mumbled, her footsteps slow like a limp in the darkness. "You were so promising. You would have made a great prefect one day. Much better than the current bunch."

Katja pressed her back against the wall and slid down to her knees. She closed her eyes, pressed her finger to her quivering lips, hummed, and whispered the magic words under her breath.

Suddenly, the chamber doors tore open, and candlelight filled the room. Several prefects armed with maces, staffs, knives, or whatever they could get hold of filled the room. Standing not even an arm's length away was Grand Maiden Argaut, dressed in her flowing nightgown and face smeared with blood.

"Grand Maiden! Bitter teeth! What is all of that noise?" Prefect Haggerty shouted, swirling around the room, looking for a culprit.

"Ms. Rosdyre. She nearly killed me!" the grand maiden wailed. "She is hiding in here as we speak!"

The prefects searched the room with their lights, inspecting under the desk, inside the cabinets, and in the back room, but returned with only more questions.

"I do not see Ms. Rosdyre. Are you certain she was here?" a prefect said.

"I am certain. She is here!"

The grand maiden looked in Katja's direction, but her gaze appeared distant, and it was apparent she could not see her.

Katja was invisible.

She delicately stepped across the room, avoiding touching any panicked prefects before slipping out the grand maiden's door, which was already open.

She carefully dashed down the spiral stairs. She spotted Ms. Humphry smoking at the front desk when she reached the bottom.

Katja put a palm to her mouth and smelled her breath, as Stav had warned her. It smelled bitter like iron. She was running out of time.

Katja carefully snuck past Ms. Humphry, wafting a cloud of smoke in her wake, down into the laundry room, to the bottom of the Maiden Tower. Inside, she found heaps of dirty clothing beneath the clothes shoot. Beside the shoot was the recognizable dumbwaiter door, which she pried open, then reached for the scroll, but her hand slid through it. It was then that she remembered Stav's teachings. *You cannot speak, touch, smell, or even hear, much like you would imagine a ghost.*

Katja nervously plucked a red hair from the back of her head, and a weariness overcame her as she became uncloaked. She reached for the scroll and tucked it under her arm.

A cold breeze blew down the shaft. It was the familiar rotten flower smell. She didn't know what she was doing, but she peered up the shaft and only saw a column of darkness. She didn't know what she expected. She imagined the grand maiden was staring back down at her, watching her every move as she did with the crystal ball.

Loud footsteps creaked down the stairs, and she knew she was running out of time. She pulled the grand maiden's hood over her face once more and ran past Ms. Humphry as shouts filled the halls.

Katja ran into the night air. As she slid down the alleyways, scroll tucked away, her feet finding footing only by the grace of the midnight moon, she looked back at the Maiden Tower, crooked in the night sky. As she pulled her hood over her face, she smiled. *I've done it.*

Her smile was short-lived when a sinking thought consumed her. *And I can never return to the Maiden Tower again.*

Chapter Twenty-One

It was a starless night as Katja wandered the zigzagging streets of the Smoker District. The entire time, she imagined Prefect Haggerty and all of the other prefects appearing on the back roads, their white aprons piercing the dark veil of night. There were a few times when someone would shout out from a distance. Every hair and fiber of her would perk up, expecting the shouts of constables and the night watch calling for her arrest. Instead, it was likely another horror—another robbery, cutthroat, or wail of misery that Theed had no shortage of in these days.

Katja wished she could say she was relieved when she reached the Warren, but her angst grew as she imagined the place torn, littered, and bloodied from the raid Claudia and the other girls had discussed during supper. Her stomach gurgled as she entered the mausoleum, and her paranoia grew. *Was coming here a mistake?* She didn't know where else to go except to return to the dreadful streets and join the wails that kept her awake all night, but she knew she had to find out what had happened.

Most of all, she needed to deliver the dossier to Kristoff before he ruined what she had with the Arkan Roth. She refused to lose two homes on the same day. She had chosen her place, and it would be the last chance she would ever get to learn magic.

Katja removed the thimble and placed the violet thistle into the gargoyle's mouth. It didn't quite have the same bright glow it had the other day, but sitting among the shelf like the toy soldier, thimble, and other tokens made her feel like she belonged. She'd half expected her token to be discarded or blown away by the wind.

To Katja's relief, the Warren was full of life. Gwith and Stav were chuckling about some story, Urie was eating a bowl of steaming soup by the fire, and Kristoff was reading in Fleck's chair, feet propped up and bare against the warm bricks. Even the strange boy, Jasper, was sleeping on a pile of hay near the jail cell.

When Stav spotted Katja, he gave her a smile, his cheeks rosy from firebrandy.

"Kat! You made it!" Stav exclaimed, pouring brandy into an empty tankard and shoving it into her hands after hugging her. "I thought you had finally given up on us! You know, I would send Jasper looking for you if you did! Have a seat! We are celebrating!"

"Celebrating . . . what?" Katja hid the scroll behind her back, catching Kristoff's suspicious gaze.

"We are celebrating the news! My ancestral homestead has been raided, and my mother has been arrested! Aren't you happy? You will never have to work for her ever again!"

"I am surprised you do not know already," Gwith grinned, her face flushed from drink. "They are blaming everything that happened at the college on her! The murder . . . everything!"

Katja's stomach sank. "The countess was arrested? Why are they saying she murdered the professor?"

"You should be joyous, Kat! That means the Magesleuths, constables, and guards won't be gunning for us anymore! It couldn't have happened to a more miserable sack of old dirt!" Stav roared.

"Must I remind you, Hugo, that is our mother you are speaking about? I think she has earned a bit more respect despite our feelings about her recent doings," Kristoff spat, eyes not leaving the book he was reading. Upon further inspection, it was the grimoire in his hands.

Stav waved off Kristoff dismissively. "Better her than us! She would have backstabbed us and done the same to her own two boys if it were the other way!"

"They never said they arrested her," Urie said, scraping the bottom of his soup bowl. "The paper only said Stavoren Manor was raided. She is a slippery old witch."

"Are you trying to ruin the evening?" Stav said, downing his tankard as Katja sat at the table where the map was splayed. "Kat, just don't spill anything on that map! We worked hard getting that thing!"

She took her tankard off the map, spotting a round stain that was bleeding into the southern Relian Sea like a monsoon.

"Nice going, Dustmage!" Gwith mocked, her cheeks flush with drink. "This is a relic!"

"Ease off, Gwith!" Kristoff snapped, wiping the spill with his handkerchief. "She is one of us now." He stared pointedly into her eyes as he delivered the words.

"Looks like Kristoff has gone soft. Since when were we ever polite to our fellow Roth?" Gwith teased.

Kristoff rapped his knuckles on the counter and retreated to the mantle, stoking the fire. "Perhaps very soon."

The chamber fell silent, the weight of his words hanging in the air—until Gwith broke the tension with a bark of laughter, and the room followed suit.

"So, why do they think the countess murdered the professor?" Katja asked, taking a sip of brandy. It felt nice to moisten her dry mouth.

Stav pondered for a moment. "Reports say they found a card with Professor Gill's face crossed off in ink."

"They found a dozen other cards, too," Urie said. "I would be very curious to know what other names there were among them."

"I think you know," Gwith said. "It isn't exactly the first time we have seen these cards. They once were an important tool of the Arkan Roth."

Katja felt chills on her neck. "The Arkan Roth used to use cards? What . . . like some kill deck?"

"Precisely that," Gwith smirked. "I wouldn't be surprised if some were hidden around the Warren from those days. Back when Fleck was just a Dustmage like you."

"Fleck . . . Dustmage?" Katja asked, hiding the scroll at her feet, away from the others.

Kristoff stood up and wandered toward his chambers at the back of the corridor as if inviting Katja to join him, but she was too curious and frustrated at what his blackmail had cost her. *He can wait*. It was time to learn more about the organization she was serving.

"Kristoff? You don't want to stay for a bit of story time?" Stav teased, but Kristoff did not falter in his stride.

"Is Jasper asleep?" Gwith asked.

Urie stood up and kicked Jasper's boot. The boy snorted but rolled onto his side in a deep dust-induced slumber. "Like a corpse."

Gwith began whispering. Her voice slurred from drinking. "Many years ago, Fleck was the Dustmage. He was likely the greatest Dustmage since the Arkan Roth was founded hundreds of years ago. I wasn't around at the time, I was barely a child, but from what I was told, Fleck was the steward to a great commodore during the Legish Wars—"

"*Stellish Wars*," Urie interrupted. "He worked under the service of Commodore Montross and was gifted a generous promotion and sum for saving the commodore's life during a surprise attack at the Mouth of Saurador."

"I'm sorry, Urie. Did I interrupt your story?" Gwith spat, but her bite softened into laughter.

"I think you are too drunk," Urie grinned.

She snorted, but then continued. "Fleck was promoted to captain and served the rest of the Stellish War until those blasted grape mashers handed their vassals to the Commonwealth, giving us everything from Duskpool to Tarclay. If you have ever been there, you will know it is mostly beautiful cliffside, so rarely worth so much blood, but kings and queens will do anything to change the borders on the map."

"Yes, it is all just one big pissing war. Same ones we boys had during summers in the wild," Stav chuckled.

"What does this have to do with him becoming a Dustmage?" Katja asked.

"Commodore Montross found out that Fleck was a wizard the day that Fleck saved him. I dunno, he never told me the specifics of the magic he used, but I reckon it was obvious," Stav said. "Turns out, Montross was a bloody warlock himself, like most of these rich blokes, and was also a secret stakeholder in the Arkan Roth, which was being rebuilt from the ashes by my father."

"Your father? Count Stavoren?" Katja said. She wondered whether the count would have brought her to the Arkan Roth if he were still alive, and whether that was part of his grander plan for her.

Stav nodded. "My father was a bit of a renegade like me. As a child, he lived through the banning of magic and the Dust Wars. He was one of the last generations of Glints to be educated in prestigious academies before they were either closed or their records burned. He met many similarly minded people at the academy, many of whom were born into powerful and wealthy families like his. After researching the fabled Arkan Roth from the forbidden texts of the academy, he and his influential friends began building a reiteration of the Arkan Roth . . . and we serve as its remains."

Katja looked at the rubble around Warren, but she could not imagine it ever looking nice. "What happened?"

"A lot happened." Stav hiccupped. "Much I don't care to talk about, but to summarize, the Arkan Roth tried to influence the elites who ruled parliament and spoke into the ears of the Crown, but there were a lot of betrayals. Moving along, my father married my mother, and more and more members got arrested, hanged, or vanished, and their numbers dwindled. Many high-profile assassinations get pinned on the Arkan Roth, and my father got too old to serve as its leader."

Gwith grinned. "Then comes Auriella Stavoren, who takes the reins away from the count, and you start to see the cards with bloody 'X's. There was conflict between her and the other leaders, such as Fleck and her sons."

"So, the countess was once your leader? Why didn't her sons take her place?" Katja asked.

Urie laughed. "Right where it hurts!"

"Stav and Kristoff hate each other and wouldn't let the other rule. Because of this, Fleck won them over," Gwith chuckled. "Not to mention, he had seniority and helped the Arkan Roth take flight in its beginnings."

Stav frowned. "It should have been me. I think everyone knows it."

Katja couldn't believe the countess once walked these halls, feeling both confused and relieved at the same time. Much of it finally made sense, including the cards, the wand, the tapestry, and why Fleck had spies watching over Stavoren Manor to keep tabs on their deranged former leader. And to think that Fleck's paranoia led them to discover her, a chambermaid employed to care for the old countess in her final years, only to uncover a secret.

"So, did Auriella have the count killed?" Katja said solemnly. "I always thought it was a murder. I was the first one to find his body."

Urie stopped scraping his bowl, and Gwith looked stunned.

"That must have been a terrible sight," Gwith said. "Truly horrific."

"So, you don't know?" Katja asked.

"Not for certain . . ." Stav spat, finishing his tankard and straightening before wobbling to his feet. "I don't think she will ever admit it if she did! Hopefully, now she feels the pain of the suffering she has caused others."

Stav dropped his tankard swiftly, stumbled to his chamber, and slammed the door.

"I shouldn't have brought it up," Katja said, picking up her scroll and wandering toward Stav's door. "I should apologize."

"Good luck," Urie chuckled. "He just needs to sleep off the brandy."

Katja was about to rap on Stav's door, but before she could, she glanced at the light under Kristoff's and wandered down the end of the corridor. She would apologize the next day when he was sober. She knocked, and before she could lift her knuckles to knock again, Kristoff opened the door ajar and reached out with a pale hand.

"You succeeded . . . very good," he whispered. "Have you told the others?"

"No," she uttered.

"Good," Kristoff smiled, his pale eyes gleaming. "Keep it that way."

"Why don't you want them to know? Shouldn't we all be working together?"

"My brother likes to think things over and get in the way," Kristoff whispered, glancing down the corridor to the others. "I will let them know in time. Now give it here."

Katja was initially reluctant, but then placed the scroll in Kristoff's hand.

"It better be worth it. I lost my job at the Maiden Tower for this," she rebutted.

Kristoff frowned. "They raided my mother's house because of those cards you turned in. My brother and the others don't realize this, but they will come straight to us once they start tearing that house apart. It is good that you brought this to me so we can start the work that the Arkan Roth has promised to deliver for centuries."

"What if they get to us first?"

"They won't," he chuckled. "Our leader is approaching as we speak, and then not even the Magesleuths will be able to stop us. Our people will get vengeance for all of those pitchforks stabbed into unmarked graves and murdered at the gallows. Today is the beginning of tomorrow."

"What are you going to do with the dossier?" Katja asked nervously.

"Everyone will know soon enough," Kristoff said.

Then Kristoff slammed his door in her face before she could utter another word. Katja stood at the door for a minute, tempted to knock again or bash it down for more answers, but she was too tired. Her arms felt heavy, her mind filled with sand, and her legs sore and weak.

She stumbled back to Gwith and Urie, tempted to tell them everything she had just gone through with the grand maiden and the dossier, but instead, she drank some more firebrandy and wandered to the goat's pen at the back of the Warren and collapsed onto the hay as a baby quail pecked at her hair.

Katja had done the impossible, but she was too tired to care.

Chapter Twenty-Two

Katja felt something kick her boots, and jolted awake.

"Sorry, I didn't mean to scare ya," Urie said, holding a basket of eggs and petting a goat. The goat bleated happily as it ate small pellets out of its hand. "I wasn't sure if you needed to return to the Maiden Tower."

Katja combed strands of hay out of her mess of hair and eyed a trough of water in the corner of the pen. Her mouth was parched, her body ached, and even dirty goat water looked like an oasis.

"You wouldn't be the first one to take a sip from there," Urie chuckled, pulling a wineskin from his belt and tossing it to her. "Start with that."

Katja desperately took a sip, and once she realized it wasn't water, she spat it out in a red mist. "Boils! What is that? It certainly isn't water!"

"It is wine, of course! After a night of tossing spirits down your gullet, the best thing to do is to chase it with some more," Urie laughed, helping her to her feet. "Come with me. I will get you some fresh water, but I swear the wine trick works."

Katja politely refused the wineskin, petted the goats as they exited the pen, and joined the others in the main chamber. Gwith was cooking sausage in a skillet over the fire and excitedly stole the quail eggs from Urie's hands, cracking them onto the empty side of the pan. The swirling smells reminded her of walking around the Market District in the summer when streetside merchants and vendors grilled every cutlet of seasoned meat you could imagine. Her stomach growled as she took a mug of water from Urie and sat at the table, fingers pinching her sore brows in an attempt to gain some relief.

Stav sat across the table from her, eyes fixed on the map and a few open letters. He shuffled a pile of schillings stacked six high, toying with them between his fingers as he scribbled letters onto the parchment between sips of tea.

"I am sorry for upsetting you," Katja whispered, interrupting the silence. "I did not know what I was saying."

Stav sighed. "You didn't do anything wrong."

"What are you working on? Can I help?" Katja asked.

"You sure are chipper for someone who woke up in a goat pen," he said, dipping his nib in ink and blowing his hair out of his face. "Aren't you supposed to be at the Maiden Tower? Perhaps you will be getting a new assignment."

How did he do it? He barely looked tired after nursing his tankard all night. Katja dismissed the thought and assumed it must have been some magic or enchanted draught that dissolved any hangover, no matter how copious the drinking.

"I no longer have my morning duties," Katja lied. "I am in no rush."

Gwith pulled the skillet from the fire, placed a few links and eggs onto plates, and handed them to everyone. Katja's stomach ached with how hungry she was, and drool dribbled from her lip when she pressed her face into the steaming pile of food. A few minutes later, they heard only the sound of scraping forks. When she finished, Gwith offered her seconds, but she was already fuller than she had ever been after supper in the Maiden Tower. *Boils!* At the Maiden Tower, she hardly ate—a bite of toast while dressing, a scant teatime snack between tasks, and supper only at the end of the day. Tonight's meal felt like the best she had ever had.

"I should have figured the thistle was yours," Gwith said. "If you are to join us on a permanent basis, you will have to use something more everlasting."

Katja acknowledged Gwith with a faint nod, though she lacked both the energy and the will to reply. Instead, she reached for a pail of stale water, lifting it in trembling hands to sip between waves of nausea. Only when her headache dulled enough, and her stomach no longer threatened revolt, did she manage a weak farewell and turn toward the exit. She climbed the worn rungs to the gallows above, where a dense crowd had gathered, their murmurings blending with the damp chill of the air and the faint tang of iron.

Fantastic, another hanging.

Katja skirted the crowded square and drifted into the narrow streets of the Smoker District, just south of the graveyard. She slipped past the rotting brick gate and ducked into tea shops, bookshops, bakeries, and other small storefronts, seeking refuge from the relentless rain that hammered against rooftops and cobblestones alike. She lingered too long in each one, though, and eventually the owners told her she would have to buy something or move along. She was used to it. The shooing felt oddly nostalgic, bringing back the days when she and the other street urchins would snatch a few hot pastries from a tray and dash in all directions so they wouldn't get caught. The taste was always more enjoyable knowing it was free. She wondered if the other kids were still alive, but it would be impossible to know for certain.

Once the crowd started swelling for lunchtime, Katja meandered down the sparser streets leading to the Brinkley District, which was not much of an improvement from the Smoker District, except it had a few more trees lining the street and perhaps fewer potholes pocking the ground. When she was younger, Brinkley was a place to take a deep breath amid the crowds, get a nap, or set up camp for the night. She thought of it like the seagulls that gathered where the careless hordes dropped their breadcrumbs during the day, only to retreat to their nests among the cliffs, far away from the madness.

She passed the old Brinkley Abbey that was run by Deacon Willis the last time she was here, but from the looks of it, had seen better days. Boards plastered one of the once vibrant stained-glass windows, and wild crabgrass and dandelion patches filled the once glorious yard that adorned the deacon's proud garden. Often, the deacon could be found on his knees with a damp towel around his neck as he plucked cucumbers and tomatoes from the vines and passed them out to the hungry urchins that walked by that afternoon, leaving nothing for himself. She still remembered his smile and the vibrant abbey during worship, when the pews were full, and the soup lines that wrapped around the alleyway during the cold winter months. Now it looked like a skeleton of itself, as fading graffiti littered its front door, the most notable one thick black lines with the word "dregu" written on it. She recognized it as a common tag by the mob that controlled the northwest side of the Brinkley District. The word came from the Bartish harbors across the Relian a long time ago. If it had a different meaning once, it did not matter, as the word was commonly known as a warning—*a warning that death is near.*

Katja tucked her head down and swiftly walked past the abbey, darting through the crossroads of the Brinkley District until she reached the Midlands. One side of its busiest street was gated, while a large wall of tall flats and condominiums rose on the western side. The storied buildings had once had pleasant balconies, but they had been welded shut with barricades and bars for as long as Katja could remember.

While it wasn't a bad place to sleep, the Midlands was mostly known as the Brig because it felt like a prison, with menacing gates, towering buildings, and closed-in atmosphere that made it easy to feel trapped. It also didn't help that the place was rampant with cutpurses, vagabonds, and bands of urchins, with whom Katja was often accused of being affiliated when she was younger.

The only time she ever got to see the other side of the gate on the eastern side of Waller Street was when she was a child, led inside by a district constable to avoid retribution from her supposed sidekicks, who were known for attacking officers who dared to arrest their friends—mostly out of fear that someone would confess after hours of sharp pins shoved beneath their fingernails or some other tortures the constables could devise.

The other side of the gate was where the constable's office was located, and they interrogated her for two hours before releasing her with a stern warning and a few lashes for not disclosing the location of her fictional teammates. She remembered the massive manors and luxurious chateaus set back among massive flowery yards as she was ushered back to the gate and tossed back to the street into a puddle with a wagging finger and a few curses before the gate squealed shut. It wasn't until she was a little older that her mother told her that was where many of the bailiffs, judges, attorneys, politicians, and lead constables lived because it was close to the city center where they worked, but avoided the slums outside their towering gates. She hadn't been that awestruck with abundance until she met the Stavorens several years later when she joined the Maiden Tower.

Just as she thought of the Maiden Tower, she realized it wasn't that far away from where she stood. In fact, despite trying to avoid it, it appeared that she had been walking toward it without even realizing it. Perhaps old habits died hard, or maybe deep down she knew she needed to take a look at it one last time before she rid that part of her past for good. Part of her didn't even feel like anything had happened, because the night she stole the dossier felt like a strange nightmare. Could she really have snuck into the grand maiden's chambers all on her own and coerced her with magic? It didn't sound like something that she could have done even a few months ago, let alone now. What if the grand maiden reported her to the constables and the Magesleuths were able to track her scent? Could they pick up magic that many hours ago? Her stomach sank at the thought as she rounded a bend in the street and darted down an alleyway, took a right, then a left, and climbed up a creaky iron-rung ladder where she came upon a small opening covered by a roofed overhang.

It was her old home. Well . . . one of them.

It was the spot where Katja and her mother had spent many of their nights when she was growing up, and the exact spot where she waited for her mother to return when she vanished. Katja admired the spot with a subtle grin, dragging her finger along the dry brick walls, its familiar gritty feeling scraping against her fingernails. She spotted the carvings on the wall that her mother had etched one night, when Katja was scared during a thunderstorm, of a flower that had eroded over time but still held its image well. Upon further inspection, she realized the flower resembled a thistle, with its sharp, budding bristles billowing from its end. For some reason, she could have sworn it was a more beautiful flower when she was younger, and had to give it a second look just to be sure. What were the odds that the same flower would be used as her token to the Arkan Roth a decade later? Chills ran down her spine and down her legs as a cool breeze swirled into the alleyway. Could her mother have known?

There was a footstep behind her, and Katja stumbled back into the wall, her back pressing against the carved thistle. She half expected to find a creature in blackened robes with a hidden face standing before her, sniffing the air, but instead, it was a lady with desperate eyes, drawn tight in a thin shawl, brandishing a dagger. The dagger looked small and too dull to break skin, but depending on how experienced the wielder was, the tip could gut a pig.

Katja reached out her hands gently. Her heart jumped in her chest as she felt a swell of warmth fill her stomach and radiate to the beds of her fingernails. "Don't do anything rash. I will leave now."

"Get out of my spot, girl!" the lady spat. "I was here first. See the little bed in the corner?"

Katja hadn't noticed the dirt- and concrete-colored blankets nestled in the corner, and her hands rose defensively. "I am not going to steal your spot."

"Why else would you be wandering down these parts?" the lady scolded, her eyes wild and pupils widened from dust. She eyed Katja's gown. "You are one of those gals working in the tower. I don't think your masters live down here. Better start running back home before someone foul guts you like a fish for whatever it is you got in them pockets!"

"I don't have anything." Katja was lying, but not by much. Jiggling inside her pockets was a sharp thistle and a ball of lint. "But if you want to find out what the Maiden Tower does to find its missing girls, you can certainly find out for yourself by hurting me."

Deep down, Katja knew she could snatch the dagger from the lady with levitation, but she didn't want to gamble that the woman wouldn't tip off the constables about a witch wearing the dress of the illustrious Maiden Tower. Let alone one with red hair that already had whispers surrounding her among her peers. She would only do it if there were no other option.

The lady lowered her dagger. "Bet you steal from your masters too, don't ya? Well . . . If you don't get out of here now, then I am gonna have to find out for meself," the lady said, fanning her knife down the alleyway. "Now shoo, girl! I don't want your trouble."

Katja slid out of the corner, across the wall, and looked back once before darting down the alleyway and spilling into Starling Street, slowing down to a brisk gait once she entered the crowd. She took a few familiar crossroads north through the Brig into the Oldgate District, past shabby gardens, fragrant street vendors, and a flock of street preachers chanting in throaty huffs that sounded more like raked gravel than that of a man. It was not long before her feet took her down a hollow side street, its balconies bowed beneath neglected flower boxes. Even in the narrow strips of sunlight between buildings, the sorrow pooling in the gutters smothered any hope of growth.

It was then that she saw it. *The Maiden Tower*. It swung between the narrow gap like a clock's pendulum as she sauntered with every stride. She didn't expect to be here and knew she shouldn't, but her feet ignored the warnings coming from her head. At the mouth of the alleyway, a loud voice echoed off the brick walls, followed by the rattle of steel that glinted only briefly off his shiny breastplate before continuing down the road.

Katja dove behind a wooden crate as her heart drummed behind her ribs. *I should not be here.* Why was she here? Was it closure that she sought after such an abrupt split with the Maiden Tower? It felt so strange knowing that not even a day ago, she was welcomed within the tower's belly, even demanded, but now she was worse than a stranger. Her thoughts were confirmed when she summoned enough courage to peek out from behind the crate and slip to the end of the alleyway and noticed four constables clad in crimson interrogating a few maidens and Prefect Haggerty, who had a solemn expression. To her surprise, among the sea of red clothing stood Miss Frisbee, belly as swollen as a pigeon, in her stained work clothes, with a look of pale horror on her face. One of the guards gestured toward the alleyway briefly, sending Katja a few steps back into the shadows, much like the yellow-eyed boy, Jasper, many days ago.

She pulled the hood over her head and fled, the soles of her feet tapping on cracked pavement like a crude drum. A man in tattered habits stared at her with wide eyes as she passed, which shouldn't have been something she would have concerned herself with if it wasn't for her remembering the bright red dress dancing at her heels and signature white apron. She had been so proud to get it after Stav fetched it for her at the tailor's the day she joined the Arkan Roth for the first time. Her stomach sank at the thought of abandoning the gracious gift that Portia had give to her before she left. She wondered if Portia already knew the news of the grand maiden and what she thought of her. Boils! *Of course, she knows*. Portia could live across town in whatever manor her family had inherited and still be better connected with the Maiden Tower than Katja. Then she remembered the strange conversation she had with Portia in the shower room after the fallout at Hartwind College, where the professor died. Portia had warned Katja that she would not be able to protect her when she was gone, but that if Katja needed a safe place, she could come to her family's estate in the Lord's Park, across from the old lighthouse.

Katja desperately dashed across a street between two moving stagecoaches, whose drivers shouted at her in her wake before she entered another alley. She muscled through a crowd of wanderers cooking mincemeat around a weak fire with the swirl of dust consuming their eyes. Down another street, her heel misstepped, sending her into a puddle shining with oil. When she got back to her feet, her dress was coated with a brackish brown slop. The only red she could see was the remains of her dress and the fresh blood on her palms. She scooped more mud and slick onto her gown and apron, rolling into it like a hog until it felt adequately ruined before standing again. The dress felt heavy and dripped at her feet, but no one would mistake her for a maiden anymore, let alone anyone worth confronting. She continued, dampening her hair in the puddle until it nearly looked black, and began scraping the fringes of her dress with the slimy brick walls until the threads were coarse and splayed.

It wasn't long until she had moused across Oldgate into an area she was less familiar with, dragging her dress against the walls, and even the lousiest dusthead stared at her as if she were feral. That was until her hand smacked into something larger. *The city walls.* She looked upward, watching the endless walls split the dimming sky like the eyelid of a massive whale with bright blue eyes preparing for slumber. Looking down the length of the wall, she noticed the craning lampposts slowly ignite as the lamplighter made his way with his tall flaming torch.

Katja pressed her palm against the stone. A faint, pulsing vibration hummed through her fingertips, though she couldn't be sure if it was real or imagined. Was that the roaring world outside the capital calling her? She often fancied this was where her mother had gone—that day she never returned. It would be tragic to hear that her mother abandoned her, but perhaps there was a reason that could justify it all. The lack of knowing was what hurt her the most. Was she a slave somewhere? Her stomach sank, and she tried to think of more pleasant thoughts, like finding a place where no one turned their head at the mention of magic, let alone the people who practiced it.

Yes, perhaps that is where she went.

"It is the winds," a faint voice said. "The gate is so big, you can feel it shake on a stormy night."

Katja looked over her shoulder to find an old man sitting in an alcove behind her.

"Sorry . . . I will just be going now," she stammered, taking her hand from the wall and skirting down the street.

"Need a dry place to stay for the night?" the man said, his eyes fluttering with dust.

Katja looked into the darkening sky.

"Give it a few minutes," he chuckled. "I have yet to be wrong."

"I already have a home, but thank you for the offer," she said, bowing before taking another step down the street.

"To each their own," the man grinned. "Find somewhere dry! A storm is brewing! Might be the biggest one in years!"

Katja briskly trailed down the sidewalk along the wall, passing the lamplighter who was whistling joyously atop his ladder. He stopped whistling when his gaze met her discolored wares, and nodded, a look of pity flashing in his eyes as she passed, as if to say, "I am sorry, I would help, but I have a job to do."

For another hour, she walked the walls, thankful to the lamplighter for the guiding light along her way. After all, trouble often happened in the shadows along the edges of the lamplight. But muggings and worse crimes have occurred in broad daylight before, even if less common.

She heard a hiss overhead, and a moment later, a cold prickle on her neck. Another hiss and another prick, but this time she felt it on her hands. Before long, rain dumped from the dark swirl of clouds swarming overhead as the sun began to flee over the city gates to the west. Darkness was rapidly spreading across the city as a cool breeze flowed through the narrow streets like a frozen river, and snuffed out the lantern flames overhead with a muffled roar. Whatever heat remained in her body was ripped from her bones as her damp dress clung to her shins and tugged at her shoulders. It wasn't long before forks of lightning flared across the sky, followed by a racket of thunder that she could feel vibrate in her lungs as it cracked.

Katja scanned the streets as they became a shallow chasm. She stumbled into a side street.

She scanned the streets for a dry spot beneath a rooftop with eaves, but when she found a place, it was already occupied, which was made abundantly clear by the weary eyes glaring at her from beneath tattered sheets. She even stumbled upon a nook that would have made a perfect place, as it protected against the slanting rain, but it was filled with a man and a woman, surrounded by a litter of countless children, peeping their heads from their nest. When she appeared, the children cried and the mother shrieked at her like a banshee, startling her so much that she nearly tripped over a puddle crossing the now empty street.

The rain fell from the sky in droplets the size of buttons, which reminded her of all the mismatched buttons she'd found at the bottom of the laundry pot at the end of her shift with Miss Frisbee. Somehow, there always seemed to be more than there were dresses missing them. Thunder cracked like a whip, and a flash lit up the tormented streets as streetlamps started to flicker and hiss. It felt like the city might flood overnight if it continued like this.

Then she stumbled upon it as she entered another alley. Her foot snagged something solid but loose, like a rotting log, sending her into a wall, but it was so cold that she couldn't feel any pain. She turned to see what had caught her leg—something dark and sodden lay draped across the path. Cold pins ran down her arms. *It was a dead body.* When she nudged the body, it was limp, like a doll, and when the lightning flared, she could see the girl's pale face, marbled skin, and distant eyes staring past her. An almost luminescent green stain dribbled down her nostrils to her chin. She was still clutching a damp napkin from which she had made her final huff before she succumbed to a fate all too common.

Katja closed the girl's eyes with her fingers and covered her face with her blanket.

Then she sat beside her and wept.

Chapter Twenty-Three

Katja didn't sleep a wink for the next few hours as the storm only intensified. Every year or so, a storm this big would strike Theed, and every time it hit, everyone was ill-prepared. This one had to have been one of the worst, as wind roared through the hallowed alleyway with such force that it rattled the glass on the windowpanes above.

A scream echoed faintly into the night, but it was quickly swallowed.

Mother. Where are you?

Another scream bellowed into the night, but this time it was so close that it made Katja jump. It sounded like it came just down the darkened path to her right. Katja huddled against the brick wall and tried to stay still, using the motionless body beside her for cover. *Perhaps whatever it is will think I'm dead, too.*

Peering down the path, she conjured the outline of something coming her way, but couldn't tell if it was just her eyes playing tricks on her. She imagined it was that same Magesleuth from Hartwind College, stalking her with that horrific half-shrew, half-owl mask and taloned feet.

Before she could find out, Katja leaped to her feet and stumbled out of the alleyway, her foot catching on the corpse's heavy leg before she spilled onto the dark streets. At this point, every lantern and lamppost was snuffed, and the only usable light was that of pinpricks coming from the fringes of curtains adorning the apartments lining the streets. To her relief, she still had her sense of direction about her and took the eastward road out of Oldgate, through the Midlands, and through the Brinkley and Smoker District until she reached a cross street heading southeast that ended at a lofty wrought-iron gate. The gate had stark concrete spires conjoined by a mouthful of sharp iron spikes to deter anyone from climbing it. Its sheer size—five times a person's height—made the spikes seem a bit severe, but Katja knew, deep down, that was the intention. *You don't belong here.*

Where did Portia say her family lived again? Was it the gate to Eastgate? No, she distinctly remembered Portia mentioning the Lord's Park back when she confronted her in the shower. She shielded her brow with her hand to make out the words on the gate, which spelled Dunrow District. The Dunrow District wasn't too far from the Lord's Park, but it would take the remainder of the night wandering the Dunrow, Little Stellen, and Harleck without light, and the storm didn't seem to be clearing any time soon. She wasn't completely familiar with the streets either. Her friend's words whispered faintly in her ear, *If you need a safe place away from the Maiden Tower, you're welcome to come to my family's estate . . . We live across from the old lighthouse . . . It is crooked, like a poorly tapped nail.*

Without an exact placename within Lord's Park, she could be looking until sunrise for the Ponvelle estate. Not to mention, she could barely see anything in the distance with the river of water pouring from the sky. A flare ignited the sky, sending glistening tendrils in every direction and filling the air with thunder. Katja pulled her damp hair out of her face. She ran parallel to the district gate until she found a familiar bakery that she knew was located on the edge of the Parliament District, which occasionally discarded day-old bread in its dumpsters. *Puffer Square is near.* Excitement filled her heart, even though she had no real direction, as she then headed down the empty streets, which were now concrete rivers, except for a few dry spots on the sidewalks.

The outline of a carriage blasted past the street with horses whining and huffing with every breath. It was the first sign of life she had seen on the street for hours, as anyone wiser was inside their warm, dry homes, waiting out this nightmare. Whoever was in that carriage had somewhere they needed to be, or they were just as lost as she was in a city submerged in shadow. She wanted to chase after the carriage and knock on their doors to ask for a ride, or at least some place dry for a few minutes, but it turned out of sight before she could make a decision.

Another scream ripped through the sky between thunderclaps. This time, it sounded like it was coming from over her shoulder, but she only let herself glance for one second before dashing down the street like a dog was nipping at her heels, and didn't stop for what felt like an hour. During that hour, she nearly lost herself on more than one occasion, twisting and backtracking again and again, but she was certain of her path when she came upon the colorful glass glowing warmly atop a soggy hilltop. It was the chapel at Puffer Square, the same one that warded the cemetery where the Warren entrance sat. She had never been inside the small chapel, nor had she felt any warm connection to it, but tonight it served as a welcoming beacon. Only seeing her mother's face could make her feel more welcomed in this moment.

This has to be a sign. She knew where she had to be, even if she didn't like it.

Katja prepared her mind and heart as she briskly passed the chapel, whose stained-glass windows depicted a split tree with sunbursts beaming between its gap—but she couldn't see much detail because looking upward brought an onslaught of raindrops into her eyes. Nearly slipping on the slick grass and dodging the eerie gravestones and pitchforks, she came upon the mausoleum on top of one of the many knolls in the cemetery. The mausoleum looked bone white in the black of night, and with the jagged pitchforks surrounding it, it resembled some skeletal crown. She entered the mausoleum cavern, her hands caressing the broken marble columns to guide her within until the rain suddenly stopped dripping on her head. Inside, it sounded like what she imagined the caves of legends sounded like, with their dwarven cities and dripping stalactites. For some reason, the smell was even worse than usual, like the scent of tossed soil, horse droppings, and moth-eaten linens. She reached for the gargoyle, her finger pressing against its sharp teeth, and placed a thorny thistle into its mouth, spat into the right coffin, but before she could rap its lid three times, she stopped as the hairs on her arms and the nape of her neck stood their full length.

Footsteps. She listened again, but could not hear the footsteps. This time, she could just make out someone approaching the mausoleum in black, the outline of their hood faintly glistening from the chapel lights overhead. It was a Magesleuth, probably the same one she sensed coming for her back in that alleyway. How had she known? She could hardly see anything in that alleyway, but somewhere deep down inside, she had a feeling.

Katja's heart pounded as she snatched her token from the gargoyle and searched for a place to hide. Looking over her shoulder, she noticed that the outline of the figure was gone, but that only scared her more, as she had no idea where the threat lay. She was tempted to run out of the mausoleum, but not knowing where the figure was and if she could outrun it made her hesitate. Not knowing any better, she eyed the coffin on the right and peeled open its lid and tucked herself into its cavity, her back pressing against something sharp that could have only been a pile of bones. There was a small crack in the coffin lid that looked toward the entrance, but it was too dark to see. Did the Magesleuth follow her all this way? The thought sent a chill down her spine.

A pair of footsteps tapped on the damp floor, and a shadow entered the chamber. Katja's stomach fluttered as she dreaded the sound of sniffing that she knew would follow. She closed her eyes, wishing more than anything that her mother was here. Even having Stav would have sufficed in this moment, but she knew no one was here to save her now. The Warren was hundreds of feet below her right now, and it appeared the Magesleuths would finally find out their hideout. The Roth was over, and all of her friends would be tortured until they begged for death if any of the rumors about the Magesleuths were true.

In that moment, the shadow played with its hood, and a stream of wet yellow hair, so pale it was nearly white, spilled out, contrasting brightly against its black robe. *It was a woman.* The lady combed her hair neatly before fiddling with the front altar when a familiar clanking sound came from the gargoyle's mouth. There was a short whisper that Katja couldn't decipher, and three loud knocks thudded on the coffin lid above her, sending coffin dust into her eyes and mouth.

Katja froze in fear, but after she rubbed the dust out of her eyes, she felt a gust of warm air. She peered through the crack, and the yellow-haired shadow was gone. *No way*, Katja thought as footsteps creaked down the left coffin steps into the Warren. Was there a member of the Arkan Roth that she had not met? Was it Gwith disguised as someone else? After all, she had seen how talented Gwith was at changing her appearance during her mission at Hartwind College. Suddenly, a terrible thought occurred to her—a Magesleuth figuring out the secrets of the Warren after all this time. Perhaps they have been monitoring them for days, weeks, or months to finally figure out the trick. What if they had been watching her all this time and figured it all out, and it was she to blame? After all, someone could hide pretty easily in this cemetery, behind a gravestone, high in the chapel, or even worse, in the very spot she was hiding now in the coffin, waiting for someone to enter. It wouldn't be the first time she hadn't noticed when someone was spying on her.

If this is true, she had to warn Stav and the others. A Magesleuth had found their entrance, and it was only a matter of time before they discovered the way in. After all, Magesleuths were supposed to be talented sorcerers, the only ones permitted to use magic in the entire city of Theed.

Katja took a deep breath, pressed her finger to her lip, and hummed while muttering, "*Tudor vasa,*" and after two tries, the cloaking spell took, and she vanished. She followed the Magesleuth down the stairs into the Warren, figuring she would find it just ahead of her, but it was nowhere to be seen. She continued down the switchback stairs, made of rotting wood and bent nails, looking down into the Warren, where only a trace amount of light came from a few glowing coals in the fire, which appeared to have been neglected for hours. Where was everyone?

Katja sniffed the air, and there was a faint scent of perfume. There was something familiar about its scent that shouldn't quite place. A door opened and then shut at the end of the corridor, startling her, but her guard fell when she realized it was Kristoff's room at the far end of the Warren.

She quietly snuck into the foyer, past the fireplace and Fleck's chair, and the empty chairs around the map. When she reached Stav's room, she took a moment to look under the crack of its door, but it was dark. Carefully, she crept down the stony corridor, past all of the doors, until she reached Kristoff's room and propped her ear against it to listen. *Whispers.* All she could hear were faint whispers.

"Does Stav know? How about Fleck?" a woman muttered.

"They don't," Kristoff's replied softly.

"How did you get hold of it?"

"The girl."

"Kitty? The Rosdyre girl?" the woman whispered.

"Indeed." Kristoff scoffed. "I thought I sent her to her death, but she is more capable than I thought. I will tell the others of your coming tonight when they arrive. They will be astonished and perhaps reluctant at first, but without Fleck in the way, they will have no choice but to hear you."

The woman muttered something indiscernible.

"Yes," Kristoff said, "she has the wand . . . and the tapestry is here. It will still suffice, but the inside requires some work."

"I will need all of your support tonight," the woman said, and the doorknob twisted. "You were the only son who believed in me. If Stav gets in the way, we must act appropriately."

Katja stumbled away from the door just as it opened. The woman in the black robe with long blonde hair exited Kristoff's room. She had a pointed chin, gaunt cheeks, a confident gaze, and those bright blue eyes—it was the countess, yet she didn't look a day over fifty.

The countess wandered into the main chamber and slowly touched everything around the room, as if she remembered something from a long time ago. Katja followed slowly behind, but her legs were growing tired. It dawned on her that she had been cloaking for nearly as long as she had the night she snuck out of the Maiden Tower, and she had far less Vigor than that night.

Katja put a hand to her mouth and smelled her breath. It smelled bitter, like steel. She knew she had to stop cloaking, or else she would faint. A wave of dizziness passed through her, and she blinked her heavy eyelids. When she opened her eyes again, the countess stared straight at her.

"All this time, you thought you were tricking me when I was the one playing tricks on you," the countess said, her voice echoing off the hallowed walls.

Katja knew she had to stop cloaking, or else she would faint.

"You thought people wouldn't notice you finish your shift before all the others without breaking a sweat? I might have been old and losing my wits, but I watched you use magic the entire time. You thought you were so clever, but you don't even know that I handpicked you from the lineup of chambermaids for that very reason," the countess said. "Hurry, you'd better pluck one of your red hairs before you faint. I wouldn't want to lose another promising Dustmage."

Katja stammered, plucked a hair while invisible, and collapsed to her knees. "Was this all just a ruse to get me to work for the Arkan Roth?"

"It isn't all about you, Kitty!" the countess scoffed. "You think I would go through all of that for you? No! You already delivered me what I wanted most of all."

The dossier.

"How did you escape from jail? The Magesleuths?" Katja asked, her lips feeling thick as she spoke.

"You know more than anyone, dear. I haven't been at Stavoren Manor in days," the countess smiled, kneeling, pinching Katja's chin and shaking it playfully. "They might have raided the manor, but they didn't find me. Kristoff told me how you fiendishly handed those cards to the Maiden Tower days ago, and that was when I knew they would be coming."

"Are you going to kill me?" Katja muttered, her breathing growing heavier.

The countess paused for a moment and stroked her hair. "You should be thankful that I strongly believe in second chances. You deserve that after all of that time combing my hair—but if you betray me again, I will not hesitate to do what I must."

She lifted Katja's dress and pulled the wand from her stocking.

"I heard you were holding onto this for me," the countess smirked. "I am afraid it misses its master."

Tears welled in Katja's eyes as her breathing strained more. She was kindling, and this time she was going to die.

The countess reached for a bright green mage serum vial and forced it between Katja's fingers. "Let's test fate tonight. If you can save yourself, you will see the fall of kingdoms and the rise of a new age, and you will be known as the greatest Dustmage that ever lived."

Katja's eyes flickered as she struggled to uncork the vial, but it slipped from her fingers onto the stone floor. Hope wavered away as she lunged for the spilled green liquid and desperately pressed her face into it, snorting and licking it off the ground, her lips and gums too numb to tell if she was smashing every tooth in her mouth.

Then, a black curtain fell over her.

Chapter Twenty-Four

Katja woke up to the sound of shouting. She winced as she struggled to move her arms and legs, which felt heavy and rigid, as if they were not entirely hers. Her eyes flickered open as she rolled onto her side to face the direction of the voice. Her head and jaws ached, and bright motes of color danced across her vision as she spotted the long iron bars surrounding her and the pile of hay she was lying in.

"She shouldn't be here! We decided long ago that Mother was not fit to run the show anymore," Stav shouted. "We must wait for Fleck to return! He makes the final call!"

"Well, Fleck isn't here, and as far as we know, he might never come back!" Kristoff said, a satisfied smile tugging at his lips as he looked to Gwith and Urie for reassurance. "What sort of leader abandons his crew and disappears like that? Not a good one, I reckon! Fleck should never have been promoted from Dustmage, and it should have been one of us Stavorens taking the reins!"

"Now you want to listen to that man? Why has your tune changed, brother? Now is our chance to do something that will finally make a difference! We've got the warlocks right where we want them! Now is the time to strike!" Kristoff spat.

"We tried that, and you know how it went!" Stav shouted. "You refuse to concede anything!"

Kristoff shoved Stav across the chest. "The successor should be chosen, and we all know who Mother favored to replace her."

Stav shoved Kristoff back, causing him to stumble over a chair. "We needed change! Not more of the same! You and Mother always treated every problem like a batch of crabgrass terrorizing our gardens. It was only a matter of time before we were all caught and hanged!"

"Better to die than sit around for years having accomplished nothing while others perish!" Kristoff barked, pulling out his wand.

"Always quick to violence! Father would never have approved!" Stav snapped, yanking his wand from the gap in his boot. He dropped into a low, wide stance while Kristoff held himself tall and composed, his posture a rigid pillar of cold control.

"You did not know Father well enough, then," Kristoff said, inhaling a dab of green magedust from his side pouch like an artist dipping their brushes in paint on a palette.

Stav's eyes widened. "*You are serious?* You would load your Vigor? Are you threatening me, brother?"

"Both of you need to calm down!" Gwith shouted, jumping between the two drawn wands with her own. "Do you want the entire square to hear you two squabble? We work together!"

"Yes, I would like to hear more about this dossier while I cook supper rather than hear you two murder one another," Urie grumbled, stirring a pot of soup over the hearth. "Where is Countess Stavoren anyway?"

A loud thud rattled from the shadows, and a foul breeze swirled around the room. Footsteps echoed through the door from the sewers, and the countess appeared, drawing her hood from her head.

"The streets are littered with guards and Magesleuths from the Dunrow District to Northgate," the countess said, marching to the back of the Warren and retrieving the dossier scroll.

"What did you expect messing with the grand maiden of the Maiden Tower?" Gwith chuckled. "We know who bankrolls that place."

"We gave them three good reasons to search for the Arkan Roth," Stav challenged, glaring at his mother. "First the professor . . . then the bloody cards . . . and now this dossier . . . this is why we were going to wait for things to cool down before infiltrating the Maiden Tower."

"Not to mention you put all your faith in a novice . . . That could have ended terribly," Gwith said, eyeing Katja in her jail cell.

Katja ducked down low, her body obscured in a heap of hay so that no one noticed her eavesdropping.

"But she didn't fail. Brother! You are her mentor, yet you have so little faith in her! Perhaps she deserves better," Kristoff rebutted. "Perhaps Fleck was too soon to award you a student. Did you even know she could successfully use a cloaking spell yet?"

Stav was silent.

"Hugo . . . you look at me like the reaper coming to bring you to your grave. We should be celebrating, son . . ." the countess said, brushing Stav's cheek, but he pulled away in disgust. "Fleck was an important part of the Arkan Roth and returning it to its former glory, but the game has outpaced him. It was a mistake to assume someone who spent most of his days nose to a spellbook had the gall to lead such a sacred covenant. You should be welcoming me with open arms!"

"You think because you sucked the life out of those poor men that you are young? You might look only a decade older than me, your son, but your mind has not changed," Stav asserted, baring his teeth. "Just a few months ago, you were clinging to your deathbed with barely a thought to bounce around in that thick skull of yours!"

Kristoff charged Stav, but the countess pushed him back with a spell.

Countess Auriella slapped the dossier on the table. "Rather than tearing at each other's throats, why don't we look at the treasure our little Dustmage has brought us? We might have taken a risk, but we have won the battle. Now we plan our strike."

"We must wait for Fleck," Stav grumbled.

"Fleck is gone," the countess grinned. "We know the warlock families will never let this dossier see the light of day if they have their way. We must act fast and ruthlessly!"

"Ruthlessly? So, we are returning to how things were done before you left. We cannot delve into such shameless violence!" Stav blurted.

"Violence was when their entire bloodlines turned their backs on us and betrayed our people," Kristoff argued. "We need to send a message. They cannot continue to live comfortably while magic prohibition leads to so many deaths! You know the plan . . . if we can terrorize the warlocks, then we can put pressure on Parliament and the Crown."

"And only then will magic be legal again," Urie said. "I have heard it repeatedly since I started working with all of you."

"And finally, we have a chance to make it happen!" Kristoff shouted.

"We only need to frighten them . . . not harm them," Stav said. "You and I both know that too much spilled blood can lead to *the opposite happening*. If you upset the warlocks, you might see more laws and crackdowns on our people. They might finish us off for good!"

"So, what do you suggest, brother?" Kristoff sneered.

"We send them a message," Stav said, lowering his voice. "Release a name every day from the dossier. Publish it in every newspaper in the Commonwealth as far as Westreach."

"I like this idea," Urie said. "Let them squirm without needing to knock on a single door."

"Boils, Hugo! It will take one name for every warlock in the realm to hunt down every publisher and journalist who leaks the next," the countess said. "And they will find a way to figure out the source through every form of terrible torture."

Stav pondered for a moment. "We will send an anonymous letter to the *Daily Kroner*."

"And they will believe you? What do you plan to write? 'I believe that this family has the blood of a witch?'" Kristoff said. "That is no better than town gossip."

"And you plan to break down the doors of every magical family listed on the dossier and murder them in their sleep?" Stav chided.

"No, but if they give us no other choice, then maybe they will die, but it will be their choice," the countess sneered. "The demands will be clear: *side with us over the Crown or perish*."

A chill ran down Katja's neck as she listened, her head throbbing and wishing she could vomit, but she knew she couldn't stop listening.

Stav looked to Gwith and Urie. "Gwith . . . Urie? What do you think? Can you stand for this?"

Gwith shrugged, and Urie frowned but did not answer. Their answer was clear despite no words being spoken.

Stav lowered his wand, defeated. "So, it has been decided then? Blood will spill, and we will stand on the side of death."

"No, that is the side you have stood on for years, listening to Fleck and his diluted dreams," Auriella said. "You might think you have lived a harmless rebellion, but Glints are murdered in city's squares every day. Doing nothing and waiting for perfection is standing on the side of death, son."

Stav took the seat across from Fleck's chair and stared into the flames.

"Who is the first name on the list? I have never been more curious?" Gwith asked.

Countess Auriella rolled out the scroll and scanned the ledger with a long finger. "Not everyone on this list is a warlock, but the grand maiden has denoted those with Glint blood with a small star next to their family name."

Kristoff joined his mother at the table, craning his neck as he scoured the list.

"Sir Alfred Blythe of the Blythe family," Kristoff blurted excitedly.

"The senator?" Urie said.

"None other . . . next on the list . . . Lord Gilbert Trumhold . . . Sir Glenn tar Breck . . . Henry Black . . . and Madame Adelaide of the Wallingford District," Kristoff jeered, "and of course they have addresses listed too."

"This map is brilliant. You can't send a chambermaid if they don't know where the chamber is located," Gwith laughed, taking a swig of firebrandy and handing it to Kristoff.

"I need to be sober for this," Kristoff said, politely refusing the bottle. "We all should be sober. We need to act fast . . . perhaps tonight if we are daring."

"Tonight?" Gwith said, surprise on her face.

"My son is right," the countess said, taking Fleck's seat and watching Stav's face as it turned white. "We cannot give the Crown another day to find our hiding spot. We must act tonight. We will meet at the address of the Blythe family . . . then the Trumholds."

"Two in one night?" Gwith asked.

"We must be bold," the countess said, glaring at Stav. "We will hit five families tonight to strike a dagger of fear in this town. Every paper will be filled with news tomorrow morning. The annals of history will remember what we have done and mark us as the beginning of retribution and a new era of magic. The families that betrayed ours to protect their own skin will finally pay for their decades of collusion!"

"And then tomorrow?" Urie asked.

The countess smiled. "We strike five more. If they do not concede to our demands, we will continue until no more names are left on this list . . . and there are thousands!"

"I agree" Gwith said, raising her bottle. "It wasn't long ago I was nearly one of those murdered witches myself. I raise this glass to those who died merely for enacting their birthright!"

"I have been prepared to die since joining the Roth," Urie said, raising his dripping ladle. "Fleck be damned!"

Stav sank his head into his lap. "You are all making a grave mistake . . ."

"*You?* Are you not coming?" Kristoff said.

"Why would I? It is not the plan," Stav barked.

"Then you are not a part of our family . . . or the Arkan Roth," the countess spat. "Join us, or join the fate of those on the dossier. After all, your father's family, the Stavorens, also turned their backs on our people. If you refuse to join us, you are no different than the other warlocks."

Stav thought deeply for a minute.

"His silence speaks for itself," Kristoff chuckled. "My brother is rarely quiet when he disagrees."

"We will all head out upon the hour then!" the countess barked. "Anyone absent is as good as an enemy of the Roth."

"What about the girl?" Gwith asked.

"The girl is weak and in the depths of kindling," Kristoff said, glaring at Stav. "If she had a better master, she would better understand her limitations."

"I wouldn't expect our Dustmage to abandon us now, especially after I saved her life," the countess smirked, glancing at the prison cell. "She will serve us better healing in her cell. Now, let's be off before sunrise. Let the entire city gasp in fear at the early light."

Chapter Twenty-Five

"**H**urry! Kat, we've got to go!"

Katja gasped awake as a hand jerked at her shoulder. When the colorful spots faded from her vision, she could make out Stav's face pressed against the bars, leaving pale lines on his cheeks. His eyes glistened in the dim light, but his face was cut and bruised, and his greasy hair slick and untamed.

Rain dripped from the vents high above and pattered on the floor in the depths of the Warren. The hearth was just a few bright coals, enough to outline the upturned furniture strewn across the chamber. *What happened here?*

"The countess . . ." Katja stammered.

"I know. Where do you think I got these?" Stav whispered, pointing at his seeping wounds. "We have to leave now before they return. They will hunt us down, knowing our scent, but perhaps we can outrun them."

"Stav . . . I kindled again," Katja whimpered, slowly rising to her feet dizzily. "Did the countess actually save me?"

"Possibly. She might find you too valuable a Dustmage to expend, but it won't feel like it living under her rule." Stav's voice was hushed as he reached his arms through the bars to help her balance. "I can't believe I am saying this . . . but I think she might be more powerful than before. She has turned back the sands of time for her body, but her mind still knows all the intricacies of advanced magic."

Katja pushed the jail cell open, but it did not budge. "Did she lock me in here, or was it Kristoff?"

Stav shook his head. "It was my mother, but it won't open as easily this time."

"What do you mean?"

"Let me make a correction. It might open with a lockpicking spell, but my mother has likely enchanted it so that there will be some trap if the lock is disarmed."

"So, how do I get out of here?" Katja said nervously.

"We go quickly. I am not sure I have the time to figure out the enchantment," Stav said, dodging her question.

Katja felt a chill in her neck. "Stav . . .what happened? Why aren't you with the rest of them?"

"I can tell you more about it later, Kat," Stav uttered, pale and grave. "But it isn't good."

Katja sighed, finding her balance. "Where will we go?"

"We have to find Fleck. I hate to say it, but he is our only hope," Stav said. He pressed his finger to the lock and took a deep breath.

"Wait!" Katja began, but it was too late. Stav uttered his mother's name, and the lock clicked open.

A flock of bats screeched out of the tiny keyhole, fluttering toward the ceiling like a swarm of bees. The jail cell bars started to wiggle and slither, falling to the floor like giant serpents hissing with dripping fangs. One of the serpents flicked its tongue at Stav and struck the heel of his boot. Another inched closer to Katja with its hooded neck and prepared to strike, but a gust blasted it away before it could.

Stav aimed his wand at the encroaching creatures and helped Katja past the slithering heap, blasting them away with spells, but no matter how quickly he moved, others replaced them. They were too swift and too fast, far more clever than typical snakes.

"Follow me!" Stav yelled, flicking his wand so that a wall of flame warded off the beasts as he pulled her forward.

"I can barely move my legs," Katja said, feeling weak. *I shouldn't even be alive.*

"Then you will be pleased by what I have in store for our escape," Stav grinned.

He led her past the blackened hearth and down the corridor before telling her to wait. He then entered his bedchambers, exiting with the grimoire in one hand, before darting off to the back of the hall to Kristoff's chambers, where he returned with his brother's glowing crystal ball in the other hand. He dashed into one more room and returned with the flowing tapestry hanging from over his shoulder with a wild expression.

"The tapestry?" Katja said as Stav plopped the grimoire in her arms. "They definitely will not be happy. You might as well take the dossier."

"If only I could. My mother won't let it leave her side," he sighed, marching back to the other side of the Warren. The snakes continued to slither in their direction as the flocks of bats circled, but he conjured a spell that belched black smoke, causing them to shriek away.

Katja followed as closely as she could as they drifted up the stone staircase Urie had told her never to use as an exit. Once they reached the top, they heard barking orders that echoed off the stone walls, which sounded remarkably like the countess's.

"Hexes! They are here . . ." Stav whispered, raising a finger to his lip and tucking the scrying ball under his jacket so it wouldn't glow as bright. "Use your cloaking spell."

"I am out of Vigor!" Katja spat. "I am barely hanging on as we speak!"

"Then, change of plan, you will need to hide," Stav said, his bright eyes flashing in the dark. "Hurry, they will be here any minute!"

"They will know I escaped the cell, not to mention all of the snakes!" Katja said.

Stav nodded. "Good observation. We will split up. Meet me at the graveyard in ten minutes."

Katja slipped down the stairs again just as the coffin door slammed open, revealing a sliver of light into the Warren. Her heart pounded as she brushed the back of her shoulders against the polished stone walls in the shadows, and footsteps flooded down the stairs. She found the door to the sewers and muttered the secret password just as Kristoff's pale face entered the chambers. She quietly shut the door so it didn't create a distraction and held her breath as she limped to the iron rungs leading to the gallows overhead, but instead decided to run past them so that the countess might be less likely to spot her. She wound down a bend in the tunnel to another set of rungs leading to the street above. Further down, there were several other exits until they vanished into the shadows around another bend. Her pulse beat like a drum in her chest as the sound of splashing water echoed loudly in every direction.

"The girl is gone!" she heard Kristoff shout.

"Kitty Kat!" the countess called. "Where are you, Kitty Kat?"

Katja climbed up the tall ladder just as she had done before, but more haggardly than usual due to the grimoire tucked under her left arm. Her calves burned, her arms tensed like coiled leather, and cold sweat beaded down her neck as she made her way up the slimy sewer walls.

The door to the sewer screeched open, and footsteps fell behind her. They had found her.

"Kitty Kat! Leaving so soon, my pet?" the countess called loudly.

Katja looked over her shoulder just in time to spot the countess's pale silhouette approaching with a curved wand. In this lighting, the wand was the color of bone, and its tip was sharp like a spike and flickered with burning sparks. She admitted it was strange seeing the same wand she had so desperately hidden in someone else's hands, even if it was true that it was the countess's wand to begin with.

"Don't make me hurt you," Auriella threatened.

Katja pulled the grimoire from her armpit and held it out like a shield. "I am not afraid to destroy it. In fact, it might be better if it were gone forever!"

The countess frowned, but didn't lower her wand as they came to a stalemate. "Oh, Kitty," she sighed before flicking her wand, and in an instant, the slick ladder began to rattle and move downward toward the floor.

Katja panicked, climbing the rungs desperately as they plummeted toward the ground. She leaped a few rungs higher, but she felt herself descend further and further from her exit. Her heart sank when she felt the concrete on the soles of her boots and smelled the scent of the countess's perfume thick in the air, followed by the tapping of footsteps.

"Is that all you have learned from my son? Empty threats?" Auriella chuckled. "Not even a simple Ward? Not that it would save you now."

"Maybe I would have learned more if he didn't need to babysit his decrepit mother!" Katja snapped.

The countess glared at her and aimed her wand at her face. "He is the weak one. Just like his pupil."

"You are a murderer," Katja said. "You and your terrible son."

The countess's eyes narrowed, and with a swipe of her wand, the ladder bent and coiled with a horrific metallic sound and swirled in a circle around Katja, closer and closer, threatening to bind her like a mouse caught by a jungle snake.

Katja held out the grimoire as the ladder swirled closer. She took one glance at the coin-shaped lid overhead—her only hope for freedom. Then she stared at the grimoire in her hands, and an idea consumed her. She had the opportunity to try something she had dreamed about, but had never done before.

"Hand it over," the countess said. "You can go live your life and leave this to people with power."

"Come get it."

Katja gritted her teeth as a fire burned in her chest. To her astonishment, a hidden reservoir of Vigor bubbled up where there had been none moments before. She channeled the newfound Vigor from her core, fixed her gaze on the grimoire's boiled-leather cover, and clung to the book as though it were the most precious thing in the world. With one surge, an invisible string attempted to pull the grimoire from her hands, but she held on as hard as her fingers could bear. The ground slipped from under her feet and the heavy sewer cover came frighteningly close, but just as she feared she might be crushed against the ceiling, the sewer lid blasted upward in a surge of power, sending rain and streaks of storm light into the black depths below. Her levitation spell began to wane, and after only a few seconds of weightless flight her body felt heavier than iron.

I'm going to die.

Desperately, she reached toward the exit, her fingers slipping on the slick concrete, then finally clinging onto a ridge that likely saved her from a brutal end. Her body dangled for a minute as she tried to summon the energy to pull herself up to the city street.

"Tsk tsk, naughty," the countess's voice echoed below.

Horror washed over Katja as a hand gripped her ankle. Looking down, she met the countess's gaze—soft blue eyes contrasting with a furious sneer. The countess was levitating on a pitchfork, her wand pressed firmly into Katja's gut.

"I will teach you everything I know about magic, which is more than Hugo ever knew! Become the great Dustmage you were destined to become!" Auriella pleaded, tightening her grip.

Katja kicked her legs and tried to pull herself free, yelling for help, but the sharp tip of the countess's wand only jutted firmer into her skin. She felt her fingers grow painful and tired as they began to slip from the ridge, but as she was going to give up, a man with a tall hat and a formal crimson frock peered his head into the hole from above. A few other curious heads peered at her too, but from a more cautious distance.

"Boils, it is a girl!" the constable shouted, his shiny badge reflecting in the pale light as rain dripped down the visor of his hat. "Let me get you out."

The constable strained as he reached for Katja's hand and heaved her onto the street, where she collapsed with exhaustion. "How did you end up like that?" he asked.

Katja looked down into the sewer, but the countess was nowhere to be seen.

"I was just crossing the street and the manhole just sort of blew up under my feet," Katja said, gasping for air. She knew it was a terrible lie, but what could she say?

"You don't say?" the constable said, scratching his thick walrus mustache. "That is a bit . . . interesting, isn't it?"

"Perhaps it was from the storm," Katja said, climbing to her feet. "I have never seen so much water in my life . . . well, aside from when I swim in the bay, of course. I wonder if it got flooded and sort of just 'popped.'"

"Stranger things have happened in these sewers," the constable said, his saber clanking on his hip as he circled the manhole covering, which was now resting in a garden across the street. He glanced at her red dress and furrowed his brow. "You are a maiden. I trust a lady of the Maiden Tower, but I will have to take down your name in case this becomes something bigger than it is."

The constable pulled out a pen and paper, which started to blot with rain before he jotted down a single word.

"Claudia Ashworth," Katja said, wiping the mud off her gown. "I really should be going. The senator isn't going to be pleased if I am late."

"Senator? Of course, be off," the constable said dismissively.

Katja massaged her fingers as she strutted across the street, taking one last glance into the sewer, but it was too dark to see much of anything. It then dawned on her that if the constable were to inspect the sewers below, they would be very close to the entrance of the Warren. All of those years of secrecy could end because of her, but at least it would be under the countess's rule and not Stav or Fleck's.

"Girl!" the constable shouted.

Katja froze, then slowly turned toward the street. He was swiftly approaching with something in his hand.

"Is this your book?"

Katja glanced at the grimoire, which was covered in puddle water. Her heart pounded in her chest, but before she could answer, the constable shoved it into her hands.

"Oh my, the senator's book," she proclaimed.

"Someone said they saw it fly out of the hole," the constable chuckled, handing her the book. "Witnesses, I tell ya . . . have a good day, mam. If the senator asks, tell them Constable Gabler was responsible for helping you this morning." He winked before walking back into the street.

When the constable was gone, she noticed that everyone who had been watching her returned to their own affairs, their umbrellas pulled down over their heads as the rain picked up. Katja tucked the grimoire back under her arm to avoid it getting wetter than it was and scanned the street to reorient herself. Ahead, the chapel's stained-glass window sparkled from its central tower, and below it was the gallows, which looked more like a wooden monster than a contraption from this distance.

Stav. She needed to meet Stav at the graveyard. That is, if he'd managed to escape the Warren.

Katja weaved through the sidewalks around Puffer Square before slipping behind the gallows, which was surprisingly empty after such an active evening the other day. When she reached the abbey, she discreetly slipped into the graveyard and wandered among the tombstones and barbed pitchforks around the Warren entrance. Her eyes fixed on the crumbling mausoleum, half expecting the countess to emerge from its shadows.

She drifted along the hill until she reached another mausoleum in a slightly better condition, further east of the cemetery. Her fingers slid across the shrine's slick marble façade, and she poked her head inside, half expecting to find a similar twin casket chamber with a waxy altar, but instead it was locked with an iron grate. She could barely see anything inside aside from a few discarded cigarettes and broken glass on the floor.

Katja crouched against the mausoleum wall and watched the Warren entrance from afar, looking for any sign of Stav along the hillside. What felt like an hour went by, and the skies started to darken as thick clouds made their course from the Relian like the night before. Never in her life had she been caught in a storm that strong, but by the looks of it, this one could get even messier.

After a few minutes, Katja began to question what Stav had told her. Did he mean to meet up at some other graveyard? That didn't make much sense, but the longer time passed, a darker thought emerged. What if he was harmed and couldn't move? Maybe he got caught or something far worse.

The shadows grew long across the graves, stretching like lion claws upon the slopes. A few candles were still lit at the feet of some wicker and pewter pitchfork tributes. She crawled up the hill, her feet sliding on the slick mud as her hands clawed the ground for traction to avoid falling. She was so tired she thought she might faint.

They should never have decided to meet in the cemetery. It was far too close to the countess for comfort. Katja had already barely escaped her once, but she wasn't sure if she would be so fortunate next time. They should have decided to meet almost anywhere else in Theed, but Stav wanted this. Perhaps it was the first place that came to mind for both of them, or maybe Stav was hiding something from her.

A rustling sound stirred somewhere among the graves.

Stav? A heavy, urgent thump echoed inside her chest. She thought about whispering, but knew no one would hear, especially over the growing storm, which hurled gales across the city like javelins.

Katja sauntered out of her hiding spot and noticed a bright patch among the graves. Hunched, she crept from grave marker to grave marker, doing her best to conceal her flowing red gown behind them before proceeding. She inched closer until she came upon the glow emanating from a small stone embedded in the ground, surrounded by glowing lanterns and fireflies. Cautiously, she inspected it, looking over her shoulder. The stone had faint letters engraved into it, covered in a thin layer of dirt.

She quickly wiped the dirt from the letters as the lanterns flickered brightly.

Rosema Rosdyre

"Mother?" she uttered under her trembling lips. *She has been here the whole time.*

Katja turned as footsteps rapidly squelched the mud behind her. It was Stav, but he was empty-handed and looked angry.

"Katja, where have you been?" he shouted, growing closer.

"I was running away from your mother," she said, eyes still focused on her mother's grave. "I could ask you the same thing. I have been looking for you for over an hour."

"I had to run an errand," Stav said mysteriously.

"Is it even safe here? The others cannot be far," Katja said, finger outlining her mother's name on the coarse stone.

"We shouldn't stay long, but it is safe for now, Miss Rosdyre," Stav said, pointing at the gravestone. "*Rosdyre*, either that is a coincidence, or perhaps you have a relation?"

Katja stammered. "*Rosema*. This is my mother's name. I have only just noticed it after all of this time. I must have passed it a dozen times."

"There are thousands of gravestones here. I imagine it would be easy to miss," Stav said, reaching out his hand. "I see you still have the grimoire. Let me hold onto that now."

Katja handed the grimoire toward Stav, but noticed something was missing.

"Where did the tapestry and ball go?" she stammered.

Stav smiled. "I hid them so the others wouldn't find them."

Katja nodded. "We should leave before the countess finds us. I nearly got picked up by the town constable. Wouldn't be surprised if they find the Warren after all of this."

"The Warren? They are coming here?" Stav asked, incredulously.

"It is possible," Katja said, still in disbelief at her mother's grave. She would have to return later if this whole graveyard wasn't sealed up after being discovered.

"Katja . . . the grimoire," Stav said, tugging at her shoulder. "I will hold onto it for now. Once we find a safe place, I have a bit of research to do before we continue your training."

She handed him the book, and he tore it from her clasp.

Katja tilted her head in confusion. "You could say thanks. I saved it from falling into your mother's slimy hands after all."

"Sure thing, girl," Stav said with a cockeyed grin.

Katja squinted her eyes, noticing something off. Something about the hue of his eyes, like they were missing his signature shine. *The way he smiles.* It was far too reserved and less toothy. She stepped away, tripping over her mother's grave. She gasped in horror, realizing that the lanterns and fireflies were gone, and the name on the gravestone was blank, just like the rest of the simple graves on the hilltop. Had she imagined it?

"Stav . . . something is wrong," Katja stammered.

"Sometimes change feels wrong at first," Stav said. "Fleck is gone, and the countess is back. So much is going to be different."

Katja started heading down the hill. "We should leave before the others find us."

Lightning crackled along the horizon, igniting the sky as rain pattered onto the gravestones so hard that it looked as if it would ricochet back toward the heavens. In the distance, a few elm trees swayed in the rising winds as their limbs scraped against each other like haunted violins commanded by a deathly orchestra. The air smelled sickly, with a mixture of salt, rotting leaves, and bile.

When Katja didn't hear anyone follow, she turned on her heel to find Stav hadn't moved.

"C'mon, Stav! What are you doing?" she shouted, her voice wavering in the wind.

"I can't leave," he said solemnly. "I should just turn back now."

"After everything you just told me about your mother! You are the one who wanted to run in the first place!" Katja said.

"It is my mother, Katja," Stav uttered, baring his teeth. "I have made a grave mistake. We can't claw at each other's necks. Only a unified Roth can save the Glint."

"Even if it means murdering innocents?"

Stav frowned. "If we break apart, the Roth will never win, and far more will die. The Crown has only just started! They will not stop until every wizard and witch is dead, and not even the warlocks will be safe in the end. They can only hide behind their gold and thick walls for so long."

Katja stared at Stav angrily, but the words would not come.

"Follow me," he said. "You won't find anything out there, especially on your own. There is nothing like the Roth. The countess can be merciful. She has a soft spot for you, I can tell."

"You are making a mistake," Katja shouted, balling her fists. She wanted to slap him across the face. "Can you live with yourself knowing you led to the death in the murder of entire bloodlines? Families? Children?"

"They won't hurt children," Stav scoffed. "Unless they get in the way."

"Do you hear yourself?" Katja said. "You sound like one of them!"

He raised his pale wand. "I don't even know what they see in you!"

The air shivered, and a ribbon of iridescent red surged towards Stav. With a hiss, he flew down the hillside and was nearly impaled by a crooked pitchfork where his body stopped. Katja screamed and dashed toward Stav, her boots slipping in the mud just as she noticed Kristoff emerging from the shadows of the tomb with a smoking wand.

"Mother, I found her!" Kristoff shouted over his shoulder.

Katja's heart raced as she weaved between the maze of pitchforks and gravestones until she came upon Stav—except it wasn't Stav. *Not anymore.* Stav's face had shifted before her eyes. His ear-length dark hair grew long and blonde, and his face turned into another, more feminine one.

Gwith.

Katja examined Gwith and was half relieved, half mortified that her chest was still rising and falling beneath her thick coat. She had seen enough dead bodies to tell that Gwith was not gone from this world just yet. Her face had too much color for that.

"Don't worry, Katja. It was just a simple stunning curse," Kristoff said, carefully plodding toward her, using his fingers to avoid the fraying and decaying iron pitchforks. "She won't be happy when she wakes up, but she won't be dead."

"Stay away from me!" Katja shouted.

"Is that how you treat the person who just saved your life?" Kristoff said, the vein in his neck bulging. "She never did like you. I suspect she was jealous of the attention you get . . . You know, being the Dustmage and everything."

"What is it about the Dustmage that makes me so special? Just leave me alone!" Katja spat.

Kristoff hesitated and braced himself against a crumbling gravestone, but he seemed disgusted at the filth now coating his sleeve. "Let's get out of this storm, Katja. Someplace warmer and drier where we can discuss things properly. We will tell you everything you need to know about what you really are."

"I am not going back in there with you!" she growled, backing away. "Besides, it is just a matter of time before the constable finds out about the Warren."

"Do not worry about that *incident*," Kristoff smiled. "It has been taken care of."

"What do you mean, it has been taken care of?"

"Come now. We will gather Gwith and have a nice chat next to the warm fire. My mother has high hopes for you, dear."

"I already gave you an answer," Katja spat.

Kristoff swirled his wand, and a liquid gold ribbon twisted around her wrists like vines with intense heat. She winced as the binds tightened, clenching so tight it might tear through her narrow bones. With a tug of his wand, Kristoff pulled her to the ground, her face planting into the mud.

"It was only a hypothetical," Kristoff said, reeling her up like a trout out of Balledore Bay.

Katja winced as she fought the devastating effectiveness of Kristoff's binding spell. She groaned as she dug her callused fingers and knees into any bit of gritty ground she could find until she flailed onto her back, causing her to slide with ease despite her using her heels to try to halt the ascent. Her teeth clenched as clay and gravel sifted into her eyes and threatened to fill her mouth.

"I'll stop if you agree to follow me," Kristoff said, but she could barely hear him over the sound of grinding stone.

Katja spat out a rock. She had an idea. Her heart raced as she imagined a line splitting down her muddied face. What if her body was scratched so badly that she could no longer pull it off? But she didn't have any other option. Her dry lips hummed.

"*Tudor vasa*," Katja whispered.

The binds crackled from the tension like a hoisting rope snapping under too much weight. Kristoff fell backward, and Katja sprinted away from the hill, using levitation to summon the grimoire that was still clutched in Gwith's hands and let it hover over her shoulder like an old, tired moth flapping near a streetlamp. In the blink of an eye, there was a whizzing sound, and something long and gray struck the soggy soil a few strides ahead of her.

A pitchfork.

She swerved, but almost immediately, another pitchfork embedded next to her, nearly plunging into her thigh. Then a dozen more pitchforks littered the ground before her, each of their wooden handles wobbling once they made impact.

Katja ran faster than ever as what felt like a hundred pitchforks fell just outside her wake. How could he see her? Then she spotted the hovering grimoire fluttering in the wind over her shoulder. She pushed the grimoire further away, and the pitchforks followed it like a swarm of bees. Her legs felt heavier with every step. If her Vigor was low just moments ago, then it was all but drained now.

Her lungs burned, and her breath tasted of blood as she scanned the horizon and spotted the glow of the chapel window far off to the right, along with the shabby towers of Puffer Square beyond the graveyard's ivy-laced walls.

She pulled a red hair, and a sickness swelled in her belly as the fuzziness of her vision refocused in a nauseating flux. Just then, a wicker pitchfork was hurled toward her, but she guarded herself behind the nearest gravestone. There was a loud crack as the wicker splintered around her, and the pitchfork handle swayed. In the corner of her eye, she spotted the grimoire splayed on the slick grass and attempted to levitate it to herself, but her Vigor was nearly gone, and she could smell the rusty taste in her mouth as she dove to the grimoire just before another pitchfork jabbed into the ground where she had just been.

Kristoff slowly walked down the hill, waving his wand like a pit orchestra conductor commanding a symphony of chaos. The earth trembled as dozens of pitchforks were ripped violently from their plots, soaring toward her like a deadly hailstorm—but to her shock, Kristoff's terrible act barely made a dent in her defense.

Katja caught her breath, tucked the grimoire beneath her arm, planted her toe firmly into the ground, and yanked a long pitchfork free from the mud. She swung it high, deflecting three that came too close, but dozens more zipped past her, whistling dangerously by, leaving only shards of jagged splinters to sting her face. Pain registered almost as an afterthought, dulled by adrenaline.

Through her semi-closed eyelids, she glimpsed a pale silhouette emerging from the mausoleum, joining Kristoff's side. The woman produced a slender wand from her dress, turning it over and over as if it were a piece of art, before drawing it through the air like a masterful stylus.

A shifting storm of cobalt smoke erupted from its tip, splitting into tendrils that snapped and lashed like living whips. In a blink, the cloudy coils wound around Katja until nothing remained in view but her hands. She swiped and stabbed at the writhing mass as she inhaled a lungful of acrid fumes. By the second breath she realized she could barely draw air.

"My son has betrayed the Arkan Roth," the countess said, her voice sounding close yet distant, like someone talking in a tunnel. "It appears you have been led astray by your 'tutor,' which means you are also a betrayer. The punishment for treason among the Roth is an infinite veil between our coven and the evildoer, in the form of death."

"Death . . . then quartered, with a dagger embedded in their heart," Kristoff said, sounding hollow.

"Yes . . . yes, we cannot allow the betrayer to trespass on us even in the dying world . . . this is true, Kristoff," the countess said. "We will spare you if you condemn my son, Hugo, and make a vow of amends for our covenant, the Arkan Roth."

Katja felt chills run down her neck. She couldn't betray Stav. Not for the countess, or anyone, if she thought about it. Stav and Portia were the only ones who seemed to care about her in this world, even a little bit, now that her mother and the count were long gone. She didn't know what Stav saw or what the countess had the Roth do tonight, but she could tell by the look she had seen on his face that it was something unforgivable.

"You would . . ." Katja choked, ". . . sentence your own son to death?"

"My son is responsible for his fate. I cannot protect him from the bylaws of our coven!" the countess snapped. "Since I left, this company has become a reckless and lawless congregation. Loyalty is paramount!"

Katja fell to her knees, choking so hard she vomited.

"I think she is dying, Mother," Kristoff said.

The countess chuckled. "I won't let her die." And then the smoky serpents let loose and crawled away from Katja, only to return to the tip of Auriella's wand like some sort of pet.

Katja fell to the ground, her fingers sinking into the mud, but she kept her arms tight around the grimoire, and a hand wrapped around the pitchfork, which was still quivering from the onslaught.

"Has she taken the oath?" the countess asked, swiftly approaching Katja and placing her cold hand against her neck. Auriella's familiar pale blue eyes stared into hers, and it was then that Katja realized how much the countess had transformed. Her hair was thick and, instead of white, was a youthful yellow, which was drawn in a bun so tight that it tugged at her wrinkleless ivory skin. Her hands were no longer bent and knobby, and the tops no longer veiny and spotty. Even her voice was subtly different, sounding far less strained and more melodic when she spoke, like a singing mother. By the looks of it, the countess could have been younger than her own son standing beside her.

"Not yet. Fleck was dragging his feet at any opportunity he could," Kristoff scoffed. "But Fleck had a valid reason for mistrusting the girl, and that reason is blossoming before your very eyes. Perhaps one of the few signs of competence from our old leader."

"But then she would be tied to me . . . to us!" the countess scolded. "I will strangle Fleck the moment I see him."

"The oath works both ways, Mother," Kristoff said meekly.

She frowned. "You know the consequences for breaking a blood oath, don't you?"

Kristoff groaned. "You know that my brother and I have taken the oath. We did under Father's leadership."

"So, none of the others? That will change. From now on, blood will spill for those who take part in the fellowship of the Arkan Roth," the countess snarled. "I will start with her."

"Her? She has done everything to betray us! We must not let someone like her into our coven!"

"I see no bigger betrayal than you permitting Fleck to instill cowardly policy in our sacred house! You were complacent!" the countess sneered, and Kristoff winced after every piercing word.

"I deserve credit for restoring the Roth by bringing us the dossier. Without it, we might still be twiddling our thumbs in the Warren!" Kristoff rebutted.

"I recall it was our brave Dustmage who brought us the dossier," the countess smiled ruthlessly.

"It was my plan. She had no choice but to follow my demands or else join these nameless graves!" Kristoff spat.

"And what if Fleck never left? What if he never abandoned you?"

Kristoff's jaw tightened. "Fleck is gone because I smothered that professor to death and got every Magesleuth in Theed sniffing for a trail!"

Katja was dizzy from this family's dynamic and too exhausted to care. It had been Kristoff who killed the professor, and she should have been wary of him this whole time. A shadow flickered in the corner of her eye, but when she turned her head, she saw a figure sauntering down from the Warren. To her surprise, it was a slender character with a red furred mask and delicate whiskers that appeared to be real. *The face of a fox.* Through the hollow eyeholes, nothing could be seen—just darkness that seemed to watch her, unreadable and unsettling, as if the mask itself were alive.

"Oh . . . is this our Dustmage?" the fox asked, tilting its head.

Kristoff nodded.

"What will you do if I refuse your oath?" Katja said weakly.

"We will make you." The countess shrugged. "There is magic far more powerful than anything you have ever seen. Complicated . . . but powerful if done correctly. I could make you do anything I wanted. If I had the ingredients, Vigor, and access, I could control kings and queens like a puppet with a swirl of my wand. That is the sort of magic you could learn under my wing, Kitty Kat. We can change this terrible Commonwealth into something good and pure."

Katja grimaced. "Can't you just leave me alone? I would rather be left to die than to serve the likes of you!"

"I don't believe you," the countess said. "No one wants to die. Not when told they are a Glint . . . let alone a *Dustmage*. They are more precious than the rarest jewels in the world, and if properly cut, can shine brighter than any gemstone. It is so sad how little you know of the blood that flows through your beating heart!"

Katja watched as three more figures joined them, each wearing a different horrific, realistic mask of varying creatures. One wore the mask of a wolf with sharp white fangs, another a horse with a chestnut mane that flowed in the storm, and the third a mole with bristled cheeks, dark eyes, and jagged teeth. There was something about the disguises that made them look uncannily real. The fur was alive and flowed like that of living animals, and their gums were slick, their teeth dripping with saliva. Each of their eyes was like a dark pit, receding far into the wearer's head. Just looking at them made her uneasy.

"Please, just let me go," Katja pleaded, hand wrapping around the pitchfork. "I just want to go home."

"Home, what home?" the countess laughed, resting her hands delicately on her wand. "We are your home. You made sure the Maiden Tower would never take you back."

Kristoff stepped forward, pulling something from his pocket and presenting his hand.

"I figured the thistle was your token, but you will need something more permanent," he said.

It was Professor Gill's mother-of-pearl amulet from the night of her initiation at Hartwind. The same night the professor was murdered and all of this chaos started. She couldn't help but sneak a grin as she took the pretty amulet and held it firmly in her hand. She could see the sincerity in Kristoff's eyes, but she also felt that if she refused, he would kill her immediately.

"I will teach you everything you want to know . . . everything Hugo and my son failed to," the countess pleaded. "I see a bright future for you, Kitty Kat, if you join our covenant and take the blood oath."

"Take the gift, girl," Kristoff said coldly. "Remember who truly taught you how to cloak."

The air vibrated overhead, and a sound hummed faintly in her ears, followed by a loud flapping, like the sound of laundry clinging to a drying line, left out in a storm.

Katja clenched the amulet in her palm and then placed the silver chain around her neck. *It felt good.* Was she making a terrible mistake? What choice did she have? There was no way the countess would let her live if she refused.

She closed her eyes and released her breath as a swoosh of wind pulled her high into the air. She screamed as hard and loud as her lungs would allow her as she clutched whatever it was that had plucked her from the hilltop. Icy tears welled in her eyes as she winced to keep them open. Her stomach sank into her bladder as the mausoleum and hills shrank beneath her feet, and cold air whipped around her body, flapping strands of red hair around her face like banners clutching to flagpoles during a storm.

"Hold on tight! She will be coming after us!" Stav's voice was strained.

"Stav?" Katja exclaimed in some relief, but clung desperately to the flapping cloth that was separating her from falling to her death. "Is this . . .?"

"Look familiar?" Stav shouted, his voice hoarse and drowned out by the wind. "Just keep holding on! I have got to lose her!"

Katja glanced over her shoulder and spotted a dark silhouette flying through the sky on an iron pitchfork, likely one of the hundreds in that graveyard. Sitting atop the pitchfork was the countess. The Countess shook out her pale hair as she released it from its tight bun, letting it flow with her red cloak like a long elegant tail. Behind her, the sky darkened as water continued to spill from the heavens. Forks of lightning ripped from the clouds and stabbed the ground like daggers. *Is she controlling this storm?*

A flash of lightning hurled across the sky toward them, barely missing. The clap was deafening as it rang deep to her bones and rattled her teeth—or was that fear? She could not tell.

Stav sat atop the carpet like a jokey on a horse's saddle. Katja dug her fingers deeper into the rug, squeezing the grimoire in her armpits, when she noticed something familiar about the carpet—the colors, patterns, and designs. Her eyes widened when she realized what they were riding because she had seen it a hundred times before, but never like this—it was the *tapestry*.

"Brace yourself!" Stav barked, gazing out at the horizon that Katja could not see.

She gripped the tapestry with all her might and tucked her face into the rough spun fabric. Rain and wind stung her eyes, making them burn. Her heart skipped a few beats as they flew off at a speed far greater than before. She felt like she might fly as they turned starkly. It took all of her willpower not to continue screaming.

Lightning rippled across the sky again, followed by a drumline of percussion.

"How much longer?" Katja yelled, feeling her body soften with exhaustion.

"I just have to get her off our tail! Stay with me, Kat!" Stav shouted.

She buried her teeth into the fabric, hoping that bit of strength might keep her from falling.

A flash pierced the edge of the tapestry. The smell of burnt linen and mothballs filled the air, but Stav extinguished the flame before it became a catastrophe with a swoosh of his wand.

"There is only one way out of this!" he shouted, turning to face her for the first time. His eyes looked as if they were glowing. What purpose would that sort of magic serve?

"Just do it! I can't hold on any longer!" Katja shouted as she spat out a wad of soggy carpet. She looked over her shoulder and spotted the countess's silhouette in the shadows as a flare of lightning ignited the sky.

"Hold my hand!" Stav commanded, reaching out his hand while the other steered the carpet.

Katja grabbed his hand as a bolt of lightning snaked across the sky and struck a watchtower that might have been the Maiden Tower, but she couldn't be too sure where they were. Another bolt of lightning hissed past her ear, and although Katja couldn't tell for sure due to the bright radiance flooding her vision, she could have sworn she saw Stav loosen his grip on the tapestry fringe and reach for the lightning bolt with his bare hands.

The ground was now spiraling toward her face, and all she could hear was the ringing in her ears, or was she screaming?

Chapter Twenty-Six

When she opened her eyes, she was swarmed with red, orange, and yellow flurries dancing along the edge of her vision, and she could still make out the flattened valley around her, speckled with squares of yellow, green, and red pastures that reminded her of a quilt.

The only freestanding building in sight was a white three-story plantation house, a red barn consumed by ivy, and a grain silo that shone like metal on the far side of the valley. A gentle breeze chased across her face as she climbed to her knees, and the sound of creaky gears and crankshafts from a giant windmill, spinning a stone's toss behind, calmed her. The windmill's paint was chipping—a dull red that looked almost pink in the morning light. It took her a minute to notice that one of the blades was missing, its broken pieces scattered in ruins across the tall grass.

"Stav?" Katja shouted, her voice echoing into the distance. She groaned as she struggled to her feet and nearly gasped when she took a step and put too much pressure on her left knee. "Stav? Where are you?"

Katja bared her teeth through the pain as she limped across the pasture to the ruined windmill wing that she could only assume they had hit on the way down. To her horror, she found the tapestry torn among the muddled heap. Her heart raced as she attempted to pull apart the wreckage to find any signs of her mentor, but she couldn't find him. Her boot kicked something heavy, pages fluttering in the wind—*the grimoire.*

Her heart sank as she dove toward the blackened tome only to spot the glistening gold lettering shimmer beneath a layer of soot that she blew off with her breath. Its gilded-edged pages flashed brilliantly in the light as she splayed them, which were without a single blemish. Relieved, she placed the grimoire beneath her arm and continued scanning the horizon for her mentor.

"Stav!" Katja shouted, and now, searching more thoroughly, found an almond grove behind the windmill, backed by a copse of cedarwood that stood like matches scraping against the blue sky.

She noticed small sparrows and robins scurry from thick bushes and a rug of wildflowers sprawling among the tall grasslands. The flowers came in all shades of color, including vibrant violet, shiny goldenrod, cobalt blue, sunset orange, pinkish reds, and a few pale blue forget-me-nots that were almost white. The air around her was buzzing, but not like that of the city, which was all chatter, grinding breaks, squealing metal, clenching rope, clopping horsecars, and ringing temple bells she was used to. Instead, it was the buzz of bees, the sigh of trees, clicking of beetles, and the hum of grass combing in the gentle breeze. She had never felt so small and exposed in her life.

It was peaceful—but unnerving. Where was she?

Katja tiptoed through the grass, as its damp sprouts tickled her bare shins. It was then she realized that there were only a few wisps of white clouds, but even those were being swiftly scraped across the sky like a painter mixing ink with a palette knife.

"Stav!" she shouted again, furrowing her brow. Worry was setting in. There weren't many places to go. She began focusing on the trees when she caught sight of something long and dark protruding from a hollowed-out blackberry bramble that served as a wall guarding the sparse forest. Katja clenched her jaw in anguish as she limped toward the misshapen hedge. Lifeless legs stuck out, and to her relief and terror, she discovered Stav lying with dark blood across his arms, neck, and face. Despite the cuts and bleeds, he looked oddly peaceful, as if he were sleeping.

"Stav!" Katja gently patted his cheeks, which felt cold. "Wake up! Stav!"

He did not respond, but she could tell by his rising chest and flaring nostrils that he was still alive. She recalled his lessons and brought her face close to his, trying to catch a whiff of his breath. *Iron.* His breath smelled like blood. *If it smells sweet like honey, then you have plenty. If it smells like iron or blood, you don't have long before the kindling begins.*

Katja feverishly rummaged through his pockets but only found a small vial of green Vigor in his left breast pocket. It would have to do. She carefully uncorked the glass vial and tilted his head upward before pouring the viscous fluid down his throat, draining every last drop. Whatever magic Stav had used to lose the countess must have depleted his reserves.

Katja watched him closely, and to her relief, his breathing grew stronger, as some color returned to his cheeks. However, he continued to sleep. Was this how she acted when she had kindled? How long had she been unconscious? She didn't have sophisticated knowledge of kindling, but she knew that the more time you spent untreated, the worse it faired. If she wasn't careful, she could also run out of Vigor. She had just started recovering from the last kindling the countess had saved her from.

Memories swam back. The countess had saved her, but also had tried to kill her. It was all very complicated and made her head hurt, and all of this was happening because everyone believed her to be a Dustmage—*whatever that really meant.*

"Kat . . .?"

Katja spun to look at Stav, who was wincing with pain but slowly wiggling among the broken branches. She tried to pull him out of the shrubs, but he was still too weak and too heavy to lift on her own. She considered levitating him to softer ground, but she knew risking magic could mean death for both of them if she were to faint.

"Take it easy. You're kindling," Katja said, holding his hand assuredly. "What is hurting most?"

Stav groaned as he crawled to his knees, gripping his left arm, which had gone limp against his flank. "I am not kindling, or else I would be dead."

"Well, if you aren't, you are very close," Katja said. "Besides, I have kindled many times and I have survived to live another day."

Stav nodded. "You and I are very different."

Katja ignored that strange remark. "Where are you hurt?"

"I busted my arm, but that will heal," Stav groaned. "I think that windmill softened our landing. Are you hurt?"

Katja inspected her arms and legs. "I busted my knee, not to mention I was bruised and beaten before we fell from the sky into a windmill in the middle of nowhere. What sort of magic was that?"

"I only used it because I didn't see any other way to escape my mother. It isn't anything I am going to teach you . . . at least not yet," Stav said, pulling his greasy hair out of his face. "I told you she was a powerful witch. She probably figured I wouldn't be so desperate to latch onto her lightning bolts to bring us somewhere else. I don't know how long we can stay hidden, though. My scent will be scattered across the Theed sky, and I wouldn't be surprised if even dims could smell it."

"Dims? I heard the Grand Maiden use that word, but I haven't heard it used anywhere else," Katja asked.

"Luckless people . . . dims. It is all the same," Stav said. "People who know nothing about magic."

"My mother referred to them as *ords*," Katja said. "As in 'ordinary people.'"

"Ords, dims, luckless, it doesn't matter what you call them," Stav said dismissively.

Katja wanted to change the subject. "I gave you what was left of this vial" she said, raising the glass for Stav to see. "It isn't much, but it appears to have broken your slumber."

"Indeed," Stav said, taking Katja's hand and climbing to his feet, falling straight back to the ground. "Boils! I will need more time to recover." He took in their surroundings, observing the distant hills and valley walls.

"I dunno where we are," Katja said. "But it isn't Theed."

Stav smirked. "Correction . . . it isn't a part of Theed you have been to. I wager we are somewhere in the Cobb District. These foothills and forests lead to the Brakken Mountains, so we are on the far outskirts of the capital. There aren't many lands like this that aren't flattened and turned into a factory or township these days."

"I thought I knew almost everything about the city," Katja said, awestruck. "You could have fooled me into believing this was beyond the city gates somewhere . . . even beyond the Relian if I am being honest."

"There is a lot we don't know about this world," Stav said dismissively. "I have only been over the wall three times, and that was from the inside of a safe cabin in a locomotive when I was a young lad. It was back when those with enough coin and a household name could pay a fare to a few nearby cities, but now even that is hard to come by."

"What was it like?" Katja asked.

Stav sighed. "I don't remember much, but you would be surprised how normal it looked. A whole lot of trees, mountains, rivers, animals, and not a lot of people, unless they were hiding. I remember distinctly riding beneath a canopy of trees that looked as tall as skyscrapers."

"What else did you see? Giant deer? Bears with two heads? Dragons flying along the crests of mountaintops?"

Stav waved at her dismissively. "We have more important things to discuss than folktales, Kat. Have you seen anyone come out of that windmill? I don't know who owns these lands, but I reckon they won't be too happy about it being broken."

"I haven't seen a soul," Katja said. "Unless you count birds."

"Maybe luck is finally in our favor. We can find a spot within those trees to camp for the night and lick our wounds. Did you find the tapestry?" Stav asked eagerly.

"Yes," Katja said solemnly, looking back at the wreckage. "But it is torn into ribbons. I had no idea it could fly."

"There is a lot you have yet to learn, Kat," Stav said. "For example, if you gather the shreds, I should be able to mend them, but it won't be easy. Do you think you could do that? I will gather my strength so we can move to that alcove."

Katja mustered her own strength and headed back to the mill to collect the tapestry's tattered violet, mauve, red, and green flaps, avoiding any jagged splinters or rusty nails riddling the wreckage. To her relief, the tapestry was not completely severed, but had a large tear near its center and a few smaller ones along its edges. When she gathered what she could, she set it at Stav's feet. "I doubt we will find any needle and thread . . ."

"Oh! We can work with this!" he said excitedly, displaying the tapestry before him as if it were a map. "It will not be able to support both of us being torn like this, but I might be able to fly it far enough to the tree line."

"Are you certain? I can try to help you across the field."

"No, we are both too weak," Stav interrupted. "If you can, hold onto one end while I hold the other, and I will try to take flight."

Katja and Stav took hold of the tapestry, extending it outward like one would a kite. He uttered a few Elddir words beneath his breath, petting the rough fabric like a mighty mare, and with a soft exhale, they were pulled into the sky, but only so that their boots dangled a few lengths from the tall grass. They flew across the field, dodging jutting boulders and a few stray bushes until they approached the woodlands at good speed.

"We are almost there!" Stav shouted, his face red and intense.

Katja turned her focus to the fast-approaching trees, anticipation filling her body when there was a sudden snap, and they both fell to the ground.

She wiped thick mud from her face as she struggled to her feet again. She coughed and gagged as she approached Stav, who was covered in brown sludge and holding the tapestry in both hands solemnly.

"She got us where we needed, but tore right in half," Stav said. "It will take an expert tailor specializing in enchantments to fix these wounds . . . but the good news is, we are alive."

Katja helped Stav drag the muddied tapestry's remains into the tree's coverings for a camp. Once out of the intense sun, they collapsed to the forest floor, panting and beaten, the cool shade acting like a nice breeze on a warm day.

A squirrel darted up a tree trunk and watched them curiously as it nibbled on a nut. Katja stared at the squirrel as its fat cheeks shifted from one side to the other, and remembered the strange fox mask the stranger had worn in the graveyard. For some reason, what was likely only a few hours ago felt like days—time had become odd ever since she'd met Fleck and his miscreants.

"Are you going to eat that squirrel, or am I?" Stav said, his eyes and teeth bright, contrasting with the mud-caked skin on his face.

"I reckon they taste better than rats," Katja said, her stomach rumbling.

"Kat, I was joking!" Stav chuckled, looking at her like she was the strangest person he had ever met. "Besides, it wouldn't be much meat for all of that work, especially without using magic. If I could use magic, I would have it rigged over the fire already."

"I saw some crops out in those fields. Also, plenty of berries."

"I don't plan on needing much," Stav said defiantly. "We won't be staying long enough. We need to find Fleck."

"You have that much confidence in a man you loathed for so long?" Katja laughed, staring at the gently swaying branches and leaves overhead.

"I might loathe him, but no one else can strike fear in my mother like he can," Stav said. "Fleck pushed my mother out of the Roth years ago. I reckon he can do the same again."

"How do you reckon you will find him?"

Stav sighed. "The Orb."

"The scrying ball?" Katja asked.

"My brother and I just called it the Orb, but yes," Stav said, producing a short purple candlestick from his pocket. "I must admit, if this weren't in my pocket, I would be all out of ideas . . . thankfully, it is right where I put it."

Katja instantly recognized the candle. "Will it still work with the tapestry being torn to bits like this?"

Stav frowned. "I . . . I don't know, but we will find out."

He pulled his wand from his pocket and pointed it at the blackened candlewick, but Katja slapped it out of his hand. "What are you doing? Do you have a death wish?"

"Oh . . . I forgot . . . I am so accustomed to using magic, especially simple cantrips like sparking a fire," Stav grumbled. "I am sure I could spare enough Vigor for one light."

"That is how it starts, and then the next moment, you are hunting squirrels and collecting tree branches . . . and then boom! You faint on me, and I am stranded in this forest without any Vigor to revive you," Katja rebutted.

Stav sighed, "Just one spell . . ."

"You mean second? Maybe this is a good time to try living like an Dim for once . . . or whatever word you use to slander them," Katja scolded, attempting to rinse the mud out of her hair with her dry fingers with not much success. "You can't leave me out here alone when you die. We can start a fire the 'Dim' way."

"Oh . . . right," Stav said, collected a few twigs, pinecones, and leaves from the forest floor around him, and put them in a pile. "You think you can create a spark?"

She stared at him incredulously. "You don't know how to start a fire?"

Stav frowned. "Of course I do! You need a lot of dry materials."

"You have never started a fire before, have you?" Katja smirked.

His silence was telling.

"Not without . . . magic," Stav finally answered, avoiding her gaze. "I wager many magic folk don't know how to do things, ironically *because* of magic. Why learn to do things the hard way?"

"You work on the tapestry. I will work on the fire," Katja said. "Today, I am *your* mentor, Mr. Stavoren."

"Yes, Ms. Rosdyre," Stav grumbled, sitting on the ground and inspecting the large tear in the tapestry.

Katja jumped to her feet, her legs sore as she stretched. Her heart started to beat quickly as she remembered standing on that cemetery hill, moments from either accepting the countess's offer to join her or likely dying and being buried beneath a pitchfork in a shallow grave.

Her hand slid to her chest. *The amulet was gone.*

"I lost it. I lost the professor's amulet!" Katja gasped, swiftly searching the tall grass.

"That old thing? Where did you put it last?" Stav said dismissively.

Katja circled their camp, but there was no sign of anything of value, let alone a pearl amulet. "I put it around my neck before we took off flying. It must have fallen off when we crashed."

"Shame," Stav said. "Somebody wandering these fields will find it one day and won't have to work another day in their life."

"Was it really worth that much? You never told me why it was so valuable," Katja said, pacing. "I should go check by the mill."

"No, someone might spot you," Stav said rather sternly. "Especially alone, and I cannot make it out there to protect you until I am healed."

"I don't require protection, Stav," Katja snapped. "I think it is you who needs protecting."

"Perhaps that is true, but we need to stick together," Stav said. "You don't know who might be watching. Who knows, maybe the countess put some sort of enchantment on the amulet."

"Alright, fine," Katja groaned. "But later I need to look for dry wood near the fields. I won't go past the tree line, but if I see that amulet sparkling in the sun, I'm fetching it."

Katja sighed and gathered more dry leaves, twigs, and a pile of dry alfalfa grass from the field. She then slowly dug a small pit with her hands and collected a few uneven stones to form a circular barrier. She tossed her muddy mop of hair over her shoulder and stuck her tongue out as she feverishly scraped the two twigs together until a bit of smoke started to trickle from a newly formed ember, catching the dry grass ablaze.

Stav stirred with shock as the fire grew, almost looking scared by its intensity.

"No magic required," Katja said, her palms raw and sweat dripping down her brow. She knew she would have blisters from all her hard work by tomorrow morning, but having a little light when it turns night will be worth the pain.

"I will serve you one better," Stav smiled, displaying the tapestry, which was now roughly stitched together with loose weaves of grass.

Katja was somewhat impressed but could tell the stitch would break under even the lightest scrutiny. "That won't hold a bunny rabbit, let alone both of us."

"I am going to try and get inside it," Stav said, ignoring her. He placed the candle into the new flame and set it on a nearby rock.

Both watched, observing the tapestry's spectacular colors, but they were not swirling. Stav grazed his hand against the fabric, but nothing happened. It acted like any ordinary tapestry. "This isn't good. We need an expert in enchanted fabrics, but we won't find one anywhere out here."

"Let me work on the stitch to see if that helps," Katja said, sticking her finger through a few gaps in Stav's patchwork. "Every fiber may need to be perfectly sealed."

"Magic is so finicky, isn't it?" he chuckled, raising his hands to the fire, which had started to tame.

By the time it was nearly dark, Katja's blistered hands were worn down to the bone after meticulously stitching the tapestry with only tall grass, which she had Stav collect more of every few hours. In the end, she barely used a single strand of Stav's stitching, but this time it was quite strong and held firm when she pulled at it, which was good enough for tonight.

Katja's eyes glazed over from exhaustion, and her body felt like it had been chiseled away like a sculptor accidentally chipping off too much marble and leaving only a mesh of something that partially resembled a person. Across from her, she now had to squint to see Stav sitting between the light and the shadow, massaging his injured leg.

"You should rest, Kat," he said, gesturing that his hands were not injured. "Let me take on the rest."

"I am almost done," she said, her eyes twitching from staring at her fingers for hours. "Besides, you will probably try to use a little magic trick to finish it when I am not looking."

"I would not," Stav said. "I might have been raised like a prince, but I rejected that life long ago. I can do a bit of stitching."

"Are you sure about that?" Katja asked. "I saw your last attempt."

Stav picked up some grass twine and fidgeted with it for a moment with his delicate fingers, but it only got caught into a couple of unsavory clumps and knots after only a few minutes.

"My mother taught me to sew! I am not that lame!" he said defensively.

Katja rolled onto her back and watched the smoke and sparks rise to the forest canopy, which was thankfully far above their heads. "Are you going to try to open the portal or not?"

Stav grunted and relit the violet candle. For a moment, nothing happened, but then the tapestry's façade started to twist, contort, and swirl like silvery moonlight contorting on churning seas at night.

"It worked!" Stav exclaimed, looking at Katja with a fiendish face. "I will be right back."

"Shouldn't I go? I did fix it after all."

There was silence between them as they stared into each other's eyes like some duel of obstinacy. The sound of crackling flames, rustling leaves, crickets, and a distant barred owl filled the silence.

"Fine. Go," Katja said, shooing him with her hands. She did not like the idea of her only ally jumping into a likely faulty portal. "If you don't return in ten minutes, I will assume something bad happened and will come looking for you."

Stav nodded, carefully palming the candle. "Make it five minutes. This won't take long."

She sighed. "Well . . . go on then."

Stav swiveled his legs into the portal, where they disappeared as if he had dipped them beneath a pool of water. He then winked before shoving himself into the portal like someone jumping off a ledge into an abyss.

Chapter Twenty-Seven

Although she had no way of telling time other than some less-than-credible guesswork, Katja knew for sure more than five minutes had passed. In fact, it felt more like half an hour before the realization truly struck her that she might never see Stav again. *Why did he fall into the portal?* Whenever she entered the portal, it was seamless, like stepping into another room. The floors in the secret chamber were perfectly aligned with the floorboards of Stavoren Manor and the Warren. So why did his legs dangle, and why did he fall?

Katja's mind spun, watching the swirling tapestry on the forest floor. She then carefully braced herself, holding onto a tree root with one hand, and slowly slipped her other hand into the portal. She could feel the warm air wrap and embalm her skin. She stuck the twig through the barrier and lifted it back up, noticing no changes to its characteristics until something grazed her finger, causing her to retreat. Was Stav playing a cruel trick on her?

She took a deep breath and counted down from ten before pressing her face against the tapestry.

Katja's face entered the warm chamber and she choked on the terrible brew of candle smoke, ashes, and dust coating the air. A little down, she spotted the dim pinprick of Stav's candle and the gentle glow of the crystal ball on his face. She also spotted his bright, toothy grin, which looked delighted to see her.

"Kat!" Stav's voice shouted hoarsely. "Kat! Help me out!"

"What happened?" she asked, bewildered at the messy hole of ash and all things gray that Stav was standing in. He looked helpless, like a child.

"Turns out the tapestry was hung on the wall for a reason!" Stav said, choking on ash. "The whole chamber is flipped on its side! I nearly broke my ankle, falling onto a rubble heap, and I cannot reach the portal!"

"I told you I should have gone in," Katja said, reaching her arm down into the pit. Then, she noticed Stav standing at the altar where the grimoire once stood, opposite the entrance. "Did you find the scrying ball?"

"Catch!" he shouted, tossing the thick glass orb in her direction.

Katja reached out her arm at the last minute and swiveled on her hips to balance the swirling ball cradled delicately in her arm. She secured the scrying ball and set it beside the fire before returning to the portal for Stav.

"What if I had dropped it? That wasn't funny!" Katja scolded.

Stav carefully picked the candle up off the floor, making her wince with anxiety. She did not like that candle anymore—not after it nearly killed her to light it.

"Hand the candle to me. If the ashes extinguish it, I am going to be headless, and you will be stuck here for an eternity," Katja said. She wasn't sure what happened when your body was partially between worlds, but it didn't seem promising.

Stav carefully leaned against the wall, which had once been the floor, and stepped on his tippy toes, extending the candle to Katja, but he could not reach her. "I don't think I should throw this one!" He choked on every word.

Katja speculated for a second, wondering if she could balance her body over the ledge inside the portal to gain more leverage, but she thought it was too risky. If both of them fell to the bottom, they wouldn't have much hope of getting out without using magic.

Magic. How much Vigor could a quick levitation spell cost? She debated in her head until she decided there was no other way.

"Set the candle down very carefully, and I will get you out first," Katja ordered.

Stav appeared to weigh the decision and set the candle down. Katja lifted herself out of the portal, bracing her feet in the tree roots like an anchor, then lunged down to Stav. He leaped a few times, finally catching her hand on the fourth attempt. Her shoulders felt like they would burst from their sockets, and she could feel her feet lose their grip as she slowly dragged him up the wall while he did most of the work, shimmying with his legs.

When Stav reached the ledge, Katja repositioned herself and helped pull him out of the portal, spilling them onto the forest floor. Both of them gasped for breath like a fish out of water, and Katja felt like she might have broken something in her arms and spine, which ached and burned in agony. But she knew she was not entirely done. She reached into the portal again, felt the warm boil in her chest, summoned the candle to her hand, and watched it float carefully up to her. She rolled onto her back out of the portal and pulled a hair from the back of her head.

Stav pointed at the violet candle, puffing black smoke from its wick.

Chills ran down Katja's neck as the realization settled within her.

He started howling with laughter. "Witches' boils! You almost lost your bloody arm!"

Katja frowned, but watching Stav laugh was almost contagious. A smile cracked, and she laughed and coughed, too tired to care, as they caught their breath. "Hexes! I almost lost my head!"

They laughed into the evening and stayed put as the flames began to wane, and twilight gave way to night. Katja was thankful they were far removed from the busy city and roads, because if any travelers had been nearby, they would likely have been horrified, believing there was a coven of witches cackling late into the night.

* * *

That morning, Katja woke up to the chirping of robins and chickadees, which made for the most peaceful morning of her life, despite how terrible her body felt. When she rolled her eyes and adjusted to the sunlight, she spotted the fire, a pit of hot embers at her feet. A platter made of thick tree bark sat next to the fire, adorned with three runny eggs boasting bright orange yolks that baked in the heat.

"Good . . . you didn't die," Stav said, studying the crystal ball between his feet across the fire. "I stumbled into a nest of robin eggs. I'm sure you're hungry."

Her stomach growled at the smell of food, but part of it ruined the serenity of birdsong that had graced her morning. She stretched her arms and legs and sat upright, watching the strange images reflecting from the orb's glowing, misty innards.

"I am impressed you knew how to crack an egg," Katja teased.

"I might have been born with servants and butlers, but I ran away from home when I was your age," Stav smiled, gaze locked on the crystal ball. "Besides, I never quite liked how rich people did their eggs with all the embellishments, so I learned to cook them correctly."

"On a worm-infested slab of tree bark next to a dying flame?" Katja chuckled.

Stav grinned. "Precisely."

"Next time, try using a stone. Something flat, like a river rock," she said with judgment in her tone. "But at this point, I will eat anything, even if it splinters my tongue."

Katja tossed a few branches and dry leaves onto the embers. There was a sprinkle of dew on everything around the camp, which made managing the flame a bit difficult, but she found it refreshing—short of taking a bath—as she used the dew droplets to scrub dirt from her face.

"There is a creek a little way from here. Perhaps we can take turns washing," Stav said.

Katja listened and heard a very faint trickle of water, more like a hum.

"Have you found Fleck yet?" she asked, carefully flipping the eggs with the tips of her callused fingers so the yolk did not break.

"I am close." Stav wiped his sweaty brow and firmly placed his hand on the top of the orb like a crown. With the other hand, he was fidgeting with a small tin soldier, similar to the ones kids would barter over on street corners during a game of dice.

"Isn't that Fleck's token? How did you get hold of it?" Katja asked.

"Do you remember me cloaking just before my mother and the other Roth returned? I slipped past them with the tapestry, crystal ball, grimoire, and token before taking flight and waiting for you to return to the graveyard. It was a bit difficult, because I had to uncloak for just a moment to pick up everything . . . you know, because you can't grab things when you are cloaking. I can show you later, but you can only hold things that were already on you when you started the cloaking spell to begin with. Everything has to be accounted for when you split your body like that."

"That would have been useful to know earlier," Katja uttered under her breath.

"You should have seen my face when I saw Gwith set her trap on you," Stav said. "I only had one chance to steal you from my mother's desperate claws."

Katja ruminated on what happened in the graveyard not even a day ago. "Kristoff said Gwith was going to kill me. It sounds like she had different plans than the countess and the rest of the Roth. I don't understand why she hates me so much."

Stav nodded. "Gwith is loyal to the Roth, but her own agenda gets in the way. She is a powerful Glint, who can cast detailed illusions—better than I have ever seen, with only a few exceptions. She also holds grudges, and I suspect she is very jealous of the attention you get from the others. It wasn't long ago that Gwith was the promising new talent."

"Jealous of me? I can cast at most three different spells, and only one with certainty," Katja said. "And why would Kristoff and the countess attack her? For a moment, I thought she was dead."

"The countess has been obsessed with finding Dustmages for decades, if not longer," Stav said. "Gwith has never been afraid to spill blood to further her aims. She justifies it in her wicked ways, much like my mother and my brother. I wager they knew Gwith wouldn't hold back and decided to stop her before she ruined everything my mother has been working for. Besides, if my mother wanted you dead, she would want to deal the final blow. She would never let Gwith get away with it. You are far to valuable to her."

"If there are other Dustmages, why does she pursue me? Could she not find another?" Katja folded her arms tighter across her chest. "I think I have made it clear I am not interested in working with her."

Stav's mouth curved faintly. "There are others, but they are few. They say one is born for every million births, but I wager it could be even fewer. The difficulty lies in that very few ever know they are a Dustmage, much less a Glint. Most die having never learned magic—perhaps only witnessing a few strange occurrences throughout their lives that made them feel different, but never discerning the reason why."

"What is so special about being a Dustmage?" Katja pressed. "I used to think I was special, being able to levitate, but after meeting the Roth, I feel rather inadequate. If I were the countess, I would rather find a dozen more like Gwith to fill my ranks."

Stav bit the inside of his lip before answering. "My mother knows more, but from my understanding, the Dustmage is a Glint unhindered by the same rules we normal Glint live by and, if properly mentored, can master magic with far more ease and tenacity. They are unburdened by magedust and cannot die through the kindling process." He rubbed a hand over his jaw. "I do not know the reasoning behind it, but from what I have heard, a Dustmage can somehow absorb Vigor from the very air we breathe. Perhaps there is something in the wind, or perhaps it has to do with the sun and stars. There is no mistaking that they survive even the worst Vigor overdraws."

"But I require magedust like the rest of you," Katja insisted. "That is painfully obvious from how many times I have kindled."

"But you have never died." Stav's gaze sharpened as he held hers. "That is the key. I would have died in nearly every instance you fell into kindling, but here you are. Alive and well."

A chill ran down Katja's spine. "I felt like I was dying each time."

"I do not doubt that," Stav replied more quietly. "I never said a Dustmage does not suffer."

Katja's thoughts scattered like bees shaken from their hive.

"So if magedust were not so costly, much of a Dustmage's advantage would vanish? With an endless supply, kindling would scarcely matter," she said after a moment. "Even with time, I doubt I could be more valuable to the Roth than, say, Urie, who can poof anywhere he wants, or Gwith, who can create mind-altering entrapments."

"When you are building something that is meant to last, you cannot only think of the moment." Stav rubbed the scrying stone with his cuff, polishing away a faint smudge. "Imagine all the time we spend acquiring enough dust and Vigor to prepare even basic spells. That does not include magic far beyond my understanding. There are spells that take a lifetime to master, and much of that delay is due to Vigor limitations. The Dustmage can learn to be unhindered by magedust, which, as you know, is rare and more precious than gold." He paused. "The specifics elude me."

She studied him. "So that is it? She wants to mentor me for decades until I can do her bidding?"

Stav exhaled slowly. "Simply put, yes. But there is more complexity than that. I do not understand much of it because she keeps it close to her chest. Most records of Dustmages have long since been removed from the libraries in Theed. Even the grimoire is missing pages, and entire appendices have been blotted out. There is much we do not know."

"So, what happened to Simon?" Katja asked, her voice carrying over the hush of the trees. "Fleck said that was the name of the last Dustmage he trained."

Stav's fingers stilled against the bright stone. He cast her a narrow look before lowering his gaze again. "He was taken by the Magesleuths," he said at last. "During one of our raids. Not one of our finest."

"Well? What happened?"

"Fleck received word that a massive reserve of magedust was stored in the city armory off Waller Street in the Brig," Stav began. "We planned it down to the minute. Urie *shimmed* inside—" He snapped his fingers softly. "—and opened the lock from within. Simon entered with Fleck and Gwith."

"Shimmed?" Katja echoed.

"That is what we call it when he vanishes." A faint ghost of amusement passed over his face. "Poof, and there he stands, within walls thick enough to resist even the heaviest artillery."

He continued, "Simon always knew where the stockpile was. We suspected some manner of foresight."

"Perhaps he was hooked on it himself," Katja muttered.

"Possibly," Stav conceded, continuing his tale. "They broke one of the codes protecting the stockpile. We intended to take only a few years' supply, enough to go unnoticed, and return once it ran dry."

"It always goes faster than you think," Katja said.

He inclined his head but did not comment. "We fled with our bags and split through the sewers. It is suspected that the Magesleuths had discovered Simon's scent weeks prior and pursued him beneath the streets. According to Fleck, Simon resisted, yet he was overcome, while Fleck made his escape."

"And they didn't pick up Fleck's scent when he fought back?" Katja asked.

"Fleck didn't go into that." Stav's jaw tightened. "He said there was nothing he could do to save Simon, and judging by his reaction to Simon's passing, I have no reason to doubt him."

Silence settled between them.

"I believe Simon died in the sewer," Stav said at last. "If the rumors of the Magesleuths' torture are true, he would have revealed the Warren eventually. Not even Simon's will was that strong."

Katja parted her lips to respond, but nothing came. She withdrew into her thoughts.

There was a moment of silence as the two sat ruminating with distant eyes that only focused when a bird and squirrel rustled a tree branch. Katja couldn't help but stare at her fingers, wondering if she had overlooked something simple about her anatomy that made her different. She wished so badly to talk to her mother and tell her about everything that she had learned. Was her mother a Dustmage, too? How about her father? Was it something you inherited? The thoughts swiveled through her mind until she was overwhelmed and focused on something tangible—something solid to ground her in the moment.

Katja reached for the tin soldier token. "Does the token do something, or is it just sentimental?"

"When scrying, it helps to have something . . . such as an item of the person you seek to find," Stav said. "A lock of hair or dirty sock would have been stronger, but this is better than nothing."

Katja scooted closer to the crystal ball, sitting opposite Stav. She stared into the reflection and saw a lonely dirt road with a willow tree in the foreground. Then the image shifted, revealing a set of iron gates with arrow tips and a dying rosebush garden. Next, she saw a small crowd of men seated at a tavern, sipping foamy ales and eating hot plates, which made Katja eye their eggs, luckily just before they burned.

Katja reached for the charred bark slab and brought the sizzling eggs between them, thankful they were only a little brown along the usually pale edge than desired. She blew on one egg and plopped it into her mouth, allowing the yoke to pop on her tongue and run down her cheek. The warmth and slightly salty taste were delightful as they burned down her throat to her belly.

"I should critique you for using wood to cook over fire, but when you haven't eaten in a while, one cannot complain about the method," Katja smirked, licking the slab without any concern for splinters.

"That is wise," Stav winked, "Isn't the old wisdom to never bite the hands that feed you?"

Katja pivoted the conversation. "So, do you believe Stav is in another city within the Commonwealth? Maybe Duskpool? Warring? Montcrest? Those are the only ones I know that are close to Theed".

"Maybe Krone? But I imagine that would be risky going all that way flying a magic carpet," Stav said, taking a bite of egg and recoiling. "A little crisp for my tastes. You can have the other."

"You warlocks are something else," Katja smiled, reaching for the egg and devouring it. "Clearly, you lot have never had to wonder where your next meal will come from."

"Wait!" Stav said, drawing his face so close to the orb that his nose pressed against it. "From the street, I can see something! It is faint, but anyone from Theed can recognize that bloody silhouette!"

Katja licked her fingers and pressed her face closer to the orb, but couldn't see anything peculiar. "Where?"

"Look in the background . . . don't you see it?" Stav jeered, punching the air with excitement. "I can't believe I did it! Kristoff was always the scryer in the family, but it turns out I can find someone if my will is strong enough!"

Katja squinted her eyes. Far in the distance was a dark silhouette barely visible off the hilltop, but it had one distinguishing feature: *three round and spiked turrets.*

"The royal palace!" she gasped. "Well, if that is true . . . that could only mean one thing."

"He is not far away in some foreign city . . . he is still in Theed," Stav said, his bright eyes wide. "The royal family built the palace high on the hill and so massive that anyone from every district could see its display of strength and wealth."

"We can't see it from here . . ."

"I am sure you could see it somewhere from the Flowing District on a clear day," Stav argued. "In the vision, the palace looks far away. That makes me think he is in one of these far-off rural districts like we are in now, like the Cobb, High Garden, or Low Garden Districts."

"That is good news!" Katja said, looking at her empty wooden slab. "Where should we look first? I don't know how long my stitch will hold up."

Stav continued staring at the ball. "Give me a minute to figure that out. I might be able to determine a name or town. How about you go wash off in the creek? By the time you come back, I will have a better answer. If we are lucky, we will be flying off today!"

Katja nodded, feeling like bathing would be a perfect addition to her delightful morning. She listened for the waters again and headed deeper into the forest, wading through sticker bushes, spiderwebs, and thick brush, constantly noting where their camp was so she would not get turned around.

It did not take long before the water became louder, and her foot stepped into a cold basin of water. She looked over her shoulder and down the narrow creek to make sure there weren't any animals or people watching. She slipped out of her dress, which had lost its pristine red color. *All that stress and money spent on a new dress was for nothing.*

Katja rinsed her dress, using a pumice stone she found on the riverbed to scrape off the dirt, but some of the stains would likely never get out without the lye and boiling waters of the Maiden Tower laundry. She set the dress to dry on a large stone, unclothed completely, and submerged into the cold waters, gasping as she plunged to her chest. When she was done scrapping every bit of caked mud and grime from her cracked and chapped skin, she untied her hair and dropped under the slow, churning current. The sound of babbling water was peaceful, and when she returned to the surface, the dark grit left her hair slick and a darker shade of red. She had never thought she would miss the firm brush of the Maiden Tower prefects.

When she was done, Katja dried off in the sun for a while, but grew impatient and slipped into her damp clothing, figuring it would dry if they flew later that day. She put her hair in braids, feeling the thinning patch near the nape of her neck where she had pulled a few too many strands over the years. She took a few swigs of water, giving her the strength she did not know she was missing. Despite being bruised, beaten, and bleeding in some spots, she felt far better than sitting in that jail cell in the Warren or under the constant gaze of prefects.

She felt truly free. *This is how the warlocks must feel inside their giant castles of stone and glass.*

When she finished drinking from the creek, her eyes locked on something from the other side of the riverbank. It was an old man with long, white hair, leathery skin, and strange ornaments, like jewelry, dangling from his neck, earlobes, nose, and wrists.

"Hello . . .?" Katja stammered, approaching the dry shore.

The man did not answer, his hair and jewelry swaying in the wind. His eyes were foggy like milk, and his smile was sunken, suggesting he was missing his teeth. A cold tremor swept through her as she noticed a curved knife glistening in his right hand.

Katja felt her heart skip a beat.

"Is this your forest? I do not mean to trespass, and I don't mean any harm," Katja said, raising her hands to show she was not a threat. "I will just go away now . . . back to my friends."

The man's hazy eyes drifted upward, where a faint black smoke drifted from the forest canopy. He licked his lips, revealing his toothless mouth.

Katja drew a deep breath and started running into the forest, ignoring spiderwebs, tree branches, and thick brush as she hurried back to their camp. When she arrived, Stav was still poring over his crystal ball as if nothing had happened.

"Stav! We have to go!" she said breathlessly, picking up the candle and grimoire frantically. "There is someone in this forest, and they don't seem happy we are here!"

"You ran into someone? Here?" Stav said. "We can talk to them and ask them for help finding where Fleck is located. Nice hair, by the way! I was just getting used to you being a brunette, but red favors you better."

"He didn't seem like the helping kind!" Katja spat.

"Are you sure? I heard the locals are kind around these parts," Stav grinned.

"He had a bloody knife!" Katja screamed. "We need to leave!"

There was a crack of a twig across the forest, and Katja jumped, picturing the man before she saw him. But instead of the old man, it was a tall, emaciated woman with long black hair dressed in deer hide. Out of the corner of her eye, Katja spotted another figure, this one a young man naked from the waist up and missing an eye. A third figure stood a ways off with a large hammer in one hand and blue tattoos inked into their skin.

Stav jumped to his feet, tucked the crystal ball under his arm, heaved the tapestry over his shoulder, and started running out of the forest without a word. Katja chased after him as something whizzed by her ankle, which she imagined was an arrow, but she was too scared to look over her shoulder to make sure. They spilled out of the forest edge into the bright grassy fields, which were still dew-licked.

"Hurry! Jump aboard!" Stav shouted, reaching a grassy knoll and spreading the tapestry over it like they would have a nice picnic.

Katja dove onto the back of the tapestry and clung her fingers to its fabric, her stomach sinking as she watched the newly stitched grass threads, fearing they might be undone at any moment. Stav sat at the helm and uttered a few words under his breath before the tapestry pushed off the ground, albeit a little crooked, but sturdy enough to hold both of them.

"Hold onto everything tightly! We don't want to drop anything!" Stav barked, tucking the crystal ball between his legs.

Below them, they spotted the strangers slowly approaching from the forest, but this time, ten . . . maybe twenty were pouring from the shadows. Arrows flew past, one piercing through the tapestry edge that had been burned by lightning the other night.

Then, with a firm mush of the tapestry flaps, they soared away, the patchwork of perfectly square fields zooming by beneath them.

"Where will we go?" Katja said, watching the scar in the fabric and feeling a leak of air whistling through the delicate weave. "I don't know how long we have."

"We are going to the nearest small town. Someplace so small they don't even have a constable. That is where Fleck would hide," Stav shouted. He looked over his shoulder and pointed east toward the city. "Do you see the palace?"

Katja looked where he was pointing and noticed the shine of the ruby red, sapphire blue, and emerald green domes sitting atop the hilltop next to the shimmering bay filled with distant white sails. Atop the domes were spiked turrets that scraped the clouds high above. She wondered about the odds of them happening to spot the royal palace just now. After all, it was usually shrouded in the thick fog from the Relian that settled on the palace roof.

"It looks almost like the same distance and angle from the vision," Stav said. "Fleck can't be far."

Katja noticed a few mossy rooftops and smoky chimneys poking from the forest just ahead, set beside a large field. Stav appeared to see the same thing and smiled before lowering the tapestry, dodging past the building windows and streets to avoid being spotted or raising suspicion.

When they reached the field, it was far less muddy than the one prior. Katja disembarked the tapestry first, grimoire and candle firmly pressed against her ribs. As she expected, she was still a little damp but far drier after flying across the sky, although she had already lost some of the cleanliness she had achieved after running across the forest from those strange forest dwellers.

"Who were those people?" Katja asked as Stav took the grimoire, candle, and crystal ball, hid them beneath the tapestry in a small hole, and buried them with leaves so they could be retrieved later.

"*Blotters*," Stav said. "I can talk more about it later."

Katja looked at the scrappy hiding spot and scanned the horizon, where they spotted a few wooden houses with stone chimneys. "Are you sure no one will stumble upon this hiding spot? It would be quite a discovery."

"It will have to serve," Stav said, "and I hope we won't be long."

He started to hobble across the field. Katja followed closely behind, the two eggs in her stomach threatening to come up as the toll of flying attempted to collect its toll. "Who were those other men we saw standing alongside your mother? I saw one of them was wearing a mask."

"Former members," Stav grumbled, picking up a long stick and using it to help his step. "But now is not the time for questions. We don't know who is in this town, and it could be anyone, even my mother's spies. So keep your questions simple and your eyes down."

When they reached the end of the field, they climbed over a small wooden gate and stepped onto a flat gravel road. Further down, there was a series of tiny half-timber houses, but the one that caught their eyes was an inn at the end of the road backed up to a small orchard. Hanging from the inn's entrance was an engraved sign swinging in the wind with the words *Thistle & Grove Inn*. As they approached, Stav stopped to point out a familiar vantage point where you might see the royal palace perched on its roost on a clear morning, but the fog had already moved in from the sea.

They entered the inn, the door creaking on its hinges, and a dozen men and a few women with rough-spun clothing and fur hats stared at them as they approached the front desk, which also served as a bar with kegs stacked behind it from floor to ceiling. Each barrel had a different branding scorched into its timbers. Across the tavern were a handful of round tables, a few beat-up sofas, and a makeshift stage in the far corner where a boy not much older than Katja was tuning a fiddle.

Stav waved to the innkeeper, who was busy talking with a few patrons at the corner of the long wooden bar top. He seemed bothered by being hailed, but smothered his cigarette and approached after taking a swig of something brown in his mug, which dripped down his long red beard. When he stood before them, his stomach plopped over the counter, his massive stature towering over them as he pulled out a pen and paper and started scribbling on it.

"What can I do for you two strangers?" the innkeeper said, his voice as deep as one of the barrels behind him. Katja noticed that he was missing three of his ten fingers, one ear, and a chunk of his nose, and he was walking on a peg leg that scraped against the hardwoods. Not to mention, he was missing an eye, which was covered with a patch.

"We are looking for someone," Stav said, leaning his weight onto the bar and combing back his greasy hair. "Have you seen a man going by 'Fleck' around these parts?"

"Fleck? Never heard of him," the innkeeper said, folding his scarred arms. "Why are you looking out here? You look dirty, but I can tell by your clothes you aren't from this district, that is for certain."

A lady from the bar with bushy honey hair pulled her pipe out of her lips and sized both of them up. She was missing several fingers as well. "Looks like you got into some trouble. We don't care for trouble here. We have seen enough of it."

Stav chuckled nervously. "We ran into a horde of blotters just west of here, so yes, we did indeed run into bloody trouble."

The whole room swiveled its attention back to them, fear painted on their faces.

"Watch that tongue, traveler," the innkeeper spat. "You are a guest for as long as I allow you to stay in my inn."

"Blotters?" "Did he say out west?" "Do you reckon that is out past Pliny Hill?" a few voices whispered in the crowd.

"There were a dozen of them, men and women. They chased us out of the woods, but I am afraid to say I couldn't tell you the name of the trees if you begged me. It was a few miles west of here, past a red barn near an old windmill," Stav said. "They were bloodthirsty, too."

The innkeeper nodded. "They all are."

"Do you have a bloody cigarette? I need a cigarette," Stav said, wiping his brow, "and maybe a glass of water. Two, if you include my friend here."

The innkeeper glared at Stav for a minute but then pulled a pack of cigarettes from his back pocket and handed him one. "The water isn't good out here. I reckon a cold and refreshing ale from our inn brewmaster's casks would serve you better."

"Ale it is then," Stav said, sitting on a stool and signaling for Katja to join him.

A few minutes later, the innkeeper plopped two foaming pewter pints in front of them and leaned onto the counter, the grain of oak straining under his weight as he lit a cigarette and blew the smoke into the air, which was already thick with it. The man had bands of scars up his arms, one of which was a thistle that reminded her of the one engraved on the grand maiden's bedchamber doors.

"So, no man by the name of Fleck, ey?" Stav said, puffing on the cigarette and flicking the ashes into a tray. It was strange how natural he looked smoking. His demeanor was also a little off, and he spoke as if his tongue was heavy or coated with molasses. It was almost as if he were playing a character. *Who is this man?*

"I am afraid not," the barkeep said, looking out to the crowd and hollering. "Anyone heard of a man named Fleck around these parts?"

No one responded, but instead continued staring at them with alien stares.

"Can you describe him?" the honey-haired lady said between sips of brandy.

"Well . . . for one, his face looks like one not even a mother could love," Stav simpered. "Burnt and scarred like a melted candle."

The innkeeper looked a little shaken by his description and took a large gulp of ale, foam dripping down his beard. "I have never seen anyone by that description. Perhaps you could try the next town . . . that is, once you pay for your drinks, of course."

Stav reached into his pocket and fetched a leather wallet. He handed the man eight knots. "I would also like a room for tonight. We are weary travelers."

"*A* room?" Katja said, sending an elbow into Stav's ribs.

"Two rooms," Stav said, reaching into his wallet. "Is that enough to keep the ale flowing, a warm meal, and our names omitted from your log books?"

The innkeeper glanced at his wallet, which was full of coins. "I see one silver crown" he said. "How about you part ways with that, and you've got a deal?"

Stav narrowed his eyes at the innkeeper but smiled, slapping the shiny silver coins on the counter. "Smart chap. Never settle when there is more coin on the table to be plucked. Fleck would have liked you."

Katja kicked Stav's boot as the innkeeper walked away. "Who are you? You have charm, but I have never seen you lay it so thick," she whispered.

Stav smiled mischievously and took a swig of from his pint.

"I was almost one of those fancy feet-kissing lawmen my mother used to meet with, like Rhys DeGrom," Stav said, blowing smoke into Katja's face, making her cough. "I also know that the innkeeper is lying. This place is a bloody blotters' den."

"Blotters? Like the ones we just saw?" Katja whispered, eyeing the faces across the inn. "They don't act like . . . blotters."

"If the innkeepers missing limbs and scars didn't make it obvious, the fact that he and everyone else in the bar didn't leap up and run when they heard blotters had been spotted a few miles away made it unmistakable," Stav uttered into her ear, his breath reeking of smoke and brew already. "Not all blotters live like nomads in the forest. Some find edges of the city where the Crown and Magesleuths have a harder time finding them."

"Just thinking about it gives me a cold shiver?" Katja trembled.

Stav pursed his lips. "It is a terrible way to live, but Magedust is incredibly expensive. Some people find another way, no matter how horrific the means."

"Are we safe?" she asked.

"Hard to say for certain. But it appears these people are trying to keep hidden. Killing a few travelers is not in their interest . . . I assume," Stav said, finishing his ale. "Try to keep low. Let's find a table, eat a meal, and then we can figure out where Fleck is hiding in this bloody place."

"They said they never heard of him."

Stav smiled. "As I mentioned, they are lying. The crystal ball does not lie. Fleck is somewhere nearby . . . I can almost smell him."

Chapter Twenty-Eight

A platter of roast duck and potatoes was gone before it could be set down on the counter. Katja didn't bother with silverware as she pulled the tender meat from the bone and washed it with a swig of brew. Stav watched, appalled, before neatly parting his duck with a fork and knife.

"I have seen goats at the Warren eat with better manners," Stav whispered, dabbing his lips with a cloth napkin. "I would have thought living in the Maiden Tower and serving my mother would have rubbed off on you."

Katja frowned. "I served your mother. I didn't sit at her table."

"Fair," Stav said, nearly choking on his overcooked potatoes. "Once you are done eating, I want you to take a look around upstairs."

"Upstairs?"

"Yes. Ask the innkeeper for your room key. While you're upstairs, see which rooms are occupied. I doubt a place like this fills many beds," Stav said matter-of-factly. "I'd wager Fleck is staying here."

"You think he is hiding here, among . . . *blotters*?" Katja whispered, looking around the room before speaking. She still caught the occasional stare from the locals who slipped in and out of the inn.

"What's a more inconspicuous place to hide?" Stav said. "I give him credit . . . it is quite genius."

"I think I would rather get back to our stuff," Katja said. "Unless someone already stumbled upon it."

Stav groaned. "Not now. Go upstairs quickly, check the rooms, and then we'll decide our next move."

"I'm a young girl in a tavern full of even stranger people," Katja spat. "There's no way I'm going upstairs alone."

"It will only take a few minutes."

"If it's so simple, why don't you do it?" Katja bemoaned. "I would rather be somewhere near the door in case I need to run away. Especially if they are what you say they are."

Stav contemplated for a minute, biting his tongue. "Fine. I will be back." He tore from his seat, fetched his room key from the innkeeper, and vanished up the stairs where the man directed him to go.

Katja's stomach growled as she eyed a few scraps from Stav's plate and decided to resume where he had left off. She gulped her pint of ale, which one of the servers refilled before she ever lost sight of the head of foam. Despite their circumstance, she felt this was how normal people lived. Not rich, but ordinary people who didn't live in the streets or were forced to work as chambermaids. How nice it must be to have even an ounce of dignity to your name, to walk into a tavern, order food and drink, and talk to others who had warm homes to return to at night's end. It felt like bliss.

The feeling was ruined when someone sat at the table behind her and took the single chair directly at her back. The stranger leaned back, reclining their chair into hers. The stranger cleared their throat before starting to speak.

"What are you doing here, Miss Rosdyre?"

She knew that voice.

Katja shuddered and looked back to see the back of a brown hood.

"Fleck?"

"Don't say that name around here," he growled. "Act like you are still eating and listen."

Katja reached down and grabbed a forkful of Stav's potatoes.

"You both are terrible at hiding and stick out like a candle in a dark cellar," Fleck uttered. "I suppose this was all Stav's idea?"

"Yes, but we came because—" Katja began.

"I don't care why! Stav knows not to come looking for me. I return when I mean to . . . on my terms," Fleck challenged. "Stav is careless, and his presence threatens everything I have built here. I could smell his scent the moment both of you landed. Someone is going to find all of that stuff, you know?"

"That is what I told him," Katja sighed.

"Reckless. I should never have allowed him to become a mentor," Fleck whispered. "He is a brilliant wizard but lacks the wisdom and decorum for training a young Glint like yourself."

"Do you still blame me for that botched mission at the college?" Katja asked, taking a bite of Stav's duck, which was getting cold. "That is why you're hiding, right? You were afraid that Magesleuth caught your scent."

"I don't blame you. We should never have rushed you into initiation without first teaching you the core tenets of archmagery. You didn't even know cloaking," Fleck spat.

"I know cloaking now," Katja couldn't help but say, like a child trying to prove their worth to their parents.

"You do? That is quite impressive in that allotted time," Fleck said. "Did Stav teach you?"

"Well, yes, but I admit Kristoff ultimately gave me a tip that led to my first successful attempt," Katja said. Just the name felt sour in her mouth. "You know he killed the professor, right? He admitted it just before Stav and I left."

"I know," Fleck said nonchalantly. "I am afraid he has been plotting this the entire time—he wanted me to disappear. Well, he won. He can have the Arkan Roth."

"But that is why we are looking for you, Fleck," Katja said, facing the back of his head. "We need you more than ever."

The doors burst open, nearly snapping from their hinges, and a gust of cold, foul air filled the room, replacing the thick cloud of smoke swirling near the ceiling with shadows. Every candle and wall sconce snuffed, plunging the inn into darkness except for the daylight spilling in from a few barred and curtained windows.

A tall figure stood at the door. It entered, draped in a gray cloak and a white mask, with a long chain clinking around its neck. After the initial screams, there was silence, followed by the sound of sniffing.

The inn grew deathly silent, as if it were frozen in time. It took a minute for the innkeeper to gain the courage to speak, but when he did, everyone stood still, holding onto every word as if each syllable shaped the rest of their lives.

"Hello! One of the queen's very own! Welcome to the Thistle & Grove Inn!" He poured a pint of ale and slid it across the bar top. "On the house! Consider it a payment of debt to the Crown!"

The Sleuth crept toward the bar, its footsteps silent as if it were floating. It did not speak, but its sniffing grew louder, and Katja felt as though she could sense the eyes shifting across the room and staring at her from behind those dark, hollow pits.

"Don't care for drink . . . do ya?" the innkeeper stammered. "Are you seeking a place to sleep? Perhaps a bit to eat?" He looked at the cockeyed mask as if trying to figure out if there was a face behind it or even a mouth to feed.

The Magesleuth sniffed the innkeeper, getting its face so close to him that it nearly grazed his neck. "I am looking for someone . . . a traitor."

"A . . . traitor?" the innkeeper stammered. "None such here. I only serve those loyal to the Crown."

The Sleuth darted its attention to the crowd of seated customers, who gasped and clenched their teeth with angst. The air was tense with fear as the Sleuth approached a middle-aged man with a stocking cap, sniffed it like a rose, and then gripped his ear with gloved fingers like a mother would to their disobedient child.

"I . . . I swear I have done nothing, milord," the man said, weeping tears of fear. "I serve our Crown in the fields to ensure we are not short on beans, corn, and chayote come Winterhour. I have never associated with magic folk, nor flirted with their wickedness!"

Katja glanced at Fleck, staring out the window and picking a scab on his face. She mouthed, "What should we do?"

Before Fleck could answer, the Sleuth approached their table, and she no longer doubted whether the void of their eyes could pierce one's soul. Katja's heart raced as she held her breath. The Sleuth sniffed Fleck first, taking note of the burns on his face, before shifting to Katja. Her knees trembled beneath the table.

When the Magesleuth was within a few inches of her, she could smell the foul scent of rotting meat and a chilling radiance seeped deep into her bones. She avoided looking into the mask and instead focused on the empty plate before her. She prayed that the bath in the river was enough to wipe away the scent of magic on her body, if that was even how it worked.

The Magesleuth stood for a while, almost basking in her fear, before sniffing the top of her head three times. The terrible rattling breath sounded sickly, as if phlegm filled its lungs and a rat scurried around its ribcage. The Sleuth reached for her jaw and forced her face into its own. Katja nearly gasped as she stared into the Magesleuth's gaze. This close, she could almost distinguish the faint appearance of eyes deep in the shadows. *Perhaps they were real people in there.* The Sleuth sniffed heavily and expelled noxious breath that had been the source of the foul stench.

Katja felt tears in her eyes, but before she could scream, the Sleuth dropped her chin and continued to the following table full of guests, who looked at her with an equal amount of dread. The Sleuth plucked a newborn baby from its mother, whose face was red with tears, and stared into its face before tossing it back into its mother's arms—the *horror.*

"Follow," Fleck said under his breath, grasping Katja's arm and darting to the other end of the tavern.

Fleck ran for the front door so fast that Katja could barely catch up, her leg still sore and weak. When they spilled out onto the gravel road, he snuck around the side of the inn and looked up at the rafters with a hand over his brow to block the bright autumn sun.

"What about Stav? He went to look for you upstairs and likely doesn't know what is coming his way!" Katja shouted, tugging Fleck's sleeve like a child. "We can't leave him!"

"The Sleuth is looking for him," Fleck said. "There isn't much we can do to stop a royal Magesleuth."

Katja swatted his shoulder. "Stav needs our help!"

"Don't ever do that again," Fleck said, eyes like daggers. "I trust Stav to get out of this without our help. He is competent when he wants to . . ."

"You just said there is not much we can do to stop a Magesleuth!" Katja shouted. "What chance does he have alone?"

"Are you willing to die for this man?" Fleck said presumptuously. "He wouldn't do the same if the roles were reversed."

"He has saved me before."

"And I am sure it was only when it was convenient," Fleck scoffed. "Or perhaps when he needed something. That man has a heart for himself and no other, much like his mother."

"What kind of leader are you? Maybe Kristoff was right all along!" Katja said, spitting at Fleck's feet. "You aren't a leader, you are a coward! That is why you have been hiding here all of this time! That is why the Roth has been essentially crippled for years while our people are hanged in the square above your head!"

Fleck furrowed his brow. "You sound just like him. His propaganda has been effective at infecting your mind. If you want to serve Kristoff, return to that Warren."

"Because they are killing people, Fleck," Katja said, wanting to cry. "Which doesn't seem much better with you abandoning your own."

Katja glared at Fleck before she entered the inn. She strutted through the front door, but almost regretted it instantly when the foul, rotting stench returned. She scanned the room, but it was nowhere in sight. When she approached the innkeeper, he was dabbing his forehead with a rag.

"Where did it go?" Katja asked.

The innkeeper pointed to the stairs. Her heart dropped.

Katja nodded, trying to steel herself before cautiously walking up the stairs. She reached the top floor, where a single door across the hall was open.

She silently crept across the hall, peering inside the dimly lit room. She jolted back as she saw the shadowy Magesleuth creeping among the shadows, sniffing intensely for something . . . someone. Katja retreated and began gently wiggling the knobs on all the other doors, but none opened. On the third door, she heard a light rustling sound and decided to knock quietly.

"Stav?" Katja whispered.

A minute seemed to pass while she looked over her shoulder to ensure the Sleuth hadn't entered the hall. She knocked again and called Stav's name, but this time, the door swung open, and she was pulled into the room before it shut again.

"Oh, good, you are alive," Stav said. She felt like she had heard that too often as of late. He locked the door and slid a desk in front of it before returning to the window, from which he seemed to contemplate jumping. "There is a Magesleuth in the inn . . . I think it's looking for Fleck, but I don't want to risk it. We might have to jump and break a leg, but it is far better than meeting face-to-face with one of those demons."

"Yes, I already met it face-to-face, but it didn't want anything to do with me . . . or Fleck," Katja said, looking down at the hard ground far beneath the window.

"Fleck? You found him?" Stav exclaimed, forgetting his place, before turning to a whisper. "Where was he hiding?"

"More like he found me," Katja said. "I don't know why we came all this way for him. He has no interest in helping us."

"He will help us. He just needs convincing," Stav said stubbornly. "I remember the old Fleck when he was fresh from the navy boat. He will turn his banner once I tell him who took his place."

"They aren't looking for Fleck . . . they are looking for you," Katja said.

"*Me?* Why me?" Stav said, just as there was a loud creak outside the door.

"I dunno, all I know is they aren't looking for Fleck. They already sniffed past him," Katja said. "You have to jump!"

"They will kill you for conspiring with me. You have to jump too," Stav whispered, frantically pacing before the window. "Perhaps I can afford one spell, something to break our fall."

The door blasted open, tearing at its hinge, and the Magesleuth entered the room with its black wand drawn. The dresser flew towards them, but they ducked just in time as it smashed through the window, littering the floor with glass.

With a flick of his wrist, Stav held his wand and blasted a gust of wind at the Magesleuth, but the Sleuth deflected it, sending the gust through the door and wreaking chaos down the hall. He hurled a chair across the room into the Magesleuth, but it swished its hands, and the chair disassembled itself, turning back toward them and battering them with its pieces.

"I can't afford much more," Stav said.

Katja cast a levitation spell on the Magesleuth, but the Sleuth laughed, reversing the spell and slamming her against the wall. When she opened her eyes, the room started spinning, and she felt warm blood down her neck. She staggered upright, just in time to see the Magesleuth hoist Stav off the ground and torture him with some invisible spell.

Stav's screams filled the air.

"Hugo Stavoren . . . by decree of the Crown, you are sentenced to die," the Magesleuth said.

Katja felt the ground beneath her shift as she vomited on the floor. She heard a distant whooshing sound followed by a gentle breeze from the broken window. Out of the corner of her eye, she spotted a large shadow outside the window and she caught a glimpse of something colorful flapping in the air.

"Hurry now! Jump aboard! I got the carpet!" a frantic voice bellowed from outside the window.

The smell of hot iron filled the small room as a hiss of bright blue flame wafted through the window toward the Magesleuth, forming a fiery cyclone that illuminated the walls with a light so bright it made the Magesleuth scream. It didn't take long for the Sleuth to use its own magic, quickly encircling itself in an egglike shell of transparent mucus that dripped to the floor as the flames were quenched to a vapid black smoke.

Katja gasped for breath, feeling like she was back in the portal, stuck in an oven of burning magedust and old parchment. She buried her lips in the crease of her arm and reached for Stav, who was gagging on the black smoke, then pushed him toward the window just as a pair of arms pulled him onto the carpet. She leaped from the window with blind faith, inhaling the crisp air as they cut through the sky.

Chapter Twenty-Nine

The sun was hanging in the middle of the sky when the land beneath them changed to water, but it wouldn't be long before it was tugged to the horizon. Katja had never seen the ocean like this, far beneath her feet and surprisingly calm the further they fled from the battered, foamy coastlines. They didn't stray far from land, always keeping it within sight, which was good, but if she had her way, she might never set foot on solid ground again.

Why would one ever walk when one could fly? she thought.

"Don't you fear some fishermen might spot us from here?" Katja asked, anxiously holding onto the carpet with pale knuckles.

"You don't have to worry about that—" Stav said, hoarsely, but before he could finish, he reached for his throat, hacking up black phlegm onto his sleeve. "Fleck . . . you tell the girl. I can barely get out a word."

Katja looked away and nearly hurled down onto the world below. As if contagious, she too coughed up a terrible black thing that she swiftly wiped on her dress. She did her best not to cough again, but she couldn't help it, and neither could Stav. It felt like tiny meat hooks had latched deep into her lungs, threatening to tear them out.

Fleck peered down below, where a couple of lazy yawls and schooners dragging long nets bobbed lazily in the tide. "The ancient carpet weavers were a lot more clever than you think. The bottom stitches are deeply entwined so that the strands blend seamlessly with the sky. If the sky is pale blue, it becomes pale blue. If it is black as night, it becomes black. If there are clouds, it becomes pale like ivory. Even if those fishers spotted us, we would become just another fisherman's story . . . and we have all heard how seriously people listen to those."

Stav seemed troubled by something. "We should land near those crags on the spit, toward the Isles of Otterham. No one will see us there."

"It is a long walk from Otterham to the city," Fleck said. "A treacherous, rocky endeavor that would likely end in a few rolled ankles and broken legs."

"What if the Magesleuth follows us?" Katja asked, looking over her shoulder, half expecting to see a Magesleuth flying on a pitchfork like the countess.

"Part of me thinks I would have been wiser to let them take you both!" Fleck bemoaned, legs folded like a neat pastry and one hand resting on the carpet, starkly contrasting Stav's chaotic equestrian riding style. "But my heart is warmer than I thought. A stony heart would have saved me a lot of headaches."

"You didn't answer me about the Magesleuth," Katja said, ignoring his complaints.

Fleck frowned. "The crown has enlisted the most loyal sorcerers in the realm, not the most talented . . . although one would argue that getting rigorous training as they do while the rest of us hide our abilities in sewers and dark places would result in them being the best sorcerers in the realm. Perhaps the world, if you exclude the Galoshi Reedwalkers and the other secretive magical enclaves across the Relian Sea."

"Why don't we seek their wisdom?" Stav asked. "If they are so talented."

"Because of how unaccepted the world has become of them, they have become unaccepting of the world. Including us," Fleck said. "These people want to remain a secret. Even if I could find them myself. Besides, if what you told me about the dossier is true, then we don't have much time until another family is murdered."

After Katja and Stav had been saved, Fleck flew them to the field to gather the tapestry, scrying ball, grimoire, and candle, which had thankfully not been disturbed, and flew east, to the coast of Draco's Spit, which insulated the city of Theed from the turbulent Relian Sea and had likely acted as a natural shield from outward invaders for millennia. At least, that is what Fleck told them as they crossed from land to sea an hour ago.

They had also exchanged news with Fleck about the countess usurping the Arkan Roth, the dossier, and Katja's role in taking it from the Maiden Tower,

Kristoff's betrayal, the recruitment of former disbanded members, the lightning chase in the sky that concluded with them scattering in a field, the torn tapestry, and an encounter with blotters in the forest. However, Katja noted that Stav still had not revealed what had happened the night before their escape.

But he didn't have to. The news had already reached every district in Theed and likely across the realm.

"The Blythe and tar Breck families . . . murdered," Fleck said as if rereading the front-page headline for the first time. "Two dead at the residence of Lord Gilbert Trumhold, three more in the Wallingford District at the home of the Adelaides. There are also reports of a break-in at the House of Black, where Henry Black has gone missing. It is all so terrible, I can barely stand it."

Stav stared out into the distance at a great white cloud. "I am glad you said it. I could barely utter those names without feelings of despair. Some of them were dear friends from our childhood in Wallingford. The others I knew of more distantly, but we were all aware of each other as fellow Glints in hiding. How my mother and brother could snuff them out . . ."

"You were with the Roth that night. What happened?" Katja asked cautiously.

"I was there for the first raid on Henry Black's house. It started relatively peacefully. We captured Henry from his chambers and interrogated him. We pleaded with him to tell the other warlock families in Theed to craft a bill in the Senate that would legalize magic in the Commonwealth, even offering concessions on scope, but only for certain districts of Theed. Still, he did not budge," Stav said, torment in his bright eyes. "All Henry had to do was say yes; after all, he is an influential member of the Senate, and people would listen to him if he built a coalition, but he feared too much about his reputation. 'They would make a mockery of me. Spit in my face. There would be men and women with clubs and knives gathering outside my door. The queen might even have my neck if not my chair,' he had said in his defense. It is maddening when we have sacrificed so much for our cause . . . but he wasn't wrong. The first person to bring this issue before their peers would likely be ruined without other backers."

"So, the countess murdered him?" Katja asked.

Stav sighed. "Not quite. They beat him, tortured him more, and then, when he finally broke, they recruited him to their ranks."

"So, it was a success?" Fleck said.

"I am afraid the blood lust had only just started," Stav said. "I was already uncertain about how they treated Henry before we razed Blythe Manor to the ground with Sir Alfred and his family locked inside. Then, jubilantly, my mother moved to the family of Glenn tar Breck, and that is where I left and snuck back to the Warren, unable to witness their rampage."

"Did you not try to save Sir Alfred and his family from their fate?" Fleck asked, his face disturbed.

Stav slumped his shoulders. "I tried to reason with my mother, brother, even Gwith and Urie, but they called me a coward and continued their dark deeds. I could sway Urie, but he seemed terrified to say anything to my mother . . . and for good reason. If I had told her I was leaving, she would have locked me in that manor with the Blythes, and I would be among the ashes."

"A grim story indeed, Stav." Fleck covered the end of his pipe from the wind, striking a light with the tip of his wand.

"Terrible," Katja uttered. "Those poor families."

"I wouldn't say *poor*, but I get your sentiment," Fleck said, puffing smoke into the breeze. "These people are the enemy, but they do not deserve death. Death is not for us to decide, just as much as it isn't for the Crown when we utter words of magic."

There was silence for a few minutes, perhaps half an hour, as clouds began to sweep from the Relian to the shoreline like a phantom. It was so quiet yet so profound, watching the entire landscape shift from robin's-egg blue to bleached-bone white. Even the sea was changing hues, turning deep, dark blue with foamy tides. Over their shoulder, the coastline was growing narrower, and you could make out a sliver of glistening water that made the mouth of Balledore Bay. Further out was the rugged island of Otterham, surrounded by flocks of seagulls and fleets of ships. They could make out the silhouettes of large cargo ships from far-off nations in the hazy distance.

Stav set his crystal ball between his legs and placed his palm on the top of the ball, closing his eyes while muttering something in the Elddir tongue beneath his breath.

"Stavorens, and your trust in scrying. It is stronger than the faith of the men and women sitting in temple pews," Fleck scoffed, spitting an ashy glob into the sea below. "I have seen witches and wizards go mad staring into those. Seeking the truths of life, distant treasures, or spying on their lovers. It isn't good."

"Silence!" Stav shouted. "I am trying to read!"

"Read?" Fleck chuckled. "I wasn't aware there was anything to read in that thing. Anything riveting? I like a good anthology or academic journal."

"I said quiet! I am trying to focus!" Stav swatted Fleck in the arm, spilling ash all over the carpet, which Fleck quickly brushed away.

"That was extremely childish of you, Stav," Fleck sneered, refilling his pipe with fresh tobacco, making the carpet sway. "You could have set this whole carpet on fire, you fool! Not to mention the waste of good pipe leaves."

"I am tired of you two fighting!" Katja shouted, driving her fist into the carpet. "Perhaps I should fly the tapestry as you children bicker!"

"A bit dramatic, wouldn't you say, Miss Rosdyre?" Fleck said. "But if that is what you want . . . I won't stop you."

"Baxter! Tartt! Varlot! Ponvelle!" Stav blurted.

"What are you rambling about now?" Fleck bellowed.

"Write them down!" Stav shouted. "They are the next names on the list."

Fleck rummaged through his pockets for a pen and parchment, but couldn't find anything.

Katja closed her eyes and focused, repeating the names, trying to burn them into her memory. *Baxter, Tartt, Varlot, and Ponvelle.*

"Do you see anymore?" she asked.

Stav pressed his eye into the glass, his greasy hair lathering the polished stone with sweat. "Wait . . . wait . . . no, they shut the dossier . . . dammit! There were so many more!"

"You were able to see the dossier from . . . that?" Fleck asked, scratching his chin. "You searched for your mother, didn't you? In doing so, you found her reading the dossier and reading it yourself. Am I correct?"

Stav nodded. "Yes, but I was searching for Kristoff. It is his crystal ball, after all. He would be most vexed to know I used it against him."

Fleck stared into the distance like he had been told a regrettable fact.

"Perhaps you aren't such a middling wizard after all," he said, puffing his pipe, his face looking more melted than usual from the sweat on his brow.

Stav didn't reply, but Katja caught a subtle grin. "I thought I might as well do something while we sit around. Did you catch those names? What was it again? Baxter, Valen, and Pons?"

"Baxter, Tartt, Varlot, and Ponvelle," Katja said, repeating the names out loud. Then suddenly, something struck her like a brick.

"Portia Ponvelle!" Katja blurted. "I know her! She was my bunkmate at the Maiden Tower!"

Stav and Fleck both exchanged confused looks.

"Perhaps it is a coincidence. I don't know how many lordlings are allowed to work at the Maiden Tower. I know a few who might employ their services, but to work there would be . . . sorry to say . . . an embarrassment that most warlock families wouldn't accept," Stav said.

"I know," Katja said. "But it can't be a coincidence. Portia's family *was* esteemed and wealthy, but faced hard times and lost nearly everything. She worked at the Maiden Tower to make some extra coin while her family rebuilt. She recently left her contract because her family became wealthy again and needed her at home."

"A strange coincidence indeed," Fleck pondered aloud. "Are you particularly close with this bunkmate?"

Katja nodded. "She was my only friend at the Maiden Tower and the only one who discovered my secret. She was even so trustworthy that when she found the wand hidden beneath my mattress in the Maiden Tower, instead of reporting me, she helped me avoid being detected." She suddenly remembered their conversation in the girls' bathroom. Portia had mentioned her family estate was across from an old lighthouse in Lord's Park.

"Could you gain an audience with her and her family?" Fleck asked.

"I think so . . . she invited me to her home for dinner before she left," Katja said, looking at her tattered red dress. She felt terrible for borrowing that money from Portia to buy a dress and having it become a dirty rag. "Her family lives in Lord's Park . . . near an old lighthouse."

"It seems too risky, Fleck," Stav said. "Any family living in the Lord's Park has royal pins skewered into their undergarments. Especially if they are the families on this list, most of whom I have probably had supper with at some point as a child. They aren't sympathetic folk and rather nasty."

"Portia is the opposite of everything you just said, and the Ponvelles raised her. Could it be that her family is different? If not her family, at least Portia deserves to know that her name is on the dossier. That is the least I could do for all she has done for me," Katja pleaded.

"And risk everything?" Stav chided.

"What do you mean?" Katja gestured around them. "We have already risked everything. Life as we knew it is over. There is no more Maiden Tower, no more Warren, and likely no more Theed!"

"I am not leaving Theed," Stav said. "I would rather die than leave my home."

"Then let's bloody fight for it," Fleck said, gripping the flying carpet, and it started veering to land.

"What are you doing?" Stav asked. "I don't want to play this game where you make some big decisions without telling anyone, Fleck. I have played that game my whole life."

"Where else do you think I am going?" Fleck grimaced. "To bloody Lord's Park. So, hold on, we should be there just before sundown!"

* * *

The distinction was painfully obvious the moment they flew over the cliffs into the crowded streets of Theed. Even the air felt thicker, wetter, and sadder as they skirted across the sky toward a section of Theed distinct for its large grassy plots, foliage, and, most apparent, the massive townhouses, manors, estates, and occasional brick-and-mortar castles with crenelated turrets and centuries-old battlements. It was very similar to the Wallingford District to the east and the Harleck District to the south, but there was a night-and-day difference between Little Stellen and the Smoker and Dunrow Districts to the west, which were closer to the city center. The Dunrow District was almost black from this distance, with nearly no greenery, worn-down houses, and brick apartments a quarter the size of the smallest manors in Lord's Park. Smoker and Little Stellen looked even worse, if possible, with even less to be desired.

"Do you know which lighthouse it is? There are dozens," Fleck asked, pointing downward at a whitewashed tower that resembled a cigarette snuffed in a pile of ashen sand.

Katja searched her memory. "She seemed to think it was quite obvious due to it being crooked. Perhaps there aren't many other lighthouses of that nature. If I recall, she said it resembled a 'poorly tapped nail.' And their estate is just across from it."

"Is it that one?" Stav said, hacking more phlegm into one sleeve as he pointed at a stout lighthouse atop a rocky crag near shore with the other. "Does it look crooked to you?"

Fleck frowned. "When I squint a little, it looks crooked."

"Perhaps that is it then," Katja said, but then she paused, looking inland from the lighthouse. "However . . . she distinctly told me they lived across from the lighthouse, and I don't see any houses anywhere near it."

"Yes, unless they dwell in a clam at the bottom of Balledore Bay," Stav jested, but no one laughed.

"There is another! Over there, hugging the southern shoreline!" Katja bellowed.

Fleck shook his head. "That is beyond the borders of Lord's Park."

Stav, coughing so hard into his arm that he had to gasp for air once the spell was over, asked, "Did you mishear her?"

Katja frowned. "Of course not, you nit!"

"Easy," Fleck said, disarming the flame. "We won't find this lighthouse if everyone is clawing at each other's necks, and it doesn't help that we're all coughing ourselves raw. I hope those Magesleuths are suffering just as much as we are, but the jury is still out on whether they have lungs to breathe to begin with."

Stav sighed. "Well, it doesn't look like anyone lives near any of these lighthouses. After all, who spends their family coffers on an heirloom estate built in the sights of a nauseating beacon? I would go sick before I went mad."

"I wouldn't know—I never had those problems," Katja sneered.

"But . . . it is a good point, isn't it?" Fleck said. "I think Stav is onto something for once."

Stav half coughed, half grumbled. "I can deal with one of you, alone, but together, you two are tyrants."

"You see that there?" Fleck said, pointing his thin fingers at a raised line along the coast, which had copses of bramble and olive trees littered upon it like uneven hair. "That is the old dyke. Don't ask me how old it is, but let's just say it has been here before anyone called this city Theed."

Katja nodded. "I knew you were old, but not that old, Fleck."

Fleck ignored her jest. "I know this because of my time at Port. The dyke moved the shoreline of Lord's Park forward, and we've been building on it ever since. Similar to how they built upon the catacombs of the Warren and then forgot about them. It appears to be a rather human thing to do."

"So, the lighthouse is even older, but how does that help us?" Katja coughed.

"It means the lighthouse is probably somewhere inland, behind that dyke, not near the sea," Fleck said, unable to hide the contentment of his revelation. It was a rare sight.

"Couldn't be that one, could it?" Stav shouted, pointing at a very crooked tower with a pointed turret and shattered windows encircling its top like a crown of glass.

"Must be," Fleck said, flying the carpet toward the cylindrical silo of brick with chipped white paint, which cast a long shadow toward the bay. "I will land just north of the tower in the alleyway beside the lighthouse. Let's hope no one notices."

"Here. You might need this," Fleck said, grabbing a couple of vials of magedust from his multicolored coat. He handed one to Stav and one to Katja. I suggest you take some now."

"Cheers," Stav said solemnly, raising his vial.

The three clattered while inhaling a third of the dust, then wiped the residue from their noses. Katja felt a coursing energy surge through her body, sinking deep into her stomach, roiling like a storm in her gut.

"What will you two do?" Katja asked.

"Are we not joining you?" Stav asked.

"The girl is right. The Ponvelle girl will not expect two men accompanying Miss Rosdyre, and that could further complicate things," Fleck said, lowering the carpet and moving it into the dark alleyway. "One must be wary of thieves these days . . . we should know, considering our profession."

When the carpet landed on the ground, Katja's legs felt wobbly as she disembarked onto the solid concrete. Something moved behind her, but when she looked to see what made the noise, it was a sleeping woman with magedust stains streaked on her face.

"Where can I find you when I am done?" Katja asked her companions, slowly walking down the alleyway.

"We won't be far." Stav winked. "I will ensure Fleck has us within a shout's distance."

Katja smiled back but then turned out of the alleyway, and when she looked back, the magic carpet was gone. She crossed the street, which was thankfully sleepy at twilight. The streetlamps were recently lit, making for a peaceful night if it wasn't for her mission. Before reaching the other side of the street, she looked up to the sky to search for Fleck and Stav, but she couldn't see anything, and she wasn't sure if she would be able to with its cloaking fabric.

Across the street, she found a line of large boxy estates, gaining in size from one end to the other as it climbed a massive hill. Spiraling up, the road led to an enormous manor, larger than the Stavorens', with flying buttresses and spires that nearly scraped the sky. She examined the nearest estates, noting their distinct colors, but only one had a large, engraved "*P*" on its iron gate, which she could only hope stood for Ponvelle.

Katja opened the gate, thankful it wasn't locked, and carefully trod the stairs to the large abode adorned with a fountain, nymph statues, and a manicured garden. She rapped the brass knocker three times and took a step back, her hands neatly tucked under her arms as a chill bit at her bones.

The door opened, and an old butler in a black frock welcomed her. "Hello? Have you got an appointment with the Ponvelles?"

Katja nodded. "I am friends with Portia Ponvelle. She invited me."

The butler looked her up and down skeptically and shut the door. Katja was about to look for another way in when he returned with an embarrassed grin. "Come on in. I apologize for keeping you out in the cold, Miss Rosdyre."

Katja walked inside, and a blanket of warmth overcame her. The butler led her through the tall entryway and through an antechamber before a large living room with a lit fire and a decorated mantlepiece.

"Make yourself comfortable. Miss Portia has informed me she will be down soon," the butler said. "While you wait, would you like something?"

Katja politely shook her head. A few minutes later, Portia entered the room with a large smile. She gave her a bone-breaking hug.

"It is so good to see you, Katja," Portia said, her hand patting on the small of Katja's back.

Katja looked at the butler, who retreated. "Portia," she whispered urgently, "you and your family are in trouble."

Portia's smile pursed into a neat pout. "Trouble? What trouble?"

"The Arkan Roth, they are the assassins you are hearing about all over in the paper," Katja said. "You are targets. This cannot wait. We must tell your family and leave."

"Katja, are you ill?" Portia said, looking her up and down. "Have you returned to your prior life? I have never seen you look so distraught."

"I am fine!" Katja snapped. "It is you I am worried about!"

Portia pressed her cheek against her friend's. Her chestnut hair brushed against Katja's temple. "Let's talk about this later. After supper."

"There isn't time!" Katja pleaded.

Portia sighed and pursed her lips. There was something different about her. Perhaps it was being under the wing of her family butler or in the presence of indulgence, but there was an invisible barrier between them that wasn't there before when they were bunkmates.

"We can't talk like this here," Portia said, her cheek twitching. "Follow me, we have supper ready. We can discuss this more afterwards. Now, tell me more about what is happening at the Maiden Tower—I feel like I have missed out on so much."

Portia led her down a luxurious hallway into the large dining room. A long wooden table was filled with roast lamb, pudding, corn, cranberry sauce, crumbly bread, and every kind of cheese laid out on a platter. The smells alone were enough to make Katja's mouth water.

"Take a seat, Miss Rosdyre! Portia has told us all about you!" said a lady with coils of gray hair and a warm smile. When she saw the state of Katja's dress, she winced, as if the sight of unruly clothes hurt her. But she said nothing of it.

"Yes, indeed! A friend of Portia's is a friend to us all!" another younger lady with blonde hair said. "We have only just started eating! You couldn't have made for better timing!"

Katja forced a smile yet felt almost overwhelmed by their kindness. She sat opposite Portia, who couldn't help but look solemnly at her with caramel eyes.

A butler poured a round of red wine and water. Then, the family said a blessing, which was followed by the rattling of silverware and the scraping of dinner plates. Katja timidly took a small piece of chicken and ate it as politely as she could, but despite her hunger, a sickening feeling welled in her stomach, knowing she wasn't here for pleasantries.

"So, Miss Rosdyre! How are things at the Maiden Tower these days? Our dear Portia has told us there have been a lot of complications lately," the gray-haired lady said.

A man wearing an apparent brown toupee whom she had not noticed raised a hand to his neck, as if appalled his companion would mention the tower. But the gray-haired lady did not seem to care and continued anyway.

"Not well, actually," Katja said. "I have lost my contract with the Maiden Tower. I no longer work there, which is why my dress looks like . . ." She looked down as red flushed her cheeks.

"I am sorry you lost your contract. You said that the job was essential to being freed from the streets," Portia smiled.

The others at the table gasped and looked at Katja in silent horror as if she had just confessed to a murder.

"We are so sorry, Miss Rosdyre . . . to hear of this news," the blonde lady said. "Perhaps you can stay awhile until you find new employment."

"Elizabeth!" the man with the toupee scolded before taking a breath to rein in his anger. "Elizabeth . . . we cannot guarantee a place in our home even to Portia's friend. We have only just met the girl."

"You can call me Katja," she said. "And I don't want a place to stay. I have come for another reason."

"Kat," Portia whispered fiercely, her face looking horrified. "We can help you. You don't have to scare them by talking about assassinations."

"Your grandpa wouldn't tolerate whispering at the dinner table," the gray-haired woman said. "Shame he had to die."

Katja remembered Portia mentioning that her grandpa had died, which led to her gaining an inheritance and leaving the Maiden Tower. Katja didn't know the whole dynamic and relationship within the family, and despite her curiosity, she knew she didn't have time.

"Your family is going to be murdered if you don't listen to me!" she spurted out.

The forks and dinner plates fell silent as everyone at the table stared at her in disbelief.

"I am sure you all read the news about the other warlock families that were murdered the other night. Well, those murders aren't going to stop anytime soon. In fact, they have only begun," Katja said. "Your family has to go into hiding in the meantime, but while you are doing so, I need your help stopping these people."

"Kat . . . what are you talking about?" Portia asked, mortified.

"It is what I was talking about earlier," Katja said, annoyed.

Tapping a napkin to her awestruck lips, Portia stated, "I told you we could talk about it after supper."

"Are you trying to scare us, girl?" the man with the toupee scoffed. "You aren't the first to come knocking on our door asking for help!"

"Perhaps she is a nutter . . . insane," said Elizabeth. "We see plenty of those people over in the other districts. I never should have sent you to work in the Maiden Tower, Portia."

Portia looked into Katja's eyes for a few seconds. Katja hoped she could read the seriousness on her face.

Portia straightened her posture before replying. "Katja isn't lying. I can tell what she says is true."

Katja let out a sigh of relief.

"Well, if that is true, then tell me one thing: why are they after us? We are not warlocks!" the man snapped.

The gray-haired lady sighed. "Well . . . we know that isn't necessarily true."

The others gasped.

"Don't say another word!" Elizabeth shouted.

"I know your family has Glint blood running through it . . . and it doesn't matter how strongly," Katja said. "Your family was marked as such in the grand maiden's dossier — the very document these murderers are using to hunt down every wealthy and powerful warlock who rules Theed. All because you turned on your own blood and refused to work to make magic legal once more."

"Legal? You think magic should be legal again?" the man shrieked. "Have you read the history books? It was a lawless and dangerous time, and when they revolted and ran into those forests, cutting off their arms and legs, our people had to turn to the voice of reason . . . the Crown."

"Do you think it is less lawless now?" Katja huffed. "People are suffering! People are hanged for minor offenses! I just walked past a duster foaming from the mouth. We know her fate! Living in your walled castles doesn't change that fact!"

"You need to change your tone," the man said.

"As if that would help sway you," Portia said. "What Katja is telling us is very disturbing. Do you really want to take the chance that we end up like the Blythes? Blacks? Or tar Brecks?"

The room grew silent, and the butler came through, refilling the wine glasses.

"Listen, even if we accept what you are saying, our family does not hold enough power to sway anyone," the gray-haired woman said, taking a swig of wine. "We are a proud and noble house, but nothing compared to those murdered. No one in our house even works in a significant role now that my son, Piers, was relieved of his role under the last ministership."

The man with the toupee grimaced. "*Retired*. I retired."

"Don't you know someone who might listen?" Katja asked.

Piers frowned. "When Prime Minister Stoker was assassinated, we all lost everything. No one in his cabinet takes anything seriously. I have tried to find even modest work, but no one wants to be part of that baggage."

"Do you know anyone, perhaps a neighbor, who might?" Katja asked.

Piers looked contemplative.

"Don't say it," Elizabeth muttered. "We should not bother them."

"Who is it?" Katja asked.

"The DeGroms," Piers blurted. Katja stiffened as he continued. "They live atop the hill and know everyone in Parliament, but they aren't decent folk if I am to be honest. They support the Crown and rarely do anything to bring controversy to their noble names. Rumor has it they have ties to the Magesleuths."

A chill ran down Katja's spine at the word *Magesleuth* as the smell of rotting meat returned to her nose.

She took a swig of wine and dabbed her lip with a napkin. "They do not happen to be related to Lord Rhys DeGrom, do they?"

Elizabeth nodded. "Lord Rhys is Lord Hoster DeGrom's heir, you know—the head of the Magesleuths. I heard a rumor that he up and vanished once the engagement fell through. You don't think his disappearance has anything to do with these people, do you?"

Katja pursed her lips, but the answer seemed clear to everyone at the table.

"Can you help me arrange a meeting with Lord Hoster?" Katja asked earnestly.

Piers cringed. "I . . . don't know . . . Hoster DeGrom and I aren't very close."

"That isn't true, Father," Portia said. "You and Hoster attend the same temple and guild! Lord Hoster is a deeply religious man who used to sit in the pew just in front of us during prayer. I know you two are friendly."

Piers stared at his daughter as if he might strangle her.

"Help the girl, Piers! Remember, it wasn't that long ago that we were begging others for help. Now it is our turn to give," Portia's grandmother said. "If you don't do it, I will march up the street myself and knock on his gates! You wouldn't do that to an old woman's knees, would you? Besides, what if the child is right?"

"Katja wouldn't lie about something like this," Portia said. "I will not sleep tonight, knowing what happened to the Blythes might happen to us!"

Katja's heart swelled with hope as Piers crossed his silverware, took a swig of wine, and stood up.

"Let us go then," Piers said. "Portia, you, and I will go to the DeGroms before Hoster resigns to his chambers." He then looked at his butler firmly. "Mr. Hatch, please be on high alert tonight and ensure all windows and doors are secured in case what the girl has said is true. We shall return soon."

Mr. Hatch escorted them to the door, placed a coat on Lord Ponvelle and Portia, marched across the front lawn, through the iron gates, and exited onto the street with Portia and Katja chasing at his heels. It only took a few minutes of walking uphill until they reached the spiked iron gates leading to Castle DeGrom. Katja searched the sky but could not find Fleck, Stav, or the flying carpet anywhere. It was very dark now, and the streetlights were not bright enough to illuminate all the shadows. Despite Lord Rhys's absence, Stav would be going bonkers knowing they were going to the homestead of his mother's former betrothed.

Lord Ponvelle spoke with the guards standing at the gate, who swiftly let them into a massive courtyard filled with pristine gardens, bubbling fountains, and neat topiaries resembling beasts of the wild, difficult to distinguish at night. When they finally reached the massive front door, Lord Ponvelle curtly tapped the lion-paw knocker, and within minutes, the door opened to a face so familiar that it made Katja nearly jump out of her skin.

Gavin?

"Lord DeGrom has been notified of your presence, Lord Ponvelle," Gavin said with a grin, not yet noticing Katja. "He is in deep prayer and will be with you once he wraps up. Please follow me, and I will escort you to his lively chambers."

Lord Ponvelle and Portia walked inside. The fine walls were decorated with massive oil paintings depicting Rhys at various stages of his life: as a baby, a young boy, and a decorated soldier. When they reached the living room, there was a gold-framed painting of Rhys in a fancy doublet riding a white horse that seemed to watch them as they entered. His stature was embellished, and his face cleared of pockmarks, but other than that, the artist captured his smug smile perfectly. In the corner of the living room was a bust of Rhys and other exciting art collectibles that looked far too breakable to breathe on.

Katja held back from the others until she stood just in front of Gavin.

"Hello, Gavin," Katja whispered.

Gavin's dark eyes widened, and his face paled. "You . . . what are you doing here?"

"I was unaware you were working for the DeGroms. Quite scandalous to be working in the home of our dearest Auriella's former fiancé, isn't it?"

"Didn't you see the news? The Stavorens were sacked. I had to find a job elsewhere, and when I told Hoster that I knew his son before he went missing, it was a swift hire," Gavin said, following closely behind her. "If you haven't noticed, the man is obsessed."

When Katja caught back up with the others, Gavin straightened his posture, feigning no interest in a conversation, although she knew he was dying to ask. He offered them to sit on a few padded chairs across from each other before a crackling hearth, adding another log to its embers. When he was done, Gavin stood firmly against the wall, watching over them awkwardly as they awaited Lord DeGrom's arrival. Gavin glared at Katja the entire time as sweat glistened on his forehead.

It felt like an hour before they heard creaking floorboards shifting from overhead as if the castle came to life. A man dressed in a fine burgundy robe with a twisted mustache and neat gray hair slipped past Gavin, an ornate cane in one hand and a bejeweled saber in the other.

Katja stood ready to run as she spotted the saber's shine, but Portia patted her hand. "It's okay. This is his thing," she whispered.

Lord DeGrom stumbled into his seat, his saber rattling and his cane falling to the floor. Gavin hurried to pick up the cane and set it propped against Hoster's velvet-cushioned chair beside the fire. Gavin then returned to his post by the door.

"I am sorry for the delay, Piers. I have been spending a lot of time with our Shining God," Hoster said solemnly, dark wrinkles across his face.

"Not a worry, Hoster. I know things have been tough since Rhys has . . . disappeared," Lord Ponvelle said carefully. "Have there been any leads or rumors about his whereabouts? Perhaps a word from the Shining God?"

Hoster looked like he might sob, but instead, he reached for a metal flask from his robe pocket, nearly exposing himself, and took a sip. "Nothing from the useless guards, but I have my Sleuths working harder than normal to pick up any scent of a trail. I have a feeling . . . a terrible feeling that this has something to do with the news earlier. It seems like too much of a coincidence not to be!"

Katja hid a grin. *This is going to be easy.*

"That is exactly what has happened," she interjected.

Hoster looked at Katja for the first time and squinted his eyes. "Is that a faint hint of a Dirkish accent on your tongue? Who is this girl? Did you pick her up from the street, Piers?"

"The girl is one of my friends. She worked with me at the Maiden Tower," Portia sneered defensively. "She is not from the street."

"It shouldn't matter," Katja said. "I know who took part in your son's disappearance."

Lord DeGrom glared at her, tapping a gold signet ring engraved with a large "D" on his armrest. "You think you know more than the guards and my Magesleuths? What would a simple . . ." he eyed Katja's attire, ". . . chambermaid know?"

"What if I were to tell you I was one of the last people to see Rhys before he vanished?" she said, although she wasn't entirely sure it was true. Her eyes were distracted by his oversized ring, catching the firelight. "The same people imprisoned me. I sat in the same jail cell he was locked up in."

"You come to my home in the middle of the night, speaking falsehoods! Who is this liar, Piers?" Hoster shouted, his tongue heavy.

"Maybe the girl is speaking the truth," Lord Ponvelle said. "She told us that she knows who murdered the Blythe and tar Breck families."

"Yes, and I know for certain that your families are all next on the list," Katja said. "I have seen who these people are targeting, and it is all neatly marked on a dossier. It is even nice enough to provide an address."

"And how do you know about this list?" Hoster asked, face flushed and eyes narrowing.

"And how do you know about this list?" Hoster asked, his face flushed and eyes narrowing.

"Because I gave it to them. I was imprisoned and coerced into stealing the dossier with all your names from the grand maiden of the Maiden Tower. They targeted me for working there and for having a contract with Countess Auriella Stavoren in the Wallingford District," Katja said.

"You did what?" Lord Ponvelle scolded. "You were working for these monsters?"

"You served Auriella?" Lord DeGrom looked surprised by all he was hearing. "My dearest Rhys's betrothed? It wasn't long after they called off their engagement that he vanished. I pray it wasn't heartbreak over an old, decrepit wench with a large coin purse. I have more coin than he could ever spend, yet he chased after that old hag!"

"I am afraid that there is no coincidence," Katja said. "Countess Auriella is their current ringleader. I think she and their rebellion have everything to do with your son's disappearance . . . actually, I know."

"Hexes! That wretched crone! I knew she was deeply wicked since we raided her estate!" Lord DeGrom shouted. "I suppose someone must have tipped her that we were coming! I should have known she was involved! When my Sleuths get hold of her . . . I will rip her apart!"

Katja sighed. "If only it were that easy."

She wanted to tell them how the countess had very likely magically used her lovers to drain their youth, but she thought it would be too complicated. She needed to divert this conversation into putting pressure on the warlock families to legalize magic in opposition to the Crown. *But how?*

"I will send a letter to my department tomorrow to put all efforts into finding the countess. I imagine by the end of the day they will have her and her band of thieves, and then the clock will tick until they reap what they deserve," Hoster grimaced, a threatening light forming in his eyes. He looked at Katja and snapped his fingers at Gavin. "Get me a black treasury bill. I am sure it is money that the girl wants."

"No, I do not require coin," Katja said. "The Roth will not stop murdering our people and every family on that list until their demands are met."

"And let me guess, you know what those are?" Lord DeGrom sneered.

"Make magic legal once more." The words felt foreign in her mouth, but they felt right. "That is the only way."

Lord DeGrom burst into laughter, his face shiny and red. "You are joking, yes?"

Katja was silent.

"You are serious?" he grinned, sliding his signet ring on and off his finger. "The crown would never allow it! Have you read your history? There was a long, bloody civil war that led to the decision we have today, and it isn't going to change because of anything we say!"

"You serve in Prime Minister Gideon's cabinet, correct?" Katja asked, wanting to scream. "If you can convince enough powerful politicians to join our cause, then perhaps the Crown might feel like there is no other option other than to fold."

"Have you met Queen Margot and her dreaded husband? They loath us more than people like you and all the Dims clogging the roadways!" Lord DeGrom cackled. "If she could wave her wand and get rid of us, she would in a heartbeat. She is probably thrilled by the news this morning. Perhaps she will give Auriella Stavoren and the rest of her team medals once they have murdered everyone on that list!"

"She is the queen, with a massive army at her whim. Why not just take out every warlock? One doesn't require magic to do that," Katja asked.

"It is more complicated than that . . . much more," Lord DeGrom scoffed. "There is *observable* power and then there is *quiet* power, and one faction has more of one than the other. And one is less noticeable when it manifests. Keep your eye out, and you will slowly understand what true power is."

Katja's fist clenched. "So . . . they'll win?"

Lord DeGrom took another swig of his flask. "I will write a letter to be sent tonight telling the Crown who is responsible for these murders. We don't need to buy into the demands of these witches and murderers! We will flush them out and chop them up!"

He wobbled as he got to his feet.

Katja dove to Lord DeGrom's side and grasped his hand before Gavin could reach him.

"Get this strange foreign wench away from me!" Hoster shouted, shoving her away. "Gavin, escort her and my guests out. I have a letter to write!"

Katja retreated, glad he hadn't felt her slide his ring off his knuckle.

"So, is that it?" she asked. "You would risk being like the Blythes?"

"Have you seen this place?" he grinned, pointing around the chamber. "There isn't a soldier in Theed who could break through these impenetrable walls! The Stellish couldn't three centuries ago, and the Glint mob eight scores ago with their massive armies! What chance do these petty assassins have? Now . . . return to your homes and be delighted that you would-be murderers will be vanquished soon," Lord DeGrom jeered, stumbling to the door. "Gavin, see that our guests are seen out with a proper goodbye!"

Gavin tried to hide his dismay for his master but instead nodded in agreement.

"We are done here, Miss Rosdyre," Lord Ponvelle said as soon as they reached the door. He gathered himself and patted the folds of his coat. "You heard the man? He will send a letter to his department to focus on the Roth you discussed. Like our family, he has little sway over issues such as the criminality of magic. I suggest *you* stop it."

Katja glanced at Portia, who shrugged and sighed, but deep down, she wanted nothing more than to leave this place. To put an entire street block away from her and Lord DeGrom.

"Fine," Katja said. She could barely hold back the urge to run as she felt the weight of the ring warm in her closed palm.

"Tell the Lord, I hope he rests well," Lord Ponvelle said to Gavin. "I hope our warnings did not disturb his evening."

When they reached the front gates, the guard was slumped, but jolted to attention when he heard them approach. They waved at the guard before walking through the gates into the cobblestone street. Katja waited for them to get ahead of her, and once they were out of earshot, she split down a side street and tucked behind a recess in a tall wall. She wasn't sure what she was hiding from. She had no obligation to return to the Ponvelles, but she didn't want anything to happen to Portia. She deserved to be saved from this mess.

Katja looked over her shoulder to make sure no one was looking, out of an abundance of paranoia, and glanced at the engraved "D" in her palm. The realization of her actions filled her with something she couldn't quite put into words. *Excitement.* Was she enjoying this?

"Who are you hiding from?" a voice said from overhead.

Katja instinctively clutched the ring to her chest and looked upward, spotting Stav's stupid grinning face peeking over a gutter. Fleck's melted visage appeared moments later as the magic carpet hovered down to the street beside her.

"No one is going to help us, so I am going to have to do it myself," Katja said.

"Imagine they are a bunch of useless wealthy heirs and heiresses like our friend Stav here," Fleck scoffed. "Being a warlock doesn't ensure you are a smart warlock."

"That was uncalled for," Stav said, punching his shoulder. "I may lack wit, but what I lack I make up for with charm, unlike you."

Fleck eyed her clawed hands suspiciously. "Are you hiding something from us, Miss Rosdyre?"

"Lord DeGrom is writing a letter to the Senate to increase funding for the Magesleuths to combat the Roth. He also wants their focus on you and the countess," Katja uttered. "He has no interest in inspiring his warlock colleagues to legalize magic."

She opened her palm, revealing the ring. "Lord DeGrom doesn't know that he is going to send a second letter."

"I am listening," Stav said.

Chapter Thirty

Katja felt unstoppable when she was invisible. It was a brisk morning in Parliament Square as she sifted through the growing crowd concentrated around the famous fountain adorned with a statue of Draco the Firebreather, who supposedly challenged the God of the Forge thousands of years ago in this very spot. Travelers from around the world made it part of their checklist to see, filling the square with their multicolored clothing, varying headdresses, and accents, like a grandmother's quilt. She passed faces and hair the color of milk, cinnamon, charcoal, and honey. She was filled with the scent of lavender, mint, sandalwood, and bergamot, which reminded her of the Dirkish tea her mother used to drink when she was lucky enough to steal from a spicer from across the Relian.

When Katja reached the feet of the massive domed Parliament building that looked more like a fortress, she marched up the daunting pale steps, which seemed needlessly steep.

The night before, after she got back to Stav and Fleck with the signet ring, they dissected her plan, adding and removing bits like chunks of stone until it looked somewhat pleasing to the eye. Stav was to go into town, pick up parchment and pen, and then, with his penmanship and knowledge of everything upper-class, draft the letter she was now holding folded under her armpit. At first, Stav volunteered to deliver the letter. However, sending him seemed too risky considering the Magesleuths were stalking him and knew his scent. Even worse, they spotted a swarm of royal guards patrolling the streets below in more significant numbers than usual, likely at the behest of the warlock families working there.

She could feel the thick stamp, embellished with Lord DeGrom's signet ring, pressed against her arm, which they had improvised with the violet wax from the tapestry candle rather than traditional sealing wax. They hoped no one would notice the difference.

Katja looked back over her shoulder, wondering if she could see Fleck and Stav hiding on some rooftop nearby, but there were too many buildings to count in the heart of the city.

She followed a well-dressed man through the swinging doors of Parliament. He wore a powdered wig, thick spectacles, and a doublet, like the dozens of others coming in and out of the ivory-white dome building.

"Good evening, Mr. Fledger!" a young guard said as they passed, his saber pressed tight against his shoulder. "Can't believe they called for a late-night assembly. Last time they called one this late, it was because Stoker died!"

Mr. Fledger acknowledged the boy but only nodded in response.

Katja diverted across the marble floor until they reached a crowd filling the massive circular chamber in the heart of the building. She could hear the hum of chatter, the screech of chairs, and the drum of gavels, which she assumed warned those entering that time was short to get seated.

When she squeezed past the line, a few grumbled with accusatory looks at their neighbors, but they were long behind her by the time she got onto the musty Senate floor. It was more of a stadium than a floor, with more chairs than most temples. High above, bedazzling chandeliers hung from the domed ceiling, which somewhat resembled a painted egg, with murals of people and events she could not name.

At the bottom of the chamber was a series of chairs erected on an altar where several important-looking people with wigs and long robes sat impatiently, occasionally bashing their gavels and barking orders at the court.

Katja noticed a man she had seen often on the front page of newspapers. His hawkish profile, graying black hair, and pox-mark scars were too distinct not to remember. Prime Minister Gideon was seated on the altar next to a white-haired woman with an unnerving wide grin and large spectacles, who must have been very important to sit there.

Katja felt someone run into her and cursed under her breath. She jumped out of the way before he could make a consequential discovery and began counting the aisle numbers.

Aisle 10 . . . 11 . . . 12 . . . Miss Bentkey.

Katja wandered down the steps just as the chamber started to slowly quiet. She sniffed her breath, smelling like freshly picked roses, and marched to the aisle with the number "12" marked on its side. She then looked down the length of the bench, reading each plaque, but she could barely make out the letters by the time she reached the tenth chair.

She spotted a tuft of chestnut-brown hair, the only woman seated among a pillar of men dressed in similar doublets. Each had a black, blue, or gray coat hanging from their seat, along with a bowler or derby hat set next to their glass of water.

Katja couldn't help but smile at her luck and squeezed between the narrow gap behind the seats, doing her best not to touch anyone or anything as she made her way to the chestnut-haired lady.

The gavel slammed thrice, and a booming voice rang through the halls. "Session has started! Please take a seat and keep your chatter in mind! We will be addressing our opening introduction of the Dusken Decree shortly, followed by first remarks, an opening of the floor, a short recess, and then voting!"

The chamber grew silent, with a few whispers and groans scattered throughout the crowd as a man in a dark coat approached the podium with a massive tome. He cracked open the pages before slamming it on the altar, spewing dust into the air.

"It is clear we have been working on this bit of legislation for a long time," the speaker said. The crowd filled with weak laughter but quickly died off.

Katja hadn't realized she had frozen in her step as all this was happening. Upon noticing, she inched across the stalls, holding her breath until she reached Miss Bentkey, who was scratching her pen into a ledger with a concentrated expression on her face.

Katja noticed a small pile of envelopes on the desk in front of the senator, but knew that someone might see her tinkering with it. She looked around and was pleased to spot a leather briefcase resting against her target's leg, which bounced anxiously.

Katja reached for the briefcase, but it slid to the floor with a loud *thump* when she did so. Miss Bentkey and her nearest neighbors glanced at the source of the unexpected noise.

Katja's heart raced as she tried to appear as small as possible, even though she knew she was invisible. As Miss Bentkey bent over to pick up the briefcase, Katja spotted her opening. She carefully dropped her letter with the violet "D" seal onto the pile of envelopes and delicately backtracked toward the tiered aisle, half expecting to see the rows upon rows of senators staring at her, catching on to her trick. But nobody even gave her a casual glance, too occupied in their own busyness or lack thereof.

She held her breath as she swiftly climbed the stairs that formed the aisle, being far less careful this time. She pressed past those walking slowly and scraped the backs of a few seated senators as she made her way up the incline toward the exit.

"Who did that? Was that you, Charles? Could you take your job seriously for once in your life?" a red-faced lawman said, wagging his finger at the man sitting behind him.

Katja ignored the rising tension and quickly stepped up the stairs as the speaker began deliberating on proposals concerning rivers and harbor defenses, garrison security, and public order ordinances. She was relieved to miss it as she slipped out the back door and descended the Parliament steps into the swelling crowd. She made her way to a secluded alleyway where she had made pitstops many times before in her youth. It was still marked with strange, unusual murals, scrawlings, and etchings on the brick that had never been cleaned in all this time.

The floral scent of her breath was gone. Now it carried a sour, curdled smell, not yet the sharp tang of iron, but a cloying mix of spoiled bread and milk. She plucked at a red strand of hair as a shadow briefly slipped overhead, low between the rooftops. She was thankful for the small mercies of cloaking. One could not grasp external objects, yet she could still touch her own body and anything in contact with her at the moment of vanishing. Without that control, the flow of her spells would continue unchecked until the last of her Vigor drained away.

Stav reached out his hand, and Katja took it and lunged onto the carpet. Before she could adequately balance, they flew off into the sky, a mixture of white and gray clouds and creeping fog, which beaded like dew on the wisps of her unruly hair.

"Did anyone see you?" Fleck asked, hands firm on the carpet's long tassels.

"Not a soul," Katja smiled. She watched as they glided past the tall towers of the Parliament District, squinting her eyes where she could see clusters of carts, stagecoaches, horses, carriages, and trolleys packed through the narrow streets like sand falling through an hourglass. In the distance, she could make out the spiked top of the Maiden Tower, but it swiftly moved out of view as it slid behind the enormous temple steeples standing before it.

"Where are we going now?" Katja asked.

"We are going to visit a few old friends," Fleck said. "We will send them the same letter, only with subtle revisions."

"When did you decide this?" She frowned.

Stav grinned. "While you were gone. I have already drafted two more letters. They only require Lord DeGrom's stamp of approval."

Stav pulled two pieces of parchment from beneath the crystal ball between his knees, which had been used as a paperweight. The letters were identical, with blocky paragraphs scribbled across their faces. He reached for his wand with a swish, summoned fire to its tip, and began melting the violet candlewax.

"Won't that open the portal?" Katja yelled, about to hit the wand from his hands.

Fleck shook his head. "The wax alone will not open it. It requires the wick to open."

"Can you fly any slower? This bloody wind is brutal!" Stav shouted.

He poured a small puddle of wax near the bottom of the two letters. "Your turn, Lord DeGrom," he said with a mischievous smile.

Katja carefully pressed the signet ring into the wax. "Who are the others you plan on sending these to?"

Stav looked over the ledge as the carpet approached Hartwind College, its tall spires scraping against the murky skies. They swiftly landed on a balcony overlooking the grassy lawns below. A black cloud appeared at the bay's far end, bringing fiercer winds and a gentle rain that was growing stronger by the minute.

"I will be back," Stav said, leaping onto the balcony with his wand in one hand and a letter in the other. He unlocked the balcony door with a lockpicking spell and vanished.

In his absence, Katja held onto the crystal ball and sat on the grimoire to avoid it getting wet from the rain. "Who is he delivering the letter to?"

Fleck stared off at the storm with an unfettered gaze. "The warden."

"The warden of Hartwind? Have you thought this through? What if they don't receive the letter well?" Katja asked nervously as she looked at the rustling tree lines dotting the pretty causeways below. "This seems like an unnecessary risk. The last time we were here, there was a Magesleuth following us!"

"Warden Howley is an old friend. He was once a member of the Arkan Roth long before he sought his career in academia," Fleck said wistfully. "If Stav isn't back in an hour, I will look for him myself."

Suddenly, the door ripped open. Stav pulled his hood over his head, which whipped about in the wind before leaping to the carpet, causing it to ripple under his weight.

"That was quick," Katja said.

"Indeed," Stav said, out of breath. "Now we only have one more stop."

Fleck mushed the carpet away from the balcony and began flying to the west, or perhaps it was more southwest, depending on how you looked at the angles of the horizon. They flew over the Northgate District, avoiding the busier town centers near the Parliament building until they made their way to what looked like the Midlands, where Katja often traversed on her route as a chambermaid. She could barely make out small apartments, fruit markets, taverns, inns, and temples. They finally reached Oldgate, where she made out the Maiden Tower tucked between toothy buildings and jagged turret rooftops that overshadowed it. Her heart skipped a beat, and her stomach sank when she saw it. Her stomach sank further when they didn't change direction and headed straight for it.

"What are we doing here?" Katja stammered.

"We are delivering the last message," Fleck said, pointing at the top window of the Maiden Tower. *The grand maiden's window.*

"You can't be serious? My contract has likely been shredded into bits and tossed into a flame! I would be unwelcome here if not arrested on sight and taken away like the other girl caught using magic," Katja snapped. "Why the grand maiden? She is no ally to us!"

"On the contrary!" Stav interjected. "She is no friend to the Arkan Roth, that is no mystery, but we are not the Arkan Roth . . . not anymore. She would be chomping at the bit to find out that the stolen dossier, her old client list, was being used to direct these murders around Theed. She has also always been a friend of the DeGroms, as she works closely with the Magesleuths. Rumor has it that Ms. Argaut herself even used to have a romantic interest in Hoster DeGrom when he was a young lad and unmarried."

Fleck groaned. "You know all of the high-society drama."

"And it is coming to use, isn't it?" Stav simpered.

"And you expect me to deliver the message?" Katja frowned.

"Precisely," Stav said. "Fleck, fly her closer to the seventh-floor window. That is where she used to sleep."

"You are such a creep," Katja muttered.

"We have been watching you for a while," Fleck said. "Don't take it too personally, dear. The Roth does it to everyone before recruitment."

The carpet pressed against the side of the Maiden Tower, and before she could prepare herself, Stav aimed his wand at the locked window, before hesitating.

"Go ahead. Open it. I can't be the only one using magic," he nudged.

"I can't go in there," Katja whispered. "I had it in my head that I would never return to this place, especially after the state I left it."

"Make one exception now, and then you never have to see this place ever again."

"Promise?"

Stav winked, then shrugged. "Maybe."

Katja looked below and noticed a few meandering silhouettes drifting through the streets. "That isn't how promises work, Stav."

"Hurry, before someone spots us," Fleck said impatiently.

Katja sighed and pressed against the crack of the window, focusing on the latch on the other side. She had never unlocked a window or a latched locking mechanism before, but she imagined it couldn't be much different. Then she realized she didn't know who last latched the window, though she would naturally know her roommates' names. Her memory spun like yarn as she tried to remember each of their names in full.

Claudia Ashworth, Astrid Dorne, Victoria and Jeane Littlejon.

"What's wrong?" Stav asked.

"I am thinking," Katja stammered. "It was normally Portia who made sure the windows were locked, but she left a little while ago. It could have been any of the other girls."

"Hurry up. Someone will see us," Fleck whispered.

Katja again focused on the window latch. *"Claudia don Ashworth."*

Nothing.

"Astrid don Dorne," she continued. *"Victoria don Littlejon. Jeane don Littlejon."*

A stone dropped from her chest, landing with a splash into the dark waters of her gut. What if they had already replaced her with a new maiden? How would she ever know her name? She would need to try all the names she knew that entered her former home.

An idea struck her in the face—the *prefects*. But could she remember their names?

Katja ruminated for a moment, thinking hard on all the times that the other prefects had conversed among each other, but not once did they deviate from *Prefect Haggerty, Prefect Primrose, Prefect Nugent*, and all the others she had gotten to know over the year.

Her fingers started to shake as she could almost hear the sound of a ticking clock in her head, followed by the growing sounds of passersby approaching down below. Then she locked onto the latch that held the window firmly shut and examined its simple mechanism. *It's more of a lever than a lock.*

Katja raised her hand to the windowpane and traced her fingers near the joint. A small fire brewed in her belly as she delicately tugged at the latch with the invisible hand she was so accustomed to using all of these years. The window latch creaked, and the window sighed as it gave way, spilling warm, stale air into her face.

"Go ahead . . . use the cloaking spell like you did earlier," Stav urged.

Fleck handed her a vial of green magedust.

"I hope I don't regret this," Katja whispered, feeling the vial in her cold hands. It was warm, like lukewarm tea, and glimmered iridescently, reminding her of the glossy eyes of dragonflies that hovered over the harbor during long summer days.

"Don't forget this," Stav whispered, pushing the letter into her free hand.

Katja hesitantly inhaled the Vigor, and a swarm of warmth filled her belly. Her heart raced as she split her face with her finger and uttered the words, again turning invisible. She carefully opened the window, trying to be quiet, and stuck a leg into the cold, dark dormitory she once called home.

She took the letter, and when half of her body was through the window, she held her breath and pulled her head into the room, freezing as she heard the sound of rustling bedsheets and a stuttered snore. As the snoring continued and her old dormmates stopped shifting in their beds, she carefully snuck across the room and crept out into the spiraling hallway. It was one of the few times she was relieved that there were no doors on any of the dormitories, as it was one less noisy thing she had to prod. She slid against the smooth stone wall past the numerous floors full of sleeping chambermaids until she ascended to the tower's darkened attic, where she had poisoned the grand maiden.

It didn't hit her until she saw the door in the distance. *My contract must not have been dissolved.* Kristoff told her that the Arkan Roth couldn't enter the Maiden Tower because a powerful enchantment hung over the building, allowing only those who worked for the tower to enter its halls. Or was that just another lie to get her to do his bidding? She continued past the peculiar oil paintings, gargoyles, moths, and owls adorning the wall. She reached the iron door separating her from the lady who had haunted her mind for so long. She observed the broken nose on the creepy relief carving of a face that appeared to be constantly winking.

She bent down to where the mail slot was on the bottom half of the door, close to an etching of a sharp thistle, and slid the letter within.

"Is somebody there?" a voice echoed from down the stairs. Katja nearly responded out of habit, but bit her tongue in silence. It sounded like Prefect Haggerty.

Footsteps tapped up the stairs. Katja forgot she was invisible for a minute and pressed herself against the wall as Prefect Haggerty entered the candlelight. Her face was pale and predatory as she scrutinized the empty hallway. When she realized no one was there, she started inspecting the grand maiden's door.

Katja held her breath and slid past Prefect Haggerty, barely avoiding the fringes of her crimson tunic that danced around her legs. She rushed back to her old dormitory and began to climb through the still-open window. She got one leg out into the cold night when a voice called out.

"Who is there? Reveal yourself or I'll scream!" Claudia whispered in the dark. Her voice sounded scared.

Katja plucked a hair from the nape of her neck. Claudia stared at her with a cat-like expression, eyes wide and pupils as dark as ink. She looked like she could faint.

"Shhh. I am just leaving," Katja uttered.

"Katja . . . how . . . how'd . . .?"" Claudia stammered. "What are you doing here?"

"Just go back to sleep, Claudia," Katja said, smelling her breath, which was sweet.

"We thought you got in trouble . . . or died."

"I suggest you keep thinking that," Katja whispered. "Go back to sleep."

Claudia groaned. "You'd better tell me what is going on, or I will scream and wake every prefect in this tower."

"I will be gone by the time the prefects arrive. And tomorrow, all the girls will blame you for keeping them from their precious sleep," Katja spat, pushing herself out the window onto the flying carpet. "Do what you will, Claudia."

Claudia gasped at the sight. "I knew you were a witch the whole time," she said defiantly. "I told the other girls, but they didn't fully believe me. Now I have my proof."

Katja eyed a heavy lamp in the corner of the room. She was just about to send it crashing into the back of Claudia's head when Stav seemingly read her mind, yanking her away from the window and cradling her into his lap before flying off into the pouring rain.

That night, Fleck found an abandoned boathouse off the Market District on Balledore Bay with just enough of a roof to shield them from the rain. Katja spread the torn tapestry on the ground and tried to use it as a blanket, but it wasn't soft, warm, or comfortable, and it was soaking wet. It did, however, keep the insects away and shielded her from the wind, which whistled through the cracks in the walls. Beneath the floorboards, they could hear the swishing of the tide, which occasionally splashed through the rotting wood, as thunder rumbled in the distance and lightning lit the black night. It was the closest she had ever felt to the despair of living on the streets, a feeling she had promised herself never to experience again. Her contract at the Maiden Tower was supposed to keep that promise. She reminded herself it was just for a night, and this was better than any place she had slept growing up.

It has a roof. It has walls. Allies surround me.

She convinced herself it wasn't the same because that was the only way her heart would let her sleep that night. She closed her eyes, watching the lightning flash bright behind her eyelids until she fell asleep and dreamed about her mother.

Chapter Thirty-One

Water droplets tapped on her cheek like a soft drum. The bright sun gleamed through the walls and onto her face as she rolled onto her back, watching as the blurry ceiling came into focus. She stretched and glanced at the spot where Stav and Fleck were sleeping, but their spots were empty. *Did I sleep that deeply?*

Katja spun around the boathouse dizzily, rubbing the sand out of her eyes, but the two men were nowhere to be found. She was completely and utterly alone.

Katja tossed the torn tapestry over her shoulder and strode across the rickety floor and unshackled the bolt on the door before stepping onto the bright street. Fish stands, tea shops, peddlers, shoeshines, hat sellers, barbers, cheap jewelers, counterfeiters, spice traders, and other flea market merchants lined the streets of the Market District, crowding the thoroughfare so tightly that not a single stone saw the light of day. She and her mother frequently visited it whenever they were looking to snag an apple or pear from the stands when the seller was too occupied with a customer. Even the scent of fresh cinnamon, coriander, turmeric, and basil, mixed in with the rotting fish, instantly brought her back to being a child wandering around with an empty stomach, so hungry that the day-old fish looked appetizing.

Thankfully, her current feeling of desperation wasn't about hunger. This somehow felt worse. *Abandonment.*

Where did they go? She stared at the sky and scanned the rooftops, half expecting to spot Stav's annoying smile as he poked his head down at her, but he was nowhere to be seen. She wandered down the busy street, listening as shoppers haggled with sellers and families let their children run amok, but always within earshot in case things went awry. She reached a bend in the road where the smell of hot cider filled the air like a warm blanket, and a young boy in a tawny coat and cap cried out to the street from atop a wooden soapbox. A stack of newspapers towered nearly up to his knees. Based on their popularity, they wouldn't last long, as passersby tossed coins into the tin can resting near his feet.

"MURDER! MURDER! BLOODY MURDER! THE WICKED ASSASSINS STRIKE AGAIN!" the boy cried, his face beet red. "PRIME MINISTER GIDEON ISSUING DISTRICT CURFEWS! EXCLUSIVE FROM THEED'S GREAT NEWSPAPER—THE DAILY KRONER!"

Katja snatched a crumpled newspaper from the muddy ground and sifted through the pages, but the blocky text was hard to read. She could, however, read the victims' names and was relieved not to see the Ponvelles among them. Perhaps Stav had read further down the list, or the countess wasn't going in order as they initially thought. She stared at the names that burned her memory: *Baxter, Crisp, Castner, Dobbins, tar Duren,* and *Driscol.* She could make out another smaller headline on the second page that stated, *QUEEN MARGOT ISSUING FUNDS TO HER "SLEUTHS." SUSPICION RISES AS IDENTITY OF ASSASSINS YET TO BE REVEALED.*

"More rich bastards are dead?" a man asked no one at a cider stand. "Serves them right!"

Another man, dressed in a dusty frock coat and a black-feathered bowler hat, nodded in agreement. "That is what they get for sitting in their mighty castles while the rest of us starve!"

"Yes, yes, but keep it down. I don't want you bringing unwanted attention to my business!" the cider seller said, busy peeling apples. "Believe it or not, some people are taking this news poorly, and I like to sell to anyone with coin."

"They aren't right in the head then!" the man said, tapping his forehead. "These people work every day to make our lives miserable! Finally, someone dares to throw their misery back in their faces! I wish I could shake their hand!"

"Go somewhere else if you are going to be belligerent," the cider merchant scoffed, his thick finger pointing down the street where the crowd was swelling like a ripening boil. "People get killed for saying less!"

"The only good warlock is a dead one," another passerby said, unwrinkling his unraveling newspaper. "I hope they never find these assassins. With any luck, there won't be any warlocks left by this time next year!"

There was a small cheer from the crowd as more passersby took newspapers from the boy's stack, now not even paying. Before long, the boy was overwhelmed, and he ran away in tears as his stack vanished. Someone took his tin can and scattered his coins onto the ground, where people picked them up like pigeons chasing after bread.

Katja avoided the scurry, which was growing more and more crazed as people wrestled in the mud for a few shiny knots that might buy a pint of decent beer at a tavern. She fought the urge to join them, but she needed to find Fleck and Stav. She walked further down the road, noticing a distinct energy in the people walking past her, as though they were boiling like porridge over a high flame. They seemed to crave an encounter, desperate for any shred of interaction, and between the jostle of shoulders and the friction of the crowd, frustrated glances were the only currency exchanged. There was something in the air that was less a smell than a static. It felt thick as tar, making each breath feel heavy.

Is it the news? It can't just be that, can it? She passed several fishhouses, brothels, inns, and piers overlooking the bay, and all were filled with miserable people in the worst conditions, bottled with anger, many shouting over breathing the same air and using the same space, which was all too intolerable for them. Even Katja started pushing back as they ran into her and cursed her unknown name as she passed. *I need to get out of here.*

Katja felt her throat close as the crowd swelled and people stomped on her toes. She held tightly to the tapestry on her shoulder as people gently tugged at it to see if it would fall. She could lose almost anything else, but refused to lose the tapestry. It was the only valuable thing she owned.

Something dark slithered through the crowd and caught her attention. *A Magesleuth.* She shuddered, spotting three more marching in her direction from the crowd, their faces covered by terrifying masks.

A realization dawned on her. *What if that is why Stav and Fleck are missing?* Her heart raced as she pushed toward a dark alleyway between a butcher and a run-down apothecary. Still, the crowd would not let her go as the Magesleuths swiftly approached.

"Watch where you're walking, hag!" a man cursed as she tried to squeeze past him.

Katja ignored the man, shoving harder, but could not reach the alleyway. The edge of the street was packed with barely moving wagons and carriages full of impatient drivers screaming at each other. However, she was beginning to hear a faint sniffing sound. *I have to get out of here.*

"What's the hold-up!" a red-faced driver shouted, fanning his face. "Was there an accident?"

Another driver glared at him. "I can see as well as you can!"

A carriage door window opened, and a well-dressed lady wearing a sunhat sneered at the crowd before barking orders at her driver. "Why did you take me through this mudflat? We would have been there had we gone through Eastgate or the Dunrow District!"

"I went this way because I was told it is even busier at Eastgate!" the driver shouted. "Bloody Magesleuths are running sweeps!"

Katja held her breath as the sniffing became louder, and the line of dark figures slowly approached. She nearly yelped as the nearest Sleuth stopped just a length beside her and began sniffing in her direction. Did they have her scent? Could they have picked it up when she used a cloaking spell in the Parliament chamber? Perhaps even the Maiden Tower? Her palms grew sweaty and started to shake nervously.

She dared not look at them—into their empty eyes. Somehow, she knew one was staring in her direction, likely right at her. She would be tortured and then executed in the morning before anyone read the letters.

Someone tugged at her hand, pulling her to the crowd's fringe and pressing her hard against the stagecoach. She half expected to see the Magesleuths' mask staring back at her and its gloved hands wrapped around her throat, but instead, it was Fleck's melted face concealed in a hood.

"We are leaving," he said. "This place is about to explode."

Katja nodded, hating how happy she was to see him. "Where have you been? Where is Stav?"

Fleck pressed a pale finger to her lips. "Do not say that name so loudly, dear. I am certain you saw the bloody Sleuths creeping about?"

Katja nodded, shoving his finger away from her face. "Boils! Yes, I saw them. Why did you two leave me?"

Fleck looked over his shoulder, grasped her hand, and dragged her between two stagecoaches into the alleyway with beggars cluttered near its mouth. Once they stepped deeper, it became relatively sparse. When no one was within earshot, he whispered in her ear.

"The Roth did it again. Six more families . . . murdered in cold blood," Fleck uttered.

"I know that part," Katja said. "It is the talk of the town."

"Alright then . . . well, I will have you know that Stav woke up in the middle of the night to scry into that crystal ball he has been rather obsessed with lately," Fleck whispered, the copper flecks in his eyes like stained blood on cut emeralds. "I woke up to him riding my flying carpet. I tried to stop him, but he flew out of reach before I could. I would have chased after him, but he was too fast. He looked earnest for once and told me he was going home."

"To the Warren?" Katja's mind whirled.

"No, I don't think he would risk it," Fleck said. "I think he has gone to the Stavoren homestead."

Stavoren Manor. But why would he go there?

"And you thought since he left you, you might as well leave me too?" Katja asked.

Fleck frowned and sighed. "I wanted to find some thread. It is a thrifty repair, but if we are going to fly that thing, I don't want it to tear and send me plummeting to my death."

There was a scream followed by rising shouts from the street, shattering glass, and a large explosion, sending a plume of black smoke high into the sky. Several people ran past them, panic-stricken.

"Perhaps I can repair it while we are flying," Katja said, tossing the tapestry onto the ground and sitting at its center. "You take the helm. I don't know how to fly yet."

Fleck grimaced, but when another shrill scream filled the air, he grasped the fringe of the tapestry and, with a few uttered words, the tapestry raised from the hard concrete and soared through the slit of the alleyway southeast toward the Wallingford District—albeit relatively slowly as not to tear its less-than-savory grassy threads.

* * *

Stavoren Manor looked nothing more than ordinary, although its gardens looked untamed and overgrown. Fleck landed the carpet so that it draped over the garden lawn and hid it beneath a rhubarb bush. Katja scanned the windows, noticing many were boarded-up near the front. When they reached the front door, Fleck turned to Katja and put a finger to his lips.

"*Hugo tar Stavoren,*" Fleck uttered, and there was a satisfying click. He pushed the door open, letting it creak, and entered. The entry was littered with broken ceramic vases and shattered glass.

"They weren't exaggerating about the place getting raided," Katja whispered, noticing the piles of glass at the foot of the boarded windowpanes.

They walked to the stairwell, but before they could take a step, Stav leaped from around a corner with his wand raised. When he realized who it was, he looked at them with a mix of disappointment and a sense of idle relief.

"Bitter teeth, Stav!" Fleck shouted, smacking Stav across the face. "You pull something like that on me again, and I will snap that wand in half!"

Stav lowered his guard but began pacing across the living room, avoiding a pile of overturned furniture, books, lampstands, and drapes. The only part that remotely resembled Countess Auriella's living room was the hearth, which was full of charred wood and a few partially burnt stacks of paper. Did the countess try to hide something from the Sleuths? Perhaps she was tipped off that they were coming, or the Sleuths were responsible for the burning. Did she have something on them?

Katja didn't have answers, but the thoughts spun in her head as she examined the room, running along a railing full of dust, remembering all the tabletops and bookshelves she had tended to over the year.

She suspiciously examined Stav's face, looking at every wrinkle around his eye and the brightness of his eyes. "If this even is the real Stav?"

"Of course I am," he said through gritted teeth. "None of you should be here."

"Prove it," Katja said, pushing against his chest. "What did you give me the day you decided to become my mentor?"

Stav thought for a moment. "Your red dress," he sighed.

"Good," she said. "I can't be too careful. I have been tricked by Gwith one too many times."

"It is good to be careful," Stav said. "Which is why you two should leave."

"I woke up completely abandoned. I'm used to working alone, but we are not working under normal circumstances. I thought the Magesleuths got you," Katja said, folding her arms and leaning against the wall. "I am tired of people leaving me in the dark."

"I left Fleck with you," Stav scoffed, a vein bulging on his forehead. "Did you leave the girl to the rats again?"

"Again? You can't seriously blame me for this? You left with barely a word! And did you find what you were looking for? Your mother?" Fleck scolded, picking a bleeding scab on his chin. "Have you considered for a minute that it could have all been a trick? A trap to lure you into her claws? Do you even think anymore, Hugo?"

Stav wagged a finger. "Don't ever call me that name! That is my father's name!"

"Okay . . . Stav . . . that is beside the point!" Fleck shouted, drawing back his hood, revealing a mess of black hair that only covered the back of his head. "Your mother is wicked, but she is also cunning! Is she even here?"

Stav shook his head. "No, when I arrived, the place was as quiet as temple mice. I thought I had her."

"Not even a trace of her?" Fleck asked, his face grave.

"No . . . she left right before I arrived," Stav muttered, kicking a turned-over table.

Fleck gave Katja a horrified look. "I am no expert on scrying, but those *things* aren't known for lying. Was she alone?"

Stav shook his head. "No, there was someone else . . . a Magesleuth. I came because I saw a vision of my mother being tortured by those . . . monsters. I might despise her, but I couldn't stand to see her die like that."

"And you believe they got away in the time it took for you to get here? Doesn't that seem a bit . . . odd?" Fleck said, and now raised a wand, his eyes searching the chambers like he had caught a glimpse of a ghost. "We should leave."

Stav pointed at the crystal ball sitting on a sofa cushion. "Don't worry. I already looked for my mother. All I see is darkness. Those Magesleuths have put her somewhere the light doesn't reach, or she is . . ."

Fleck sniffed the air. "Something doesn't smell right."

"Smell?" Katja asked.

A cold gust of wind swirled around the room. The sofas, broken lamps, shattered glass, boarded windows, bent chandeliers, overturned tables, dismantled picture frames, stained rugs, and peeled paint had shifted to their once pristine conditions better than Katja could have ever done with her levitation spells. She couldn't repair broken or torn things with levitation. *No, this is something very different.* Light spilled in from the gardens, blinding them as silhouettes stepped down the stairs and surrounded them.

Fleck swiveled his wand above his head like a crown, summoning a bright light surrounding them. "I knew it was a bloody trap!"

The countess, Gwith, Urie, Kristoff, and several others, wearing assorted animalistic masks, shuffled around them like eerie statues, each with wands, staffs, or arms reaching out towards them threateningly. It was all an illusion. She was tricked again, and Gwith's smug smile rubbed salt into the wound. Even now, the image of her mother's grave jolted her like a sharp strike to the jaw, making Gwith's smug satisfaction impossible to bear.

"Mother," Stav grimaced.

"Hugo . . . oh, Hugo . . . you were always so gullible," the countess said sadly. "Hexes! It is what always made you so damn likable, and far easier to rear than your brother."

"Gullible is putting it lightly, mother," Kristoff bemoaned. "More like—"

The countess raised a finger to silence him.

"I came here because I thought you were being tortured! I am sorry my heart isn't as stony as yours!" Stav bit out. "We were a family . . . all of us . . . the Roth, but now we are torn to shreds! All because you can't contain your bloodlust! Have you seen the paper? They know what you have done and are coming for you!"

"I am so glad you came here to save little old me and were important enough for your friends to follow," the countess grinned, ignoring her son's words as her long heels tapped on the wooden floor. "I was beginning to think they abandoned you, too. Yet here we all are, all I needed was a bit of an illusion!"

"A little spilled blood is often needed to gather Theed's unfettered attention!" Kristoff spat. "They don't care about a few burglaries and mysterious oaths whispered in the shadows. That got us nowhere, and you can blame Fleck for the countless deaths of our people over the last few years! I reckon that bloody hill would have far fewer pitchforks if not for Fleck!"

Fleck sighed, "And look what murder has gotten you? More dead Glints, but by your very own hands! Are you proud?"

"For every traitorous warlock we kill, we save hundreds," the countess droned as if tired of explaining herself. She walked around them like a cat circling their prey. "It is a bloody beginning that ushers in a peaceful end."

"Just wait until the warlocks read Lord Hoster DeGrom's letter. When his allies find out that Lord DeGrom is leading a stand for magic freedoms on the behest of these deaths, then you will realize the power of the pen over the blade . . . or should I say *wand*?"

"And what evil did you perform to get Hoster DeGrom to endorse such a letter? That would damn his family for an eternity if they aren't tried immediately for treason," the countess huffed.

Stav revealed the golden ring on his pointer finger, which featured a large, embellished "D." The countess and Kristoff looked visibly flustered for a heartbeat.

"For once, I am impressed, brother," Kristoff grinned. "I didn't think you had it in you to think of something so clever. Perhaps you aren't so useless after all."

The countess glared at him and then returned her gaze to Stav.

"How?" she said, her bright blue eyes glowing in the light and her coils of pale hair dangling to her shoulders.

"Lord Hoster isn't well after what happened to his beloved son, Rhys," Stav said.

The countess's eyes narrowed at the name.

"He was quite vulnerable, but our Dustmage—" Stav stopped after Fleck nudged him.

Everyone looked at Katja as if realizing she was in the room for the first time.

The countess smiled warmly. "Kitty Kat? But of course. You *fetched* the ring?"

"It was almost as easy as fetching the dossier," Katja smiled.

Kristoff frowned. "You could have almost had it all. Remember who taught you how to cloak? If you thought Gwith was a good illusionist, imagine what I could teach you? Gwith was my student, and I taught her everything she knows."

Gwith's eyes darted to the floor.

Fleck chuckled. "Kristoff, you have always weighed your contributions like they were plated in gold when they are only coated in pig iron! If you could convince enough people, you would claim the blue sky was your invention!"

Kristoff barked a laugh. "Fitting coming from you! You never knew what I was doing behind your back while you thought you were in charge! Do you think that my mother is here by mere coincidence? How about the dead professor who led you to flee the Warren like a coward? Have you considered that I might have known exactly how you would act when our great heist and initiation night turned into a botched murder? How about the Magesleuth, summoned to the college because it smelled the magic off of my breath? I knew I had succeeded when you flew off into the night!"

Fleck stared at Kristoff, his jaw clenched. "Are you saying you lured a Magesleuth to sabotage our plan?"

Kristoff grinned. It wasn't a friendly grin like his brother's, but a somewhat misplaced one.

"Oh, you both are such good boys," the countess grimaced. "Fleck, I knew the Roth were loyal to you at the time, and we couldn't just murder you, so we relied on your best skill . . . running away when times get scary."

Fleck's fists whitened around his wand. "I didn't want to compromise our hideout! Do you think secret places like the Warren are just places you often stumble upon?"

"Don't you get it? I knew you would flee the moment you knew the Magesleuths might have caught your scent after that mission. My intention was to get you to leave your seat here at the Warren. Catching your scent was only a bonus," Kristoff laughed. "Your predictability was your downfall. It always has been."

Kristoff aimed his wand at Fleck's throat, which signaled to his followers to join him in near unison.

"You are a traitor." Fleck coughed. "Gwith? Urie? How can any of you stand for this man? He has tricked us all! He would do anything for power! How do you think this will end?"

Gwith and Urie flinched but did not falter with their wands.

"We need change," Urie stammered. "Our people need our help. Sorry, Fleck."

Stav aimed his wand at Kristoff. "You would murder me in our family home? The same place where you and I climbed the trees in the garden and ran up and down these halls? Whatever happened to you, Toff? Father would be rolling in his grave."

"Father? Father would be standing by Mother's side," Kristoff seethed.

"Father never approved of bloodshed! It is part of why he left the Roth!" Stav shouted.

"And why she killed him," Katja urged. Stav and Kristoff froze, their eyes darting to their mother.

A slow grin crossed the countess's face. "Your father was of the same flock as our friend Fleck—a brilliant wizard but a coward. When he threatened to leave me and disinherit me to live a life of squalor, I took from him what I knew could not be bought with gold."

The room grew very silent.

"I know that you took some of his life force, but you didn't kill him, did you?" Kristoff asked, his face troubled. "Did you . . .?"

"I always thought I was the first person to find his body, but I wasn't, was I?" Katja continued, the memories of the count's body resting at the bottom of the lion-paw bathtub roared back to life. "His face was almost unrecognizable . . . and strained . . . unlike an old man drowning in his bathwater. Then, when you took everything you could from him, you left. However, you started to age again and even became demented, so you found a new victim . . . Rhys DeGrom, and who knows how many after he was disposed of."

The countess pursed her lips, but her silence was deafening.

"I can't tell all of my secrets," she whispered.

Bright green lightning flashed across the room, splintering into forked tendrils that stabbed the wall, shattered the windows, and ignited the rug. Stav clutched his chest, where a sizzling wound sent pale wisps of smoke into the air. He seemed shocked and fell to his knees, but instead of collapsing, he summoned a ball of blinding light at Kristoff, which sent him crashing into the wall with a thud, stunning those who watched.

Katja rubbed her eyes, imprinted by Stav's spell, and felt a hot dagger in her arm. When she pressed her finger to the pain, it returned with bright blood. She had been hit, too. She retreated to the window, her boots shuffling on the glass as a warmth bubbled in her chest. She sent a wooden table crashing across the room, striking a man with a mask fashioned like a peacock, who countered it, splintering it into pieces.

Urie disappeared in a poof of smoke, and Gwith flicked her wand, changing the living room into a house of mirrors and disorienting everyone as hundreds of reflections surrounded them. Stav summoned fire, which ignited one of the Roth's robes, before charging his brother.

Fleck clashed with the countess, unleashing colorful spells of mysterious origin, ranging from fire, air, light, liquid, steam, lightning, and other strange forms that Katja could not identify if she had time. Urie appeared behind her and reached for her arms.

"Stop, girl!" Urie grumbled. "Don't make me hurt you."

Katja tried wrestling her arms from Urie's grip, but he was too strong. She sent sharp elbows into his ribs, but aside from a few groans, she could not slip free. She bashed her head backward into his teeth twice and bit the loose skin on his arm until he screamed, finally releasing her. Once free, she tried to focus, took a deep breath, dragged her finger down her face, and vanished.

Brilliant ribbons of every color ripped across the room, shattering furniture and thickening the air they breathed with electricity that tugged at the hair on her neck and arms. The disorienting forces of wind and space pushed and pulled at everyone and everything in the room. Wood planks flew, the fire roared, smoke-choked screams filled the room, along with a loud buzzing that was vibrating in Katja's ears. Funnels of black smoke plumed toward the ceiling, bloodied bodies were tossed across the floor, and guttural shouts rattled off the manor walls and foundation.

Katja summoned a broken vase from the ground and threw it at Urie, only for him to vanish in a puff of smoke before it struck. Fleck nearly backed into her, sweat dripping from his melted face as he countered spell after spell that the countess battered at him.

"Fleck! We can't win this!" Katja said, but nothing came out, like the silence of a rudderless sinking ship moments after being swallowed by the sea.

Fleck ducked as a spell the color of molten iron and the shape of a crude sword blasted through the wall behind him, slicing it in half. He swirled his wand, summoning a fiery arrow toward the countess, who warded it, flicking it toward the ceiling and catching it on fire.

Katja levitated a table leg from the ground and raised it high above her head. She bashed it onto one of the masked Roth and slammed it into their knee, sending them to the ground. Then she looked for Stav and Kristoff, who were now battling up the stairs in a vigorous standoff as the duel sucked them deeper and deeper into the manor's depths.

"Stav! We have to leave and fight another day!" Fleck shouted over the roars of magic.

"We can hold them," Stav shouted. He swirled on his hip, looking for something. "Kat! Wherever you are . . . run!"

Katja sighed and watched the countess walk gently past her with her wand firmly aimed at Fleck's chest. Her hair was long and white like silk, but its fringes were burnt, and the wrinkles on her face appeared deeper than moments before. The veins in her arms and hands appeared thicker, and her age spots were growing darker and more widespread. *She's aging by the minute*. There was a limit to this sort of magic.

Before she could even process the moment, Katja yanked a hair free, and the table leg slammed to the floor. She lunged for the countess, driving her down hard. They hit the ground together, Katja scrambling on top, hammering her shoulder before the countess could knock her aside. Katja clawed for the wand—the same one she had once carried—and pried back each slick finger until it clattered onto the floor.

The countess looked invigorated. Her widening pupils darkened her pale blue eyes.

"I saved you," Auriella whispered. Staring straight into her eyes. "What a pity you must die."

Their eyes met like two flames coming together.

The countess yanked on Katja's hair before lunging for her wand, but before Katja could react, her body was weightless and levitated off the ground. A surge of red lightning swarmed her, its fiery prongs penetrating her skin. Currents ran through her limbs, and jolts blurred her vision as drool spilled from her lips. Everything went silent. She watched the countess pick herself up and grin as the lightning coursed from the fibers of her wand. Countess Auriella looked at the mess surrounding her, like some work of art hanging on the wall. The lightning ceased.

"Poor Kitty Kat. You would have made a great Dustmage. What it took to get the dossier, DeGrom's ring, and the letters was all quite clever," the countess said. She pinched Katja's chin, but the contact shocked her. "Oops."

Katja tried not to groan as every muscle in her body contracted rigidly.

"At least you aren't bleeding much," the countess smirked, her bright eyes observing the entrance wounds. "The heat is so hot that it cauterizes the wounds. Lord Blythe wasn't so lucky."

Katja spotted a large burning log on the floor, and with what energy she had, hurled it through the air and smashed into the back of the countess's skull, disorienting her enough to drop Katja. But when Katja found her feet, she nearly collapsed. Her hands were shaking, and she could smell a metallic bitterness on her breath. *I can't fight anymore.*

She limped down the hall, past a nameless Roth maimed on the floor. Gasping, she focused on the front door. Her heart plummeted when the door vanished, transforming into a mirror. The mirror showed Gwith's reflection standing behind her, but shadows swallowed her figure before Katja could turn. *I just want to lie down.*

"Gwith . . . let me go . . . I can't fight anymore," Katja gasped, her heart racing as she reached through the darkness but felt nothing.

"You think you can just run away? Fleck trained you well," Gwith said, shoving Katja into a wall.

"I couldn't live with murdering innocent people!" Katja shouted, swiping the darkness weakly. "Please, Gwith. Remember how Kristoff side-blinded you in the cemetery, saving me only to further his twisted agenda. He doesn't care about anyone but himself!"

Gwith nudged her again, pressing into one of her fresh wounds. Then a light appeared, glowing on Gwith's face—she looked ghostly.

"I can't let you live," Gwith said. "You know too much."

"When they read the letters we delivered, then all of this fighting will seem pointless," Katja pleaded, tears running down her cheek. "We just have to wait one more day! We don't need to hurt each other!"

Gwith snuffed out the light, and darkness swallowed her once more. A shriek tore through the room—and then the shadows were gone.

The sudden brightness left Katja reeling as she turned toward the front door that already stood open. Framed in the doorway was a towering Magesleuth, draped in long, dark robes that gleamed like spent oil. Its face was hidden behind a horrific mask studded with countless eyes, each black as coal.

Katja stumbled backward as the Magesleuth menacingly stepped toward her. Six more Magesleuths covered every corner of the house. Gwith was wincing painfully on the carpet. Loud creaks came from the stairs as another Sleuth walked down. Stav and Kristoff retreated, their wands raised and their faces bloodied.

"This is all your fault! You led them here!" Kristoff shouted at his brother.

"It was you who lured me here to begin with!" Stav spat, smacking his brother.

Gwith began weaving an illusion, but a Magesleuth's blast struck her chest and sent her flying through the window into the garden beyond.

The countess stared at the Magesleuths like she might take them herself. When a Sleuth reached for its scepter, she attacked, but a spell knocked her off balance before she could finish. Stav looked at his mother with a peculiar expression that Katja had never seen him wear before: fear and *sadness*.

"Mother," he uttered, joining her in the center of the living room next to Urie, and a few other masked Roth, and now Katja.

Kristoff cast a fiery spell at the Magesleuths, but they reflected it back at them in the shape of a sword, which Stav broke up with a swish of his wand before it could strike his brother. With one swoop, the countess reached a clawed hand toward the ceiling and sent the expensive chandelier crashing down onto a pair of Sleuths. Before the ornament could find its mark, it was sliced in two, barely scathing their thick robes.

"They are too powerful, Mother," Stav said. "We can't beat this."

"We don't have any other choice," the countess said, her expression tight. "We must fight. I should never have brought you here, son."

The Magesleuths stepped closer, scepters drawn like daggers.

Stav sent another spell across the room at them, but it was adequately guarded.

The Sleuths took another resounding step forward.

Urie poofed into smoke, but before the last wisps faded, a Sleuth snapped its scepter toward the haze, ripping him free like a net tearing a fish from dark water and flinging him across the floor.

"Stav . . ." Katja said. "I might kindle."

Kristoff slowly reached for his pocket and pressed a glass vial of Vigor into her palm without a word.

Was he helping her?

The Sleuths stepped closer—so close that Katja could almost hear their breaths behind their masks.

A coil of bright shards spun in the air like a pinwheel and assaulted one of the Magesleuth's chests, revealing bloodied pale skin beneath its cloth. *They can bleed.* The Sleuth bellowed a guttural gasp before falling into a heap of robes. Standing behind the Sleuth was Fleck, who was now summoning a whip of fire and lashing it at the Sleuths' robes, catching them aflame as they retreated. As the flames roared, Fleck made his way to their circle, avoiding even a glance at the fire. With hope, the countess and the others started to fight back, filling the living room with flashes of light and all the terrible sounds one could only imagine in nightmares.

Stav buried his wand into the Magesleuth behind Katja and ignited it, nearly catching his arm on fire. The Magesleuth countered by extinguishing the flame and blasting Stav to the ground.

"Stav, you have to run!" the countess shouted, pulling her son to his feet by the cuff of his tunic.

"They know my scent! I will always be hunted! I cannot live like this anymore!" Stav shouted, shoving his mother away.

The countess stared at him solemnly, a tear running down her wrinkled cheek. She rested her hand affectionately on his cheek before thrusting a small dagger into his gut that had been hidden on her thighs.

"Stav!" Katja screamed in utter horror, limping toward him as he fell to his knees.

The countess lowered to his eye level, placed her finger into his wound as he screamed, and closed her eyes. Her white hair turned yellow like honey, and her wrinkles smoothed like a river stone. In return, Stav's dark hair turned gray, and his hairline receded, leaving his scalp marred by brown spots. His skin sagged and marbled, his eyes dimmed and died, his forehead creased with wrinkles, his posture hunched, and his cheeks became gaunt, all within seconds.

"What have you done!" Katja shouted.

The Magesleuth tore the countess from Stav and bound her with a glowing rope that pulled tight against her chest. She looked young, like someone in her fourth decade rather than her eighth—just like how the light had returned to her eyes when Rhys had entered her life.

Three Magesleuths approached Stav with drawn scepters, but before they could obliterate him, Fleck leaped in the way with his wand outward, casting a warding spell.

"You two have to leave now! I will catch up with you later!" Fleck cried. "Take the tapestry. Fly far away from here and don't return! Never look back!"

"We can't leave you!" Katja said, but her arms and legs were too weak. She took Kristoff's vial of Vigor and inhaled a small amount, feeling the warmth fill her stomach.

"I am afraid we aren't winning this fight." Fleck frowned. "Go now before it is too late!"

Katja looked down at Stav's rapidly aging face. He would not make it if they didn't get help soon. She had to find a doctor or someone to stitch him back up.

"Hurry!" Fleck shouted. "And remember the words to fly are '*ava winslet.*'"

Katja felt conflicted as she watched Fleck, Kristoff, and all the other remaining Roth form a line against the oncoming Magesleuths, whose cloaks were scorched and smoking but no longer flaming. On the floor, the lone dead Sleuth lay sprawled, a pool of red blood leaking from its ribcage. She wanted to see what lay behind those black eyes, but the blood was enough to prove that they were mortal. *Perhaps they are human, after all.*

"Where are we?" Stav asked. "Where is father? He isn't hurt, is he?"

Katja used all her strength to pull Stav's frail body off the ground. He was lighter now that he was old. She stepped through the broken window into the garden and pushed Stav through the sill into a fern. When they were on the lawn, she rushed to the rhubarb bush where Fleck had hidden the tapestry. She tossed it onto the grass flat by Stav, not worrying about the creases, before throwing him onto it and taking the reins like Fleck had done multiple times before.

What if she couldn't steer it? She remembered the words Fleck had said and repeated them, "*Ava winslet!*"

"Katja, wait!" Gwith shouted. Despair flashed in her eyes. "Don't leave me behind."

Katja spotted Gwith slowly dragging herself across a turnip garden, blood leaking from the corner of her mouth. Katja cursed, debating what to do. Leaving another witch to die seemed cruel. She sighed before rushing to Gwith and rolling her onto the carpet.

"Do you know how to fly this thing?" Katja asked.

Gwith nodded, coughing blood onto the fabric. She placed her palm on the carpet and uttered, "*Ava winslet . . .*" The carpet began floating above the garden, then higher above Stavoren Manor. With a tug of the reins, they began to float across the sky.

They flew swiftly to Puffer Square, where crowds of hundreds lined the streets. When they landed near the mouth of the abandoned tunnel where Katja had chased her strange stalker Jasper, so long ago, they could hear chants roaring from the crowd. Guards dashed around the square with bats drawn, trying to quell the crowd, but with little success. The tension in the air was palpable.

Gwith hovered the carpet as low as she could without touching the ground, flying down the stairs covered in shadow. She grazed her hand along the wall, and when she found the stony spider, she let it bite her finger. The wall opened, and they floated down to the Warren floor. The secret door slid shut, and the spider crawled back to its web.

Katja rushed to retrieve the antidote and turned to Gwith, who was already showing signs of the spider venom's effects. Gwith collapsed onto one knee, kindled and now poisoned. She sighed with relief and reached for the vial, but Katja clutched it in her palm.

"If you go into the cell, I will give you the antidote," Katja said.

Gwith glared at her with narrowing eyes as her breath began to labor. A grin formed on her face. "You are cleverer than I thought."

Katja shook the vial. "Death or the cell. Your choice."

Chapter Thirty-Two

"**T**off! Toff! Father, help me!"

Katja woke from her slumber, morning light blinding her as she woke in Fleck's old rocking chair and rushed toward Stav, who was flailing on the floor. She rested a hand on his shoulder, and he reached for her face, grasping her cheeks so tightly that they could bruise.

His eyes stared into hers, once like two magnificent blue sapphires, now muted by a milky haze. They looked all too much like Countess Auriella's eyes before she pulled the hands of time backward. By the looks of it, he was also nearly as delusional as his mother had been, as his eyes seemed to chase invisible bats fluttering around. He ungripped her face and swatted at the air, what was left of his long gray hair bouncing like tangled spiderwebs over his face. There was a red stain where the Countess's knife had plunged into his belly, bandaged last night with strips of cloth she found in a backroom that were already soaked through.

"Stav . . . your brother isn't here. You're seeing things," Katja whispered calmly, replacing the soaked bandages with fresh ones.

It was then that she noticed Gwith stirring inside the jail cell. Her arms and legs were shivering, and her teeth clattered like broken glass in a jar. Last night, before Katja succumbed to sleep, she had dragged the weakened illusionist into the cell. She locked it, knowing Gwith didn't have the spare Vigor to unlock it, no matter if she knew her name. *Was it cruel?* Perhaps. But she was still bitter about her mother's grave. *That was true cruelty.*

"Mother, is that you?" Stav said, scratching his head. "Where did Mother go?"

"It's Kat," Katja said. She did not know where the countess was, but she could speculate that it wasn't good. She might have escaped, but the chances of going up against so many Magesleuths seemed low. "I dunno where your mother is, but I am here."

Stav frowned. "Who are you? Where am I?"

"It is Katja . . . your pupil. We are at the Warren. Don't you remember?" Katja uttered, rubbing his hand.

Stav pulled his age-spotted hand from her and looked around the Warren like it was a place of nightmares. "Did you capture me? This is not my home!"

"Stav . . . this is where you live," Katja said, measuredly. She pointed to his bedchamber across the room. "That is where you sleep."

"Here in this place? I would never! I am a lord! Not a beggar!" Stav said indignantly. "Let me out of here! I want to go home!"

"He has lost his marbles . . . or what was left of them," Gwith stammered, spitting dirt from her lips. "Just like his mother."

"What is wrong with you?" Katja scolded. "Why did you betray Fleck and Stav for that . . . foul lady anyways?"

Gwith grinned, her teeth stained red with blood. "I am a thief, not a patron knight. You know who you were working for, right, *Dustmage*?"

"We broke bread and lived under the same roof!" Katja scoffed. "You didn't mind taking those lives?"

"Not one bit," Gwith spat. "We will all be joining them in the grave soon enough. Every one of our breaths is counted by the maker, and I reckon mine is few. Stav will be drawing his last soon if you don't stop his bleeding."

Katja approached the cell bars and looked down at Gwith, who was prone and shaking like a rabid dog. "I don't have to smell your breath to know you are kindling."

"You don't happen to have more magedust, do you?" Gwith asked. "No, I don't expect you to save me again . . . unless . . ."

"Unless, what?" Katja pried.

Gwith rolled to her side. "No, you wouldn't be interested in learning a thing from me. You got Stav for that . . . after all, he taught you how to use a cloaking spell, right?"

Katja turned to leave.

"I will tell you what the Dustmage really is . . . that is, if you give me that vial in your pocket. Why would a Dustmage need dust anyway?" Gwith said, her expression severe. She was weak, but her desperation was growing. "Don't you wonder why the countess wanted you so dearly?"

A cold chill ran the length of Katja's spine. She knew the Dustmage was special, and Stav had mentioned at least one of their abilities, but he had also said there was even more he did not fully understand. Whatever Gwith was about to reveal might be something Katja had never been told.

"Do you know what makes a Dustmage truly dangerous?" Gwith pressed, running her fingers along the bars.

"I've survived kindling enough times to know I'm not ordinary. But you already know that," Katja replied, her voice steady despite the unease curling in her stomach.

"Ah, yes. You've survived, but surviving isn't the only thing," Gwith said, her grin widening. "Have you ever wondered how the Magesleuths hunt down Glint? Why they are always sniffing?"

"They pick up your scent and they never forget it," Katja said, frowning.

"Exactly," Gwith nodded. "But do you know how they do it?"

"Really, Gwith? Even children know they sniff out magic . . . it has a scent," Katja scoffed.

Gwith's smile grew as her tone grew reverent, "Maybe... but every trace of magic has a scent, every hint of its aroma clinging to the air. Like dust."

Katja's lips curved in a sharp line. "I am glad you are wasting time as you kindle, Gwith. Do let me know when you actually have something to useful to barter with."

Gwith chuckled softly, eyes glinting. "*Dust*, Kitty. Where do you think the term Dustmage comes from? You carry that ability too."

Katja frowned, unease creeping into her face. "Are you trying to say that I am one of *them*?"

"No," Gwith said, voice tight, "but you are more alike than you think."

"I have never been able to smell magic before," Katja admitted, disbelief sharp in her tone.

"You haven't been able to do it *yet*," Gwith smirked. "And it isn't only magic. It includes magedust too."

Katja's heart raced. "So . . . I could track anyone who's used magic near me? I could have found Fleck on my own?"

"Precisely," Gwith said, leaning closer to the bars. "Even now, you could follow the trails of Stav, Fleck... even the countess herself if you wanted. But only with the proper training." She paused, tilting her head. "And that, little one, is why the countess wants you more than anything."

Katja's mind swirled as she paced near the hearth, just as Fleck had done many times before. Was she one of them? The same cut of cloth as the Magesleuths? She thought back to Hartwind College, where the Magesleuth had watched them as they exited, and she could have sworn the Sleuth had talons for feet, just like the stories in the legends. She knew her mother's feet were normal, only a little callused and dirtied from walking the streets, but she had never seen her father's feet. Were Dustmage abilities passed through the father, or were they entirely random? She had so many questions, but her lips could not form the words.

"You have no idea how fortunate you are, Katja Rosdyre," Gwith said, her eyes glinting with something like hunger. "I would give anything—"

"I should never have even made it to the initiation at the college where Professor Gill was murdered," Katja interrupted, her voice hollow but steady. "The night you tricked me for the first time. I won't forget what you've done, and I won't let it happen again."

Gwith seemed to almost laugh at her comment. "How do you know you aren't in an illusion now?"

Suddenly, the crowd grew thunderous overhead. The vents were bright from the morning sun, but the shadows of passersby flickered like a blinking eye as people spilled into the square. It wasn't long before she could make out a few united chants followed by the whistle of guards. A bugle blasted, and a voice boomed over the crowd, but was still mostly drowned out by the Warren's thick walls. She didn't need to distinguish the words. She knew what it meant.

"Another execution?" Katja said, noticing her hands were clenched in white-knuckled balls. "Or is this just another one of your spells?"

"I don't have enough Vigor to conjure a fly, Kitty," Gwith said, raising her hands meekly.

The crowd's chants roared, muted by the distance overhead, but the words were as clear as day. "DEATH TO WITCHES! DEATH TO WARLOCKS!"

"What is that?" Stav shouted, cowering beneath the table. "Mother! Father! They are coming!"

"I wager they have caught someone. Possibly one of us," Gwith said, angrily. "We cannot let them get away with this!"

"Stav, I am going to get a better look. I want to make sure the Warren is safe and maybe catch a glimpse of the mayhem," Katja said. She stepped beneath the vents, and dust fell into the pale beams of sunlight, appearing like snow.

Katja reached for the tapestry, tossed it over her shoulder, and walked to the sewer door where Fleck's magic carpet used to rest. She unlocked the door, using several names, until it finally clicked open for Kristoff Stavoren. She stepped across the small sewage river, splitting the long cylindrical tunnel, and climbed up the metal rungs to the coin-shaped manhole in the ceiling. Further down the tunnel, she spotted the rungs and cover through which she had narrowly escaped the countess just days prior, and shivered.

Carefully, she slid the cover across the pavement and pulled herself through the hole beneath the gallows. The long wooden planks and beams that held up the stage creaked as guards moved along their surface above her head. She noticed three perfectly square doors where the bodies would drop and swing to their deaths, and a chill ran down her spine. A few guards stood on each corner of the gallows, but thankfully, they could not see her, even though she could make out their ironclad boots clattering on the wooden planks. In addition, she could see the legs of the first few rows of the boisterous crowd as they chanted and screamed in the city square.

Katja's pulse quickened as she found a crack wide enough to spy through. She pressed her face to the wood and searched, but could only see the pale sky and the rope dancing in the wind. An awkward, sunny rain began tapping gently around them, forming a faint rainbow over the horizon.

Then she poked her head out from under the stage as a group of men and women dragged over a frail man in a dirtied frock coat, dusty penny loafers, and a knotted tie that flailed over his shoulder like a kite. The man screamed for his mother as his legs kicked like a hardened toddler, cursing those who captured him in the same breath as pleading for his and his family's lives. It took four strong men to drag the inconsolable man up the creaking wooden monstrosity and only two to hoist his head into the noose. By the time he was standing, a short drop away from death, he was too weak to fight, and he stared out into the crowd with defeated eyes and trembling lips.

A voice shouted from a horn that echoed across the square. "Today is a monumental day for justice in our un-royal city! This morning, the Crown has decided who she prefers to dine with in her crumbling Commonwealth! She would defend the wickedness of her deep coffered friends than serve the people who built her throne with the blood spilled from our veins and the bones broken in our backs and the toil of our ancestors! If the Crown will not spill warlock blood, then someone will!"

The crowd roared, "WE WANT WARLOCK BLOOD! BLOOD! BLOOD! BLOOD!"

The man continued, dabbing his forehead with a handkerchief. "Their trials have been speedy, and the highest court in the realm has signed their death warrants . . . not those that live in the Parliament District, but instead the Court of Common Law!"

"KILL THE GLINT! KILL THE GLINT!" the crowd shouted, even more unruly than moments prior.

The crier signaled to the executioner. "Peerless, you will die, Lord Horace Redd, a spiritually surrendered man! May shame fill your family's house! And may the eternal one grant you mercy."

The crowd roared and rang silverware on dinner plates, pots, and pans until there was a sharp crack, and a silence filled the square as Horace Redd fell limp at the end of his rope. The silence did not last long, though, as the chants continued, calling for more names that Katja recognized from the dossier's list. Then the leader of the crowd began shouting again.

"Prime Minister Gideon and his warlocks think they can silence us and keep us away from the dishonorable execution of the heroic men and women of the Roth who risked their lives to give us the flame of truth! They think they can hide their tragedy inside their safe little cradle in the halls of Parliament, but no wall, no matter how thick, will stop the ringing of our voices and the swinging of iron!" the crier shouted.

The crowd erupted with cheers.

Fleck. Are they going to execute them in the Parliament building? The thought set a boundless weight on her shoulders, like anchors hanging from her heart and embedded deep in her bones. *He is lost.* There was no way she could ever save someone with the fixed eyes of every powerful warlock in the entire city counting their every heartbeat. No magic could save the poor man now.

"Rumors swirl that some of the Roth have yet to be captured! Their leader has escaped the tyrannical fist of the queen's inquisitors, and we must make sure that never changes! We will fight! Their very own have turned against them! The Roth have risen in honorable defiance against the tyranny that has stolen our blood-borne rights!" the crowd's leader bellowed from his roost. "Auriella Stavoren, if you are out there, we are here to fight alongside you! The warlocks will pay for their lies!"

The countess escaped? Katja's stomach sank like a rock in Balledore Bay. For some reason, deep down, she knew it to be true, but the question still lingered . . . *how?* There were so many Magesleuths and so much chaos, but if the countess was as fearsome as those around her spoke of her, perhaps she had the upper hand. Could there be hope that Fleck escaped, too?

Katja crawled back to the sewer door and dropped down the iron-rung ladder back into the Warren. Shadows consumed her as she splashed across the subterranean creek dividing the tunnel, entering the secret door, before collapsing down into Fleck's cold leather chair. It wasn't nearly as charming a stop to sit without a warm fire to keep the chill away, and the hearth had never looked blacker and lifeless than this moment.

"Who is there!" Stav shouted frantically, brandishing a large rock.

Katja sighed. "It is just me—Kat. They are going to execute Fleck and the others at Parliament."

"Fleck? Fleck of what?" Stav said, his pale eyes ablaze. "Paint? Dirt?"

"Fleck, your old friend, remember! Oh, right, you don't remember anything!" she yelled, slamming her fists on the armrests. "What am I supposed to do with you?"

"What you did for the countess when she was sick," Gwith said, her quiet voice echoing from her cell. "I imagine you did a fine job if she was willing to let you return every afternoon."

"Didn't you hear me? Fleck and all of your friends are doomed," Katja said, her breathing turning frantic and her heart trying to beat out of her chest. "Saving them was already going to be impossible if they were locked in a holding cell or sentenced to hang from Puffer Square above our heads, but breaking into Parliament while tensions are so high will be . . . impossible."

Gwith pressed her face between the bars, her bright green eyes sparkling in the faint light.

"I am listening," she said.

"It easily could have been us in their place hanging from a rope!" Katja rebutted. "I feel disgusted . . . no, more than disgusted. I feel like I have crossed a river I might never return from. I feel haunted, like the only steps forward lead to a terrible ending, and we are running out of road to wander."

"How profound," Gwith uttered. "I can give a bit more road to wander if you give me some dust. There are always more options. You just have to ask.

Katja groaned. "What am I missing, Gwith?"

"That I am a master of illusions. The warlocks are smart, but they are distracted, and their minds are solely on revenge," she said. "They are bloodthirsty, but they will allow the details to slip through the cracks."

"You are saying you think you can pull an illusion big enough to get into the Parliament building?" Katja asked, standing from the chair and pacing before the cold hearth. "Without alerting the Sleuths?"

"Well, not unless you let me out of here," Gwith stated. "I don't have the Vigor to pick the lock."

Katja clenched her jaw, but when she remembered she was cornered, she stuck her finger in the padlock, uttered *Katja don Rosdyre,* and watched the woman who tricked her multiple times pass her and sit in Fleck's chair like it was any other day. But it was almost nostalgic to find Gwith wandering in the shadows of the Warren, and although Katja had that gut feeling she had made a mistake, it somehow also felt right. After all, Gwith was a friend of Stav's and Fleck's at one point, and there must have been some good inside her heart somewhere, even if it was buried deeper than ore.

Gwith placed a few cores of wood in the hearth and looked at Katja expectantly. Katja shrugged. Gwith rolled her eyes, pulling a matchbox stuffed in the corner of the chair and starting a fire with a few scraps of newspaper and a few pieces of wood from the woodpile. The shouting and stomping overhead was beginning to disappear as the constable's whistles filled the streets. Finally, Katja could hear herself breathe for a moment, and she took a seat at the table, relieved not to be rid of the cold draft that filled the Warren as the city crept and sighed as if from its own weight of mistaken grandeur.

"Do you want to hear my plan?" Gwith said, waving her closer.

"You don't deserve to sit there," Katja grunted, dragging a wooden chair opposite her. "Seeing as you betrayed the man who owns that seat."

"I can see we are having a civil start," Gwith said, her green eyes flashing. "I have no problem if you want to trade places."

Katja sighed, realizing she was being childish. "Please, continue."

Gwith pursed her lips, and used a stick to draw a rough outline of the Parliament building.

"If you are correct, there will be a swelling crowd just out front and in the back of the Parliament building. We will want to avoid this crowd by entering the building here. I will use an illusion to appear like Lord Tristen tar Breck, the governor of the Harleck District, who is about as average in appearance as anyone else I have met in the entire Commonwealth," Gwith said. "We will have to change your appearance, too. I could cast a further net with my illusion, but I don't want to risk us getting split up or the Magesleuths catching my scent, as the place will likely be packed with them."

"We will need to get you out of the red dress. I also have a special ointment to dye your hair black. I would say you could choose, but I don't think you could pull off honey-yellow hair or something brighter. You have a gloominess about your complexion that bodes better dark."

"Gee, thanks," Katja muttered. "And what about Stav?"

Gwith glanced at Stav from the corner of her eye. "He has aged nearly thirty years. No one would recognize him, nor believe who he was, even if he pleaded in court. But that won't matter—Stav will have to be stowed away somewhere safe nearby. I would keep him here, but I cannot guarantee we will be able to return once our plan is in action."

Katja bit her tongue. Gwith was right. Stav would only hinder their mission, but could they leave him somewhere alone? What if he wandered or got lost? What if he ran into a Magesleuth? She wasn't certain that they knew his scent after everything that happened the other day. She wasn't even certain if they knew *her* scent.

"I don't know exactly how they will lay out the execution, but I have been inside the Parliament building and know my way around," Gwith said. "We will then wait for Countess Auriella to arrive, and that is when we join her in saving our dear friends."

"Wait for the countess?" Katja spat. "So that's your plan? Nothing and hope the countess shows up? I don't want anything to do with that vile murderer. Do you really think she cares enough to save them?"

Gwith's jade eyes twitched subtly.

"No, but she will do anything to save her precious son," Gwith said, her eyes hardening. "She wouldn't let them get away with murdering her Kristoff, especially in front of every eye that she vowed to sew shut."

"I can't . . ." Katja stammered.

Gwith scorned. "I can talk to her. You won't have to pledge an official declaration of alliance to her, but you would be foolish not to fly under her wings as she soars toward the enemies. You can save Fleck, and she will save Kristoff. It is a win-win situation."

"And what if she doesn't come?"

"She will come," Gwith smiled. "I have known that lady a long time, and if there is anything I have learned about her, it is that she is loyal to her family."

"Like the count?" Katja uttered. "Was that loyalty?"

Gwith's nostrils flared and her teeth ground, but she took a deep breath and erased what tension was building. "Fine, let Fleck die."

She bit her lip and continued softly, "Sometimes a monster is necessary."

"Can I ever convince you to come back?" Katja said. There was only silence. "When do we leave?"

Gwith nodded. "I only have one requirement for my illusion to work."

Katja tapped the bulging vial in her pocket. She knew that was where Gwith's attention was going next. She clenched her jaw, imagining Fleck facing his final moments. She pulled the vial of Vigor from her pocket and pinched it between her fingers, mere inches from Gwith's grasp.

"If I give this to you, you must promise never to betray me again," Katja spat, her fingers firm against the glass.

"You know I can't promise that," Gwith said.

"Okay, teach me how to snap my fingers and make fire," Katja said, eyes fixed on the fire.

Gwith chuckled, revealing yellow teeth. She had never seen Gwith laugh so unhindered before.

"Deal. I can teach you that on our way."

Katja exhaled and handed the vial to her new ally. "I hope I am not making a mistake."

"You are lost without me, Kitty," Gwith said, feverishly ripping the vial from Katja's palm and gulping it down, leaving a few sparkling droplets at its end. She then tore off Stav's fresh bandages, causing him to roar with pain.

"What are you doing?" Katja said in horror.

"Magedust helps it clot quicker," Gwith said, sprinkling the last drops on his gash. "It's no miracle cure—less every street-ridden addict would be immortal, assuming they'd ever trade their fix for survival. Nonetheless, it will stop a bleed."

"Thank you," Katja said, puzzled by her kindness.

"I don't want anyone dragging us behind where we're going," Gwith said, gazing at the grates overhead as she noticed them darkening. "It won't be easy."

"No, it won't," Katja uttered.

"Now get out of that dress and let's take a look at all of that red hair," Gwith said. "Tonight, we move."

Chapter Thirty-Three

They arrived at the Parliament District when it was still dark, and landed atop the towering turrets with crenels and slits, reminding all of a bygone era when the building needed to be fortified. Towering over their shoulders was the enormous globe, etched with fine lines, gargoyles, spires, and ornamental relief carvings that crowned the world-renowned dome of the capital. From below, the dome appeared more like a massive statue, carved clean out of stone, but from up close, the details came alive, and its magnificence almost hummed with its own gravity.

A pigeon landed on the banister in front of Katja and side-eyed her with its reddish-yellow eyes as if questioning why a human was up at such great heights. *Even the birds are suspicious of me.* She peered over the edge, watching a small crowd press its way from the famous fountain of Draco the Firebreather onto the tall steps of Parliament, which had been barricaded and lined with crimson-clad guards, with gold plumes erupting from their shiny helmets. Their chests puffed, and their sabers rattled in their hilts as the crowd approached. Each guard had a long gun strapped to their back, but it was clear that it was reserved for a higher escalation.

"Stav, stop scaring the pigeons," Katja snapped.

Stav waved at Katja dismissively and continued chasing a flock of cooing pigeons who left a cluster of white drippings in their wake. How were they ever going to keep him from running off? Perhaps if he got lost, it wouldn't be as bad as she thought. He could begin a new chapter as an old man, conversing with the birds, and known fondly as the village eccentric until his last day.

A splayed, inky hand seemed to stroke the stone balcony, sending a shiver through her, before she remembered for the dozenth time that it was just her hair. It would take getting used to having such dark hair once more, the familiar disguise sitting uneasily after a lifetime of red frizz crowning her vision. She didn't realize how much of what she saw every day included her hair. Gwith had scrubbed her hair with a strange black tarry substance she had concocted like a witch's brew. Since then, Katja hadn't felt like the same person, as if she were looking through the eyes of someone with a different name.

There was a distant hollow knock, and Katja turned just in time to find Gwith returning from the top of a busted vent that looked like it had been abandoned a few centuries ago. She shooed a few pigeons from the top and waved them onward.

"Come," Gwith whispered. "But be quiet."

She pointed to a pair of guards walking the perimeter of the rooftop a few stone tosses away.

"What do I do with the tapestry?" Katja asked, feeling its weight on her shoulder. "I can't bring that down there."

"Hand it here," Gwith said, taking the tapestry and stuffing it into one of the large gargoyle's mouths, looking over the lush Parliament gardens facing north. "I will come back for it."

It made Katja feel uneasy letting the tapestry go, but she knew it would have caught the attention of many eyes in the halls of Parliament. There was a sense of pride and ownership in that piece of fabric since she first learned it existed at Stavoren Manor, and now had flown on it and stitched it into a flightworthy state. She took note of the wide-mouthed gargoyle, embedding its image into her mind for the day that she would have to find it, but Gwith tugged her shoulder as the sound of oncoming boots clacked nearer.

Katja got up and pulled Stav's hand, which felt leathery and cold in hers. He fought back for a moment, but she was able to steer him toward the rickety vent with some ease. Stav was so frail that she imagined a strong breeze could wisp him away, a far cry from his younger self.

"C'mon, Stav, this way," Katja said, assuredly.

Katja climbed the vent and hoisted Stav up with Gwith's help, before climbing a ladder, rung by rung down into the Parliament building just as the guards entered the terraced rooftop, unaware of their presence mere seconds before.

"That was too close," Katja uttered, her face dangerously encroaching on Stav's rapidly descending bony rear. "Stav, you are going to crush me."

"Sorry," he said, slowing his pace.

"Be quiet, you two," Gwith whispered. "I checked that it was clear, but you never know who might have just walked in. This place is a labyrinth."

One by one, the three of them reached the last rung, finally spilling into a strange storage chamber, with hammered crates, dusty wardrobes, broken chairs, towering cabinets, and other objects covered in sheets to ward off the lifetime of dust covering every exposed surface that dared to sit upright. Katja sneezed as a cloud of motes filled the air.

"So much for a vent," she jeered.

"Follow me," Gwith said, walking across the room until she reached a door. She pulled it ajar and peered outside before closing it. "Okay, it is time."

"To teach me fire?" Katja asked.

Gwith turned toward them. "No, that would be far too dangerous here. Would probably burn the whole building down."

"That doesn't seem too bad."

Gwith smirked, and then uttered something under her breath, twirled three times, and miraculously, upon the third turn, her blonde braid vanished, her bosom faded, her eyes narrowed and darkened, her teeth straightened and whitened, her hair formed into dark tight curls, her nose turned red at its tip, her chin broadened, her legs lengthened, her crude tunic transformed into a tweed coat and pants, with leather penny loafers and a black fedora, and to perfect the illusion, a graying mustache squeezed out of the pores on her upper lip. Although Katja had never met him, she knew Gwith was now Tristen tar Beck, and she wore someone else's face better than any warlock Katja had ever seen.

"Boils," Katja uttered, her jaw dropped. "It looks so real."

"That is the point," Gwith said, twirling the ends of her mustache. "It is actually quite fun. One day, if you allow me, I could try and teach you."

"Like you did with fire," Katja groaned.

Gwith winked her dark eyes, which was almost horrific coming from Lord tar Breck.

"Soon, my apprentice," she said, exiting the door slowly and leading them out into an empty hallway.

After wandering the halls and descending a few old staircases, the hum of hundreds of voices began to echo off the walls and buzz in the air, indicating they were close. A few well-dressed bailiffs, clerks, and other people of note swept past them in a flurry, ties flying over their shoulders like banners, and oily hair dancing on their foreheads as they passed by. A few guards looked Gwith, Katja, and Stav up and down as they passed, but their eyes softened reassuringly when they noticed Lord tar Breck leading the charge with the confidence of a shoeshine on the corner of Dabbord Square.

Katja tugged Gwith's sleeve delicately as they passed a barricade of guards standing at either end of the doorway ahead, their rifles gleaming on their shoulders. Gwith pulled her away.

"Keep your head down," she uttered. "Stay close to me and make sure Stav doesn't fall behind."

Katja grasped Stav's hand, his knees shaking as they tried to keep up with Gwith's metronomic pace. "You need to slow down. Remember, Stav is nearly as old as the countess was—"

"The countess could walk this with ease," Gwith scoffed.

"I think I would know what the countess could or could not do," Katja rebutted. "Just slow down a little."

"I don't want to miss it," Gwith said, but she slowed down slightly, allowing Katja and Stav to trail close behind.

When they reached the towering guards, one of them nodded their head and opened the door. "Welcome back, Governor. We are in for a real show."

"Yes, we are," Gwith said, before walking through the door into the massive domed belly of Parliament.

Katja and Stav followed Gwith without a word from the guards, who offered neither challenge nor objection. The Parliament floor was crowded, with hundreds, if not thousands, of swaying heads of every shade of color, from frosty white to spiderweb gray to inkwell black, and many that were shiny and bald, glistening in the bright lights like polished marble. Calling the chamber stuffy felt like an understatement, as every scent and fragrance assaulted their noses—lavender, bergamot, sandalwood, licorice, sweet plums, and the foul stench of too many people wearing too many layers of socks, shirts, vests, and every coat anyone could ever need on any occasion. To summarize, the rich and well-connected smelled terrible.

Gwith led them down the narrow stairs, as they clung onto the creaky railings dividing the way like mice clinging to a sinking ship. The fall would be brutal at this height, and looking down made Katja wonder how they managed to pack so many people of varying abilities into a place like this without multiple deadly falls every session. It seemed like an absolute miracle that Stav hadn't fallen, but Katja made sure he was on a short leash behind her, and that every fallen step or slip was accounted for with herself as his safeguard.

"Hello, Breck!" a voice shouted from the side. A gray-haired man with a forked beard waved at them. "Come sit over here with me! It is going to be a joyous occasion, and I would love some company other than Mr. Gibbs and Mrs. Norris over here from the bailiffs' office!"

Gwith paused and twirled his black mustache. "Sorry, not today, old codger. I have a front row seat."

"Front row, ey?" the man said, clearly flustered, eyeing Katja and Stav with a perplexed grimace. "Who have you brought?"

Gwith looked back at Katja with coal-dust eyes. "My niece, Katherine, and my father, Eustace. They wanted to see the spectacle for themselves! Cheers, old friend!"

The man smiled. "Cheers! Come to my office on Merchant Street and we will celebrate with a glass or two! After all, our names were on that list! We shall call it an 'escaping death' celebration!"

Gwith narrowed her eyes and smiled before continuing down the stairs until they reached a blockage.

In the middle of the floor was the tall wooden podium and seats where the prime minister, speakers, whips, and delegates sat, at the center of attention like priests adorning an altar. Just in front of the tall seats was a cleared floor, with chairs stacked in neat rows to the side, and in its place stood a makeshift gallows with crude wooden blocks and freshly cut timber beams. It appeared they wasted little time getting this execution underway. On an oak placard above the pully contraption read the words "TRAITOR" in red paint, which was still shining because it had not been given time to dry.

Gwith then paused at a section of tiered seats and squeezed down a row, bumping knees along the way, until they reached two empty seats.

"You are going to have to move, sir," Gwith said sternly to the large man with a broad face that looked red like a furnace-stoked iron who was sitting in their sought-after third seat. "These seats are reserved for the tar Breck family."

"The tar Breck family?" the man said, his face shiny from sweat. "I have been sitting in this seat since the break of dawn. How can they possibly be reserved?"

Gwith frowned. "What is your name, sir?"

The man smiled. "Dunsten—"

"—Family name, you dunce," Gwith scoffed.

"Rundel," the man said, his eyes wide with offense. "Dunsten Rundel, sir."

"Never heard of it," Gwith sneered. "My name was on the bloody list. Now get out of my seat!"

The man stood up, tugged at his lapels, tucked in his shirt into his tight trousers, and, with a huff, sauntered down the row angrily. "Too bad they didn't get caught later, Mr. tar Breck."

Gwith cursed the man away, and the three of them took a seat in the noisy crowd.

"Nicely done," Katja said, but her voice barely traveled.

Gwith pressed her lips to Katja's ear. "Once the chamber is called into session, I am going to get up and head to a spot with a better view. I know the countess will probably arrive sometime once they bring the prisoners out to the gallows. Keep an eye out."

"Is Stav going to be safe here alone?"

"Safe is never a promise in these missions," Gwith said. "But he will be safer here than anywhere else. His job is to blend in and not move until we need to get him. Your job will be to wait for the signal and levitate anyone who puts a rope around their neck so they do not die if the countess comes too late. In the meantime, stay vigilant."

"What if they find me?" Katja said. "I am sure there are Sleuths somewhere out there."

"Oh, there are for certain," Gwith said. "They might even already have an idea that something is going on. Our goal is to make sure it happens anyway."

"And if the countess doesn't come?" Katja asked.

"She will," Gwith said. "It is more the matter and method of her arrival that you should keep an eye out for."

Katja nodded as unease settled in her gut. She leaned forward in her seat, watching as the chamber filled even more. She was used to being in crowds—

after all, the numerous city squares often got packed during the mornings, afternoons, and night shifts—but this was another level. Not even the trolley during Hearthward festivals got this packed. It made it almost hard to breathe, even though no one was sitting directly on her chest.

A deafening bang erupted from one of the highest seats near the chamber's center, ringing like metal striking a fiery anvil. The man who swung the gavel had graying temples, a black goatee, a pointed jaw, long ears with sagging earlobes, and hooded eyes that cast a shadow over his face, matching his raven-black tunic and trousers. The man was instantly recognizable as the face of the prime minister shown in drawings on the *Daily Kroner*'s front page nearly every day since the last one died—a mystery that still hung in parliament's rafters like a ghost.

"Order!" the crow-like man shouted hoarsely. He had clearly been yelling a lot as of late.

If the room was like an orchestra, the prime minister's gavel was like the maestro's wand. The chamber came to a drawn silence except for the faint noise of shifting garments, creaking seats, and the occasional guttural cough that filled the lulls. Prime Minister Gideon pursed his lips and shuffled a stack of paper on the podium before setting his spectacles lower onto the bridge of his drooping nose. He licked his finger each time he flipped the page until he found what he needed, cleared his throat, and looked out at the crowd with a gaze made of steel and contempt.

"Today, I thank the Theed constables and all employed under the proud banner of justice that serve the Crown, who were able to bring forth the traitors who have brought harm to our civil order here in our glorious capital! Your sacrifices will not be forgotten, and your contributions will be commemorated for years and generations to come," the prime minister clamored. "I would like to additionally thank the great investigative detective prowess of our Magesleuths in finding the murderers and capturing them before they could do irreversible damage to the fabric of our great Commonwealth, despite recent controversies surrounding its leadership."

The crowd clapped thunderously until the prime minister raised a finger and spoke again.

"This morning, after a thorough discussion, the royal family and a few delegates have decided to summon you all here to demonstrate an expeditious demonstration of justice that will help our house turn the page on this terrible chapter in our history," Prime Minister Gideon said, wiping sweat from his brow with a handkerchief. "Normally, we would have held a lengthy trial for the crime of murder, but in this rare situation where there is a syndication of murderers, the Crown has made a royal exception. There is nothing to argue about and no defense for the actions taken against our private citizens, not to mention the sense of security we often take for granted. It is a grand betrayal and warrants swift justice!"

Roars of applause refilled the chamber.

The Prime Minister then looked higher into the chamber and smiled before reaching a palm out toward the wooden contraption on the chamber floor. "This morning, we will perform a penal action that is reserved for only the worst crimes in our history. It was the Eldrelska royal family that first brought such public penalties to our halls. The last time such a calling occurred was nearly half a century ago, when the same group that acts upon our Commonwealth today committed a great atrocity against our Crown—the vile and wicked, Arkan Roth, and their sick followers . . . no more!"

"GIDEON! GIDEON! GIDEON!" the crowd chanted. "KILL THEM! KILL THEM! KILL THEM!"

Prime Minister Gideon smiled and signaled to one of the constables at the door, who exited the back of the chamber with excellent promptness.

"Let's bring out our traitors!" Prime Minister Gideon shouted.

A few moments later, nearly a hundred armed guards funneled out of a back chamber through swinging doors. Near their center was a line of seven prisoners, each in ragged black clothes, with a burlap sack over their heads. Each was chained together at their wrists, hips, and ankles, which made a terrible clanking sound that adorned the consuming shouts ringing in the chamber. People sitting around the bowl-shaped galleries stood up, shook their fists, and spat, their faces pink.

"DOWN WITH THE ROTH! KILL THEM! VENGENCE!" they shouted.

Katja stood awkwardly as those around her rose, pretending to join in on the dour occasion.

"I am going while they are distracted," Gwith whispered.

"What if—" Katja began, feeling like she wanted to vomit.

Gwith grinned and pinched the air before them. "If you want to use fire, hold your finger like so, and willingly give the skin of your thumb in exchange for a spark. Do this while whispering '*duraan*' until you get so good at it you only need to think it."

Katja found herself grinning back. She distracted herself from the ebbing nerves with Gwith's words, even placing her thumb and middle finger together as if to try now. However, it didn't last long, as those sitting around her grew rowdier and rowdier. She looked at Stav, who was wide-eyed and frantically rocking his head back and forth in his seat. She patted his shoulder and caressed his trembling hand, but it didn't seem to make much of a difference. *Is this a mistake?* The next time she looked back, Gwith was already gone, swallowed by the rows of the crowd.

Chapter Thirty-Four

Sound engulfed the chamber, a tide so fierce it seemed to hide the world itself. And yet, in that chaos, two subtle acts emerged—the first like the prelude to a play, though no stage or speech could prepare anyone for its sudden revelation.

A bright red shadow approached the altar, a dazzling blood red cape, silky like a flag, behind its back. There was an audible gasp as Queen Margot, bedazzled in gold and rubies and adorned with a thin crownlet, stood before the highest seat, with golden armrests, velvet cushions, and lion-paw feet, that looked more for staring at than sitting. By the look on Prime Minister Gideon's face, this was all a terrible shock, as his pallor paled and his jaw dropped like a wooden doll.

"Queen Margot . . . your majesty!" Prime Minister Gideon said, combing back his sweat-drenched hair. "I was not expecting you."

"You never do," Queen Margot said, eyes narrowing. She pulled off the bone-white gloves that clung to her forearms and set them on her seat before staring down at the prisoners. "But alas, here I am, in my seat where I belong."

"Of course." The prime minister bowed. He returned his attention to the crowd. "It appears the queen herself has come to witness history!"

The crowd was silent with a few mixed cheers. Most appeared to be terrified to say anything.

A clap and a whistle came from nearby, piercing the veil of silence, and when Katja looked to her side, she realized it was Stav, who was joyously clapping and cheering like a child at a pony show.

Katja smothered Stav, pressing him back down into his seat, but not before he let out more clamoring.

"All hail, Queen of Queens!"

"What has got into you, old codger!" Katja said, pale fingers pressing into his jowls.

"Control your old man, girl," someone in a long trench coat said from behind.

Katja wanted to strangle the man himself, but she knew now was not the time for gaining any more attention than they had already received.

Queen Margot smiled brilliantly, "Thank you, Count Hugo. You are a true subject of the Crown."

"Stay here!" Katja said. "I will be back. I promise."

Stav seemed to barely notice her as his eyes glazed over, much like the countess only a season ago, retreating into the vacancy of his mind. He drooped back into his seat and began singing some lullaby or children's tale under his wispy breath.

"Thank you for attending our gracious halls, Your Majesty," Prime Minister Gideon said, with furrowed brows. "It isn't often we get blessed with your presence in our court. Welcome! If it suits you, let the trial proceed."

"Yes, please," the queen said, raising a palm permissively.

"We have our prisoners. We have discovered their treachery. The judges have given us their united decision just this morning," Prime Minister Gideon said, looking sideways at a man with a powdered white wig, sunken eyes, a red nose, and sweat bleeding through his white tunic. "Please, read us the court's decision, bailiff!"

The bailiff adjusted the thick spectacles on the end of his bulbous nose and cleared his throat of gravel. "The highest court, decreed under the Crown of Queen Margot and the compliments of our Parliament, has decided that the plaintiff, the people of Theed, and their commencement to pursue the actions of damages brought on by the accused, Auriella Stavoren, Kristoff Stavoren, Hugo Stavoren, Urie Mastbilt, Sabrine Plum, Peter Higsby, Horace Powers, Lucinda Dyce, Gwith don Goste, and Archibald Fleck, be sentenced for their crimes against the Crown and its people with death."

The chamber roared, refilling the room like a mighty sea as people stomped on the wooden floor, shaking the ground like a rocking ship.

A chill ran down Katja's neck. Even hearing Hugo Stavoren caused her to catch her breath as she watched the old man fumble in his seat, unbeknownst to him that he was missing his execution date. She looked at the lineup of seven prisoners and tried to find a glimpse of who might be who, but most of them she didn't even know or recognize. Perhaps, the names listed were some of the countess's followers who had been wearing masks in the graveyard or at the ambush at Stavoren Manor. One of the prisoners had a hunched appearance to him, which must have been Fleck, and another stood tall like a rod of the building's foundation, which she deduced must be Kristoff, but a few of the names listed weren't in attendance.

And they didn't even list my name.

Katja mustered down the row, to the center aisle, taking note of where Stav was sitting in case her legs got crossed. When she reached a dense spot, she pretended to reach for something on the floor, meanwhile running a finger down her nose, and vanishing. She looked around to be sure, but there were no sideways glances. She took a deep breath of relief—they were all too distracted.

As she continued down, closer to the Parliament floor, she practiced levitating with her hands as if she hadn't done it several hundred times before. The moment was coming soon, but despite being able to levitate small apples out of food carts since she was a young girl under her mother's watch, she had never levitated something as awkward and heavy as another human. She wasn't even sure if it was possible, but she would have to try.

"Executioners, please proceed," Prime Minister Gideon said.

Three large men with covered faces approached the lineup of chained prisoners and released their connecting chain with a loud clang. They picked the first one from the lineup, who wrestled the executioner's grip, only to surrender when all three hoisted him onto the gallows and ran the noose over his head.

"Remove the mask," Queen Margot spat. "We want to see our trespassers when they breathe their last breath."

A face emerged, revealing a young boy with ear-length red hair, a dusting of freckles, and missing teeth. His forehead was slick with sweat as he winced at the bright, overwhelming room. Tears ran down his cheek.

"Any last words?" the bailiff asked, wiping sweat from his temples.

The boy sorted through words, but nothing came from his mouth.

"No last words for traitors," Prime Minister Gideon spat. "Peter Higsby, I sentence you to die."

There was a loud crack, and the boy named Peter Higsby was no more, his body dangling like a fish at the end of a line. The room grew cold, as if the boy sucked all the warmth from the air in his death, but it wasn't long before the chanting grew and the chamber became stuffy like pea soup moments after.

Why wasn't the countess here yet? Where was Gwith? Katja's eyes scanned the small lineup of seven prisoners, settling on the queen, who watched with a grave expression. Had Gwith been caught somewhere she didn't know about? Had the Sleuths tracked her down after catching her scent? They'd listed the countess's name—maybe she was among the seven, and Katja had simply overlooked her. Was this all one giant mistake?

"Remove his body. We will quarter him and put his remains in an unmarked pit," Prime Minister Gideon roared. "No one will ever utter his name again."

Katja felt sick to her stomach as another prisoner was dragged to the gallows and fastened to the end of the hangman's rope. She counted the lineup—five remaining—but they didn't have Gwith or Stav, and the rioters from earlier had said Auriella got away. Was she mistaken? She knew some of the names were there, missing from the small crowd standing before her.

The executioner removed the prisoner's mask, revealing Urie's round face. His long beard had been cut away into terrible tufts, and his eyes and lips were red and bloated like raw meat left to swell in the sun.

"Urie Mastbilt, I sentence you to die," Prime Minister Gideon said.

Katja felt like time slowed to a halt as her fingers tingled. She was now as close to the Parliament floor as she could get without breaching the barrier. Reaching out her hands, she felt the warmth well in her belly, closed her eyes, and focused on Urie's feet.

The trapdoor squealed. Katja could feel the tug of Urie's weight as he fell, but her hold snapped, sending her to the ground, and a loud thud rang through the hall.

Urie.

A fire ignited inside her, sharp and relentless. It felt as if she had sentenced him to die. Before she could even process it, another prisoner was dragged to the gallows, and a fierce determination seized her—there would be no more death on her watch. Mourning could come later. Her gaze locked on the next prisoner's feet. Cinnamon-colored skin, chestnut hair tumbling in wiry waves to narrow shoulders. A bruised, battered face looked up, lips trembling as they struggled to form a shout.

"Free the Glint!"

"Defiant even when facing death," Gideon scoffed. "Lucinda Dyce, I sentence you to die!"

Katja pulled herself to her feet and changed her stance for another attempt, but once again, the trapdoor flung open, and another lifeless body dangled mere inches from the ground. *How much of a difference a few spare inches made.* She swallowed down bile, repeating the woman's name—she would not go nameless.

Next from the lineup was a prisoner with strong shoulders, proud and stoic. When the executioner removed their mask, golden hair spilled out onto her face, obscuring her face except for a prominent brow and chin that looked like *. . . No, it can't be . . .*

"Gwith don Goste, such a shame," the prime minister said, almost sympathetically. "Your parents would be rolling in their graves."

Gwith? The coldest chill spilled down Katja's spine and sank into the base of her feet. Who is sitting in the body of Tristen tar Breck? Who had been in the cell mere hours ago?

"I wish I had been the one to send them to their graves myself," Gwith shouted, glaring at the crowd as they screamed and spat at her. "Perhaps I'll have the chance to kill them in the next life!"

Katja stared at her. It was definitely Gwith. Her voice, her stance, and her bite. Her mind raced back to every interaction she had with Gwith, and she should have known something was awry with the imposter mingling with her all this time.

"Goodbye, Gwith don Goste," Gideon said. "I sentence you to die."

The trapdoor opened. Katja sprang to action to no avail, and Gwith was no more.

Katja felt dizzy. Was she going to kindle? She knew, as the Dustmage, that she could not die from kindling—if Gwith hadn't lied, if it had even been her. Nonetheless, she could certainly faint. No, it was something else. Then she recalled the things she and Gwith talked about, looking for any sign, and then a realization settled over her like lead.

Gwith had been calling Katja "Kitty" and Stav "Hugo," but Katja just assumed it was from her being near the countess. Also, Gwith had always despised Katja, testing her and speaking foul of her since the first day Katja fell out of the tapestry. But the Gwith she had been over the last day was more like a mentor, winning her over minute by minute. Yes, this Gwith was harsh and even blunt sometimes, but it was always to win her over. Katja thought it was just a method of survival, a way to get out of the jail cell and to win her trust. Then it struck her.

The only person seeking Katja's admiration had been the countess. Even when the countess was angry and willing to destroy everything Katja stood for, she had tried to win her trust, and Katja never gave it to her—until now. Her eyes flew to the throne. How would Queen Margot, the recluse, who rarely met her constituents, have recognized an aged Stav cheering from the stands? Where were her guards? Images of Tristen tar Breck, and fake Gwith flew through her mind. The countess had taught Gwith, of course—she was a master of illusions. Katja's mouth went dry. The countess had won, and now she was standing high on the podium, crown in her hair, as she waited for her beloved son's name to be called.

It was all so obvious. Katja was trembling, but what a clever ruse. How had she done it? Katja had Gwith locked in that cell for hours, and she was not particularly merciful until her hands were forced. She needed Gwith . . . and the countess knew it. How long had this horrible switch been in place? How long had she been deceived and been talking to the one person she promised to unravel? Her hands balled into fists. How could she be so foolish? Gwith even stated that she knew more than anything that the countess would arrive today, and she was bloody right, but how was she going to make her move?

Katja glared at the queen, noticing the grimace that should have put her on the countess's trail the moment she shapeshifted into Gwith, Tristen, or the queen. She wished more than anything to reveal her now and have every constable in the realm chain her up. *Why hasn't she done something already? Why wouldn't she save the Roth? Gwith? The boy, Peter? And what about Lucinda?*

Their lives were on her, the countess, their bloody queen. She deserved to hang in their place!

Katja screamed, her nails dug into her palms. She was still invisible, and it was good she was or else the whole chamber would have heard her torment, even over the rising hollers and the distant rumble on the plank floors.

When she looked back at the gallows, a burlap sack was being torn from Fleck's scarred face, but it was hard to notice behind the brutal red swellings and lacerations that were still glistening bright red in the light.

Katja's eyes shifted from Fleck to Gideon and finally to the queen, who didn't budge her composure. Even worse, she was grinning from ear to ear. *This is what she wanted.*

"Archibald Fleck, your reign of terror on this city is over. You have hidden long enough, but justice has shone a beacon over your wickedness. The madness is over. I don't know what happened between you becoming a hero of war to . . . this, but the latter is what will be remembered through the annals of our great history! Hero no more!" Gideon shouted, gritting his teeth so hard that it looked as if his jaw might crack. "I sentence you to die!"

* * *

The second act was impeccably timed. Glass shattered through the halls, followed by the bashing of pine and oak. The perimeter doors splintered to the floor, covering the guards and anyone sitting in the furthest back seats with shrapnel as long as knives. Hundreds of attackers plowed through the frantic guards, who were screaming sweet mercies before being swallowed by the advancing ants. The sounds ringing in the dome transformed from profane cheers to wails of outright terror as fire, blood, and raging metal spewed about the chamber.

"Guards! Take care of this disorder!" Gideon screamed, face bright red as he pounded his gavel on his desk.

This only seemed to invigorate the oncoming hordes, as hundreds, if not thousands, continued to rip through the doors in every form of dress ranging from ragtag aprons to flowing skirts of every color, which stood out from the overwhelming black-, white-, and gray-clad crowd of Parliament who were now screaming in terror and jumping from their seats, away from the onslaught.

It wasn't long until the hall began smelling of smoke and iron, as dark pools of blood and red footprints covered the once bright Parliament floor. The mob advanced, taking disheveled prisoners in their hands, tying them with rope, while a pile of bodies littered the floor so thick that the advancing riot had to step over them and often slipped on the slick blood on the floor.

"HANG THE GlINT! SPARE THE ROTH! HANG THE GLINT! SPARE THE ROTH!" they shouted.

They weren't cheering on the execution. *They were protesting it.*

"KILL THEM ALL! HANG DEGROM! HANG GIDEON!" they continued violently.

Prime Minister Gideon watched the crowd, his brow furrowed with fear and hatred. He glanced at the gallows and screamed at the executioners who were fleeing to the back exit.

"Get back to your stand and finish the bloody job!"

The bailiff cowered behind his stand, but also retreated out the back door along with all the other ranking members of Parliament, leaving Gideon and Queen Margot alone at the altar, like captains of a sinking ship.

What now, Auriella? Your plans have failed.

"Hang him!" the prime minister ordered.

One of the executioners returned to his stand. Katja panicked as Fleck wrestled with his noose. She wondered if the Magesleuths had made sure they came with Vigor so low that they couldn't use even a simple cantrip.

The trapdoor swung open. Katja focused her mind, sending the tips of her fingers toward Fleck's feet, imagining them stretching long and narrow beyond her own body, brushing against the edge of the gallows. Warmth bloomed in her ribcage, and just as Fleck was about to test the hangman's knot with his neck, his weight pressed down onto Katja's shoulders, and he hovered in place.

Fleck's eyes darted across the chamber, bewilderment etched into his face. For a fleeting mercy, he realized his time was short. He tested his footing along the edge of the open trapdoor, searching for balance, but there was none to spare.

Katja focused intensely, feeling and hearing the crack of her tendons and bones shift under his weight. She would need to cut him free —how? Slowly, she pressed forward toward the knee-high barrier separating the seats and Parliament floor and managed to slide over it, holding desperately to his weight, which felt like being pulled down to the ground with heavy chains. The crowd was now advancing beyond the barrier, and the mayhem was approaching as lawmen frantically ran toward her, their ties loosened and flailing in their wake.

Something ran into her, sending her to the bloodied ground. Her levitation gave way. She wanted to scream in horror, but she was too shocked as the crushing weight of Fleck vanished from her grasp.

She flung upwards away from stampeding feet, running to the gallows, imagining Fleck's dangling lifeless body, but to her relief, multiple men were heaving him onto the floor, and cutting away his noose with a sharp sword. The remaining sacks were pulled from the prisoners' faces, revealing the two who had somehow survived. Kristoff's sly grin shone the moment he realized he was free.

A bright flare erupted toward the ceiling, the color of sapphires.

Even the rioters took a moment to observe as the flare bedazzled the intricate artwork on the Parliament dome before it came crashing down, sending more debris to litter the ground.

"I am your queen, and you will listen to my words!" the countess shouted, her face fierce like a drawn blade. "This is a historical day! The people's chambers have been ripped open like a wound, and there is bloodshed filling its halls! We must crush these invaders with the might given to you by our ancestors, our Shining God, and cleanse the filth they have spread with their treachery! At all costs—use your magic, my proud Glint!"

There was some confusion among the mayhem, but it didn't take long before a swirl of black fog, like smoke along the perimeter of the room, snuffed out the fires and consumed the light with shadow. Bright forks of lightning streaked across the room, striking souls and turning them into poofs of glowing dust. More lightning stabbed the floor, sending the crowd screaming blindly in every direction, guided only by the brief flash of death.

Katja slid through the darkness, tripping over something heavy as people crashed into her from every direction. Her vision narrowed as she heard the faint wheezing of dying men and women as they clung to the tearing thread of their lives. Another flash filled the chamber, and for a minute, she could see the outline of a pale man with blood leaking from his ears and eyes, and another with their long tongue lying serpentine on the floor.

She thought of Stav in this mess. It all felt hopeless.

"Stav!" Katja shouted, her voice hoarse.

But all she could hear was death and destruction.

She climbed back to her weary feet and smelled the metallic scent of her breath. Even if Gwith—or rather, the countess—told her the Dustmage was immune to kindling, it didn't feel like it. She would need to test the theory again.

"Fleck!" Katja shouted. "Stav!"

Another body crashed into her, but this time she was barely able to keep her balance. The air glowed brilliantly again, and she saw the wooden beams of the gallows a few strides in front of her. She reached out and steadied herself on a beam and caught her breath, but the air felt like thick molasses on her tongue.

"Stav!" Katja shouted.

Just as her voice wailed, the ground rumbled and a hole broke from the ceiling, erupting pale light into the chamber, streaming like bands of ribbon in the wavering black fog. She could see the silhouettes of the crowd running in all directions, flailing and slashing their weapons in every direction. The whistle of a saber disturbed the air beside her and impaled the throat of someone she had never seen nor would ever know, as they fell to the ground beside her with gurgles.

Katja shrank to the ground, trying to be as small as possible as rubble plummeted down upon them and a few pinpricks of black appeared floating in the pale sky like motes of ash. She rubbed the dirt out of her eyes as the black silhouettes entered the dome, floating on something long but formless. They wore long, flowing garbs the color of night, and their faces were nothing but pits behind their hoods.

"Stav!" she screamed.

A muffled voice called back, faint but unmistakably familiar. "Katja?"

Her heart leaped. She crawled across the floor toward the sound, hands sliding along the bulky, uneven edge of something massive. A hand shot out and brushed hers, slick with blood.

"Fleck?" she whispered, recognition seizing her despite the hoarse, muffled sound. "Is that you?"

"Yes . . . Yes, it's me. What are you doing here?" Fleck said, his voice hoarse. "You must escape!"

Katja leaned closer, feeling her hands along the heavy object barely lit by the sky overhead. Fleck was pinned beneath a large section of ceiling, blood splattered across his tortured face.

"Let's get you out of here," she said, mustering her strength to lift the debris, but it wouldn't budge. "Please tell me that isn't your blood."

"I dunno," Fleck said. "I'm not dead yet, but I can't move either. Leave now, the Magesleuths are here!"

"I came all this way to save you. I am not going to quit now," Katja said, continuing to heave at the debris, but nothing moved an inch. "Stav is out there somewhere. The countess is impersonating the queen."

"Of course," Fleck gasped.

"I am going to try to levitate it," Katja said, focusing on the massive heap of rubble and reaching deep within her boiling chest. She aimed her fingers at her target and felt its weight start to press on her shoulders, but before it could crush her, she released her spell. "It is too heavy for magic," Katja said frantically.

Fleck gasped with pain. "There is no time to save me or Stav." His hands reached for one of the protestors' bloody pitchforks an arm's reach away, and put it in her hands. "Use this. Get out of here."

Katja wasn't sure if Fleck intended her to fly with it or use it as a weapon, but then she thought of another idea. She grasped the pitchfork and set its blades beneath the rubble, wedging it deep in the crevice, making sure she avoided Fleck's pinned legs. Using all of her body, she pushed onto the hilt, but the rubble only slightly budged.

"There is no time, Katja! Leave!" Fleck screamed, bashing his fists. "I am an old man. I have lived a fine life. You have so much to live for. If someone doesn't survive, then our Roth is gone forever!"

"There is nothing out there for me without you and Stav," Katja snapped, pulling her mop of black hair from her face as sweat dripped down her temples.

"Then forget the Roth! Live your life! Do not die here alongside me," Fleck begged. "Boils! You are a Dustmage! One in a billion stars in the sky!"

Katja fell to her knees and watched as people continued dying all around her. Arcs of light split the dense air like hot knives. Was she so special that she couldn't die like everyone else? Just because she was a Dustmage? Plenty of better people have died here just the same.

"I have an idea. But I don't have another if this fails," Katja said. She closed her eyes and took a deep breath. Then she placed her hand on the rubble and felt the deepest pits of fire swell beneath her ribcage like never before. All around her, she could feel every grain of fog, ash, blood, sweat, tears, fear, and agony vibrate through her skin like pebbles on a beach tumbling as the tide breaches from the sea. It grew louder like an oncoming storm, and the hairs on her arms, legs, and neck pricked like quills on a frightened bird.

She inhaled, and the burden of a thousand stones eased onto her shoulders and steadily slid back off in one smooth motion. When she opened her eyes, the rubble had moved, and Fleck was now freed, with a mangled knee.

"Katja . . . you . . . you did it . . ." he stammered.

She collapsed, feeling a chill run down her arms and legs.

Fleck shifted on his side, moving away from his prior captor, and reached for Katja, keeping her from planting her face into the hard ground.

They sat trying to catch their breath as bodies flew and metal rang and blood spilled around them.

We have to find Stav. Katja reached for the pitchfork beside Fleck and tiredly raised it to her gaze, noticing the three crooked, but sharp prongs shine with a pinkish sheen in the limelight. Out of the shadows, the clanking of steel came at her with a swish of silver, striking her shoulder and clawing deep before spraying red mist onto the ground. The Parliament guard towered over her, and with his armor, his arms and legs appeared as thick as tree roots as he lifted his blade to strike again, but this time, meeting the space between the pitchfork's teeth with a terrible ring and a hint of a spark.

"Stand down!" the guard shouted, blood marking his face. He pulled the saber back and swiped the tip of his blade across the ground, spraying sparks in a threatening way before swinging toward her hips.

The attack narrowly missed her stomach.

"Terrible hag! The whole lot of you should be hanged!" he spat, swinging at her again. This time, from a higher angle that, if struck, would cleave her neck in two.

Katja rolled, dodging the guard's barrage. If she were going to fight, she would at least fight standing. Adrenalin surged through her as she sprang up and shoved him back. Before the guard could regain his footing, she disarmed him, levitating the saber out of his grip. When the guard noticed his lack of a weapon, he reached for the rifle strapped to his back and pulled back the hammer, but before he aimed, she swept his gun downward, causing the bullet to ricochet into oblivion. She charged and drove her pitchfork into his belly, but the prongs were not sharp enough to pierce his armor, and it caused him to stumble backwards, dropping his rifle into the rubble. Terror filled his eyes. He knew he was in trouble.

He lunged for the pitchfork, tearing it from her grip and raising it over his head to strike—just as a fork of lightning ignited sparks and flames. He went down beside her in a coil of smoke and charred iron, hissing and popping like a greasy pan broiling on a hot stove.

"Watch out, another one's coming!" Fleck shouted from the gallows post.

A man who looked more like a legal clerk than a soldier stormed Fleck from the side, his tweed suit torn and stained, and his pomaded hair wild and slick with blood splatter. In his hand was a small wooden wand.

Katja threw herself at the man, knocking him to the ground. Fleck pinned him on the floor with what strength he could muster, prying the man's fingers from around his wand. The man stared at Fleck's beaten face with horror, but refused to let go as a green ribbon sparked from its end and tore into someone at the far side of the chamber.

"You killed my family!" the man screamed, biting Fleck's fingers with chomping teeth. "You will pay for that, Roth!"

Fleck winced, letting loose the wand.

Katja summoned her strength and picked up the blackened pitchfork from the guard's rigid fingers and sent its end into Fleck's assailant's chest. The man fell limp as blood squirted out of his teeth.

"Great," Fleck said through gritted teeth, picking up the man's wand. "Another dead warlock."

"He was trying to kill you!" Katja protested.

"I know, but every time we choose to kill, we lose something," Fleck said, examining the wand and wiping the blood from its hilt. "Even when violence is justified."

The cold breeze tugged at the back of her hair, making her suddenly aware of it standing up on her neck like sharp arrows.

"Katja!" Fleck shouted before he was flung backwards.

Katja turned as something tall and narrow approached from the shadows. It stepped closer, illuminating a long quarterstaff that looked to be made of yellowing bone with a marbled green stone embedded in its tip that resembled an unhatched egg. Two more shades followed closely behind, brandishing crude daggers that appeared to be made of blackened glass, which seemed to shine with a mystical reflection, like the opaque gleam reflecting off a calm sea. Everything seemed to go completely still when she heard the sniffs whispering through the screams and chaos, as if they were hovering just a few inches over her shoulder.

"Hexes! Magesleuths! Katja, run!" she heard Fleck shout from wherever he had ended up.

"I am not going without you and Stav," Katja shouted.

She attempted to cloak, splitting her face with her finger and uttering the words, but her Vigor was too low, or she was too nervous. Her fingers shook as she crossed her lips several times before deciding to abandon her plan. She felt a warm breath run down her arm, only to find it was blood, trickling like a creek from the gash in her shoulder, but she thankfully couldn't feel a thing. If she had any sense, she would run, just like Fleck demanded, but she wasn't going to leave him here to die.

The lead Magesleuth tapped its quarterstaff onto the ground, summoning a ball of blue flame that sucked all the chill from the air, and hurled it toward her. Fleck flung her to the ground just as the gallows burst into an inferno. She felt him groaning in pain. Seconds later, the beams sagged as the wood blackened, and a sharp pop sent the burning structure collapsing, hurling those standing on it into the embers with terrifying screams. Flaming ashes, coals, and debris rained over them as Katja flung herself over Fleck. The smell of burnt hair stung her nostrils as both swatted lumps of red coals from their shoulders and the back of their heads, collapsing out of exhaustion.

For a moment, all they could hear was distant screaming, the popping of burning wood, and their heavy breathing. When Katja had the chance, she looked at Fleck, who stared at the fiery mess with wide, fearful eyes.

She gazed back at the gathering Magesleuths, who were closing in on them like an oncoming storm with no escape. The lead Magesleuth groaned and hummed a terrifying sound, as a fiery whip was conjured from the end of its staff. It swung the whip toward Fleck, who thankfully refocused in time to cast an icy spell that froze the whip solid for a minute before it burned more intensely.

Another Magesleuth stepped into the firelight. It swirled its glass dagger over its head, summoning what looked like bright red moths. It slammed the staff onto the ground, and the slick stones vibrated beneath them. Dust fell from the walls as they shook harder by the minute until chunks crumbled about like some horrific god's wrath. A flaming wall collapsed and slid into Fleck's flank, sending him into agonizing screams.

Katja levitated the rubble away from Fleck, and his legs both appeared misshapen.

The Magesleuths stopped and watched them silently from behind their horrific masks.

Katja raised her pitchfork, standing in front of Fleck like a wild beast, moving her sights from one swiftly approaching shade to the next. There were at least a dozen now. *This is it—this is where I will die.*

A bright blaze of green came from over their heads and hurled towards one of the Magesleuths, but it was deflected at the last minute with a flick of a gloved finger, causing it to barely graze the Sleuth's hood and explode into a hailstorm of jade splinters far off into the shadows. If it had landed as intended, it would have struck the Magesleuth square in the mask.

Kristoff appeared in a poof of smoke, stepping in front of her with his hands splayed outward. His golden hair shining with sweat and blood, and his face beaten, but it added to his fierce grimace. He summoned another spell, hurling what was left of the flaming gallows at the Sleuths like he was hurling heavy stones, nearly stumbling forward as they crashed toward the hooded creatures, sending hellfire into their wake.

The leader of the Magesleuths tapped its quarterstaff on the ground, sending a pulse through the chamber that rattled them as the flaming rubble suspended in the air. When it looked like the shade might toss the rubble back into their faces, a high-pitched screech filled the chamber, causing Katja to cover her ringing ears. The Sleuths' masks turned toward the sound in unison before darting into the shadows.

When Kristoff was done, he turned to Katja and Fleck, his eyes wild like a demon.

"What are you two waiting for?" he spat, breathing heavily and walking towards them, combing his black hair back into an untidy mess. "We finally did it. The city is burning, and the warlocks are dead. All of our hard work and planning has finally paid off."

Fleck groaned, nursing his legs and watching the death surrounding them. "You call this winning? At what cost?"

"An unfortunate but necessary cost," Kristoff grimaced, wiping blood from his chin. "The people have spoken. The queen has taken her stance. The warlocks are bleeding, and the Crown has picked her side. No one is leaving today without knowing that the throne has picked her chosen people—the wrong people. And she will die by their side. The city will continue burning until the flames lick that monstrosity on Artem's Roost—the imperial palace! Magic will return to the hands of every Glint, and we will rule without nobility."

Fleck shook his head. "The Commonwealth is much bigger than this chamber . . . than the palace . . . than Theed. Those here know that wasn't Queen Margot making those orders. She would never."

"It doesn't matter because the people knocking on hell's door believe she did," Kristoff said, between gasping breaths. "Perception is everything. This is what you never understood and why you lost the Roth, old man."

"I want no part of this," Fleck spat. "I would rather have joined them in death than live in the world you want to build. A world built on death is not one built for the living."

Kristoff shook his head. "You are free to jump into the flames if you wish to join them. But I know you are too much of a coward." He summoned an ember of flame and tossed it toward Fleck's face, who rolled out of the way. "I know what you fear."

"As do I . . ." Fleck said.

A few more people limped toward them from the shadows, their prisoner tunics still intact. Each of them looked beaten, but they smiled when they found Kristoff and the flaming pile of death burning before them.

"Raven?" one of the women asked. Katja didn't recognize her.

"It is," Kristoff smiled, embracing her. "Good to see you three survived. Are there any other survivors?"

"Howl died heroically," another man said, shaking his head. "It will be hard to find his replacement. Bravest Howl we have ever had. Shame."

The air chilled again, and the countess, as beautiful as a fox, appeared from the shadows as swiftly as the wind. In her hand was something bloodied and hard that dripped down her wrist.

"Gideon is dead," she smiled.

"That will be two prime ministers to your scorecard now, countess," the woman who embraced Kristoff said. "I look forward to crossing off that card when we meet again."

The cards. Katja's mind flashed back to the grimoire and the cards she had fetched for the grand maiden.

A man lunged at them from the corner, two constables close behind, but the countess struck back with a vicious snap of motion, detonating a wave of invisible magic that slammed forward with crushing force.

"There are still hundreds more to kill," the countess said. "Since persuading has failed." She looked at Fleck. "I see you have survived yet again."

Fleck scowled. "You prove dying isn't the worst thing. He pointed to her face with disgust. "You might see youth and beauty, but I see the horror behind each ironed-out wrinkle and unwhitened hair. How much suffering did each cost?"

Auriella only smiled before turning to Katja. "My Dustmage . . . I am so proud of you."

Katja frowned. "You tricked me."

"Our bond grew closer than ever—what does it matter who you thought I was?" the countess said softly. "We were perfect together. You and I are an unbreakable team."

Katja's eyes caught on a haggard figure behind her.

"Stav," she gasped as a weight lifted from her chest.

The countess smiled, pointing at the figure sitting on the edge of the shadow. "He is alive. You think I would let anything happen to my own son?"

Kristoff seemed annoyed at her words, but held his tongue. He looked exhausted, the toll of his spellcasting evident in his posture. Katja wagered a hint of iron would scent his breath.

She dashed toward Stav, checking him up and down, but he didn't have a single mark or blemish outside of the look of his extreme age. He looked very confused and mesmerized by the dancing flames.

"Mother saved me," Stav said.

"We need to go," Katja said, looking at Fleck. "Now, before it is too late."

"I agree with the Dustmage," the countess said. "We have won the battle, but the war continues. We will storm every office in the district, and if they fight back, we will give them the same treatment. And then if we must, we will march upon Artem's Roost, together."

The fire wavered and recoiled, roaring as if a giant had just breathed upon it, before snuffing out, plummeting them once more into darkness except for the bits of daylight beaming from the hole above them. Katja glared at the countess, only to freeze as an unmistakable expression flickered across the countess's face. *Fear.*

Chapter Thirty-Five

The Magesleuths slid in like ghosts, unnoticeable at first, until the hum and horrific sniffing consumed the entire chamber. Their robes were still tattered, and many were completely disrobed, revealing a once concealed plate of armor that contoured perfectly to their sleek form, the color of coal dust. In their gauntleted hands were an assortment of glass daggers, quarterstaffs, scepters of various forms, and one held a long-bladed scimitar that curved like an eagle's talon. It was hard to tell when disguise met flesh and where the barriers of humanity started.

"I thought they left," Katja said.

"They are Magesleuths. Once they get your scent, they always come back." Fleck frowned, almost laughing at their predicament.

Kristoff reached for a vial in his pocket, uncorked it, and drank it in one gulp. His shoulders raised as the fatigue lifted from his body, and his gaze focused on his challengers. He bent down to his knees and placed his fingers into the pools of blood, closing his eyes. Moments later, the blood thickened and hardened into large, sharp crystalline spikes, tearing through their cloaks, the spikes holding their shape like icicles dangling from sheer rooftops in winter.

Katja's jaw hung as she watched Kristoff swing his hands intricately, causing the spikes to shatter into a million shards, ripping the blackened robes into tiny shreds of fraying cloth. However, the Magesleuths still stood unbothered by what looked lethal enough to kill a small battalion.

Kristoff stared back at his mother for direction, but there was no solace to be found in her face.

Katja raised the pitchfork as the Magesleuths marched upon them.

"We can't fight this!" Fleck whispered. "We have to leave. Take Stav and live for another day if it isn't too late."

"I wish you would say something useful, Fleck," the countess sneered, staring sharp daggers. "I will not be threatened anymore by the Crown's monstrosities!"

The countess raised a long wand into the sky and pressed it into her chest in one swift motion. She then pointed the tip of her wand into the ground, sending a transparent edge of brilliant scarlet to encircle them in a dome. When the Magesleuths approached, they halted and examined it silently for a moment before barraging it with a bright fury of magic of various origins, painting the dome like fireworks.

Kristoff joined his mother's side, and the other Roth joined the effort, but Katja could tell, through their almost cult-like allegiance, that even they were worried.

Katja moved closer to Fleck and Stav, brandishing her pitchfork in case anything broke through, as if a simple tool could save her from utter demise. If she were honest, she hadn't ever expected to live this long. When her mother left her, it was the pit of Winterhour, and the streets were filled with death and despair. Even with what little magic she knew, it would have been only a matter of time before she overreached her hand and someone reported her to the constables, her magic sniffed out by the very creatures standing before them now. It was only because of the Maiden Tower that she had managed to live as long as she had, and now it had all been tarnished by the Roth.

Magic isn't a blessing. It's a terrible curse. The same curse that likely took my mother.

She couldn't die the same way. She would forget magic ever existed and live the rest of her days wandering the streets of Theed with another name, straying far from the Maiden Tower and anywhere she might be recognized. She would find a way and look for her mother, if she was even alive, or maybe jump on a ship to sail across the Relian with nothing and start over. She didn't care that she was the so-called *Dustmage*—it didn't mean she had to claim it. No one could force her to do anything.

"How can we escape?" Katja turned to Fleck, a resolution forming on her now stony face.

He gazed up at the hole in the building. "There is no other way than up. I reckon you didn't bring the carpet with you?"

Katja shook her head. "No, there has to be another way. You told me the Warren was escapeless, too."

Stav looked up at the bright sky above, his pale blue eyes shining as drool crept down his chin.

"Even if we had the carpet, we couldn't get through the countess's ward," Fleck said. "It protects from the outside just as much as within. As long as it continues, we are trapped."

"Kat . . . Kat . . ." Stav muttered, eyes still fixed on the sky. "Let's fly!"

Katja ignored Stav's muttering and patted him on the shoulder. She looked back at the ward, which had a thin, cloudy veneer that glistened like rubies. It couldn't be that strong, could it?

Outside the ward, she noticed people continuing to fight through the thick fog, many limping, cursing, and falling to their knees as the onslaught continued near the Parliament doors, which were now engulfed in flame. The whole Parliament floor was now covered with bodies, and although the battle was waning, no one was winning.

The Magesleuths' barrage continued, the spellbinding curses sending magnificent sparks, and drippings of something she had never seen fell to their feet like melted candle wax. The countess looked weaker in the dim light and a bit older than before, as sweat dripped down the nape of her neck and beaded on her face. Kristoff heaved as he cast mightily, but it was apparent he was growing weary, too. The ward was failing.

Stav placed the pitchfork between his legs and pretended to be a flying witch like the old children's tales. Fleck glared at him like he was a fool.

"What are you doing?" Fleck shouted. "This is no time for play!"

"Look, Mother, I am flying! I am flying!" Stav hollered playfully.

The countess looked at her son with pity, and then hope filled her eyes as her attention turned to the pitchfork. She flashed an expressionless glance at Katja.

"Kitty, get on the pitchfork."

"What are you up to, Auriella?" Fleck asked. "I don't like the look in your eyes. You are plotting something!"

Katja froze, taken aback by the countess's outlandish request.

"At least I have a plan," Auriella snapped. "Dustmage . . . get on the pitchfork."

"Don't listen to her, Katja. The countess only has bad intentions for you. If she wants you to survive this, it is only because there is a benefit for her later." Stav beckoned.

Katja's eyes danced back and forth between Fleck, the countess, and the flickering ward that looked close to falling apart. Images of Auriella chasing her on a pitchfork and igniting the sky with flashes of lightning flooded her mind. She could have killed Katja there and then, and this would all be over, but here the countess was, offering to spare her life, and it wasn't the first time.

There was a loud creak like the sound of a rope clenching moments before snapping. The ruby shield surrounding them shattered and fell to the ground like ribbon. The Magesleuths took a step forward, their weapons drawn, their numbers seeming to have grown.

"Hexes! Here we go!" Kristoff shouted, summoning what little Vigor he had left into the tips of his fingers for one final spell. "Fight for your lives! Fight for the Glint!"

"Katja, go!" the countess shouted, aiming her wand at the approaching wall of black.

Katja looked to Fleck for assurance, but he was already joining the others in a makeshift formation around her. Stav was staring at the glowing magelight that was beginning to fill the air around them. The pitchfork scratched the bloodied tile floor as he pretended to fly among the bodies and wreckage like some macabre reaper, dancing among the fallen whose souls they had yet to retrieve from the battlefield.

"Stav, come with us!" Katja pleaded, but he could not hear her voice.

She ran to Fleck to get his attention, but before she reached him, a bolt of blue lightning ripped into his chest, and he fell motionless to the ground in a sizzling heap. Katja bit her tongue as she wanted to scream. She ran to Fleck's side, but a dark shadow stepped over him and stood between them. It had a cruel mask, with eyes so deep and black they appeared like holes.

Katja ran away, toward Stav, but her foot slipped on the blood, sending her to her knees. She picked herself back up, but the Magesleuth was closing in with its raised scepter. She turned to cast levitation on its weapon, but the Sleuth seemed unbothered as the spell went unnoticed.

The Magesleuth flicked its scepter, sending her flailing onto her spine.

Katja raised her hand to cast a spell, anything that could put distance between her and the monster approaching, but to no avail. The Sleuth stomped closer until it was standing towering above her like a statue. It aimed its scepter at her heart, and a bright light formed at the tip.

Katja tried to crawl away, but her hands slid on the slick tiles. Her hand grazed something cold and solid, which summoned a boiling warmth from behind her ribs. She splayed her fingers on the stone, and as her body trembled, a scraping sound rose as hundreds of pebbles, stones, and motes of dust suspended in the air between her and the Magesleuth, obscuring their vision of each other like a screen.

The Magesleuth sniffed the air and cautiously combed through the suspended dust and rubble. Before it could press any closer, Katja hurled the large stone in her palm at its head, shattering its mask like delicate porcelain and revealing its right flank. The Magesleuth recoiled, shielding its face from any further attacks, but when it dropped its stance, Katja saw its face.

It had sickly pale skin, a shaven chin, gaunt cheeks, and pink lips with dull teeth.

It's human.

Katja broke her stare and lunged onto the pitchfork, anchoring her grip around Stav's ribs.

"Auriella!" Katja shouted.

The countess glanced over her shoulder and smiled before deflecting a barrage of flaming javelins being sent her way from the Magesleuths' offense. She evaporated into a plume of smoke and reappeared in a haze of what smelled like burning gunpowder. She gripped the pitchfork and stared into Katja's eyes.

"Come back to me," the countess said.

An explosion of hissing steam detonated the ground beneath their feet, sending them stumbling backwards, but Katja and Stav kept their grips as they soared upward toward the sky. The battlefield shrank beneath them, and she could see the broken masked Magesleuths' gaze follow them with deathly determination.

"I have your scent, Dustmage!" a deep, guttural voice shouted.

Before she could react, the pitchfork soared toward the cratered rooftop of Parliament that she had been standing upon mere hours before. Stav roared with excitement, his white hair wild as he kicked the pitchfork's heel, and they soared out of the shadows through the hole in the ceiling, blinding them with brilliant light.

Katja's eyes teared as the cold wind whipped against her face. She tucked her head down as they flew through the sky like a hissing arrow. When Katja dared to look back, all she could see was a chimney of ghostly smoke bellowing from the once magnificent Parliament building dome that was slowly shrinking over their shoulders. And it wasn't long before the terrible sight was a mere chalky aberration, but the madness didn't end there. Flowing outside the square through the Parliament District and far beyond was a scene Katja would never forget—utter calamity.

Chapter Thirty-Six

Katja struggled to tilt the pitchfork toward the ground, only for it to counter her every move. Everywhere she could see was a gray, brick, and concrete labyrinth filled with meandering crowds. A few children pointed up at them with the excitement of seeing a circus, while their parents ignored them and continued on their way. Wherever they landed, if it was on any of these busy roadways, someone would notice, and the city constables would not be far if they weren't preoccupied on the other side of town.

"Stav, how do we fly this thing?" Katja clamored.

Stav ignored her as he held firmly to the pitchfork and laughed.

The pitchfork whizzed faster, its cold metal humming against her thigh as they narrowly dodged the iron pendant atop a towering temple spire. A flock of startled pigeons took off in every direction. Stav pulled up, toward the pale sky, the cool autumn breeze stinging her nostrils as she clenched to his hindquarters so hard that he yelped. Regardless, the pitchfork persisted on its determined path.

Katja took a moment to breathe, looking behind her as if half expecting to find someone or something following them. Down below, she recognized a few buildings, and across the street, she spotted the south side of the Oldgate District. *The Maiden Tower isn't far.* Her beliefs were confirmed when she scanned northwesterly and saw the pathetic leaning tower among a cluster of taller buildings. Now that she had her bearings, she knew they were heading westward.

"Can we land?" Katja asked. "Do you have any control at all?"

Stav shifted the fork with his hips, moving it subtly left and right, but the pitchfork seemed determined to go in whatever direction it was instructed to go. *Of course, the countess's enchantment will not give us free rein to fly anywhere we please. There always had to be a contingent.*

Hexes! Katja's heart skipped a beat. Looming ahead was the towering monstrosity, which was part wall, part citadel, that guarded the city's edge like a knife cutting stale bread. At the foot of the gate were large barracks and sentries, likely manned by hundreds of carefully chosen city watch, with yellow pinpricks of lantern light dotting the dark stone walls like stars. She shoved her arms past Stav's and pinned them to his chest, in an awkward embrace, using her hands to hold onto the fork desperately. It was the one time she was thankful that Stav was old and meek as he failed to break free of her grasp.

"Let go!" he roared. "It is my turn!"

She yanked the fork's handle upward, lifting its nose toward the sky, but a stronger force dragged it back into a steady, unyielding glide. They were far too high to survive a fall, and too powerless to steer it in any other direction. All they could do was sit, and wait.

Looking down, they crossed into a street Katja barely recognized. She wondered if the Countess kept a secret refuge somewhere on the outskirts of Oldgate, or Watcher's Row, which stretched along the foot of the city gates. Along the road that ran beside the city gate, a gathering of armored cavalry and steel-plated coaches stood in grim formation. Crates of ammunition were stacked in neat heaps, and clusters of soldiers huddled around scattered bonfires that shivered in the wind. As the pitchfork swept overhead, a few guards rose from the firelight, staring up in disbelief.

What was the countess plotting? They were swiftly approaching the end of the world, according to her, and if they were to land anywhere near the city gate, it would be a swift chase and a hanging by next sunrise, especially after news came from the capital of their crimes, if it hadn't already.

Katja frowned as the gray monolith loomed closer, swallowing the horizon. The last chance to turn toward the sparser districts was slipping away. Her heartbeat thudded in her chest, and she held her breath, closing her eyes as if she were about to plunge into an icy sea. She half expected a surge of strange magic to blaze across the sky or for the gate itself to close in and crush them between the city's gnashing teeth. At the very least, she expected the air to change, to thicken like fog or ripple with a charge that raised the hairs on her arms. But no such thing happened.

The pitchfork soared peacefully and indifferently into the unknown.

She couldn't believe it. They were over the wall.

They were leaving Theed.

Acknowledgements

Many thanks to everyone whose encouragement, inspiration, and steadfast support carried me through the writing of this book.

To my wife, Sarah "Curls," I thank you endlessly for reading every iteration of these pages, from rough draft to final line, and for the larger manuscripts I have labored over through the years that have not yet seen the light of day. Without you, I might never have found my way back to writing after falling off the deep end. Your faith in me never faltered, even when mine did.

To my son, Edmund, and my daughter, Emmalyn, thank you for being my constant inspiration and for reminding me how to see the world again through childlike eyes still full of wonder. Because of you, the ordinary feels miraculous.

To my mom and dad, thank you for putting up with a son who was late to dinner, shut away in his bedroom writing while listening to terrible teenage angst music, a habit that, it seems, never entirely left.

To all of my family, who have rallied around me and lifted me along the way, I am deeply grateful.

Stay tuned.
More to come.

About the Author

N. A. Woltzen

N. A. Woltzen is an author from the Pacific Northwest. He chose to use his initials because of a lifelong belief that being mysterious and using one's initials is the key to a successful fiction-writing career. *Whether this proves wise remains to be seen.*

His debut novel, *The Dustmage*, was inspired by his lifelong love of storytelling, drawing on folklore, magic, history, power struggles, addiction, and familial discord, all woven together to make the city of Theed feel vivid, well lived, and tethered to our world.

When he's not writing, Nick spends his time daydreaming, wading in the local lake when the weather permits, tumbling down rabbit holes of local mysteries and treasure hunts while chasing his children, and contemplating reheating his perpetually lukewarm coffee.

Visit him online at https://nickwoltzen.substack.com/ to join his mailing list for exclusive stories and announcements.

www.ingramcontent.com/pod-product-compliance
Lightning Source LLC
Chambersburg PA
CBHW031108160726
47991CB00004B/1286